THE LAST TOQEPH

Gateway to Gannah 4

Yvonne Anderson

The Last Toqeph (Gateway to Gannah #4)

©2014 by Yvonne Anderson. All rights reserved.
http://www.YsWords.com

Edited by Emily Anderson

Scripture quotations are from the Holy Bible, King James Version.

This novel is a work of fiction. Characters, plot, and incidents are products of the author's imagination, and any similarity to people living or dead, whether on Earth, Karkar, or Gannah, is pretty much coincidental. Except for the Yasha, of course, who is real—and whose every promise is true.

ISBN-13: 978-1502449825

Cover design by
Ken Raney
Clash Creative, Inc.

Great deliverance giveth he to his king; and sheweth mercy to his anointed, to David, and to his seed for evermore.
Psalm 18:50

Dear Earthish traveler:

If you're a first-time visitor to Gannah, welcome! To help you get the most out of your trip, we who are blessed to live here would like to provide you with this brief history so you might orient yourself to the surroundings.

If you have visited before, you feel free to skip ahead to Chapter 1-- unless you want to keep reading to refresh your memory.

Almost a millennium before this story takes place, the population of Gannah was comprised of one race ruled by one king, a descendant of a man named Atarah. Since his day, every king took his name. Unlike Earthish humans, the ancient Gannahans were of an obedient nature, and Atarah's authority was seldom disputed, if ever.

The planet had never known war except for battles with weather, natural disaster, and animal attacks—which were frequent and often organized. Animals here are intelligent, able to communicate with people through a gland all natives of Gannah have, man and beast alike, called a meah. Located at the base of the brain, it enables us to perceive mental and emotional signals from others who possess the gland.

The early Gannahans had no fascination with technology. They understood a great deal about natural science, and they learned to maintain optimal health, strength, and longevity through what we might consider scientific advancements. But their lifestyles were quite simple, and they had little curiosity about mechanics or gadgetry.

Until, that is, visitors from the neighboring planet of Feuraq invaded. Gannah had never seen flying machines, let alone spacecraft. They had no concept of astronomy and were unaware there were other beings in the universe. Moreover, the only weapons they knew were of the manual variety, such as the personal blade called a lahab that each person carries for defense against animals. This alien invasion took them by complete surprise.

Their civilization may have been backward, but the Gannahans were fast learners. Once they'd caught their collective breath, they figured out how to turn the invaders' technology against them. They also learned to kill fellow humans (for all these extraterrestrials are, in fact, different branches of the human race). They became possessed by a global bloodlust. The more Feuraqis they killed, the stronger their madness gripped them. Not content to repel the invasion and rid Gannah of every trace of the Outsiders, they

THE LAST TOQEPH

built spaceships, traveled to Feuraq, and reduced the planet to a cinder.

But that only fueled their blooddrunk, and they searched the galaxy for more worlds to conquer. In two generations, their once-peaceful agrarian society had become centered around bloodshed and war.

In their galactic rampage, Gannah attacked the planet Karkar. Its people were multiracial and argumentative, its history amounting to one layer of war upon another. As a result, it seemed they had already accomplished much of the work of their own destruction before the Gannahan warships arrived. Gannah's king, Atarah Hoseh, launched an attack and remained at Karkar until total victory was imminent, then took off in a small ship with a scouting team to look for the next world to attack.

Hoseh had an insatiable appetite not only for blood, but also for knowledge of the people and cultures he devoured. One thing in particular caught his attention: the earliest history of every planet he encountered, including his own, had similar legends concerning the stars. The ancient peoples saw shapes formed by the stars in the night skies, images only the wildest leaps of imagination could reveal. Different stars formed the constellations above each planet, but the formations had similar names and were found in roughly the same locations in the skies. Individually, the legends made no sense to Hoseh. Put together, the mystery drove him mad. His desire to find new worlds to conquer was fueled by the hunger to understand this puzzle as much as it was by bloodlust.

The next planet Hoseh reconnoitered was Earth. It was there that he learned about the Creator God who had put the stars in the skies in deliberate arrangements to illustrate a story. Moreover, it was on Earth that Atarah Hoseh discovered what that universal story was: the gospel of redemption through Jesus Christ.

Meanwhile, back on Karkar, the natives of the planet engineered a microscopic organism that attacked Gannahan muscle tissue. They introduced this musculophage into the ventilation systems of the orbiting starships. The plan worked better than they'd hoped: the Gannahans all sickened, but the disease had no affect on the Karkar people. In a short space of time, the invaders had gathered their sick and dying soldiers and pointed their ships toward home. By the time the warships found their way back to Gannah, every occupant was dead of the plague. When Atarah Hoseh later arrived from Earth, carrying the gospel of salvation, he ordered the ships brought down from orbit and submerged in the sea forever, lest

THE LAST TOQEPH

the plague be loosed into Gannah's own atmosphere.

Sadly, certain factions on Karkar took advantage of the chaos the Gannahans left behind and continued the civil war the invaders had interrupted. By the time the dust settled, only one race remained, and the planet was uninhabitable outside the domes they'd built to protect themselves from the toxicity.

Speaking of toxic, their hatred of Gannah was as deadly as the atmosphere. They blamed all their world's ills on the invaders, and hatred of the Gannahans became deeply entrenched in the Karkar psyche.

Book #1, *The Story in the Stars*, opens with a woman, Dassa, completing the last requirement for entrance into the Gannahan knighthood. While she's off on her quest, a global disaster strikes: Her father, the ruler of Gannah, ordered the raising of the ancient warships that returned from Karkar centuries before. The first was brought up without incident. The second, however, exploded as it reached the surface, flinging tainted air into Gannah's atmosphere. Before Dassa's quest is completed, a significant portion of the world's population has died, and the rest are infected.

Gannah sends a distress call into space. The call is picked up by the LSS *Barton,* a medical research vessel. The captain orders Dr. Pik, chief of the infectious disease unit, to come up with an antidote to the Karkar plague while the ship races to Gannah's rescue.

All fine and good, except that Dr. Pik is a Karkar. Though it goes against every fiber of his being, he finds records of how the virus worked and figures out how to thwart it. As the *Barton* nears Gannah, he and the people in his lab have prepared several thousand doses. It's nowhere near enough, considering the distress call said the entire planet is infected. But he has his team working around the clock to manufacture more.

When the *Barton* arrives, however, they find only one living Gannahan: Dassa. And she's barely alive. They take her onto the ship and try to bring her back to health, despite the fact that no one on board knows much about Gannahan physiology.

Because of their deep-seated racial animosity, Pik and Dassa are revolted by the very sight of one another. Throughout the course of her treatment, however, they come to see each other in a somewhat different light. They go through various adventures together, including an attack by space pirates and, later, a voyage back to Gannah.

THE LAST TOQEPH

Dassa shares with Pik the "story in the stars" that her forefather, Atarah Hoseh, discovered centuries ago on Earth. Pik is disgusted with the tale and is particularly angered by the suggestion that it was the gospel that changed the Gannahans' warlike habits rather than their humiliation at the hands of his Karkar forebears.

Nevertheless, by the end of the first book, Dassa and Pik have come to understand each other. Somewhat.

In book #2, *Words in the Wind*, Pik and Dassa have married. Together, they recruited a group of Earthers to travel to Gannah to establish a new settlement with the intention of repopulating the planet. Though relations between the two planets are still strained, a ship has come to Gannah requesting Dassa's help in translating ancient documents Karkar archaeologists found dating from Gannah's invasion centuries before. At Pik's insistence, she goes to the ship to complete the task, but on her return to the planet, her shuttle crashes and strands her 10,000 kilometers from home.

Weather and technical difficulties thwart rescue attempts. In her absence, Pik is left in charge of the settlement—and also of their two children, ten-year-old Adam and five-year-old Lileela. He must deal with Lileela acting out, a rebellious faction among the settlers, and a threatened uprising by the wildlife.

Lileela's behavior steadily degrades, as she believes her mother abandoned her. One snowy day, she disobeys Pik and goes sledding alone. She has an accident and breaks her neck, causing paralysis. Because the settlement's medical resources are not sophisticated enough to treat a spinal cord injury, Pik has no choice but to send Lileela to Karkar, where help is available.

The rebellious faction steals valuable resources from the settlement and goes out to start a separate colony. The settlers are left with food shortages and no means of transportation to pursue the thieves.

On the other side of the world, Dassa is beset by a blizzard. She seeks refuge in a canyon, where she finds some ruins that figure prominently in ancient legends that she had always thought were mere fairy tales. What she discovers forces her to acknowledge that much of what she thought she knew about Gannah's history was a lie. Her isolation from the rest of the settlement and the eroding of everything she'd once thought true combine

THE LAST TOQEPH

to drive her nearly mad. The only thing that keeps her together is her faith in the God of her father Hoseh and the constant reliability of His word.

Pik and Dassa eventually reunite, but both Dassa and the settlement are irrevocably changed.

In Book #3, *Ransom in the Rock*, Lileela returns to Gannah after ten years on Karkar. She's able to walk again, but she bears bitter resentment toward her parents. First they rejected her, and now, after she's finally gotten comfortable on Karkar, they force her to return. She vows to leave Gannah once and for all the first chance she gets.

The Karkar ship that brought her home is commissioned to pick up quantities of valuable ores Gannah is giving Karkar as payment for Lileela's medical treatment. However, the ship's crew has another motive for being there. Karkar's resources are strained to the breaking point, and, since they believe the problem was caused by Gannah to begin with, it would be poetic justice if they could take over the resource-rich planet once owned by the ancient marauders.

Meanwhile, on Earth, a Special Starforces team led by Commander Faris is ordered to pick up an insurrectionist, Philip Dengel, and his family and take them to a penal colony for interrogation. One problem: Dengel's crime is preaching Christianity, and Faris is a secret convert. Faris leads his team to capture the family, but then, through subterfuge of which he is not proud, he steals a starship and whisks the Dengels toward Gannah and what he hopes will be safety.

On that distant world, the settlers learn of the Karkar's intentions, but they have no weapons to repel an attack. All they can do is pray.

A short time later, massive magnetic storms on Gannah's sun cause severe disturbances in space, disabling the Karkar ship and creating catastrophic weather and seismological events on the planet. None of the settlers die, however, and they see the situation as God having prevented their annihilation by the Karkar. Dassa chooses to respond to the would-be attackers with mercy rather than vengeance. In order to save the remaining Karkar lives, she brings the survivors down to the planet until the settlers can figure out how to send them home.

Right about then, Faris and his crew of renegades arrive at Gannah. They are amazed to see the empty Karkar ship orbiting helplessly, and the planet that formerly had only one landmass now divided into a number of

THE LAST TOQEPH

continents.

When Dassa questions the visitors as to their purpose, she discovers that Faris and his men were created through genetic engineering—using genetic material that Pik took from her and sold to the League of Planets when she was his patient decades before. The League used it to try to create a race of super-soldiers using DNA from the fabled Gannahan warriors.

Through all the upheavals, both emotional and meteorological, that Lileela endured since her return to Gannah, she comes to grips with who she is—and Who God is. When Faris offers his ship to the Karkar refugees so they can return home, instead of asking to go with them as she'd previously planned, Lileela decides to stay on Gannah, where she now feels she belongs. The fact that she's keenly attracted to Faris might have something to do with it.

And that's where we pick up with this, the final book in the series. We hope you have a wonderful time exploring our lovely planet.

Sincerely,

Atarah Adam Pik
Last Toqeph of Gannah

THE LAST TOQEPH

1

When Adam lifted his head to survey his surroundings, rainwater spilled down his back from his hat brim. Again.

Being soaked already, he ignored the indignity as he scanned the land before him. Hovering vapor blurred every outline of the treeless scenery, and the downpour's rhythmic song pattered across the sodden world in a soft cadence.

He squeezed water from his ponytail. Despite the damp, the air held no chill. Once the sun went down, though, it would be another story.

He strode on, boots pressing water from the fragrant loam as if from a sponge. He was grateful the mud had a solid base, thanks to what may have once been a paved highway. Who could say? The countryside bore no resemblance to the photos he'd seen of the old Yereq.

The Great Disaster six years ago had transformed this once fruitful plain into a jumble of rock-strewn hills and valleys, bogs, quicksand, and mounds of decay. A series of tremendous earthquakes—still occurring from time to time—had divided Gannah's single landmass into three continents, breaking off Yereq along the natural boundary of the Nazal River. Now they called it the Nazal Sea, and, too broad to swim, it cut him off from the settlement of the New Gannah. If he were to ever see it again—if he were to lead it, as was his birthright—he must complete this quest.

Adam slogged on until the path vanished ahead where the ground fell away sharply. He approached the edge and peered through the sheeting rain.

Below, a tangle of uprooted trees formed a ghostly thicket of limbs, trunks, and twisted roots. These logjams were wholly impenetrable. Any man who thought he could walk across from tree to tree would soon learn otherwise. He knew, because he'd tried it earlier.

THE LAST TOQEPH

He'd emerged from that fiasco scraped and torn but with no broken bones. Soon afterward, he'd discovered this semblance of a road heading in the direction he wanted to go. For the past three days, its firm footing had allowed him to make excellent time. If he could keep that pace, he'd arrive at the pick-up point with days to spare.

He stared into the tangled abyss beneath him and sighed. So much for efficient traveling. But then, all good things come to an end. "And so do all things painful," his mother would often add.

His emma was full of the wisdom of Old Gannah. Where her supply of adages left a gap, his abba had a Karkar homily to fill it. Adam's multiracial gene pool gave him a galaxy of proverbs for every occasion.

The precipice he stood upon continued as far as he could see in both directions. The path of least resistance seemed to lie to the north, so he followed the ridge to the right. A few paces later, his feet sank into the muck.

He plunged onward, step by desperate, sucking step, until at last he reached firm footing on the edge of a gray slab of scarred rock. Jutting from the ground at an angle, it looked like the floor of some ancient hall, broken and tipped upward.

He slipped in the slime on its muddy shoulder and grabbed at the leaning slab. His hand smeared a swath nearly clean before he'd caught his balance. He stared.

This was no random chunk of rock. The mud concealed a polished surface. Where it wasn't scored and cracked, it seemed to display a design of sorts. A deliberate pattern. He rubbed again.

The black mud ran in frantic rivulets before the driving rain, and the pattern grew clearer. Within a circle of gold on a green field, the letter *aleph* crowned with light: the royal symbol of Atarah.

Adam stared, trying to make sense of it, while the remainder of the mud he'd loosened trickled away, clearing the circle on the floor.

For that's what this certainly was. A piece of the floor from the throne room of one of the old provincial palaces. The nearest would be Saba, the old toqeph's residence at Yereq. But how could this be? Had he lost his bearings and wandered off course? The ancient palace had stood many leagues east of where he now journeyed.

THE LAST TOQEPH

Though shrouded in clouds, the lowering sun lit the western sky with a weak, watery glow. No, he hadn't strayed. He'd been heading steadily west by northwest since he'd parachuted out of the topeller almost a week ago.

He reviewed his knowledge of geography, picturing maps and images in his near-photographic mind, fixing first on Saba and then his own location. He was not mistaken. This slab had traveled hundreds of kilometers.

Adam turned in a full circle, scanning the soggy terrain for anything else out of place. All he saw was scrubby brush cringing against the downpour. If any other vestige of humanity existed here, it was buried beneath a meter of mud.

He faced the slab once more, and his skin prickled as he watched the rain rinse the sign of Atarah, leaving it mud-free and gleaming. He shivered from an inner chill.

What sort of inheritance had he been born to? The throne of a dead, broken planet.

He stiffened his jaw with resolve. Old Gannah was dead, yes. Wiped out by the Plague almost half a century ago, sparing only his emma as the heir of Atarah. Sole survivor of her race, she'd been carried away on a stretcher by the rescue team sent by the League of Planets, leaving Gannah utterly desolate.

But by the Yasha's grace, Emma and Abba had married on Earth, gathered a group of adventurers, and come here to establish the New Gannah. Now she ruled over a thriving community of two thousand people.

A small population, yes. But growing. And the people had a proud legacy. They deserved a good person to lead them.

Adam ran his hand across the symbol on the slab. No one could say he wasn't a good man. Since childhood he'd striven for perfection in knowledge, in character, in obedience to Emma and to the Yasha. He was a strong and loving husband to Elise, a kind and supportive father to his son, and had the good of Gannah foremost in his ambitions.

But to wear the Ring of Atarah? He traced the gold circle on the floor with his finger — the third finger of six.

Something clumped in his gut like a not-quite-done Cephargian blood pudding. No ruler of Gannah should be of Karkar blood. It would be a sacrilege.

9

THE LAST TOQEPH

He lowered his hand and stared at the circle. He'd seen that same sign on the floor in Emma's throne room beneath a round skylight. In Old Gannah, when a man was convicted of a capital crime, he was required to stand in that circle in a column of sunlight while the toqeph carried out the penalty: death by a swift breaking of the neck.

Adam knew how it was done. He'd been trained in the process, among other violent arts, in preparation for the Nasihood. But he'd never performed it on a man.

How many had stood on this very circle and surrendered obediently to their fates? He envisioned it—a dark, bearded, curly-haired man like the Gannahans of old, short of stature but powerful of build. Head bowed in submission, regret in his heart, but loyalty to the toqeph overriding his fear.

If Adam were justly condemned of some crime, would he have the courage to take his punishment standing in silence? Or would he bring shame to himself and all Gannah by struggling or pleading for mercy?

The ancient toqephs might consider him worthy of death for even thinking to inherit the throne. But wasn't that the destiny to which he was born? Was he not the rightful heir of Atarah?

The rain poured harder. Another chill shook him from hat to boots, and a sick feeling spread throughout his midsection. Must be a combination of hunger, the exertion of a day-long hike through the rain, and the eeriness of stumbling upon a relic of the former civilization.

It might be wise to rest. He'd been moving almost nonstop for days on end, and even the Old Gannahans couldn't keep that up indefinitely. With one last look at the symbol, he sidled around the upward-slanting floor. The footing was fairly firm, as if pieces of the slab had broken off and lay beneath the mud. But would he start sinking again on the other side?

The ground remained solid for the next few paces. A well-worn animal trail led from beneath the angled rock, where it appeared a family of qaran had taken up residence. Adam followed the narrow track. If the qaran didn't sink into the mud, he wouldn't either.

After several minutes, the meandering trail petered out in a grassy area littered with small boulders. The mother qaran and two half-grown fawns, their neck spines not yet emerged, browsed on berries growing on tall shrubs amongst the rocks.

THE LAST TOQEPH

Seeing him, they snorted and bounded away, and he made no effort to follow. He didn't need to hunt this evening. The berries would be nice, though. He approached the shrub the deer had been nibbling from.

Chophen fruits looked like closed fists. Two centimeters in diameter, the shining yellow lumps grew here in abundance. He'd never seen them before but recognized them from photos.

The first he picked was so soft it turned to mush in his hand. The second was firmer, but when a worm stuck its head out a hole and wagged at him, he let that one go too. He gave the third a good inspection before biting it in half then discovered it was inhabited as well. He flicked the worm out and ate the rest of the berry.

It was full of gritty seeds and wasn't very juicy. Perhaps it wasn't quite ripe.

He spent the next several minutes exploring the berry patch, eating enough to take the edge off his hunger. The sun sank lower, the rain still poured, and the ravine still stood between him and his destination. He'd have to climb down eventually, and sooner seemed better than later.

He headed westward, relieved the mud no longer tried to suck his boots off, until he found the ridge again. The drop-off was more gradual here, and nothing blocked his way. He followed another qaran trail downward with the rain.

Yasha willing, he'd have no trouble making the rendezvous. But the feeling of ill-ease remained, and the image of that yellow circle still burned in his mind.

Lileela rose from bending over a row of third-year powl plants in the kitchen garden. "There's got to be an easier way to do this."

She smoothed back a spiral curl that had escaped her braid. Though the hair flopped forward again as soon as she pulled her hand away, she was too busy massaging the kinks out of her back to care.

"What do you mean? It's fun." Six-year-old Tamah opened her hand and shook out four bright orange, centimeter-long larvae into the collection can.

"So you say." Lileela smiled at her sister despite the backache. "But you're a lot younger than me." And Tamah had never fractured her spine.

THE LAST TOQEPH

Their three-year-old nephew, Everett, worked on his hands and knees between the rows. "Is tonight Wormfest?" He picked a larva off a leaf and examined it before dropping it into the can beside him.

"Not for a couple weeks yet." Tamah, dark braids dangling as she resumed her search for larvae, answered for Lileela. "But we need to pick all these now, or they'll eat the powl plants to the ground."

Lileela wondered about that. Had anyone tried leaving the little critters alone to see what would happen? "Just this one row to finish, and we'll be done."

Everett sat cross-legged. "Then can we eat?" He studied a larva before depositing it in the can, as if contemplating it for lunch. "These make me hungry."

Tamah wrinkled her nose. "Eww. They're no good raw."

He sniffed the can's opening then imitated his aunt's expression. "They're stinky."

"They're only good when they're popped." Lileela had a hard time believing such disgusting things could be edible under any circumstances. But when heated over a bonfire, the larvae exploded, casting their orange skins to the winds and leaving behind tender morsels of unsurpassed deliciousness.

Everett shook the can and peered inside. "Why can't we do it now?"

"'Cause we save 'em up till we have enough." Tamah searched among a cluster of hole-riddled foliage for offending nibblers.

Lileela bent again. Using a leaf to protect her hands, she clasped a worm's fat body and pulled it off what was left of its perch. They sure were hungry little things. They might, indeed, do serious damage if left to feed. She picked off two more from the next plant.

Everett hopped up, tipping over his can. "Emma!"

After righting his worm collection, Lileela turned. She tossed a casual wave at her sister-in-law emerging from the alley but continued her work, unwilling to stop again until she'd finished the job. "Hi, Elise. How'd it go with Dr. Jane?"

Everett ran to his mother and threw his arms around her legs, almost tripping her.

Elise grabbed both his shoulders. "Easy, there, bruiser. Don't knock me over."

THE LAST TOQEPH

He grinned and patted her bulging abdomen. "Would it knock Baby out of you?"

She chuckled. "No, but it would make me plenty sore." She spanned her abdomen with splayed fingers. "Dr. Jane says everything's okay. But it'll be two or three weeks yet, and Junior here is getting bigger by the moment. Must be the Karkar in him."

Everett pressed his ear against his mother's belly then pulled away quickly. "He kicked me!"

Elise caressed her son's head. "He kicks everything that gets in his way. Including my bladder."

She tossed her copper-colored ponytail over her shoulder and turned to Lileela. "What do you hear from your brother?" She sounded as if she was almost afraid to ask.

Lileela plucked the last worm and dropped it in the can in Tamah's hands. She sympathized with Elise's inability to keep in touch with her husband through the Gannahan *meah* communication. "I don't feel much from him, but I don't get the impression anything's wrong."

She gave Elise a smile of sympathy. If it were Faris making his quest, she'd worry for him like Elise did for Adam. Both couples paired a half-Gannahan with a mate of off-world heritage. But there was one difference.

Lileela felt her own flat abdomen. Then, embarrassed by the unconscious gesture, she hurried to pick up the other collection can and hand it to Tamah. "After you empty these in the wormfarm, you'd better run home and get cleaned up for lunch. You have lessons to do this afternoon, as I recall."

Tamah flashed one of her frequent gap-toothed grins. "Do I have to run, or can I walk?"

"You must run." Lileela answered in mock-sternness. "Walking is for the weak."

Laughing, Tamah darted off, a collection can in each arm. Lileela called after her. "But don't run so fast you lose those crawlies! If they spill, you'll have to pick them all up again."

Tamah immediately slowed but disappeared into the alley without turning around.

Everett pulled on Elise's hand. "I'm hungry, Emma."

THE LAST TOQEPH

"You're right, it's lunchtime. And I need to visit the restroom. I think we should see what they're serving at Hu House today. It'll be quicker than going all the way home." She turned to Lileela. "Want to come?"

Lileela glanced at the house. "No, Faris will be home soon, and I promised to make him some fryrolls for lunch."

Elise winked. "I'm looking forward to giving some of those to Adam in a few days." Allowing Everett to drag her away, she faced Lileela as she walked backward. "Thanks for watching this one for me."

Lileela made a visor with her hand to block sunlight reflecting from a neighbor's window. "Don't mention it. And thank you, Everett, for helping in the garden."

Intent on tugging his emma's hand, the boy didn't answer. Elise stopped and pulled him to her side. "What do you say to your auntie when she thanks you?"

Everett scowled. "I thought we were going to Hu's."

"After you respond politely. When someone thanks you, you mustn't ignore them. Now, what do you say?"

Pouting, he turned to Lileela. Then, with evident reluctance, he let go of his emma's hand and made a little bow. "It was a pleasure to help you, Auntie."

Lileela nodded. "The pleasure was all mine. Now, go eat your lunch."

"That's better," Elise told him, but he'd already scampered on ahead.

Lileela headed for the cool of the house. Elise was too easy on the boy. He should have been reprimanded for not having given the proper response immediately, and no mother should tolerate pouting. A child must be taught prompt obedience right from the start. She knew from experience that these things were harder to learn when you're older.

She entered through the back door then slipped off her shoes and set them neatly on the mat. Faris didn't like it when she tossed things every which-way. Remembering his lessons in that regard, a rueful chuckle bubbled up.

Faris's deep voice came from the kitchen. "What's so amusing?"

She stopped in her tracks, a warm blade of pleasure twisting in her gut as he came through the doorway. "I was, ah..." The feeling rushed throughout her whole body under that brilliant azure gaze. "Just thinking about how cute Everett is." She stepped forward and greeted her husband

THE LAST TOQEPH

with a kiss. "It was funny, the way he and Tamah had such a good time picking those nasty beetle larvae off the powl plants."

Holding her gaze captive in his, Faris ran his hands down her hips. "Sorry I missed them. Did you remember I was coming home for lunch?"

"Of course. I just didn't expect you quite so soon." She combed his hair with her fingers. "Have time for your daily trim?"

"It can wait."

She traced his jawline with a finger. "Everyone else on this planet wears their hair long. Why so determined to keep yours short?"

He brushed her curls back from her face. "Not everyone."

"Well, almost everyone. They get tired of cutting it every day."

He lifted his chin to tickle her face with his beard. "And they wear these long and bushy too, but that's not for me. I'd rather cut my hair and beard every day than look like a shaggy-maned arych."

"I'm glad." She kissed him. "I like it short."

"And at least I'm not like old Dmitry, shaving his whole face and head three times a day."

She chuckled. "He likes the look, I guess. Won't let it go no matter how hard it is to keep up."

"That's his problem. As for me" — his brows lifted — "I'm on my lunch break, so…"

"The rolls are almost ready. I've mixed the filling and the dough's made, so I can put them together and fry them up in just a few minutes."

He drew her close. "Mmm. That's not exactly the kind of roll I had in mind."

THE LAST TOQEPH

2

When the last fryroll was done to golden perfection, Lileela tonged it from the oil and set it on the rack with the rest. After extinguishing the fire under the grid, she moved the pan off the burner. "No chance of getting those satellites working again? I miss the days when we could use all the electricity we wanted."

Faris sat at the table, pencil in hand, studying three pages of neat diagrams. He didn't glance up. "The toqeph doesn't consider it a priority."

She slid the rolls into a bowl then tossed them with an herb-salt mixture. "I'd think she'd want to restore things to the way they were before." She set the bowl on the table beside a vase bristling with mintwood sticks and nodded at his diagrams. "If you don't put those away, you'll get grease on them."

His piercing gaze sent a beam of warmth coursing through her.

"Just a respectful suggestion, my husband."

His eyes crinkled in a gentle smile. "And a good one." He picked up his paperwork and slid it into the thin briefcase that leaned against the table leg. "You've been a challenge to train, but my efforts are paying off."

He grasped her upper arms, pulled her close, and planted a kiss that made her heart race. "Lunch smells wonderful."

The change of subject left her a little disappointed. But only a little, because the food did smell good, and she was hungry. She set a plate in front of him. "I think they turned out rather well this time." She laid the bowl containing a wet handcloth to the left of his plate, a bottle of everyday blend and a glass to the right.

He put two rolls on his plate. "They look perfect."

After she'd laid out her own lunch, he rose, and together they closed their eyes, lifted their hands, and sang the midday blessing.

THE LAST TOQEPH

Although her lips sang praises to the Yasha, her mind went to her husband. It wasn't right that someone so strong and intense, so perfectly formed—so perfectly virile—should be unable to father a child.

The geneticists from the League of Planets who'd engineered his conception and development had seen to that. Until they were sure which gene controlled what and which mix created the desired results, they didn't want their creations reproducing. Or was it merely job security? Whatever the scientists' motivation, none of the renegades who'd come here seeking asylum six years ago were equipped to boost New Gannah's population.

And Lileela, of all people, had no business marrying one. As one of a mere five young settlers with Old Gannahan blood, she shouldn't have been permitted to waste that rare heritage. She and her siblings should all be fruitful and multiply and fill the planet with as much true Gannahan DNA as they could.

But the law gave the toqeph no power to say who married whom, and Lileela had no inclination to be reasonable.

Near the end of the prayer she opened her eyes a slit and stole a glance at her husband's chiseled face framed by a neat black beard—his broad shoulders and chest, gnarled with muscle—thick, powerful hands raised in joyful surrender to the Yasha.

Her voice broke. She quickly closed her eyes, swallowed, and sang the last notes of the refrain.

The blessing finished, they sat. He took her hand in his and spoke in Old Gannahan. "Thou art a joy to me, my wife. In every regard."

She squeezed his fingers. "As art thou to me."

Morning birdsong filtered through Adam's dream and pulled him to consciousness. How long had he slept?

He opened his eyes. No light yet grayed the western sky, but the *aphaph* birds announced the dawn.

Groaning, he tried to move, but didn't have room. This fissure in the hillside had seemed cozy when he'd settled into it a couple hours ago, but it was intolerable now. He pushed past the shrub that guarded the entrance into the pre-dawn chill. The rain had stopped, the sky cleared.

It felt good to stretch his limbs to their fullest. No stars had been visible behind the clouds when he'd crawled into his den, but now they spread across the black western sky like a spray of sparks, with the constellation

THE LAST TOQEPH

Ar, the roaring lion, leading the host. Eastward, they paled in the gray glow. He calculated his position. Still on course and ahead of schedule.

He allowed his limbs a final stretch, then, on the edge of shivering, crawled behind the bush again and pulled his belongings from the cleft in the rock. The tiny birds flittered everywhere, singing to the morning, as he shook out his clothes. Still damp, of course, but they'd dry quickly once they were on.

As the sun rose, the birdsong almost made his ears ring. Brown-and-orange aphaphs, no bigger than his thumb, flitted and hopped and ran across the ground welcoming the dawn with joy.

Or so it seemed. Actually, they devoured the infinitesimal *ednats* that swarmed in a near-invisible mist at sunrise. As the insects rose from the ground, the birds rose to chase them. In half an hour, they'd split the air just overhead, forming a noisy, gyrating ceiling. Then the ednats' short lifespan would end and they'd fall like dust. The birds' song would turn to mourning as they scratched the ground searching for survivors. Finally they'd grow silent until the next generation of food emerged at dawn.

With the birds now at knee level, Adam moved slowly through the swirling masses of feathery glee. He smiled. Every morning in Yereq had been like this. He doubted he'd ever see another sunrise without recalling the music of this joyful rite.

A head-high tangle of thorny growth, much of it studded with moldy fruit, blocked his route. He swung southward around it, plucking any fruits that still looked edible and eating them as he went. The sun and the birds rose higher, and the air grew warmer.

Something glinted on the ground, and he bent to get a closer look. Broken glass. He frowned. The Great Disaster had scattered brokenness everywhere. But when glass was found, it was usually intact. The sturdiness of Gannahan glass was legendary.

He'd found a variety of odd things on this journey. Not just broken and rotting manmade artifacts, but also natural ones far out of place, like seashells. All this supported the theory that the Great Disaster had sent a towering wave from the sea that reached thousands of kilometers inland, washing away everything that stood and changing the lay of the land forever.

THE LAST TOQEPH

If the Old Gannahans hadn't died in the Plague forty years ago, they'd have been wiped out by the Disaster, like the ancient Earthers in their biblical Flood.

Though the sun now filled the world with fresh, hopeful light, a shadow clouded Adam's soul. The Yasha knew best, of course. But why would He cause such destruction?

Adam reached for the Yasha in his meah, and connected, as always. But the answer wasn't what he was looking for.

I AM, was all He said.

Adam paused in his steps and bowed deeply. *Yea, Lord. Thou art.*

He kept moving, and the land grew rockier. Whenever he tried to recover his westward direction, another obstacle rerouted him to the south. Finally he found a shallow stream flowing north. The temperature had been climbing all morning, and the cool, clear water refreshed him. Moreover, its minerals and nutrients should be sufficient for a midday meal. He drank deeply, splashed water on his face before following the stream northward.

Since the brook continued to meander in roughly the direction he wanted to go, Adam stayed with it the rest of the day. Despite having to skirt a few boggy areas or detour around dense thorn-brakes, he made good time. Half a dozen shallow tributaries, easily crossed in his waterproof *hezir*-hide boots, swelled the stream.

In the second hour of Green Afternoon, Adam paused for another drink. Above the burble of the growing river, he heard the steady rumble of falling waters. He looked that direction, but boulders, bushes and hillocks prevented him from seeing very far ahead.

On the other side of a house-sized boulder planted in his way along the bank, the river sluiced steeply downward through a rocky chute and over a cliff. He strode to the edge and, careful to make sure the ground beneath him was stable, he looked down.

A well-worn animal trail descended the slope to a broad plain where the river resumed its journey. On the far side, a herd of ayal grazed among scattered saplings, the first real trees Adam had seen in Yereq. He turned his attention to the water pouring over the ledge near his feet.

It fell a few meters to fill a pool on a shelf below then spilled over onto a tall... what was that? Its color was silver-gray, whereas the rock in this area was a browner shade.

THE LAST TOQEPH

Following the animal trail, he descended the slope toward the valley, alternately studying the waterfall and watching his footing. Whatever that thing was, it wasn't rock. Too deliberately shaped, too smooth. Almost aerodynamic. The water tumbled onto the object's pointed apex then flowed evenly down its sides.

Halfway down the slope, he stopped to take a better look. He still couldn't identify the thing, but it was certainly man-made. Gouges and scrapes were visible in its surface. It seemed to have been planted there on purpose, rising out of the riverbed perfectly centered beneath the waterfall.

He continued his descent. Of all the unexpected things he'd come across, this was the strangest.

He wondered if any other fledgling Nasi had explored lands never seen before. This province had once been peopled, of course. But Adam was the first human to set foot in Yereq since the Disaster had altered it.

At the bottom of the slope, he stopped again and studied the object protruding from the base of the falls. It was as much a mystery from this view as it had been from above. Standing beside a young *zayith* tree about his own height, he faced the valley. When a sudden brightness assaulted his eye, he turned from the glare.

A glass bottle was imbedded in the sapling to his left. Apparently it had once been buried and the zayith's branches grew around it, lifting it ever higher as the tree grew taller. Now, the sun reflected off the glass and into his face.

This place was full of oddities. He directed his attention toward the herd of ayal that meandered along the far bank. Confident they wouldn't charge him because of the river between them, he kept his lahab in its pocket.

But what was that? Something whizzed from behind a rock toward a young buck on the edge of the herd. Even from here, Adam could see a spurt of blood from the animal's neck as it fell to its knees and then dropped over.

He gasped, confused. What could have done that?

He shifted his gaze from the deer in its death throes to the rock from behind which the missile had silently flown.

A man stepped from behind it and strode toward the ayal.

20

3

Sitting at the dressing table, Lileela watched Faris's reflection in the mirror as he brushed her hair. Eyes heavy-lidded and expression mellow, he stroked until her scalp tingled. Then he made a tight braid with practiced fingers.

She shifted her gaze from his face to her own and was amused to find their expressions the same. The near-smile that had played around the corners of her lips blossomed full.

After fastening the braid's end, he glanced up. "What?"

"Nothing. I just like watching you."

He nuzzled her neck. "That's good."

A thrill like a low dose of electricity shot through her then intensified when his nuzzling turned to a nibble. She giggled. "Don't you ever get enough?"

He paused and met her glance again. "Of you? Never." Then he kissed the spots he'd nibbled. "How about you?"

She closed her eyes. "No. At least, not yet."

"Not yet?" He reached past her and opened the top drawer of the dressing table. "What's that supposed to mean?"

She watched him pull out the pink embroidered collar. "How can I know how I'll feel thirty years from now?" She lifted her chin as he gently wrapped the soft band around her throat. Once it was in position, she lowered her head to let him fasten it behind her neck. "We might be sick to death of each other by the time we're old and gray."

"I don't believe that's possible. Too tight?"

She fingered the ornament as she studied her reflection. "Not at all." The collar was just right. And her hair never looked so smooth when she

THE LAST TOQEPH

fixed it. "But don't you think old people might get tired of one another after a while?"

"That's not what I meant." His teasing smile contradicted his words. "I don't think we'll ever turn gray. Gannahans' hair is dark their whole lives, isn't it?"

She rose, welling with the conviction that their love would never fade. "The Old Gannahans' was. At least, Emma says, until a month or so before they died of old age, usually some time after their hundred and tenth birthday. Then their hair would turn white almost overnight, letting them know the end was near. But seeing neither of us are full-blooded Gannahans, we don't know how we'll age." She ran her hands along his perfect face, the beard sharp and clean from its morning trim, then down his neck and along his hard-muscled shoulders. "If I get grotesque and ugly, will you still love me?"

"You won't get ugly, because I won't permit it. Not until your hundred and fiftieth birthday. Then you may grow a beard."

She laughed. "You'd be a hundred and sixty-three. I don't care how much Gannahan DNA you have, you'll never live that long."

"No?" He straightened her collar, though it wasn't crooked. "Cute as a Nobian kitbug."

She allowed him one kiss before pressing her finger to his lips. "We're supposed to meet them before the first hour of Yellow Morning."

"What time is it now?" Glancing at the timedial on the wall, he straightened. "Whoa, we'd better get going. Look what you've done. When I was with League Special Forces, I never lost track of time." He grabbed his tunic from the garment stand and pulled it over his head. "I should beat you for distracting me."

Stifling a chuckle, she put on a frown for him to see when his head came through the shirt's opening. "We could have been halfway there by now if you didn't insist on fixing my hair for me. I am capable of dressing myself, you know." She regretted her cutting tone the moment the words passed her lips. She'd only intended to *look* like a nagging Karkar, not sound like one.

"If you're not careful, I'll change out that pink collar for the red." He headed toward the door.

Chagrined, she followed him out of the bedroom.

THE LAST TOQEPH

Under Old Gannahan tradition, a married woman wearing a pink collar was permitted to move about the community and conduct her business as if she were single and free. It indicated her husband's approval of her activities. A wife wearing a red collar, however, was not permitted to leave home unless accompanied by her husband. It marked the loss of his trust, and it was a painful burden to bear.

Faris had already proven his readiness to make her wear the red. True, she sometimes pushed him. Tested his limits and his willingness to enforce them. But she had no desire to provoke him now.

After following him to the kitchen, she bowed. "I am sorry, my husband. I meant no disrespect."

He picked up his backpack. "No apology needed. I knew you weren't serious. So neither was I." He grinned. "Fact is, we both like the distractions."

She matched his grin as she grabbed her bag. "Too bad we're out of time this morning."

They passed through the front room and out the door, where they stepped into a thick morning mist. He clattered down the one flight of stairs to the ground level. Lileela made her way more slowly, emerging beneath the fog into what felt like a vast, outdoor room with a misty ceiling above.

This had been the city of Qatsyr's central chatsr before the plague wiped out the Old Gannahans. Emma still called it Qatsyr One, but to everyone else, the first chatsr the New Gannahan settlers renovated for their use was First Town.

Lileela breathed in the sweet Gannahan air as they passed through the courtyard. Despite being pressed for time, they kept to the pavement rather than wetting their feet by cutting across the dewy grass in the central common.

In the muted light, the village resembled an oil painting. Though it was primitive by the standards she'd grown up with on Karkar, Lileela viewed it with pride and contentment. The beautiful community represented her Old Gannahan heritage, her newlywed bliss, and New Gannah's promising future all in one hopeful scene.

Hand in hand, Faris and Lileela hurried toward the traveltube entrance. Their footsteps echoed wetly off the buildings. Lights twinkled in windows. Somewhere a door opened and closed. Ahead and to their left, a man called, "Good morning!" and Faris waved. "Morning, Michael."

THE LAST TOQEPH

Lileela smiled and waved as well, though she didn't speak for lack of breath. Faris had a hard time remembering her limp, and she hated to remind him, but it was all she could do to keep up.

Almost as if he felt her distress in his meah—but he couldn't, because the Earthish genetic engineers who'd designed him hadn't the sense to give him that gene—he slowed his stride and squeezed her hand. "We don't need to be in such a hurry. They won't leave without us."

She squeezed back. "If they do, they'll be leaving early, because the dial hasn't rolled into the first Yellow yet."

He tossed a glance back at the timedial tower in the middle of the courtyard, its upper third swallowed up by the fog. "How can you see it?"

"I can't. But I haven't heard the chime."

At the railway entrance, the door slid open, activating the interior lights and the moving stairway. Faris motioned for Lileela to take the stairs first. With him close behind, she stepped on and started the descent, walking down the moving steps in order to hurry things along. Before they reached the bottom, the dial tower tolled the Yellow chord, a major triad.

She smiled. "I'm so glad Roshan repaired that. The Old Gannahan way of measuring time is crazy, but their chiming timedials are delightful."

Faris snorted. "Not when it means we're late."

"You have so little appreciation of the Old music. Must be the Earther in you."

At the bottom of the stairs, he took her bag. "One thing I do appreciate is timeliness." He quickened his pace. "Save your breath for walking, because you've already told me: Gannah's not so concerned with these things. But I was trained to be prompt, and I don't like to go against training."

Biting back a snappy retort, Lileela slowed and let him stride on ahead. He could knock himself out if he wanted to, but there was no reason for her to be dragged along with him. A distant rumble indicated the others were en route.

By the time she reached the platform, he'd removed the pack from his back, set her bag beside it on a bench, and was staring down the track. The rumble grew louder, the warning lights flashed, and a pod slid into view along its rail.

He glanced at her as she approached. "I guess I needn't have worried, huh?"

THE LAST TOQEPH

She smiled. He could admit his error. Did she have the perfect man or what? "By local standards, they're surprisingly prompt."

Sleek, smooth, and shining despite its age, the pod slowed and came to a stop precisely where it was supposed to. Inside, Phinehas Yuang and Safiy tossed them welcoming nods, while Kughurrrro feigned sleep. He couldn't really be sleeping, because the trip from his station took all of five minutes. He was merely being unsociable. As usual.

Faris picked up the bags as the door slid open. Lileela would have entered, but Kughurrrro's huge feet, stretched out as far as possible in the Gannahan-sized space, were in the way. "Excuse me," she said in her best shrill Karkar.

Safiy leaned forward and swatted Kughurrrro's knee. "Hey, Kughie, didn't I tell you to move those bony slabs? The lady can't get past."

Kughurrrro grunted something that sounded vaguely like the Karkar for, "Let her climb over." The phrase had off-color connotations, but since no one but Lileela understood, he probably felt safe in saying it. Nevertheless, without opening his eyes, he shuffled his feet back just far enough that she could squeeze past.

He wanted her to have to touch him, she knew. For a Karkar, he'd adapted remarkably well to the Gannahan culture, except for the prohibition against physical contact of any sort between unrelated males and females. He seemed to be constantly looking for ways to bend the rules.

Despite her ungraceful limp, she managed to get past without loss of virtue and took a seat on the far side of the car, leaving the one between her and Kughurrrro empty.

Faris entered and, while stowing the bags in the overhead compartment, stepped on one of the Karkar's feet with his full weight. "Oops."

Eyes flying open, Kughurrrro let out a roar and drew his legs up until his knees nearly hit his chin. He blurted out in broken Standard Language, "You did that on purpose!" Because of the physical limitation of his Karkar facial muscles, it sounded more like "Oo did dat on trrrtus!"

As the door slid closed, Faris took his seat, which required him to press so close against Kughurrrro he was nearly in his lap. "Did I?"

Lileela rolled her eyes. "You're just rude, Kughurrrro. Don't play the innocent victim, it makes you look ridiculous." He had no difficulty understanding the Standard Language, just pronouncing it.

THE LAST TOQEPH

His ears tilted back in annoyance. "Ih tis too urrrli thor dis."

Safiy snorted. "Too early? The morning's half gone already. We'd have gotten here on time if you hadn't been dawdling like an overgrown toddler."

Lileela wrapped her arm around Faris's. He and Safiy were cut from the same cloth. "You were right on time. We just got here ourselves."

Phinehas set their destination on the control panel. "As far as we're concerned, Kughie, you can go back to sleep. Just so you move out of the way at Chashabba so we can get off."

The pod slid into motion and immediately picked up speed until the walls outside were a blur. Extending his legs again, Kughurrrro made disgruntled clicking noises, folded his arms across his chest, and resumed his pretense at sleep.

Phinehas looked toward Lileela. "I'm glad it's you who's got to spend the day with him, not me."

Faris answered for her. "She knows how to handle him. She lived on Karkar for ten years."

Safiy grinned. "So where'd you learn to handle *her*?"

"I've had combat training, remember?"

Even Kughurrrro laughed, though he didn't open his eyes. Lileela kept her expression bland, but her ears scowled like a Karkar's as she let go of Faris's arm and shifted as far from him as the seat allowed.

Faris took the opportunity to get all businesslike, as if she wasn't there anymore. "So how many of those machines are we moving?"

Safiy reclined his seat. Being no bigger than an Old Gannahan, it fit him perfectly. "Dmitri says the entire line."

"Which line?"

"Finishing. Scour, mercerize and bleach, sanforize, dye. The whole thing."

Phinehas took a sip from his travel mug then wiped his lips with a knuckle. "Fiber process is up and running in the plant in Shesh, and so's the spinning. The looms are all assembled, and Vin has people training on them this week. Once production's fully under way, we'll need to be ready to finish the textiles so they can be distributed."

Faris nodded. "If we don't do something soon, we'll be wearing animal skins."

THE LAST TOQEPH

Lileela shuddered. "Then by all means, get those machines up and running."

"You sound like your father." Faris chuckled. "I hear he's pushed for textile production since the settlement's first year."

Phinehas drained his cup and set it on the floor. "And he's been right. The way we use fabrics for everything from clothing to wall coverings, I don't know how we've gotten by this long without manufacturing new."

Safiy picked a bit of lint from the front of his tunic and dropped it on the floor. "Good thing the Old Gannahans left such stockpiles. Although I suppose if they didn't, it would have been a higher priority." He turned his attention to Lileela. "So what's this story you're going to research with Kughie? Something about that weird Orville Vigneron digging holes in the ground?"

Lileela sat up straighter. For once, she got to report on important news instead of the usual mundane details the Ministry of Information Dissemination kept track of. "He's weird, that's for sure. Even by New Gannahan standards. But apparently in his nosing around, he's discovered a rare element or something. And he's crafting some pretty amazing stuff out of it."

Safiy shrugged. "I've heard a little. Tell me more."

"I can't tell you what I don't know. But the geologist over there—" she tossed her head toward Kughurrrro- "and I are going to check it out. See what the stuff is, where he's getting it, how he's processing it, that sort of thing."

Kughurrrro's ears pricked, indicating he was listening.

Faris took her hand. "Once we offload at Chassabba, these two will take the tube to the end of the line. Vigneron says there'll be a car there for her to drive, and he told her how to find where he's been working. Sounds like it'll be a bit of a trek."

"Does that mean you won't be joining us for dinner at Chassabba tonight?" Safiy asked. "Esposito's got a pretty good food service going there. He serves the evening meal through all three hours of Purple. "

"Oh, we'll be there by then. We're just going to take a look around, get samples, and bring them back to analyze them. Neither of us wants to spend any more time out there than we have to. From what Faris tells me, Chassabba sounds primitive enough. Orville's camp has got to be the absolute dregs."

THE LAST TOQEPH

Phinehas crossed his legs. "Being half Gannahan, you should like venturing into the wilds, getting in touch with your inner savage and all that." He grinned. "I'll bet once you're out there, Kughurrrro'll have a hard time dragging you back. You'll never want to see civilization again."

Lileela scowled. "I haven't seen anything resembling civilization since I left Karkar."

Kughurrrro expelled a grunt of agreement, but still didn't open his eyes.

It would be a long day to be sure. She leaned her head against Faris's firm shoulder, already wishing they were back in First Town.

4

Like any good son, Natsach Daviyd Natasch had only been trying to please his em.

"It be warm now, but winter shall come." Em had sat cross-legged with a scarred wooden bowl between her knees, her brows meeting above her nose with the force of her scowl. "All those animals out there wearing fur coats, but we shiver in the cold months?" Her chopping knife worked its way around the bowl with a vengeance. If she kept it up, there would be nothing left of the nuts but an oily pulp. "Now is the time to start curing hides. And I expect someone in the village could find use for fresh meat as well."

Daviyd bowed deeply. "Thou art wise, mine em. We cannot wait for frost to bite before we prepare."

"Hmph." Apparently she thought the nuts sufficiently punished, for she set the bowl aside. "So thou sayest. But still, there thou standest."

He bowed again, scorched by the fire of her blazing violet eyes. "I leave now, mine em." Still bent, he stepped forward, kissed her forehead, and backed away. "I shall not return empty-handed."

"See to it, then. Since thou refusest to take a wife, at least thou canst take care of thy poor widowed em."

The words were hurtful enough, but the unspoken thoughts bent his back like a hundredweight bundle. *Quit wasting time listening for what is not there*, she scolded through her meah. *Is it not enough that my husband heard voices? My only son would embarrass me further by trying to hear them too?*

Accepting the chafing load of her scorn, Daviyd straightened his shoulders then strode across the chatsr and through the gate, away from the

THE LAST TOQEPH

circular cluster of huts. He felt his neighbors' eyes and thoughts following him. But not their feet. None wanted to share his em's chastisement, so they kept their distance.

Yes, Ab had heard a voice that he couldn't identify. Not regularly, but reliably. When that unfamiliar voice spoke, it had authority. It directed Ab rightly. If he hadn't heard it and followed its command, that terrible wave would have washed them all away.

Daviyd mulled these matters as he descended the hillside path. Ayal often grazed by the river on a clear day such as this. He should have no trouble finding one to satisfy his em's command. But he didn't like to go there without spending time at the Tebah, listening in silence for a voice in the wind or the falling water. And that would displease Em.

So he searched for game closer to home. If it were just meat he was after, he could have had success early on, for he found small animals. But Em wanted an ayal hide, and an ayal hide she would have. Daviyd would not have it be said that his em's son was not a true one.

The sun had soared high and was on the descent again when at last he extended his search to the valley he'd tried to avoid. There, as if waiting for him, a herd of some twenty ayal grazed on this side of the river. The breeze was in his favor. If he moved cautiously, he could reach that boulder and watch from behind it until the animals drew within range of his lahab.

Buoyed by hope, he made his slow way from the cover of the bushes into the vale, making no more noise than an ednat and blocking his meah from any intrusion. His movements wouldn't appear threatening so long as the ayal didn't discern his intentions.

Concealed by the boulder at last, he turned his gaze to the water falling with a constant, comforting rumble. As usual, a rainbow ringed the Tebah. The sight filled him with awe. Its shimmering beauty never grew tedious. But more than that, it reminded him of the promise the Voice had given Ab twenty years ago.

Ab and a hunting party had been caught in a rain. When it ended, a rainbow arched across the land. That was when Ab heard the Voice for the first time: *A young man shall come, tall as a tree and standing in the prism's light. He will speak the truth.*

Startled, Ab sought the source of the Voice. It didn't belong to any of his three companions. He had heard it in his meah, not his ears. And when

THE LAST TOQEPH

he asked, "Did you hear that?" they didn't know what he was talking about. The words, apparently, had been for Ab alone.

After that day, Ab heard the Voice twice more. He was alone on both occasions. The second communication was very short, perhaps in answer to a question he'd been contemplating: *His truth shall lead to your redemption.*

The third, which came six years ago, was a warning: *Those who would be saved will gather in the Tebah on Arawts Peak.*

Though no one else heard the Voice, when he told the people, they went to the Tebah as Ab had said. He was the heir of Atarah Natsach, so none doubted him or called him daft.

But neither did they now wish his son to hear voices too.

Daviyd gazed at the Tebah's broken remains at the base of the waterfall. Listening for a voice, though no one was near. Straining his meah toward the lifeless vessel in the water, though only living things possessed a meah. Wondering…

After long, fruitless moments he directed his attention to the grazing ayal. He knew nothing of the Voice, but he knew ayal. He knew how to please his em. He knew his lahab and how to fling it with deadly precision. When a beast came into range, it would be his, as sure as the aphaph greet the sunrise.

The ayal drew closer, and he singled out the nearest—a young buck protecting the herd's flank. Slowly, Daviyd drew his lahab from its pocket.

The sound of falling water masked the click when he opened the blade. He took aim and threw.

The creature lifted its head at the approaching whiz then fell with its throat sliced wide. A perfect throw. The beast hadn't felt a thing.

The herd raised the alarm and took off with a clamor of drumming hooves and snorting terror. Daviyd stepped from behind the boulder and hurried to retrieve his lahab, without which he felt empty and vulnerable.

It was then that, like the sudden grab of a hand, an unfamiliar meah rammed into his. He froze. No Voice, just a horrified amazement that made him lightheaded. His gaze jerked toward the Tebah. The relic hadn't changed since the last time he'd looked.

But on the far bank, a young man stood, as tall as the tree beside him— the tree with the bottle stuck in its branches. The sun shining through the bottle cast a rainbow across the man's pale face.

THE LAST TOQEPH

The rules of the quest forbade Adam from communing with anyone other than the Yasha except in time of grave need. Adam wasn't sure if this qualified, but the way his heart pounded, it certainly seemed like it.

Emergency or not, he had been seen, and common courtesy required him to acknowledge the man. He raised his hand in greeting and shouted, "Hail, mighty hunter!"

He spoke in the Gannahan language because his brief meah communication with the stranger told him that would be appropriate. But he couldn't fathom who this man was, nor how he got here. He looked like a character out of a film about ancient Gannahan history. This wasn't real. It couldn't be real.

The apparition raised its hand. "Hail, promised one!"

Even at this distance, the voice was deep and rich, the accent thick as breakfast micken. And the greeting did nothing to reassure. Promised one? Who did this person think Adam was?

Emma had trained each of her children in the detailed conventions of Old Gannahan society. If the man spoke the language (but how could he?), he might also follow the protocol. Adam took a step forward and made a small bow. "I have not made thy acquaintance."

Sure enough, the man also took a step. "Nor I thine." He mirrored Adam's bow. "I am pleased to do so, if thou wouldst."

"I would."

Both men moved forward. Courtesy dictated that they meet at a point midway between them, but that would mean standing in the river.

Apparently the wild man — or was he a vision? — had no qualms about that, for when he reached the bank, he waded in without pause. Adam did the same, never taking his eyes off the smaller man. They met mid-stream, where the water didn't quite reach Adam's hips but rose past the wild thing's waist.

The fellow planted his feet and stood like a rock, his fiery glare raised to Adam like a challenge. "Natsach Daviyd Natsach."

Adam's head spun. Natsach was a name of Gannahan legend. Moreover, the man Emma had been married to before the Plague was a Natsach. Masking his shock, he responded with perfect decorum. "Pik Adam Atarah."

The man's eyes widened. "Atarah!"

THE LAST TOQEPH

Why did that surprise him so? "Yea. Mine em is the toqeph."

This person who couldn't possibly exist stared at him. Who was he? Adam had every right and reason to be here. The wild man had no business breathing, let alone interrupting his mission.

Following protocol, Adam waited for the apparition to speak, but all the while his mind grappled with this incomprehensible turn of events.

"Let us speak on land," the man finally said. He gestured toward the far bank.

"Yea. But—" Adam extended his hand toward the shore he'd come from. "We will speak on this side."

Staring at Adam's hand, the man's eyes widened further, and Adam felt his horror. Six fingers, especially when combined with Adam's considerable height, identified him as being of Karkar breeding. And this little man knew what that meant.

"Mine ab is half Karkar." Adam answered the unvoiced question. "Mine em is Atarah Hadassah Haga Natsach Pik." The man stiffened at hearing his own name, and Adam explained. "Her first husband was Natsach."

Every emotion played across the wild man's expressive face. But his only reply was a grunt as he waded past Adam to the shore. Adam turned and went with him. Despite their difference in size, they reached land together.

Apparently finding his tongue with the firm footing as he strode onto the bank, the fellow turned to Adam. "Thou art an Outsider. Thou canst not be the one who was promised."

The man's movements were efficient and confident. But his words came out slurred. That whole speech sounded like "Thartousider. Cnstnotbe thunhoospromst." If Adam had not been able to listen with his meah as well as his ears, it would have been incomprehensible.

As it was, he understood far more vividly than he'd have liked. He was anathema to this man.

And yet, he'd come to Adam's side of the river, indicating a willingness to listen even while assuming Adam had nothing to say. But as Adam prepared to speak, the stranger continued. "Why dost thou violate this place with thy cursed Karkar feet and thy filthy Outside ways? Thou standest upon sacred ground." He gestured with an angry fling of his arm

THE LAST TOQEPH

toward the waterfall. "Thou insultest mine eyes with thy pale and arrogant face. Thou foulest the sweet air with thy stinking, lying breath."

Adam bristled, his fingers tingling with the desire to silence the man's voice with a firm slice across that short, thick neck. But he couldn't attack an unarmed man, and this one's lahab lay beside the fallen beast. Steeling his jaw against all the things he might have said, Adam merely answered the last accusation first. "I speak the truth."

As the words fell, they must have stabbed a hole in the man's defiance, for it seemed to seep out and drip to the ground with the water from his animal-skin skirt. "Thou speakest the truth." His steady gaze softened and his voice grew less harsh. "Thou standest tall as a tree. Thou cometh in the prism's light." His expression turned baffled. Plaintive. "How canst *thou* be the promised one?"

Adam was so confused he hardly knew how to respond. "Who hast promised this?"

Natsach turned wary again, as if this were something Adam should know. "The Voice."

Adam hesitated. If he asked *what voice*, would the man's anger return? But he couldn't answer without more information. "What hath this voice said?"

Natsach replied with unslurred words, obviously reciting the message by rote. "A young man shall come, tall as a tree and standing in the prism's light. He shall speak the truth."

Adam's skin prickled. "The prism's light?"

The wild man gestured toward the zayith sapling. "When first I saw thee, the sun shone off the bottle and cast a rainbow on thy face. Thou didst stand tall as the tree and in the prism's light."

A prophecy. Adam felt his hair stand on end. "The voice must have been that of the Yasha, for only He can see the future." But what did all this mean? How could Adam be the promised one, when the Yasha Himself held that title? And who was this man standing before him?

In response to the word *Yasha*, the wild thing took a step back.

Adam was more confused than ever. "What—?"

"The second time the voice did come, it spake of redemption." The little man stared up at him in awe.

Yasha, of course, meant Redeemer. Somehow, this person who shouldn't exist had been contacted by the Yasha. "What was the message?"

THE LAST TOQEPH

Again, the words came clearly. "His truth shall lead to your redemption."

Adam hadn't felt so directionless since he was a ten-year-old. His confusion was all the greater because the prophecy was for "your" redemption, which was plural, rather than the singular "thy." He stared at the stranger, but in his meah, he reached for the Yasha. *What is happening, my Lord? How must I respond?*

He received no answer other than the reassurance that the Yasha knew of this and supervised the events.

He swallowed. "I know of redemption, for I have been redeemed, praise His name. But who art thou? The voice spake of *your* redemption. Thou art not alone here?"

The man's face darkened with a frown. "Few survived the Great Death. Fewer still live after the wave. But nay, I am not alone."

Adam's heart plummeted and he felt as if he would faint. "Mine em was the only one. She said she was."

Natsach spat on the ground. "Plainly, thine em knoweth nought."

5

Unable to keep up with Kughurrrro's long stride, Lileela fell behind as she followed him along the narrow forest trail. Half-buried roots did their best to trip her. Thorny branches snagged her hair, and twice she twisted an ankle on the uneven ground.

Why did the mine have to be so far from civilization? Oh, wait. Gannah had no civilization. So then, why did it have to be so far from anything familiar?

They'd taken a car—Old Gannah's ridiculous oval version with a clear glass dome on top—as far as they could. Orville Vigneron had said they could go most of the distance on the old Almanah Road. "Shortly past the fallen-down signpost pointing the way to Towb, the road washes away," he'd said. "But at the bottom of the hill just before the wash-out, you can pull off and park. That's where you'll find a path on the left leading into the woods."

Lileela didn't bother taking notes except in her retentive mind. "And then what?"

"Just follow the trail."

Skeptical, her ears twitched. "How far?"

"You go in a ways, then up and down and around." He demonstrated with his hand. "It's a nice little road with birds and things. You walk a bit, and then you're there."

"Half a kilometer? More?" Lileela hoped he'd say less.

"Not sure. But you won't get lost. I got the path worn down pretty good."

Now, as she stumbled through this brutal Gannahan wilderness, she doubted she was the right person for this assignment.

After leaving Faris and the others at Chassabba, Kughurrrro had managed to actually sleep, sprawled across a whole row of seats, as he and

THE LAST TOQEPH

Lileela continued on the tube another hour or so. Glad of the quiet, she took out her notebook and started a draft of her article, sketching out the basic structure but leaving the details to fill in later.

When she'd gone as far as she could, she closed the file. After a careful glance at Kughurrrro to make sure he was really sleeping, she unlocked another document entitled "FFO," which she alone knew meant *For Faris Only*. It was the only file in her notebook with access restricted by password protection, and her blood ran cold at the thought of anyone reading it.

But the fear soon faded and a smile emerged as she re-read the poem she'd started writing earlier. Continuing the thoughts and polishing the verses to a warm glow kept her fully engrossed until the pod slowed then eased to a stop at Sepheth.

That was as far as they could go, for a kilometer or two after that, the tunnel became one of the many casualties of the Great Disaster.

She saved the document as Kughurrrro lifted his head and rubbed his neck. He blinked his yellow eyes, ears tilting back in distaste at awakening in such surroundings. Privately, she shared his unvoiced opinion, preferring the fantasy world about which she'd just been waxing poetic to the one outside the window.

She slid the notebook into her satchel then glared at the giant nearly filling the car with his massive body. "Have a nice nap?"

He grunted, which she interpreted to mean, "Not hardly." He pressed the button to slide the pod's door open then clambered out with a rumble of Karkar complaints about primitive planets. Though she didn't reply, her mind shouted a hearty *amen*.

In places, Gannah had a sort of poetic charm. This dimly lit, echoing, vermin-infested underground tube station, with its deathly emptiness tugging the soul into its invisible depths, was not one of them.

They hurried to the exit as fast as their stiff legs could carry them. Behind her, Kughurrrro yawned loudly as they climbed the rubble-strewn stairs to ground level, but all six of Lileela's senses were alert for signs of danger. No human foot had trodden these steps, nor human lungs breathed this chatsr's air, since the Plague a generation earlier. None but weird Orville's, that is. And he hardly qualified as human.

Lileela felt the stares of countless creatures as she and Kughurrrro emerged above ground. The vacant chatsr seemed to hold its breath at their appearance.

THE LAST TOQEPH

From the way Kughurrrro cried with delight upon seeing the promised car and hurried toward it, he must have felt as uncomfortable as she. He wouldn't have been eager to cram himself into the tiny vehicle otherwise.

Once safe within the car's confines, Lileela breathed a sigh of relief. Her sigh became a prayer of thanks when the motor started at the first press of the button, with the indicator showing a full charge in the fuel cell.

Lileela urged the vehicle forward. "Looks like we're good to go."

Kughurrrro seemed to be trying to shrink his body to fit into the seat. "I hope young Vigneron's mine will be worth all this suffering."

So did Lileela. She failed to see how anything Orville did could be worth a journey to the end of the world. But if she hoped one day to be head of the Ministry of Information Dissemination, she must be willing to do whatever it took to gather information to disseminate.

First, to locate the Migrash — the Old Gannahan designation for whatever road led away from a chatsr. That turned out to be easy, as the layout of all Gannahan towns was more or less the same. Once outside the walls, she had no difficulty locating the Almanah Road as Orville had instructed. They traveled it for some fifty kilometers.

With the vehicle's control console providing a buffer between them, Lileela's gigantic companion sat with his knees grazing his chin. He stared through the bubble at the vast wasteland tumbling past. The pavement had crumbled, and the encroaching flora left little over a car's-width of unobstructed road. It was almost like being encased in the underground tube, but with walls of foliage instead of concrete.

The going was much slower — and bumpier — than by rail. Though it robbed power from the battery, Lileela shifted into hover mode to avoid jarring their teeth loose on the broken excuse of a highway.

They passed several other roads branching off. But if any headed for the old town of Towb, as Orville had indicated, they saw no fallen-down signpost. Eventually reaching the highway's abrupt end at the edge of a ravine, she backtracked, looking for a path at the bottom of some hill.

In the first nondescript hollow they came to, she noticed the remains of a road. Probably paved at one time, it would be indiscernible now except that it bore signs of recent use.

"That must be it." Lileela turned onto it. Wondering how much power they'd expended in their meanderings, she glanced at the gauge. What? The indicator hadn't moved. Was it not functioning? Great. How would she

THE LAST TOQEPH

know if they had enough power to get back? If she survived this ordeal, she'd never leave First Town again.

The trees closed in tighter as they went, and the road was nothing more than flattened undergrowth. Kughurrrro had been oddly quiet throughout the drive, making only occasional snide comments. The close quarters must have stifled his usual garrulous nature.

After traveling over a kilometer into a forest that seemed to grow ever denser, if that were possible, she pulled to a stop behind an abandoned truck blocking the way and peered through the dusty glass of her car's dome. "Is that Orville?"

"I believe it is a truck." Kughurrrro groaned as he shifted his cramped position.

She rolled her eyes. "Yes. But is he the one who left it there?"

He unlatched his door, lifted it, and began the laborious process of removing his seven-foot frame from the vehicle. "Let's see if there's a path anywhere near."

Lileela exited slowly then stretched. "I'm beginning to think that path doesn't exist. But at least we can take a break."

After grabbing their gear from the vehicle's storage compartment, they examined the area. Lileela soon spied a narrow track disappearing into the woods, and they followed it.

The hard-packed trail was ten centimeters wide at its broadest. It was surely the one Orville told them about, because it meandered the way his conversation did.

Mocking Orville's directions, Lileela muttered under her breath as she disengaged a bramble from her tunic sleeve. "It's a nice little road."

Kughurrrro's lumbering form drew farther ahead by the minute, but she couldn't move any faster.

"With birds and things." A flapping flock of black oreb darkened the sky as they rose, screaming, from the trees ahead. The approach of Kughurrrro, who trod as daintily as a bulb-footed Eutarian pachyderm, had undoubtedly spooked them.

The trail took a sharp bend then plunged into a gully through which oozed a slimy, leaf-covered stream. Fortunately, Orville had been considerate enough to cut steps into the steepest part of the descent, or Lileela wouldn't have made it down alive.

THE LAST TOQEPH

The long-legged Kughurrrro hopped the stream without wetting his feet, but Lileela had to pick her way across slippery steppingstones. Even the stern Gannahan sun couldn't penetrate the depth of the forest canopy down here. Glowing eyestalks protruding from the water at the far bank made her jump and almost fall in. But the poisonous tsphardeq the eyes belonged to didn't spring at her. Must have still been recovering from the shock of seeing the giant Kughie soar over it a minute earlier.

By the time she'd climbed the slope on the other side, she'd lost sight of her companion. Panic welled up, but she fought it down with logic. Orville was right: the path was well trodden and easy to follow. Wherever they were going, she'd find the Karkar waiting once she got there.

But, to her relief, she found him around the next bend, standing in a patch of sunlight examining a rock in his big, six-fingered hands.

She limped toward him. "Find something good?"

"I don't think so." He brushed dirt from its surface. "The rock is ordinary, but the insect was not. Two pairs of pink wings and a tail like a spring. It flew before I could get a good look at it." He dropped the rock and turned his attention to her. "I forgot about your affliction. I'll move more slowly to accommodate you."

She scowled. "It's not an affliction."

"Your *condition*, then." Once she caught up, he stepped off the path, bravely standing on a tussock of some unidentified vegetation that probably sheltered an army of small, unfriendly creatures, and gestured for her to go in front of him. "If our brilliant Karkar neurological specialists had not reversed your paralysis? Now, that would be an affliction."

"I'm told my distinctive limp adds charm to my character."

Kughurrrro's laugh made the forest vibrate. "It does indeed. I suppose it's your dear little husband who says that?"

Did he *try* to be annoying, or did it come naturally? "Everyone on the planet is little compared to you."

"Mostly, yes, excepting your father, Adam, and your auntie. But your husband? He's small by any standard. And I'm surprised he'd allow you to traipse through the wilderness alone with your handsome uncle."

His bulk towering behind her made her skin crawl. "You're not my uncle. You're the geologist who's going to help me report about this mine, because you know more about these things than I do."

THE LAST TOQEPH

He snorted. "I know more about most things than you. And I married your aunt. That makes me as much your uncle as the late Ogliziizzl was, bless him. Moreover—" It sounded like a branch had slapped him, and he sputtered. "Moreover, it is you who accompany me on *my* errand. I am here to examine the mine, and you to record the event."

"Same beast, different stripe." Would this trail ever end? They could have walked to Ayin by now. And being in the lead, she ran into a new weaverrat web slung across the trail every few steps, usually just about face-level.

"But does he mind? Being alone in the forest with—"

She stopped and turned to him. "Of course not. Because I'm a chronicler for the Ministry of Information Dissemination, and you're a geologist, and we're—"

He drew himself up to his full height. "I'm the foremost geologist on the planet."

"You're the *only* geologist on this planet. But as I was trying to say, we're here as professionals. Quit trying to make it sound tawdry."

He laughed, and she spun around and plunged forward along the trail. "I'd think after being here for six years, you'd have learned to behave like a Gannahan."

"I do, mostly. I just like to indulge in a little honest Karkar humor every now and then. You know, with someone who understands." He heaved a sigh. "Most people don't."

She shook her head. "I'm not sure I do anymore either. But I do understand how different things are here than what you were used to."

He grunted. "Different. That's one way to put it." After a few more steps, he added, "I shall never understand how anyone finds pleasure in hiking."

Though she felt like she should defend her planet to this ungainly Outsider, she wholeheartedly agreed. "I'm not fond of it myself. But, of course, my *condition*, as you put it, does hamper me a bit. You don't have that problem."

The worst part about this long walk was knowing they'd have to retrace their steps later. It would be she who slept on the tube ride back to Chassabba that evening.

THE LAST TOQEPH

The thought of her reunion there with Faris gave her new energy. Waving her arms to knock down the ubiquitous webs, she hastened her pace.

At the top of a rise, however, she paused, staring. Kughurrrro uttered a Karkar expletive behind her.

The world as they knew it ended here.

6

"Plainly, thy em knoweth naught."

More than anything else at that moment, Adam wanted the little man standing before him to vanish like a bad dream. But he was solid. Thickly muscled, eyes blazing.

Adam stiffened. He couldn't stand here sparring with an obnoxious impossibility, no matter how insistent it was. "Mine em hath seen and done more than thou canst imagine. Moreover, she hath given me a mission, and I cannot allow thee to keep me from it. I pray thee, stand aside."

"A mission?" The fellow was as immovable as a boulder. "If thou art indeed the one the Voice promised, is it not thy mission to bring us redemption?"

Adam's stomach rolled over. His mind couldn't deal with these events, and his feet refused to consider changing their course.

"I am bound for Dadan. I must be at the Point of Chen in six days."

Natsach's black brows rose. "Thou lookest not like a fish."

Through his meah, Adam discerned what he meant. "The Point is under water?"

The man nodded. "Yea, as is much of the region once called Dadan. What is thy mission thence?"

"I cannot say."

But the little man could read meahs too, and his expression revealed incredulity as his critical gaze scanned Adam from high head to long foot, lingering on the twelve digits in between. "Thou hopest to be a Nasi?" He almost choked on a mouthful of what must have been contempt. "How? Thou art no true Gannahan."

THE LAST TOQEPH

Adam's head buzzed. He'd heard of pure hatred, but this was the first time he'd experienced it. He spoke through clenched teeth. "I was born on Gannah. Descendant of Atarah. I am more Gannahan than most in this world."

The violet eyes narrowed. "Thou art the one of whom the Voice did speak. Yet thou wouldst pass by on a mission to serve a people as polluted as thyself, rather than bringing true Gannah the promised redemption. Am I to let thee go thy faithless way, or kill thee where thou standest?"

As Adam considered pulling out his lahab, his fingers twitched—a fact he could see his adversary's quick eye observed. Adam sensed no dread in the other man's heart. Though unarmed and dwarfed, Natsach was ready for a fight.

Adam struggled to wrest his reason from the grip of hate, confusion, and cold, hard fear. "Thou shalt return to thy kill on the other side of the river, and I shall go my way. When my quest is fulfilled, we shall meet again."

At the mention of the ayal, the sharpness faded from the other man's glare and his thoughts turned inward. So, he was on a mission of his own, was he? Not for position and power, but survival in this harsh wilderness.

Adam's anger ebbed just a little. "Then, we shall speak more freely, I hope."

Natsach bowed stiffly. "We shall. Until then, I have much to contemplate."

Adam returned the bow. The man's contempt was still apparent, and still stung. Sharply. But Adam wanted to get away as quickly as possible. "Until then."

Natsach made a deeper bow. "Gannah lives."

It was the ancient farewell, not one the New Gannahans used. But Adam matched the other man's bow. "Gannah lives."

Natsach turned away and plunged back into the river. Adam watched for a moment, but the apparition never looked back.

Shaken, Adam turned his gaze to the west. He had no reason to doubt what the man said, that the Point of Chen no longer existed. Had this happened in the Great Disaster, or was it a more recent development? Whatever the case, he sensed no deceit in his meah. Moreover, a Gannahan—a genuine Old Gannahan, which this Natsach must be, impossible though it was—didn't lie.

THE LAST TOQEPH

If he couldn't meet the toppeller at the Point of Chen, he'd get as close as possible and pray the toppeller found him. What more could he do?

He wouldn't stand here any longer, that was for sure. Visualizing the outdated map of Gannah as he'd memorized it, he analyzed the angle of the sun and set out with long strides for what used to be Dadan.

It seemed everything mocked him. The sun burned his Karkar-pale skin. Insects swarmed in his face, and birds swooped near, eyeing him with suspicion. He walked faster. When he couldn't outpace his inner disquiet, he accelerated to a jog.

That was better, somehow. It made him feel in control. His legs were long and agile, the ground a blur beneath his feet. No one could say he wasn't a Gannahan. No one could call him an aberration. He was a fine specimen of a man in body, mind, and character. He was heir of Atarah. One day, he would rule all Gannah. See what that wild Natsach would say then!

He barely saw the land he passed through. He trotted straight, more or less, west and northwest, certain of his footing, his destination, his purpose. His pedigree. His rightness in leaving Natsach and continuing his quest.

After a long while, he slowed to a brisk walk. The thoughts he'd been trying to escape caught up with him: the Yasha had told that man he was coming. A young man tall as a tree who stood in the prism's light. What else could the prophecy mean, but Adam standing in that spot with the sunlight refracting through the bottle? The Yasha had foretold it and brought it to pass.

The sun sat poised above the horizon. Adam had run all afternoon, but his confusion kept pace with him.

He wished — oh, how he wished! — he'd never met Natsach Daviyd Natsach. But they *had* met.

He had to tell Emma.

And he had promised to return.

Nothing would ever be the same. He was sure of it.

Squinting against the sun, Lileela stared at the endless plain below. A treeless expanse spread from the bottom of the cliff beneath her feet to the hazy horizon. Small pools dotted the ground, and a fishy odor wafted up.

THE LAST TOQEPH

Behind her, Kughurrrro voiced her thoughts. "It's like a different planet."

After surveying the scene a few moments longer, Lileela pointed at a cluster of strange, crude structures far below. "It's Planet Orville. There's his camp."

The trail they'd been following skirted the cliff's edge a short distance before plummeting downward in an exhausting series of slopes, steps, flats, and switchbacks that, presumably, led to their destination. Lileela wanted to cry. Getting down would be difficult. Climbing back up would be nearly impossible.

She set her jaw. This would be her last field trip. If she couldn't report from the palace or one of the chatsrs of Qatsyr, she wouldn't take the assignment. And if that cost her a career, she'd find another one.

Kughurrrro snorted as only a Karkar could. "We're supposed to walk down there? On that ridiculous excuse for a road?" Despite his grumbling, he moved forward with determination. "Too bad there's no such thing as an elevator on this backward world."

Resigning herself to her fate, Lileela followed him along the rim. "We do have elevators here."

He didn't stop. "Point me to one, then, if you please."

"I don't mean *here* here. I mean at home. You know, in Qatsyr. In Gullach." At least he kept the pace slow.

He didn't answer. Just followed the trail, with Lileela tagging along.

She'd expected an arduous journey, but this got more ridiculous by the minute. It was long past lunchtime, and they hadn't even arrived at their destination. It was plain to see they wouldn't be back at Chassabba by nightfall, and out here, she had no way to communicate with Faris. He'd worry about her if she didn't show up.

From the way Kughurrrro stopped every now and then to examine things, he appeared to be enjoying himself. Or did he pause to let her catch up? No, he seemed truly intent on studying the wall to their left, the crumbles of rock at their feet, and features of the sheer drop-off to their right, with professional interest.

Lileela, however, stayed as close to the wall as possible without scraping her shoulder raw, and didn't toss so much as a glance toward the abyss beside them.

THE LAST TOQEPH

By the time they reached the bottom, she was rubber-legged, damp with sweat, and grimy with grit. In contrast, her long-limbed companion seemed energized by the sight of the rustic huts—was that the right word? More like the misbegotten, misshapen jumble of cobbled-together rocks, sticks, grasses, and mud—at the foot of the cliff.

"Ah!" Kughurrrro bellowed. "Civilization!"

Now it was Lileela's turn to snort. "Is that what you call this?"

Three structures stood in a semi-circle against the cliff face, with a fourth pressed to the wall like a smashed bug. All were dome-shaped, built of rubble, and artful as a child's mud pie.

The largest probably housed Orville's kiln, if the massive stone chimney rising from the top was a reliable clue. Another hut might have been his sleeping quarters, and the one with the most windows was probably his workshop. How about that one against the cliff? Was that supposed to be the mine entrance?

Lileela surveyed the area for their host. "Hello, Orville? Are you here? This is the afternoon you said we should come."

No answer but the cry of the *neshar* soaring overhead.

The compound was floored with small broken stones, which Orville had probably strewn across the muddy ground to make things less sloppy. Seeing no one about, Kughurrrro strode past Lileela and crunched across to the little building against the cliff face. He opened the door, bent double to look in, then bellowed into it in the Standard Tongue. "OrrrrrrrDIL? ORRRRRRRRdil!"

Lileela realized with a flush of embarrassment that her real purpose here was merely to interpret; Kughurrrro could easily record his findings without her help. As he'd said, her role was to assist him rather than the other way around.

But Orville answered neither Kughurrrro's teeth-grating shriek nor Lileela's more decorous hail. After the echoes died, the giant straightened himself and spoke in his own language. "He is not here."

She limped across the compound to the dwelling and knocked. It had no windows, and the door was closed. A faint, unpleasant smell surrounded it. In fact, the same odor hung in the air throughout the entire area. "Are you here, Orville?" When he didn't respond, she had no desire to open the door and see who or what was inside.

THE LAST TOQEPH

Kughurro's ears tilted back in a Karkar frown. "I'm here to see this mine, and that is what I shall do. I do not need an escort."

Lileela bit her lip. "Don't you think we should wait until he gets back?"

"He's scattered in his mind. Likely he's forgotten we were coming and won't be back for days."

Her stomach growled. She sank onto a pile of rock near Orville's door and rummaged in her bag. "I can't go any farther without a break. Let's have lunch, and maybe he'll be here by the time we're done." She pulled out her water bottle and took a long drink.

Kughurrrro hesitated. "I could eat." He looked about, probably searching for a place to sit. "But..." He shrugged. "I suppose this will do." He brushed off the top of another pile of rock near the mine entrance and lowered himself onto it. His ears twitched with distaste as he opened his bag. "At least I thought to bring hand disinfectant."

Lileela had a fryroll left over from yesterday as well as a summerfruit. Kughurrrro produced two containers of something pureed. A Karkar's mouth was small and offered limited chewing abilities, and their foods were always soft. Hard to believe she'd grown up on that stuff. The thought turned her stomach these days.

While he cleaned his hands, she sang one verse of the midday prayer of thanks. Her hands shook with hunger, and she didn't want to delay her lunch by singing the whole thing. Kughurrrro probably wouldn't have appreciated it anyway.

When she finished, he tipped his head in a Karkar nod of agreement. "Amen."

Lileela's brows rose with surprise. Since when did Kughurrrro participate in prayer, however cursory? "Amen," she echoed, then unwrapped her roll.

They ate in a strangely companionable silence, each wrapped in private thoughts — which Lileela suspected overlapped. Where was Orville? Would this trip be for nothing? How long would they be here, and how much difficulty would they have getting back?

They finished their lunches at about the same time, and Kughurrrro replaced the empty containers in his pack. "Orville is not here. I will visit the mine without him." He rose and turned to the entrance.

Lileela stowed her food wrappings in her bag and limped after him. "I'm not sure that's a good idea."

THE LAST TOQEPH

"Why not? I didn't come all this way to sit in the sun." He bent again and peered in. "Will I fit, though? It must widen further in, or he wouldn't have room to work."

"Isn't it too dark in there to see anything?"

He reached in and pulled out a lantern. "He left this just inside."

The idea of Kughurrrro disappearing into that dark hole and leaving her alone gave her a bad feeling. "If you get stuck, I'm not pulling you out."

He got on his hands and knees and pushed his bag into the opening. "You wouldn't come in after me?"

"Not on your life." She doubted he heard, since his upper half had already vanished into the hole with the rest of him sliding after.

For several moments, she stood listening to the scrape of his movements and a succession of grunts and expletives. Apparently the channel had not widened further in. Not yet, at least. Or not enough.

She went to the entrance and peered in. A short distance down the tunnel, the lantern cast a weird, dancing gleam on a ceiling ridged with dig marks. His body blocked the rest of the light, and his house-sized boots waggled as he elbowed after it. The damp, earthy smell had overtones of burning lantern, grunting Karkar, and that other strange odor she couldn't identify. "You okay?"

"It looks like it opens out ahead. All I have to do is get there. Then I'll be fine."

The light continued to dance slowly along the ceiling as he wormed his way in. He shouldn't be doing this without Orville.

When her back ached from stooping, she withdrew but left the door open. Orville said he'd be here. Had seemed eager for Kughurrrro to see his discovery. Where was he hiding?

She went back to the dwelling hut and rapped again. No answer. The door was latched on the outside, so he couldn't be in there. She opened it anyway. "Orville?"

The structure contained a sleeping mat—probably crawling with vermin—a chest of some sort, and a few cooking pots and other utilitarian items piled on a table made of lashed-together sticks. But no Orville.

She backed out.

As no smoke came from the third building's chimney, he wasn't likely to be there. But she had to look.

THE LAST TOQEPH

The shack housed a dome-shaped kiln with a chimney that went through a hole in the rounded roof. Both the kiln and the chimney looked as if they'd been made from the ground itself. Nearby stood a rack of unfamiliar metal tools and other items, and near the door, a huge mound of reddish rock. Leaving the door open for light, she stepped to the rock pile and picked up a sample. It was gritty and odorous. Whatever sort of mineral it was, its scent was what permeated the whole area.

She dropped the rock onto the pile and exited the building, making sure to latch the door. Then she crossed the small courtyard to the mine entrance. "How are you doing, Mr. Kughurrrro?"

He didn't answer. Great. She got down on hands and knees and stuck her head and shoulders into the opening. "Mr. Kughurrrro? Everything okay?"

"Yes! It's wonderful!" His voice had the weird quality of both echoing and sounding muffled.

She breathed a sigh of relief. "You have room to move, then?"

"I'm no longer on my belly, if that's what you mean. But it's good I'm not claustrophobic. You must see this. Where are you?"

"I'm out here. Shouting through the door."

His excitement was audible. "This is amazing. You must come."

Peering into the darkness, she wrinkled her nose at the thought.

A light shone in the distant dimness. "Why are you standing out there? You are a reporter, aren't you? How can you report on what you can't see?"

She gritted her teeth. Hard to argue with that. "Okay, I'm coming. Keep shining that light on the tunnel. I'll head for it."

"Small as you are, you should have no trouble." His chuckle, bouncing off the walls, sounded like it came from nowhere and everywhere at once. "I might even have widened the passage for you with my splendid bulk."

Lileela had never been fond of dampness, darkness, worms, or tight spaces. But it was worse after her spinal cord injury as a five-year-old. Since then, it terrified her to be immobilized. The prospect of crawling into that dark hole filled her with dread. She'd be trapped. Helpless.

Paralyzed.

She closed her eyes and took a deep breath. She was the daughter of the toqeph. Not only that, but the wife of the bravest man in the galaxy. If Faris knew how scared she was, he'd laugh at her.

THE LAST TOQEPH

Keeping her eyes on the light ahead, she held her breath and plunged in.

Once she'd made the decision, it wasn't bad going. Crawling on hands and knees, she moved far easier than Kughurrrro must have. A few more meters, and she'd be in the opening beyond, standing upright.

But that torch was bright. "Could you lower the light a little? You're blinding me."

"Sorry." He cast the beam across the opening but not directly into it. "Can you see the walls in here? Can you see what they're made of?"

She paused to blink hard. "All I see is spots. But I'll be fine once my eyes—ouch!" She pitched sideways and banged her head on the side of the tunnel. Why was she so dizzy? And what was that rumbling? Kughurrrro let out a yell. The light went out and the ceiling pressed down on her, knocking her flat.

"Mr. Kughurrrro!" Chin pressed on the floor, she choked on swirling dust and grit while Gannah writhed and growled all around her. "Mr. Kughurrrro! Is this an earthquake?"

THE LAST TOQEPH

7

Lileela lay in utter darkness, pressed against the tunnel's floor and choking on dust. Every movement caused pain in her legs, but at least she could feel them.

She tugged the neck of her tunic over her face to filter the air. But, because the fabric was permeated with dust, it only made things worse. It took several moments to bring her coughing under control and assess her situation.

It wasn't good. No matter what angle she came at it from.

Put it in a positive light. Any light would be nice about now. Well, okay, she was alive. She wiggled her toes—and gasped with pain. Nothing wrong with her spine, but she couldn't say the same for her legs. Hands and arms were functional. She closed her eyes and tried to will the world from spinning, her stomach from churning. A wave of bright diamonds sparked across her vision in a swirling pattern that narrowed into nothing, sucking her consciousness away with it.

Squeezed into a chair at the kid-sized table in the playroom, Ra'anan tried to summon more patience. Her little sister Tamah was bright enough, but she had a dense streak where arithmetic was concerned.

"No, sweet. Just the opposite. The larger the number on the bottom of a fraction, the smaller the portion. It's easy to see a half is bigger than a quarter, right?" She wrote the fractions on Tamah's whiteboard then drew a pie diagram below each. "Even though two is a smaller number than four?"

Ears tilting back, Tamah made a show of crossing her arms and scowling darkly. "Well, that's just stupid. A bigger number should be a bigger piece."

THE LAST TOQEPH

Was she just doing this to be difficult? "Let me show you again." Ra'anan pointed to the pie divided in half. "How many pieces?"

Tamah bent her head down, refusing to look. "I'm tired of this game. Can we play someth—"

Tamah's expression changed from defiance to alarm as sudden pang of terror tore through Ra'anan's meah.

"Lileela?" they said together.

Tamah threw herself into Ra'anan's arms. "What just happened to Lileela? She's scared!"

Holding the trembling eight-year-old, Ra'anan tried to analyze the panic they both felt on behalf of their older sister. "She's scared, all right." She jerked as a pain shot through her lower legs. "And I think she's hurt." She extricated herself from Tamah's grasp and staggered up from the tiny chair. "We'd better talk to Emma."

Eleven-year-old Hushai puffed an insect away from his face as he pushed the mower. The rolling blades sliced off the grass with a smooth, rhythmic swish. He'd been at it for a couple of hours, and the grassy strips between the rows of powlroot seemed to grow longer with each pass.

He turned and made the last cut along the edge of the long, straw-covered mound. One more row after this, and then lunchtime.

Watching at the end of the mound, Mr. Mutombo removed his wide-brimmed hat and mopped his forehead with a handkerchief. "You still here?"

Hushai pushed the machine past Mr. Mutombo, around the end of the row, then onto the last dividing strip. "Yes, sir. It's a good morning for mowing."

The farm manager replaced his hat and tucked his handkerchief in his back pocket. "Hot as blazes, though, ain't it?"

"Not too bad." Hushai kept mowing. He knew the man didn't expect him to stop.

When Hushai turned and made the second pass, his boss was behind him. "Once you're finished here, you're done for the day. I don't want your em to accuse me of keeping you from your schoolwork."

Hushai shrugged. "She likes that I help you."

THE LAST TOQEPH

"I don't doubt it. But you've got to learn other things besides farm work. I'll take the mower back when you're through. Run over and eat your lunch." Mr. Mutombo pointed toward the shaqad grove. "Then head on home."

The powlcurd-cheese-and-radish sandwich Hushai had made for himself that morning called to his stomach. Had Ittai brought it yet? "Yes, sir."

It was true about the schoolwork. He had a report to write about the ancient Wildlife Wars. Last night, when Emma had asked about his progress, he'd promised to finish today. But it was too beautiful a morning to be indoors struggling with words. He'd rather be at the farm, getting his hands dirty and coaxing plants to thrive.

Mr. Mutombo shared his passion for agriculture. Even now, he puttered among the plants, pulling out a weed here and there from among the powl foliage. He'd just weeded and mulched with fresh straw, but a few stray invaders always got missed the first time through.

Mr. Mutombo met him at the end of the row. "I think I just saw your little brother run into the grove with a basket. Better get a move on before he eats his lunch and yours too."

Hushai relinquished the mower's handle. "I wouldn't put it past him." He started for the grove then turned back. "See you tomorrow?"

Mr. Mutombo waved. "I'll let you know if I need you. Get out of here."

Hushai waved back and trotted toward the trees. When he reached the grove, the lunch basket sat on the ground, but Ittai was nowhere in sight.

A leafy rustling in a tree above made Hushai's pulse quicken. Was that an etshaphan? He reached for his lahab. The furry animals weren't very big, but they could do some damage with those sharp little teeth. A few years ago, his big brother Adam had caught one stealing nuts in this very grove. The beast had leaped from the tree and bitten him, and the poison in the wound made his arm swell up almost twice its normal size.

But that was no etshaphan. It was Ittai, climbing toward a hanging pod of ripe nuts, their husks brown and dry.

The kid climbed like an arnebeth, balancing on one branch and stretching for the nuts that dangled from another just out of reach. Now he had them. He gave a tug, and the pod broke away from the branch.

Holding the tree trunk for stability, Ittai hugged the nuts to his chest and grinned down at Hushai. "Come 'ere and I'll drop these down to you."

THE LAST TOQEPH

Hushai stared up at him. "That branch doesn't look very strong. You'd better come down from there before—" A flash of terror cut through his meah. He gasped. "Lileela!"

At the same instant, Ittai lost his balance and fell with a cry, arms waving.

Hushai bounded forward, plowing through the long-thorned shrubs between him and his falling brother. Barbs tore his clothes and skin, but he hardly felt it as he watched Ittai crash to the ground just beyond the reach of his outstretched arms.

Hushai fell beside the motionless form. "'Tai! Are you alive?"

The boy moaned and blinked. "I think so. Ow. Oh, ow." He gasped for breath and grimaced. "But what was that? Did you feel it?"

Hushai wiped away the blood running into his eye from a cut on his forehead. "You mean with Lileela? I don't know. But I think something terrible happened to her."

Ittai tried to sit up but let out a yelp and fell back. "I think something happened to me, too." Tears welled from his eyes and he bit his lip.

"Are you hurt? Is it your back?" Hushai had never known such fear. What if the kid were paralyzed, like Lileela had been? What if they had to send him away to Karkar?

"I don't know." Ittai's words came in short gasps. "I can move. But, oh, it hurts!"

Lileela wandered toward a group of men sitting around a campfire. Around and above them, a blaze of stars swirled and shone with a brightness that almost shamed the dancing flames.

Her focus zoomed in on the campers, and she realized it was Faris and his men. Uniformed, and with their hair cropped close and faces shaven, they looked fresh off the ship they'd arrived on six years ago. Their Special Starforces insignia flashed in the firelight.

They laughed at something. As she stood behind Faris, she couldn't make her legs take her closer. But no, they weren't around a campfire, they were in a building of some sort, and the lights overhead weren't stars, but fixtures in the ceiling. The men sat around a table, eating. Round noodles were mounded in their bowls, covered with a scoop of Karkar kcht balls in rallalta sauce. Elbows on the table, the men ate with their fingers. The sauce dribbled down their chins, and they didn't wipe it off.

THE LAST TOQEPH

"Faris!" she said. But he ignored her. Though she stood behind him, she was also before him. She could see his face or his back, depending on which eye she peered through. He didn't look at her. Just laughed and popped a ktch ball into his mouth, and before it was chewed, sucked up noodles in disgusting slurps.

"Faris! Stop that!" Shrieking in Karkar, she wanted to grab the bowl and throw it across the room.

The ground moved. The lights flashed. Faris and the others looked up.

"What's that?" he asked, a noodle swaying from his lip. "Another earthquake?"

Safaiy rubbed the back of his hand across his mouth, smearing it with more sauce than it had before. "Yeah, I guess. I think both Lileela's legs are broken."

"She'll be okay." Faris licked his fingers. "She knows how to handle a Karkar. If he gives her any trouble, she'll cut off his ears."

Lileela felt herself flying backward and away from the men until they were tiny specks, with Faris illuminated by the stars. But what was that sound? She turned toward it and saw a herd of ayal clambering up a mountain in the moonlight. Their movements sent an avalanche of loose rock tumbling down with a clatter that grew louder as the rocks rumbled nearer. She wanted to run, but her legs were pinned by the rubble. From the midst of the herd, a dowb rose up, and the ayal took flight. No, it wasn't a dowb, it was Kughurrrro, with rallalta sauce on his face and one ear hanging limp.

"Lileela!" Kughurrrro's voice sounded like it was wrapped in fog.

She coughed. And banged her head on the ceiling.

"Lileela! You're alive!"

She was paralyzed again. No, her legs hurt. They didn't move, but she sure could feel them. Every cough made the pain worse, bringing her to full consciousness.

"Kughurrrro!" Her voice was stopped by a pile of rock forming a wall directly in front of her. Digging sounds came from the other side. Something big, like a dowb.

She imagined its curved, six-centimeter claws raking away the rocks, moving ever closer, until the creature's giant paw would break through and—she stifled a scream, and it turned into more coughing.

"Lileela!"

THE LAST TOQEPH

Of course. It was Kughurrrro. She must be losing her mind. "I'm here!" But where was *here*? Orville's mine, that was it. The tunnel had collapsed on her.

The digging continued. Not with claws, but something metallic. Orville must have left tools in there.

Was she running out of air? Or was she hyperventilating? Didn't panic sometimes make you think you were suffocating? Maybe she'd breathe better if she could just quit coughing. She had to quit coughing. It jarred her and hurt her legs terribly. But it was so dusty in here, she couldn't inhale without choking. Why couldn't she faint again? She closed her eyes but couldn't make her mind slide into unconsciousness.

The digging didn't stop. Would Kughurrrro be able to open the passage before she suffocated? She'd died once before. Or thought she had. Wished she had. When she broke her neck as a five-year-old. She'd lain on her back in the snow all day, it seemed, before they found her. Adam found her. He'd led them to her. But he couldn't help her now.

Faris. She strained for him in her meah, but it was like talking to a deaf man whose back was turned.

Kughurrrro was all she had. And he was on the other side of that wall. By the time he reached her, she'd be dead.

She must breathe more shallowly. That should make the air last longer.

The tunnel rolled. No, it was her head spinning. Her body was still, but it felt like she rolled over and over. She wanted to call Kughurrrro but couldn't waste the air. She'd die in here. Alone.

Thou art not alone.

Her eyes flew open. The Yasha! How foolish of her to forget about Him. *Yes, my Yasha. You're with me. I'm sorry I didn't think of that.*

Thou seldom thinkest of me, though I am always with thee.

A choking sob escaped her. *Am I dying, my Yasha?*

With Him here, the thought was less terrifying. With Him, she was safe forever. But what of Faris? He'd miss her so. And her parents? They'd almost lost her once; it would kill them to lose her again after all they'd sacrificed to obtain her treatment and bring her back home.

For Emma's sake, and Abba's. Don't take me yet, my Yasha, please? I've been sorrow enough to them. And Faris...

She couldn't stop her tears. *Oh, Faris! I don't want to leave you, Faris!*

THE LAST TOQEPH

8

Outside the dining room door, Ra'anan stood by the sidelight with Tamah clinging to her like a vine. Something terrible was happening, and only Emma would know what to do. But Ra'anan couldn't interrupt a council meeting. Watching through the window, she reached for Emma in her meah.

She'd stood there only a moment when Emma rose from her chair. Her instruction to the council that they should continue without her came through the wall muffled and distant. When she headed for the door, Ra'anan stepped back, moving Tamah out of the way as well.

Emma spoke softly as the door closed behind her. "What's happened? I sense fear from Lileela. And something from the boys."

Tamah threw herself at Emma and burst into tears. Ra'anan restrained herself from doing the same. "I don't know." She couldn't keep from trembling as Emma guided them into the sitting room.

Emma sat on a sofa with one girl on each side as Ra'anan continued. "I know Lileela's trapped somewhere in the dark. Her legs are hurt, and she's scared. Like she's in a cave or something."

Emma stared at nothing, probably concentrating on trying to contact her oldest daughter's meah. "An accident at Orville's mine, perhaps."

Ra'anan nodded. "That makes sense."

"And the boys? I sense something from them, too."

Tamah wiped her nose on her sleeve, leaving a wide, nasty smear. "They're both hurt. But mostly scared."

Emma's brow furrowed. "The boys are nearby, and they'll find help. I must focus on Lileela." She took Ra'anan's hand and squeezed. "An earthquake is likely. I'll check the seismic records. I know the approximate location of Orville's mine, so I'll send out the air ambulance in any event."

THE LAST TOQEPH

She gave Ra'anan's hand another squeeze then released it. "You may come upstairs with me if you'd like."

Ra'anan was almost never allowed into Emma's private offices, and it would have been an exciting occasion if not for her overwhelming concern for Lileela. "Yes, ma'am."

Emma rose, and Ra'anan and Tamah stood with her. "I wanna come too!" Tamah wiped her nose on her sleeve again.

Emma turned to the child. "Tamah. What did I tell you about using your clothing as a handkerchief?"

Tamah lowered her gaze. Her lower lip trembled, but she didn't speak.

"What did I tell you?" Emma's tone made Ra'anan wince.

"That I shouldn't."

"Why shouldn't you?"

She sniffed deeply. "'Cause Abba doesn't approve. He—he doesn't want to see me ever do it again."

"That's right. And wha—"

Tamah lifted her head, eyes brimming. "But Abba's not here."

"It's rude to interrupt. What did I tell you would happen the next time I caught you wiping your nose on your sleeve?"

Tamah paled and turned her attention to the floor. "That I'd have to sit in the greyroom."

"That's right. And you've been smearing mucus on your sleeve since I came out of the council meeting. Fear is no excuse for disobedience. Go get yourself a proper handkerchief and sit in the greyroom until I release you."

Ra'anan held her breath until her little sister finally, reluctantly, responded in the prescribed manner. Going to her knees and pressing forehead and forearms to the floor, she said, "Your penalty is just. You are wise to punish me."

Emma nodded. "Go."

Tamah rose and moved toward the doorway, her whimper promising to blossom into sobs in short order.

Emma turned toward a door on the opposite side of the room, and Ra'anan followed.

"You feel sorry for her?" Emma opened the door and started up the spiral stairs without looking back.

Ra'anan followed her up the dizzying steps. "You're kinda scary when you're, um, displeased."

THE LAST TOQEPH

Emma grunted in reply as she quickly wound her way toward the bright skylight. When Abba climbed these stairs, his pace grew slower the higher he went. But nothing seemed to tire Emma. "It's an em's job, you know. To teach Gannah's children obedience. The earlier you learn it, the easier your lives will be."

"Yes, Emma. You are wise." Being well trained, Ra'anan reflexively bobbed her head in a bow even though Emma couldn't see it.

Finishing her climb into the sunshine, Emma almost scampered the last few steps before hurrying into the hallway at the top. "I pray for more wisdom every hour. What's to be done for our Lileela?"

Ra'anan didn't figure Emma expected an answer, so she offered none. Just followed her into the control room on the right side of the curving hall. She stared at all the unfamiliar equipment. Some of it had been rendered inoperable in the Great Disaster six years ago, and Emma hadn't seen fit to have it repaired. Ra'anan wondered at this but didn't voice her puzzlement. Emma was the toqeph. That was enough.

Emma strode to one of the computers and pressed a couple of places on the touch screen. A wall-sized monitor across the room revealed a jumble of data in Old Gannahan characters. Ra'anan was fairly fluent in her em's mother tongue, but this was technical stuff, incomprehensible in any language.

Frowning, Emma studied it for several moments. "Well, we know there was, in fact, a significant earthquake."

Ra'anan wanted to say, "We do?" but held her tongue.

"The question is, where? All the coordinates relate to the old configuration. Now that the continent's broken up and the pieces are shifting, we're going to have to translate all this." She picked up a tablet lying nearby and brushed off the dust, then opened it. "I really should clean every now and then."

The toqeph's servants kept the living quarters spotless, but they weren't permitted in the tower. This place was off-limits to everyone except the toqeph and whomever she invited.

Having downloaded the information from the main computer to the tablet, Emma brought up a map on the monitor across the room. "Do you have any idea where that place of Orville's is? I know it's east of here, past Chassabba but before what used to be the Lower Nagad River." She isolated

THE LAST TOQEPH

the province of Periy on the map, enlarged it, and added the detail of railtube routes and major highways. "Did Lileela tell you anything?"

So that's why Emma had invited her up here. Ra'anan tried to recall everything Lileela had said about her trip. "Mostly, she worried about having to spend so much time with Mr. Kughurrrro. But she did say they'd take the rail past Chassabba until they reached the point where it was too damaged to continue."

Carrying the tablet, Emma moved across the room to the map on the wall. She drew a circle with her finger around the railtube route where it passed under the river. "Reports have the break-off occurring at the riverbed and the tunnel ending at that point. So we can guess they stopped here, at Sepheth, and went above ground." She indicated a station just before the river. "Do you know what they planned to do next?"

"Orville told them there were a bunch of cars parked at the depot left from —" It had to be painful for Emma to be reminded of the Plague. "Left from before. He'd fixed one of them so they could use it, and they were supposed to drive the Migrashah until it ended." She found the highway and traced it with her finger. "Not sure how far it goes. But somewhere off the road, they'd find a path."

Emma peered at the map. "Which direction did the path go?"

"I don't think she said. Just that it was at the end of the road at the end of the rail." Ra'anan's meah went back to Lileela, and she trembled. "What's going to happen to her?"

Emma had been entering something into the tablet, but looked up quickly. Then, holding the tablet in her right hand, she put her good arm around Ra'anan. "The Yasha is with her, sweet."

Her words sounded confident, but her meah, impaired though it was, radiated concern.

Hushai remembered his first aid lessons. "Don't try to get up." He laid his hand on his brother's shoulder. "Just lie here, I'll get help."

Pushing up on one elbow, Ittai brushed off Hushai's hand with an impatient gesture. "I'm a Gannahan. I don't lie down if I can stand."

Hushai nodded, approving. He'd have said the same thing. "Well, you're moving. So I guess that means your back's not broke." He helped him up.

THE LAST TOQEPH

Ittai winced with every movement. On his feet, he pulled himself upright, biting off a cry. "I think I can walk. Just give me a minute." He wavered a little and Hushai supported him. Face pale and eyes wide, Ittai breathed deeply. Then he glanced at Hushai. "You're bleeding. Everywhere."

"You would be too, if you'd just run through a qots bush." With his arm still around his brother, he looked over the powlfield beyond the grove. Mr. Mutombo was gone, and no one else was in sight. "Maybe you should sit on the lunch basket or something. I can run and get someone out here."

Ittai shook his head. "No, I can walk." But he made no effort to move. "What—what do you think happened to Lileela?"

"I don't know." A wave of nausea rolled over him. He clung to his brother to keep his own balance as much as to help Ittai. A trickle of blood ran into his eye from a cut on his head, and he wiped it away with the back of his hand. "We've got to go get help."

L ileela blinked her gritty eyelids. Was that a crack of light? And had the sound of scraping returned?

Wedged like a peg in the half-collapsed tunnel, she strained to focus on that flickering thread of yellow.

When she tried to shift her position for a better look, she hit her head on the rock above. Then she wiggled her toes to make sure they were still there. Either her legs were going numb or her mind was, because the pain was less intense.

The light widened, and a breath of air wafted in. Her heart fluttered. Was it true? She wasn't going to die here after all?

Another rumble shook the ground.

She screamed as the floor rippled, sending a new spasm of pain through her legs. Then the ground shuddered violently, and she was jiggled about like a powlroot on a shaking table. When that trip through hell finally ended, she lay on her side, right arm beneath her.

Though still in the hole, it seemed less dark. Particles sifted from above in a fine, dusty cascade, covering her with a blanket of red-brown material that she could see, hear, and smell. But all she could feel was her injured legs. The searing pain flew through her body and out her mouth in a shriek that would do a Karkar proud.

THE LAST TOQEPH

The agony grew by the millisecond. Ducking to avoid the dribbling rivulets of grit, she screamed again. And again. But she couldn't scream away the pain.

"Lileela!"

Kughurrrro was still there. But she had no spare breath to answer.

Metal scraped against rock again, and enough light trickled in that she closed her eyes against the unaccustomed brightness. Or maybe it was the pain that made her want to shut out the world.

After coughing up a gob of putty from her lungs and vomiting her lunch, she kept her eyes closed.

The pain in her legs leveled out at the farthest boundary of bearable. *Don't think about it. Try to occupy your mind.*

The metal scraping ceased but she still heard rocks moving. Kughurrrro must be clearing the opening with his shovel-sized hands. And making good headway, from the way the world brightened on the other side of her closed eyes.

She reached her free arm toward the source of the sounds and the light. Her attempt at calling him turned into a helpless gargle. "Kughghgh."

"Lileela! Are you hurt?"

Darkness took over again. A huge hand engulfed hers, and the tactile sensation revived her enough to open her eyes and tip her head toward him. The smell of sweaty Karkar mingled with underground odors took what little breath she had. Her eyes might be open, but pain drenched her vision and every other sense. She coughed once, yelped at the agony, and croaked a response through her gravel-filled throat. "No, of course not. Why would you think I was?"

He'd been able to fit only his arm through the small opening, and his shoulder blocked most of the light. He released her hand and withdrew. A moment later, his face appeared at the opening. "Because you were screaming. I thought—" He cut off his words with a click of his tongue. "Oh, you were joking. I see." He grunted. "I'd think you could see this is not a humorous situation. I was nearly knocked out in the first barrage. I've banged my knee quite painfully. Somehow, my ear was torn in the fracas. It's bleeding profusely. And you're stuck in a hole. I've moved all the loose rock, but it will take more than this little trowel to get through this wall. Tell me, then, what is there to make jokes about?"

THE LAST TOQEPH

She breathed deeply of the fresher air drifting her way through the opening — and didn't cough. "It was a dumb question, that's what."

And didn't Faris say sometimes humor keeps you alive? Yes. Special Starforces survival training involved attitude exercises as well as physical skills.

But she was out of jokes.

"Where are you, Kughurrrro?"

He must have been on the floor before, because now it sounded like he clambered to his feet. "In the belly of your inhospitable planet. Where did you think I was?"

No one could lift the spirits like a Karkar. "I mean, are you in the tunnel too? Didn't you get out into a bigger area before the earthquake?"

"Oh. Yes. I suppose I should be glad for that, at least. If I'd still been where you are, I'd have been bitten in pieces and chewed, not swallowed whole." He moved as he spoke, with uneven steps, as if limping. His body cast an intermittent shadow into the tunnel.

"Where's that light coming from? It's not from outside?"

"Outside? I wish. Your absent friend Orville was kind enough to provide us some primitive illumination, even though he didn't see fit to meet us here as arranged."

Where *was* Orville, anyway? "It's good he's not here, isn't it? Because then he'd be trapped with us. Since he's above ground somewhere, he'll be able to dig us out. Right?"

It sounded like Kughurrrro stopped pacing. "Dig us out? He doesn't even know we're here." His footsteps started again.

"He knew we were coming. Besides — " She closed her eyes and tried to disconnect herself from the pain in her legs. "I have a meah, remember? I've let people know what happened. My mother's hard to reach, but my sisters and my two younger brothers know. They'll tell Emma, and she'll send someone. If Orville doesn't get to us first."

He moved near the entrance. "You can communicate over such distances? Even through solid rock? How does this Gannahan meah work, exactly?"

"I don't know how to explain it. I guess you could say it's a spiritual connection. If two people have a meah, they can sense things about one another. What they're feeling, even what they're thinking, to a degree."

THE LAST TOQEPH

"This knee is killing me. I need a cold pack." With a noisy effort, he sat down. Perhaps their absent friend had provided them with a primitive chair as well. "A spiritual connection, you say?"

"I suppose. I don't know any other way to say it."

He paused. "I can't stop this ear from bleeding. If I pass out suddenly, you'll know why."

Her smile was more like a wince. "Thanks for the warning. What should I do if that happens?"

"About that spiritual connection you mention. Can you—can you talk to that Yasha of yours?"

She let out a long, slow breath. "Yes." And then, "I do sometimes. But, I don't communicate with Him a lot. I figure He's too busy to bother. And besides, I have Faris to take care of me."

Faris! If only he had a meah.

Kughurrrro snorted. "A lot of good that little *ghaannikik* is to you now. He's not the god you seem to think."

"What?" Her violent objection to the slur made her response so shrill, it rang in her own ears. On Karkar, *ghaannikik* was a derivative of *Gannahan* meaning a weak, insignificant person of small stature who considers himself powerful and authoritative. And it certainly didn't apply to Faris.

"He treats you like a Karkar gikdog. Putting a collar on you, making you heel. I know it's the Old Gannahan way, but it's horrifying. No woman should submit to that. As you should know, having spent most of your childhood in a proper civilization."

She was angry enough to slap him, if he were in reach. "I don't expect someone like you to understand. Faris is—"

"Faris is useless to this discussion. It is your Yasha I wish to speak with. If I had the means of communicating with such a Being, I would do it. Frequently. And in depth."

She didn't know how to respond.

"And right now? I would ask Him why He has done this. Will you ask Him for me? Or are you too busy lying there in pain to talk to your Redeemer?"

A chill passed through her body. "How do you know I'm in pain?"

"I am not deaf, my dear. Not that your screams weren't enough to destroy my hearing. But even now, I hear from the sounds coming from that hole that you are struggling with pain."

THE LAST TOQEPH

"I—"

"And it grieves me." He spoke so softly she wondered if he was speaking to himself. "I wish I could help you."

"I wish you could too, bu—"

"And that is why—" His voice rose again—"I want you to talk to your Yasha. Ask Him what He thinks He's doing. Oh, I know. You people always say He has a plan. And sometimes, I can see that. I understand why He sent those rays of energy shooting out from your sun to destroy our ship six years ago. He was protecting the settlers. That was obvious. I suppose the fact that the storms also damaged your planet was unavoidable. But He protected you people through it all. Not a one of you was lost. So why does He not help you now? Ask Him that. See what He tells you. Because I, Kughurrrro, want to know. And He does not speak to me."

This sort of talk coming from Kughurrrro? Lileela couldn't believe her ears. "Have you ever tried?"

"Have *I* ever tried? It's He who won't speak to me, not I to Him."

"So you *have* spoken to Him? I thought you didn't believe He even existed."

It sounded as though he shuffled his feet. "How could I not? The evidence is everywhere. I can scarcely believe I lived my whole life without seeing it. But why are you evading the issue? Talk to Him." He shuffled again. "Or don't you believe He can help you? You're the Gannahan. You're the one who's supposed to have all the faith."

"I don't—" She was going to say *have all the faith*, but didn't want to admit it. Abba and Emma had faith. So did Adam and Elise, and several other people she knew. Even Faris. But Lileela's relationship with the Yasha was more casual.

Even as she tried to come up with a response, the Yasha spoke to her. *I AM.*

In her meah, she heard the Old Gannahan words and understood their meaning with new depth. Her body shuddered under the power of them. "He says to trust Him. He's got it under control."

Another shuffle—or perhaps a jerk. "The Yasha spoke to you? Just like that? You asked Him my question, and He answered?"

"I didn't ask the question. He heard *you* ask it. And He didn't tell me anything He hasn't already said in His book."

"So what is He doing? Why has this happened to us?"

THE LAST TOQEPH

Lileela closed her eyes and breathed slowly. The pain in her legs made it hard to think. "I don't know, Kughie. I can't understand all this stuff. He just says to trust Him."

R a'anan followed Emma down the spiral staircase. Without turning, Emma said, "Though I wouldn't ordinarily want you to interrupt a council meeting, you made the right decision."

Ra'anan wasn't sure of the correct response. "Uh-huh."

At the bottom of the stairs, Emma gave Ra'anan a hug with her good arm, holding the tablet in her other hand. "You've helped me get a pretty good idea of where your sister is, and we're going to find her. I'm confident of that." Emma moved toward the dining room. "It would save a little time if you'd call your ab at the clinic and let him know what's going on. He and Rocco can assemble the emergency team so they'll be ready to take off immediately once I have a location for them."

Ra'anan bobbed a little bow. "I'll do that right away."

At the door, Emma paused. "We should also contact Faris. But he's out of messenger range. Send Danzig to Chassaba. Have him tell Faris what's going on. I'll have Rocco stop there to pick him up to help in the search." She paused, frowning in thought. "Better find Danzig first and send him on his way before calling Abba. Even then, he'll barely get to Chassaba before the medipeller."

Ra'anan bowed again. "Yes, Emma. I will."

Emma gave her a quick kiss. "Thank you, Ra'anan. You're a good Gannahan." Then she opened the door and returned to the meeting.

Despite her concern for Lileela, Ra'anan couldn't help but glow at Emma's praise. Not only her words, but especially the trust she'd placed in her. The assignment was one the toqeph would give an adult, not a girl of fourteen.

Stepping away from the doorway, she messaged Danzig. "Where are you?" she asked when he responded.

"In the garden near the front gate, miss. Repairing the edging those blasted little *chapharperah* dug up."

"That will have to wait." She tried to keep her voice from quavering with tension. "The toqeph has another task for you, and she needs you to do it right away."

THE LAST TOQEPH

"Yes, Miss. What does the toqeph require?" She imagined him bowing deeply. With no one near for him to be bowing to, it would be a funny sight should someone happen to see him.

"It's best I explain it face to face. I'll meet you in the Greatroom in two minutes. Just leave your shovel where it is. This is urgent."

"Very good, Miss. I'm leaving now. Thank you, Miss."

She disconnected the call and took a step toward the door, then remembered Tamah. She was supposed to be tending her while Emma was in the meeting.

Ra'anan went to the kitchen, where a servant hummed as she washed the round windows. "Miami?"

The woman turned and bowed, cleaning towel in her hand. "Miss?"

"I must go out on an errand for the toqeph. Tamah is in the greyroom until Emma releases her. Could you keep an eye on her for me until I get back? I shouldn't be long."

Miami bowed again. "Of course, Miss. Thank you."

Ra'anan hurried from the apartment, heart pounding. She'd enter adulthood in less than two years. She hoped by then, the weight of responsibility wouldn't overwhelm her like it did now. How did Emma stand having the whole world looking to her to lead them?

THE LAST TOQEPH

9

Squeezed between Ittai and the passenger door of the rattling farm truck, Hushai tried to keep his worry at bay as Mr. Mutombo drove to the clinic.

In the garage beneath the second chatsr, the farm manager parked near the exit and set the brake. "Here we are, boys." He patted Ittai's knee. "Need any help?"

Pale and wide-eyed, Ittai shook his head. "No, sir, I'll be okay."

Hushai lifted the door and slid out. Ittai scooted, wincing, to the edge of the seat and lowered himself to the pavement. He must be hurt pretty bad.

The empty parking area echoed weirdly. Darkness shrouded the far end, and this side was only dimly lit. Cracks spidered the stained walls, and pieces of ceiling lay on the floor. Ordinarily, the boys would have run outside to escape the gloom. But today, Ittai couldn't have moved quickly if an arych were after him, and Hushai wasn't about to leave him behind.

Mr. Mutombo watched Ittai with evident concern. "I think your dad's on duty today." He placed a hand on each boy's back and walked between them up the ramp into the yellow daylight. "You'll both be good as new in no time."

What about Lileela? Hushai wanted to ask. But Mr. Mutombo wouldn't know anything about that.

The clinic towering on the other side of the spacious courtyard was Adam's pet project. Although he and Abba both saw patients there, they also did something they called research. Adam and his family lived in an apartment on the third floor of the same building, while the research lab was on the second floor.

THE LAST TOQEPH

In the center of the chatsr, water tumbled from the fountain shaped like a tree. It filled the air with a cool, soothing music. Hushai's scratches and punctures lit his skin on fire. It would sure feel good to stand beneath that tree and let the water pour over him. Sometimes when he was a kid, Abba used to let him play in it, until Emma said he was too old for such nonsense. But since when was it nonsense to cool off on a hot day?

He bit his lip. It was wicked to complain about anything Emma said, even in his mind. As Abba said, rebellion starts with a thought. But as they passed the fountain on their way to the clinic, he couldn't help imagining how good that water would feel.

In the sun's glare, the walk across the courtyard had never seemed so far. Mr. Mutombo kept his steps slow, probably for Ittai's sake. Finally the falling waters were behind them and the clinic drew near. As they approached, the door opened, and they entered the cool interior.

A woman's cheery voice called from somewhere within the depths. "Be right with you!"

Mr. Mutombo put a hand on Ittai's shoulder. "Maybe you should sit down."

In a nearby chair, Mr. Esposito glanced up from a book. "Hello, boys. Here to see your dad?" Then his brows rose and he straightened himself in his chair. "Looks like a business visit rather than personal."

Ittai let out a long breath as he sat. "Yes, sir. I fell out of a tree."

Mr. Esposito's gaze shifted to Hushai, who took the chair beside Ittai. "And what happened to you? Looks like you had a fight with a dowb."

Hushai shook his head. "No, sir, just a qots bush."

Mr. Mutombo remained standing. "Are you waiting to see the doctor too, Adelio?"

"No, my wife. That is, the doc did a minor surgical procedure on her. I'm waiting for the okay to take her home."

He and Mr. Mutombo chatted only a minute or two before the nurse, Mrs. Lyfar, bustled out from wherever she'd been.

"Adelio? Your wife's awake. Would you like to come on back?" She glanced up at Mr. Mutombo. "Hello, Mikaiah." Then she saw the boys. "What happened to you guys?"

Mr. Mutombo answered for them. "Ittai here fell out of a tree, and Hushai got a little scratched up trying to go to his rescue. We thought Dr. Pik should take a look at them."

THE LAST TOQEPH

"Oh, my." She eyed them with motherly sympathy. "He was just called away a few minutes ago. I'd like to ask you boys about that. But just a minute while I take Adelio back to see his wife."

Mr. Esposito followed her away, leaving Hushai to wonder why the nurse wanted to ask them about Abba. He and Ittai didn't know what was going on.

She returned a few moments later. "Come on back. I'll take a look at you."

Hushai hopped up from his chair, but Ittai moved like an old man.

Mr. Mutombo cleared his throat. "If it's okay with you, Bets, I'll leave these fellas in your capable hands. I, uh, have some things to take care of."

She smiled. "I know, Kai, you've told me before. The smell of the clinic makes you want to hurl." She made a shooing motion. "They'll be fine. Go on back to your fields."

"Well, okay, then. I'll be going." He gave the boys a strained smile then hurried for the door.

Hushai and Ittai followed Mrs. Lyfar down the hall and into an exam room. She directed Hushai to a chair then turned to Ittai. "I don't like your color, young man." She offered her hand to help him climb the step to the table. "Where does it hurt?"

He put a hand on his back. "Mr. Mutombo said it looks like I broke a couple of ribs."

She winced. "Ow. That doesn't sound good." She helped him lie down then turned to Hushai. "And how about you? Looks like you tangled with a dowb."

That joke was getting old. He shook his head. "A qots bush."

"You two sure are having a bad day. And I hate to ask, but since you have meahs, you might know something about why your dad was called away in a big hurry." Her gaze went back and forth between them.

Hushai swallowed a lump of concern. "I don't know much, ma'am. Just that Lileela got hurt. Emma thinks there was probably an earthquake, and she might be stuck in a cave-in somewhere." He tossed a glance at Ittai, whose meah and expression showed he shared his worry. "So Abba went to go help her? Do you think she'll be all right?"

Mrs. Lyfar gave both boys an unconvincing smile. "I'm sure she will. Your dad's a fine doctor. Has lots of experience in all sorts of situations. But in the meantime, let me do a scan on you, Ittai, so we can see what's going

THE LAST TOQEPH

on in there. I'll be right back." She left the room and returned a minute later pushing a long-armed piece of equipment on a wheeled cart.

A scanner. Adam had showed them how it worked once. It took a picture of everything beneath a person's skin.

She wheeled it to the table where Ittai lay. "I'm going to have to ask you to roll over onto your stomach."

Ittai groaned but complied while she keyed instructions into the machine. She adjusted the height of the scanner arm to a few centimeters above his body then slid it slowly across his torso. With a tuneless hum, it cast a thin line of green light across him as it traveled from shoulders to waist.

She had him change positions a few times and repeated the procedure.

"Okay, we're done. Let's see what we've got." She retracted the arm and folded it over top of the machine, then studied the image displayed on a screen on the wall. "Congratulations, young man. We'll let your dad make the official diagnosis when he gets back, but you appear to be the proud owner of two fractured ribs." She gave the pictures more consideration before speaking again. "Now, let's sit you up and take off your shirt."

Mrs. Lyfar helped Ittai up then had him raise his arms so he could remove his tunic. She nodded as she palpated his back and chest with gentle fingers. "I'll bet it hurts to breathe, doesn't it?"

Ittai nodded. "A little."

She listened to Ittai's lungs and heart with a stethoscope then checked him all over. "I don't see any sign of internal injuries or other broken bones. But between the ribs and some bruising, you'll be uncomfortable for quite some time." She picked up Ittai's tunic. "Let me help you get this back on. Then you can lie down and rest while we clean up your brother."

She turned to Hushai. "I'll need you to get undressed."

He hesitated, and she smiled. "Just your shirt and pants. You can keep your underwear on."

She examined each tear and puncture. "You have some deep ones there. They'll all need to be cleaned, and two or three of them sutured." She opened a cabinet and removed a bottle and some gauze. "You're worried about your sister, aren't you?"

The boys answered at once. "Yes, ma'am."

She set down the things in her hand. "Let me tell you what your ab said when he left. It's the same thing he told Ra'anan when she called."

THE LAST TOQEPH

Hushai had a hard time finding his voice, but Ittai squeaked the question for him. "What was that, ma'am?"

"He said *don't worry, just pray*." She laid a hand on each of the boys. "And I think that would be his advice to you as well."

THE LAST TOQEPH

10

Lileela would have killed for one minute of relief. Just one minute.

But there was no one within reach to kill.

The pain in her legs was bad enough. Now her body lay on one arm, crushing it. Numbness crept to her fingers, and a stone dug into her shoulder. But the low ceiling prevented her from lifting her body to relieve the pressure.

At the end of the narrow opening in which she lay, the unseen Kughurrrro shifted his weight and groaned.

She supposed she'd been doing her share of groaning herself. "You okay out there?"

"Couldn't be better. My knee throbs like a pulsating *dindunskghiskallala* in its first season of growth. My shirt is soaked through with a good half litre of blood streaming from my ear, which, if it isn't stitched back on soon, will likely dry up and fall off for lack of nourishment. But I don't suppose that matters, as I'm quite certain the rest of me will die in this hole too, eventually. It altogether adds up to a strikingly fabulous day."

Lileela's ears tipped back in annoyance then rose with amusement. By the time his speech ended, she chuckled silently. The Karkar language was perfectly suited for howling a lament, and he'd chosen his words to contain a minimum of six vibrant syllables each. The impassioned recitation rang through the mine like an epic poem.

"I'm glad, Kughurrrro. I was afraid you might be upset by this turn of events." She devised the vocabulary to patter dryly against the walls like pebbles.

A guffaw bubbled from his chest and exploded with a thundering blast. "It's a rare pleasure in these parts," he said between brays of hilarity,

THE LAST TOQEPH

"to exchange poetry with a connoisseur of the rich and colorful Karkar language."

Her laugh was scarcely daintier than his. Faris was right; humor smoothed fear's bitter edge. "How about Aunt Skiskii? I've never known her to be at a loss."

His honk settled to a dull rumble. "True enough. She has a ready tongue. But she throws out words with abandon. No real artistry to it."

Remembering Skiskii's shrillness, Lileela giggled again. "But she's sincere."

Only a Karkar would find that amusing. A Karkar frantic for a lifeline. He chortled until Lileela feared he'd faint from lack of air. Either that, or cause another cave-in.

"Can I ask you something, Kughurrrro?"

He brought his laughter more or less under control. "Can I stop you?"

"No." She chuckled at his wry inflection. "Why did you stay? On Gannah, I mean. When the rest of the Karkar delegation went home."

He laughed again. "You have an interesting way with words, little madam. 'Delegation' isn't the term I'd use." It sounded like he rose. "I don't know if it hurts my knee more to sit or to walk."

A rhythm of thud, shuffle — thud, shuffle sifted into the tunnel as he paced, apparently dragging the injured leg. "We were not the most gracious of guests. I'm embarrassed to think of my behavior in those days." Thud, shuffle — thud, shuffle. The light dimmed as he passed in front of the lantern. "But why did I stay? Curiosity, I suppose."

When he didn't elaborate, Lileela spoke again. "What could you have possibly been so curious about?"

"A number of things." His shuffling ceased just outside the opening where it sounded as if he sat again, uttering a long, guttural groan. "Not the least of which was whether my powers of seduction could win over your grieving auntie."

She rolled her eyes. "You wouldn't have sacrificed so much for *that*."

His booming laugh echoed weirdly. "You think you and your little Faris have a monopoly on love?"

"Of course not." It was true, though, that she often felt no one else loved so well or so rightly. "But you had a wife on Karkar. And a child, if I'm not mistaken."

THE LAST TOQEPH

"Ah, yes. My wife Dittaaark. You never met her, did you?" He didn't wait for a response. "I thought not. If you did, you'd understand. She was intolerable. It was no loss when she left me after our daughter was born, our reproductive obligations being fulfilled."

As a child, Lileela considered the Karkar marital practices normal and acceptable. Now they seemed tragic. "She took your daughter with her?"

"Yes. I paid support as required, but I never met the child. Other than the financial responsibility, it was not an unpleasant arrangement."

Nor an unusual one, more was the pity. "I just don't understand why you were allowed to marry Skiskii."

"In the eyes of Karkar, I was a defector and therefore legally dead. That meant my marriage to Dittaaark was dissolved."

Lileela tried to shift some of the weight off her arm, wiggling her fingers to encourage the blood to circulate. "Skiskii wasn't the whole reason you stayed. What else were you curious about?"

He grunted. "What do you think? This place. It's a treasure. Having once experienced it, how could I ever be satisfied on Karkar again? What is that saying your ancients had?"

"I've breathed the air, drunk the water, and eaten the food grown on Gannah. I am Gannah," she recited. "But if that's true, why did the others leave?"

"Because they're blind. Their kind doesn't notice the rainbow above because they're too absorbed with looking down, reveling in the perfect number of their toes. Gannah displayed its glory and power, but all they were aware of was the discomfort it caused. They didn't hear what it was trying to tell them."

Lileela remembered those tumultuous days. She'd been pretty uncomfortable herself. "What *was* it trying to tell them?"

"That they are wrong, of course. About everything. The answer to saving Karkar is not pride and revenge, but—" He stopped.

"But what?"

"You're a follower of the Yasha. You know. Salvation can only be found through repentance."

Goosebumps skittered across her body.

"But my people were not yet ready to accept the inevitable."

She swallowed a dry lump. "Why did you, then? If nobody else did?"

THE LAST TOQEPH

"Because—" He rose again, moaning. "—my thought processes were more logical. I was less moved by emotion. I didn't like what I saw, but I couldn't deny it. And I wanted to learn more. If I'd left Gannah, all that would be lost to me." Thud, shuffle— "Your father had a similar experience, you know." Thud, shuffle— "When he first came here, he was helplessly lost in pride and error. What he saw opened his eyes to something new. It took awhile before it made sense to him."

"How long did it take you to see it?"

He snorted. "I was as obtuse as any. It took years. You see, long before I came here, I had read some of the great Dr. Pik's writings on the subject, his explanation of a concept he called the story in the stars."

Lileela gasped. "You read that book? He translated and adapted an ancient manuscript by one of my Gannahan ancestors, Atarah Hoseh Charash, for the Karkar people."

"I know that now, but I didn't then. If I'd known it was a translation of your Hoseh's words, I wouldn't have let it contaminate my mind. But even unaware of its origins, it angered me. What your father wrote was so radical, I was certain he'd been the victim of some sort of brainwashing procedure carried out by your mother. But then I ran across another scientist who believed the same, named Kohz. He'd worked with your father at his research facility. His arguments were difficult to logically refute."

His shuffling grew less pronounced as he paced. "I still didn't believe it, of course, and it ate away at me. That was the primary reason I pulled every string to get myself onto that ship. It cost me a fortune. But I was determined to see the lies emanating from this place put to rest once and for all." He chuckled. "The truth has a way of asserting itself in a manner we least expect."

Lileela was still in pain, but it seemed more bearable somehow. "Are you saying—you really believe in the Yasha?"

"Of course I do. I told you before, the evidence is everywhere. How can I not believe?"

She ran her tongue around the inside of her parched mouth. "So why— that is, I seldom see you at the worship meetings, and—"

"Your auntie and I worship regularly, but not at First Town where you and Faris go. We are still Karkar, you know. We prefer to sing and pray in our own language."

THE LAST TOQEPH

That made sense. But why hadn't she known this? "So who do you meet with? Is it just you and Skiskii?"

"Often your father is there. We meet on Firstday afternoons, and we discuss what was shared in the earlier assemblies. We have a wonderful time, actually. You should join us."

"Thank you, Kughurrrro. I'd like that. I'm amazed I wasn't aware of all this before."

He stopped pacing, but it didn't sound like he sat. "You and Faris have had other things on your minds, and much of your social life involves his old comrades. You really should come to visit us more. Your auntie commented just last week how much she misses you."

"You're right." She bit her lip. But it was so hard to see Skiskii with a baby.

When Lileela was growing up, she'd been her auntie's favorite plaything. Now Auntie had a child of her own—and Lileela never would. Though a woman of Skiskii's age could never have conceived on Karkar, something on this planet made her fertile late in life, much like a native Gannahan. Lileela found the whole situation grossly unfair.

"We've been busy, but so's everyone. That's no excuse." She sighed. "I'll talk to Faris about it. Where do you meet? Next week, maybe we can worship with you. Do you eat supper afterward? I'll bring three-tongue stew. Emma taught me to make it the way her em did, and it's the best thing you've ever tasted, I guarantee."

Kughurrrro grew silent, and Lileela knew what he was thinking.

For them, there might not be a next week.

11

Daviyd carried the freshly killed ayal across his shoulders toward home. Not far from the village, his friend Jether bounded down a grassy slope toward him.

A grin lit his friend's black-bearded face. "Ah, thou hast a fine one! Wouldst thou like help up the hill?" Then their meahs met, and his smile faded. "What aileth thee? Thy hunt was a success, but thou art distressed." He drew closer, studying Daviyd's face.

Daviyd avoided his friend's eye. "As thou sayest, it is a fine beast. It will please mine em." He shrugged off the load and lowered it to the ground. Bristly hairs from the animal's coat stuck to his skin, and its blood mingled with his sweat. "If thou wishest to besmear thyself, I would accept thy help." He wiped his brow with the back of his hand.

Jether's breath caught as he probed Daviyd's meah. "What is it? Nay, tell me not — thou didst not hear the Voice?"

Daviyd shook his head. "Nay." How much should he tell him? "And yea."

Jether's dark brows rose. Daviyd would rather not discuss the matter, but he couldn't keep it from one who knew him so well. "I have seen him. The young man, tall as a tree, standing in the prism's light."

The brilliant violet of Jether's eyes grew darker as his thoughts reached toward Daviyd's mind. "What?"

Daviyd grabbed the ayal's front legs. "Take the hind end. I shall take the head so thou dost not tear thyself on the spikes."

"Ha!" Jether grabbed the back legs and lifted. "It was our cousin Azar, not I, who bled more than the ayal he killed."

THE LAST TOQEPH

Taking care to avoid the animal's razor-toothed antlers, Daviyd started up the hill. Carrying the other end, Jether kept talking. "Tell me what thou didst see. Was it truly a man? Or seest thou visions as thy father heard voices?"

David gritted his teeth. "I know not." He spoke in halting phrases as they lugged the heavy load up the slope. "But solid or vapor, seeing it filled me with none of the joy that hearing the Voice caused my ab."

"Thou speakest strangely. Should I worry about thee?"

Jether carried his portion as if it were nothing. Why did the burden seem so heavy to Daviyd? Meeting that apparition in the meadow seemed to have drained his strength.

"Nay." Daviyd continued at a steady pace, trying not to show his weariness, until they reached the top of the rise. "I can take it from here, friend. The way is neither long nor hard."

"It is thy right to carry thy kill into camp alone." Jether helped Daviyd hoist the carcass onto his shoulders. "But I shall walk beside thee, and thou shalt tell thy tale. Or dost thou prefer to tell it by the fireside and frighten the children?"

"I shall tell thee." Daviyd moved on, trying to determine through his meah if anyone else was within earshot. "And we shall not speak of it with another until I have made sense of it."

Beside him, Jether nodded. "Tell on, friend."

Daviyd sighed. "Thou wilt think me mad. I think myself mad. But I flung my blade and felled my quarry in the meadow, and —"

"By the Tebah?"

"Yea. I'd hid from the herd behind the rock. The brave ayal died well, feeling neither pain nor fear. I stepped out and felt him looking at me. He stood across the river."

"Who did?"

"The man of whom the Voice spake. Tall as the tree he stood beside. Thou knowest the one, with the bottle within its branches. The sun's rays did strike the glass and cast a rainbow across his face."

Jether's meah probed his gently. Daviyd was relieved to sense he didn't doubt his words, but merely sought to understand.

"Did he speak, this man?"

"Yea, though with a strange accent." He related their greetings, his wading across the river to converse, and the man's unwillingness to linger.

THE LAST TOQEPH

Jether was silent for several moments, frowning. "Are there truly others?"

"I know not what to think." Daviyd sighed. "He seemed to be the one the Voice spoke of, but—" He stopped and turned to Jether. "He had six fingers. Each hand had six fingers! And he was taller than the tallest Gannahan."

Jether's jaw dropped and his eyes widened. "Was— was his skin and hair pale? Like a—"

Daviyd's stomach clenched with disgust. "Paler than a doe's. And his eyes? Almost yellow were they, like those of an arych. And he told me—" He swallowed a lump of anger. "He told me his father is half bloody Karkar."

"What of the other half?" Jether's eyes glowed bright.

"He spake no more of his ab. But his em? He told me of her."

"What hath he told thee?"

Daviyd wished he could un-hear it. "His em is the toqeph."

Jether uttered a long, drawn-out expletive. "Nay!"

"Yea. The Toqephites still live. They travel the world freely. They rule it unjustly, just as they have since the days of our father, Natsach the Great. And this foreigner thinks himself the evil one's heir."

"The Toqephites did not perish in the Plague and the flood?"

Daviyd hated the thought, but it was the only conclusion. "It would appear not."

"I thought Gannah had finally punished them as they deserved. Natsach would take Atarah's throne as in the days of old." Jether swore. "Did not thy father say the Voice promised thou wouldst take back that which was lost?"

Daviyd shook his head. "The Voice spake of redemption. It stated not what should be redeemed." They walked in thoughtful silence for several paces. "Nonetheless, the promised one seemed not eager to bring us redemption of any sort. Should we even accept it from such a one." He spat. "Six fingers."

The fragrance of cook fires wafted on the breeze along with the sound of children's voices.

"We will speak more later," Jether muttered, and Daviyd grunted his agreement.

THE LAST TOQEPH

A moment later, a small herd of children ran toward them, nearly hidden in the tall, waving grasses. "Daviyd hath an ayal! Daviyd hath an ayal!"

"I shall tell Em Naomi!" Eight-year-old Kenaz broke away from the group and took off for the village.

The others surrounded Daviyd and Jether, clamoring. "We shall have meat this night!"

Jether laughed and grabbed his niece, Anna. He tucked the violet-eyed four-year-old under his arm and tickled her. "The mighty hunter bringeth the beast home to his mother, not to thee. What Em Naomi shall do with it is for Em Naomi to decide."

Anna giggled and kicked until Jether flipped her, heels over head, and plopped her feet on the ground. Once freed from his grasp, she dashed out of reach, laughing. "We shall eat it! Em Naomi told us this morning that Daviyd hath gone to bring meat for our pot."

Relief surged through Daviyd when the village came into view. Now he could pass on the carcass to Emma to dress and then go bathe. Perhaps he and Jether could continue their conversation as well. But until then, he closed his meah to all.

"**T**here!" In the medipeller cockpit, Faris pointed toward the ground. "Ten o'clock. A moving light. See it?"

Rocco Stein peered through the dark to where Faris pointed. "I don't see it. Let me get closer."

Whoever held the light appeared to be swinging it to catch their attention. It had caught Faris's, at least. After a few agonizing seconds, the pilot nodded. "Got it."

He wasted no time zeroing in on the target but then slowed his descent. "It looks like a lake or something. I'm not equipped for a water landing."

Faris ground his teeth. "What are the readings?"

Beside the pilot, Roshan Tewodros studied the instruments. Though young, he understood Gannahan technology as well as anyone on the planet. "This used to be dry land before the Disaster. But—oh, I see. The water comes in from the sea and flows out again with the tides. Right now, it's shallow, and the ground beneath it appears to be solid. We ought to be able to land, no problem."

THE LAST TOQEPH

Roshan peered at the scanner. "Look there. The guy waving that lantern is moving pretty good. Doesn't appear to be sticking in thick mud or anything, and the water's only up to his knees."

"Who is it?" Pik voiced Faris's question. If it was Kughurrrro, that would mean he'd gotten out of the mine. If so, maybe Lileela had too.

"I can't tell." Roshan shook his head. "But it's no Karkar. Wrong shape."

Faris's heart plummeted as the aircraft continued to descend. Where was Lileela? How badly was she injured? Was she even still alive?

The pilot lowered the machine until the tidal pool rippled beneath them. "What's it look like, Roshan?"

"We'll get wet feet, but not much worse."

They landed. As the hatch opened and the rescue party prepared to disembark, movement outside caught Faris's eye. A man entered the glow of the 'peller's lights, shielding his eyes with his hand.

It was Orville Vigneron, slogging through the water slow and stupid as ever, his clothes filthy. Faris twitched with desire to throttle him. Why was he walking around above ground while Lileela was buried alive?

Pik splashed out of the 'peller, and, white beard and hair flapping in the wind, strode through the black water toward Orville. He shouted above the engines as Rocco powered down. "What news?"

Orville looked down in childlike shame. "I dunno. That big Karkar guy who likes rocks? Him and Miss Lileela was supposed to come and see my mine. But I wasn't here, so I missed 'em. I guess they got tired of waitin' for me and took off." He looked up, squinting in the 'peller's lights as Faris jumped into the receding tide.

"And now," Orville went on, "what with the earthquake and all, the mine's fallen in. I'll hafta dig it out again before I can show it to them."

Pik's voice squawked. "They didn't leave, Orville. They were in it when it collapsed."

Orville's jaw dropped.

Faris waded toward the gaping idiot. "Show us the mine, Vigneron. We've no time to waste."

Orville took a step back, and Pik raised his hand as if to stop him from fleeing. "He's right, Orville. We need to see the mine entrance."

The oaf glanced from Faris to Pik, then to the others who disembarked wetly from the toppeller. Its rotors were disengaged but still swept quietly

THE LAST TOQEPH

in ever-slowing circles, and its lights remained on. "I didn't see nobody. What makes you think they're down there?"

Faris clenched his jaw. "Lileela has a meah. She's been in communication with the others in her family who are likewise so blessed." Too bad this man wasn't blessed with a brain.

Orville continued glancing from one face to another. "But— they can't be in the mine. It's all closed up."

Pik expelled a sound like a Karkar curse bitten off before it had fully formed. "Just show us the entrance. Please."

"I—" Orville's face was a picture of utter confusion. "I don't think you can get—"

Faris took another step toward him. "I'm about ready to use your head for a battering r—"

Pik grabbed Faris's arm, and those long fingers conducted their owner's tension like an electrical current.

A flood of shame washed through Faris. He wasn't the only one who loved Lileela like life itself.

When Pik released his arm, Faris let out a sigh then bobbed a small bow toward Orville. "My apologies, Mr. Vigneron. My emotions got the better of me. Let's go to the mine and see what we can do, shall we?"

Orville ran his hand down the back of his head. "You're not gonna use my head for nothin', are you? 'Cause it's a little sore." When he removed his hand, the palm was smeared with something dark.

Pik grabbed it to look. The stain was mud-caked blood, still wet.

The doctor took Orville by the shoulders and turned him around. "What happened?" He pulled a flashlight from his belt and turned it on.

"I don't remember, but I think I fell. I was climbing, then next thing, I woke up lyin' on my back on a pile of rocks. That's why I missed Mr. K and Miss Lileela when they come. I was sittin' there tryin' to figure out what happened when the ground started shakin' and rumblin'."

While Orville spoke, Pik parted the man's hair and examined the wound. Even from where he stood, Faris could see it was filthy, oozing blood, and the size and purple color of a *challa* egg.

Pik turned Orville back around to face him. "You've got a nasty bump there. I'd like to take another look at it, but we need to see the mine first, if it's not too far. Do you feel up to taking us?"

THE LAST TOQEPH

Orville nodded then winced and put his hand to his head. "Yeah. It's just over there." He gestured into the darkness beyond the 'peller's sphere. "But it's all full of rock and stuff. You can't get in."

"We know." Pik pointed his flashlight beam in the direction Orville had indicated. "Just take us there, please. Then we'll see what we can do for your headache."

Orville stole a glance toward Faris. "You're not gonna hurt me?"

Faris tried to soften his expression. "Nobody's going to hurt you."

Pik put his hand on Orville's shoulder. "Lead on." He waved his light toward the darkness.

With Orville at point, the rescue team splashed through the tide. The ground rose steadily until they exited the water, soaked from the knees down.

Fortunately, their guide's feet were more agile than his mind, and he took them at a brisk, squishy pace through the night. Envisioning Lileela pinned in utter darkness, Faris would have run ahead if he'd known their destination.

The air smelled of mud and decayed vegetation with fishy overtones. Distant insect chirrups and beastly calls answered one another, but nearby, the only sound was the swish of their clothes and the tromp of their soggy footsteps.

Above, the stars stood out in stark relief like brilliant tacks studding the heavens. Directly overhead loomed the constellation of Arar. Recognizing it, Faris's skin prickled. Just two days ago, he'd read a book about that, *The Story in the Stars: Selected Writings of Atarah Hoseh Charash.* Written by an ancient ancestor of the toqeph, it described how the constellations were put in the heavens above every planet by the Creator and arranged in such a way that they told the story of the Yasha's work of redemption. The constellation Arar went by different names in various cultures and was formed by different stars above each planet, but it was always cross-shaped, and it always represented the same thing: eternal hope.

Faris breathed a prayer of thanks for the reminder. No one loved Lileela more than the Yasha, nor was any more powerful to save. "Be with her, my Lord," he whispered. "Hold her hand and tell her help is coming."

The stars twinkled in reply.

THE LAST TOQEPH

12

Sitting on the ground a little apart from the others, Daviyd inhaled the scent of roasting ayal. The smallest children slept on skins near their parents, while others played within the chatsr's safe arms or took their turns cranking the spit.

Or clambered up Daviyd's back.

Three-year-old Na'arah swung one leg over his shoulder and then the other and grabbed his hair with both hands. "Up, Uncle! Up! I would ride!" She bounced on her perch.

Reaching up to grasp her, Daviyd bowed his head and pulled her off his shoulders. "Thou hast ridden enough this even, child. Methinks thou shouldst carry *me* now." He set her on the ground in front of him and wrapped his arms around her.

She wriggled wildly and screamed with laughter. "Nay, thou canst not ride me. Thou art big as a giant zeeb!"

"And hungry as one." He opened his mouth wide and bent toward her neck, but allowed her to escape just before his teeth snapped together.

The firelight cast dancing shadows across her face. "I too am hungry. When will the ayal be ready to eat?"

Daviyd's stomach rumbled. "Whenever the cooks decree. They labor to prepare a magnificent feast. If we interfere, they may forbid us to dine."

Standing before him, Na'arah opened her mouth to speak, but the answering voice came from behind him. "None can forbid thee, mighty hunter. It is thou who provided the meat."

THE LAST TOQEPH

Na'arah's sister, Nechama, approached shyly, holding a bottle. A few days ago, before her sixteenth birthday, she would have taken his hand. Now she stood at a respectful distance. Near enough that Daviyd could feel her warmth and smell her scent, but not so close that they might touch, even by chance.

She spoke to Na'arah. "Our em hath need of thee, sister."

Na'arah peered across the chatsr. "I didst not hear her call."

"She sent me to find thee. Thou hast played with thine uncle long enough. Now thou must let the man rest."

He eyed the bottle in her hand. "And willst thou let the man drink as well? Or didst thou bring the blend to torture me?"

Nechama giggled. Even in the dim light, he saw her flush. "It is for thee." She handed him the bottle, holding it by the neck so he could easily grasp the base without brushing her hand with his. She spoke to Na'arah again. "Go, child."

Na'arah bobbed a quick bow then giggled as she ran off. It apparently amused her to treat her sister like the adult she now was.

Daviyd drank as Nechama sat beside him on the ground, a hand span separating them. He offered her the bottle, holding it by the neck as she had. "Thank thee. For the drink as well as the rescue."

The fact was, he'd rather be alone. But he hadn't the heart to send either girl away.

She took the bottle and drank, then replaced the stopper and set it down between them.

After making sure his skirt covered him decently, he lay back, hands behind his head, and gazed at the stars. "Think ye ever of them? Those who live on other worlds?"

She glanced upward briefly then studied the ground. "Nay. Our task is to make this world live. To fill Gannah with people once more, to regain what was lost." Turning, she looked down at him. "Thine ab oft spake of this mission. I was but a child, but still I remember. 'That which was taken shall be given again.' Those were his words, were they not?"

Daviyd sighed. "His words, yea. And the words of many who came before. Since the days of Natsach the Great, that has been our hope. That Atarah would see the light of truth. That he would restore to Gannah her rightful lord."

THE LAST TOQEPH

The stars crowned Nechama's head with glittering jewels. "But why wait we longer? Thou art Atarah. The Toqephites are no more. Shouldst thou not take what is thine?"

Daviyd had often asked himself the same question, just as he had asked his ab when he still lived. He recited the eternal answer. "Patience. We accept naught that is not freely given. He who hath taken it must himself return it."

She grunted. "He who hath taken it is long dead. Wilt thou let the prize lie in the mud, unclaimed?"

Yesterday, he'd have agreed with her. Today, after having seen the man who stood tall as a tree, the ancient words almost made sense. "Those who are wiser than I have decreed that we wait." He fingered the bottle beside him. "Moreover, how can I lawfully take the throne when I am not Nasi?"

She drew up her knees and wrapped her arms around them. "There is that, yea. But even the old ones said that while we wait, we carry on."

Their hands couldn't touch, but their meahs could — and did. "Yea, we carry on. My mind hath not changed since last we spoke of this, my little Nechama. Thou art lovely. Thy spirit is tall and thy hands strong. Thou wilt make a worthy wife."

She studied his face, and the fire's reflection flamed in her eyes. "I am a woman now, Daviyd. Free to give myself to whomever I will."

"Aye." He closed his eyes. But that didn't block the probing of her thoughts. "Yet I am not ready to be chosen."

Nechama rose and grasped the bottle as if to strangle it. "It be time to cease playing with children and take up the burden of manhood."

She turned and strode toward the women at the serving table, her long braid twitching angrily behind her.

Faris emerged from the hole, breathing heavily as he pushed a cart piled with rock. Several paces from the entrance, he set it down and paused to breathe deeply of the clean air.

Exhaustion took the sharp edge off his desperation, but enough remained to keep him going.

A distant rumble prompted him to lift his eyes to the northern sky, darkening in the dusk. Thunder.

THE LAST TOQEPH

Lileela had been in that hole for two and a half days, and neither he nor the other rescuers had any way to know if she was even still alive. For the thousandth time, he cursed the genetic designers who'd neglected to give him a meah.

She could communicate with her native Gannahan mother, brothers, and sisters. But none of them were here; and with the satellites still not functioning, the rescuers were cut off from them as well.

As Faris resumed his labors, Orville approached. "I'll get that. Dr. Pik said you should take a break now." He reached for the cart. "You're supposed to get some dinner before you go back in."

Faris glanced toward the camp at the foot of the cliff, where three of the others sat eating. "Will do." After stepping back and allowing Orville to take over, he removed first his gloves then his hard hat and laid them on a pile of rubble. Then, his legs like lead, he turned away from the excavation.

The idiot Orville had proved useful. He knew this area well. Brought them food and water to supplement their supplies. When he wasn't hunting, foraging, or cooking, he offered his strong back to the rescue efforts.

A bucket of murky water sat on a flat rock near the table under the canopy. Faris plunged in his hands and forearms and scrubbed them as clean as he could. The water was barely cooler than his skin, and not a lot cleaner.

"Hey, I was gonna drink that." Safiy bit a mouthful of meat from a barbarbird thigh bone.

Faris filled his cupped hands with water to wash his face. "I won't use it all." Short as it was, his beard trapped plenty of grit. The water in a rain-swollen stream would be clearer than what trickled from his chin.

Safiy gave a weary half-smile. "I saved you a bite. Wasn't going to, but Dr. Pik insisted."

Beard still dripping, Faris shook the water from his hands then wiped his face with them. "Where is he?" After giving his head and hands another shake, he sat on the folding chair beside Safiy.

Safiy handed him a water bottle. "Went to Orville's cabin to lie down for a bit."

Faris drank deeply as Safiy continued. "Those Karkar are such weaklings. Having to rest after only twenty hours' work."

THE LAST TOQEPH

"Yeah, can you believe it?" Faris set down the bottle. Though Pik rested more than once every twenty hours, he did admirably for a man his age. "Where's that food you saved for me?"

Mathis Makris rose from his seat on the other side of the table and went to the fire a short distance away. "Right here." He picked up a plate covered with what appeared to be bandage material from the medipeller. "Saved from the hungry Safiy as well as the flies." He brought it to the table and set it in front of Faris before sitting down again.

"Thanks." Faris lifted the cover to reveal a meaty barbar drumstick twenty centimeters long. "Now that you mention it, I guess I am a little hungry."

He regretted the mention, though. He'd rather ignore his physical needs for several more hours and continue the dig until Lileela was found. The Old Gannahans were supposed to have been able to keep going day and night for days on end, so why not he?

Safiy tore the last of the meat from the thighbone. "Have you been hearing thunder the past few minutes?"

Chewing, Faris nodded. "Since I came out of the hole just now."

Mathis rose. "I didn't hear anything." He flung a denuded bone onto the tidal flats then rinsed off his plate with the water in the bucket. Once the tide came in, they could refresh the water, and the bones would be swept out to sea.

"That's because your Earthish ears are near useless." Safiy licked his fingers. "A storm, I can live with. But we don't need another temblor."

Faris swallowed a mouthful. "No. We're just now reaching the point where we were yesterday before that aftershock collapsed it again."

He should be digging, not sitting here eating. He tried not to envision Lileela's broken body crushed under the mountain. But the image wouldn't leave him, and his stomach tied in a knot.

Safiy rose. "We'll get her, brother. We're almost there." He gave Faris's shoulder a squeeze as he passed on his way back to the dig.

Faris grunted.

The chewy meat formed a gooey glob in his mouth. He forced it down then chased it with a swallow of water. It wouldn't do Lileela any good if he fainted from hunger. Besides that, he had his orders. Determined to finish so he could get back to work, he took another bite.

THE LAST TOQEPH

The rumble he heard this time was not thunder, but the now-familiar sound of the rotoscoop rooting its way into the rock that blocked his way to Lileela.

To the east, a flock of clumsy *qa'athbirds* rose from the tidal pool with enough splashing to fill a small pond. Faris wondered what had spooked them, until a *behalah* swooped down toward the stragglers. An unexpected surge of relief washed over him when the last of them escaped the monster bird.

Its attempt foiled, it came to the ground and waded in the shallow basin, scooping up great beakfuls of water along with everything that swam or floated in it. Then it tipped its head back to swallow the solids, allowing the water to pour out the corners of its beak.

Faris swallowed the bite and took another, looking down at the plate. It was one of Orville's creations, no two of which were alike. This one had a picture of a behalah bird much like the one wading a short distance away. He could swear the water pouring from its beak was flowing. No, that was grease shimmering on the plate, viewed through weary eyes.

Still, the artistry was amazing. He laid down the drumstick and picked up Safiy's empty plate to examine it. A blue *chaburah* fish flashed across it, leaping from sun-glinted water to catch a gold-winged *tanniym* fly flitting among some greenery around the plate's edge. The plate was heavy for its size. He turned it over. Though the front was smooth and glossy, he could see something that looked like faint chisel marks on the back, as if it had been cut out of a solid piece of some sort of rock. Just left of the center, two Old Gannahan characters had been cut: ו ד. Faris scratched his beard. What could that mean?

He turned the plate over again and took a closer look. Beneath the paint and glaze, he could make out chisel marks on the front, too. But Orville had created the design in such a way that his brush strokes obscured them. Rather than distracting, the chisel marks enhanced the painting, giving it depth and the illusion of liveliness. The effect was astonishing.

Weary as he was, Faris didn't know whether to caress the plate or smash it against the cliff face. This was what Lileela and the geologist had come to see. The strange new rock, never before seen on Gannah, that Orville lifted from the ground in big flakes. The material he called flakestone, which he shaped, decorated, and glazed through a process of his own invention. If not for that plate and others like it, she wouldn't have

THE LAST TOQEPH

come here. Wouldn't have crawled into that space to be trapped, and maybe killed, when the ground moved.

Thoughts of his wife lay heavy on his heart. His weary arms lay heavy on the table. He must get up, or he'd fall asleep sitting there.

He rose, finished the water in the bottle, and headed back for the dig, leaving the remains of the meal on the table.

Daylight was fading. But it was always dark in the hole. Mounds of rock they'd removed from the opening lined the entrance. The rotoscoop's thunder had ceased, and Joel Samuelson emerged, pushing a cart full of more material to add to the mountains. As he approached, Faris nodded a greeting, and Joel paused, breathing heavily. "We gotta be getting close now, I'd think."

"That's what you said six hours ago." Seeing the man's exhaustion, Faris regretted the remark. The situation was discouraging enough without sarcasm. "But you're right. We're getting closer all the time."

Everyone was dragging. How much longer could they keep this up?

And how much longer could Lileela and Kughurrrro survive?

Joel took another grip on the cart and moved it to the piles alongside the path. "That's right. Every scoop is one scoop nearer." He coughed. "Sure does smell in there, though."

"Let me help you unload." Faris had picked up his hard hat but set it down again, deciding to give Joel a hand before going back into the hole.

But instead he spun and ran toward the entrance, bareheaded, at the muffled shout that came from within. "I hear them! They're alive!"

Sitting on the grassy shore, Adam watched the sun set into the western sea. The warm wind combed through his freshly washed hair, and his clothes dried on his body.

As the wild man had told him, the Point of Chen was no more. Adam had come as far as he could.

The truth of Abba's Karkarish adage wrapped around him. *You can't hurry a profit, and there's no profit in hurrying.*

Emma had a saying too. And her proverb *Hasteth, and thou shalt arrive nowhere quickly* described the situation perfectly.

Adam was nowhere. But at least he was ahead of schedule.

With time to kill, he'd explored the area. Located a fresh water source, built a small shelter against a boulder. Killed and plucked a *shalak*, which

THE LAST TOQEPH

now roasted over a fire made of dried seaweed that had washed ashore by the ton. Basic survival was simple. It was his thoughts that gave him trouble.

He longed for Elise. Hoped the child wouldn't be born before he returned. Considered his son Everett. At one time, he'd hoped the boy would have a meah. Though it didn't appear he was so gifted, he avoided trying to reach toward him now for fear of making a forbidden connection.

He turned from the ocean and strode toward his shelter that nestled in one of the erosion furrows that scored the landscape in ripples. It was easy to locate the spot by the smoke from his cook fire that smeared the sky.

Rodents he thought were called groundjumpers leapt about him as he strode toward his camp. It would be easy to reach out and snatch one in the air. Why were there no carnivores on this coastal plain to keep them under control?

And what were beasts doing here in the first place? If the wave had wiped this part of the planet clean, shouldn't it be as barren of animal life as it was of trees and buildings?

He reached the stream and waded across, remembering Natsach in the valley by the waterfall. That man should no more be on Yereq than these hopping pests.

But his existence was as undeniable as it was unexplainable.

Adam looked to the heavens and moaned. How would he tell the toqeph she was not the last Gannahan?

13

At the end of a long and restless night, Ra'anan rose before the sun. It was hot in her room, so she'd left the bed curtain open, but it wasn't the heat that kept her awake. Mostly, she couldn't stop thinking about Lileela.

She slipped out of the bed alcove, and her sweat-dampened nightclothes felt clammy against her skin. A shower might help, but the plumbing sometimes banged when the water turned on, and she didn't want to disturb the rest of the family.

Her thoughts went to Abba somewhere out there trying to locate Lileela, and Adam on his quest—from which sometimes a fledgling Nasi didn't return. The weight of it all made her sag back onto the bed. What could she do for them? Any of them? She felt utterly helpless.

The sound of someone walking upstairs caught her attention, and she listened with meah and ears. It was Emma–whose heart seemed light, considering the circumstances. Had she heard good news?

Ra'anan jumped up. "Emma?" she stage-whispered when she reached the main floor. "Was that you I heard?" The kitchen light was on.

Standing at the table and pouring tea, Emma greeted her with a smile. "Did I wake you, sweet?"

Ra'anan pulled out a chair and sat. "I've been awake half the night. But you seem awfully cheerful. Have you heard from the rescuers or something?"

Emma's smile broadened. "I don't have a complete report yet, but yes. I was in the tower, praying, when a message came in."

"I thought they were out of messenger range." Ra'anan eyed Emma's teapot, enjoying the minty smell. Perhaps she'd make some for herself.

THE LAST TOQEPH

"They are." Emma went to the cabinet and pulled out another cup. "Would you like some wakey-up?"

Ra'anan smiled at her childhood name for the breakfast tea. "I don't want to take yours, I'll make my own."

She started to rise, but Emma raised her hand. "No need. I made a whole pot but I only want one cup. Sit down, and I'll tell you what I know."

"Oh, yes, please!"

Ra'anan took the cup and poured tea through the strainer while Emma gave her the news.

"After Abba and the rescue team left for the mine, Mr. Esam loaded another 'peller with men and equipment and flew to the site." Emma sipped her tea. "They helped with the search. But once they located Lileela and Kughurrrro and determined they were alive, Abba sent Esam back to Chassabba, where there's a communications link. He knew we'd want to know."

Ra'anan's heart thudded. "They found them? But ... they're still trapped?"

Emma's green gaze held her captive. "What do you hear from her? Is she in communication with you?"

That was the problem. One she hadn't wanted to bring up. "I lost her. That is, I know she's still alive, but she can't seem to stay with me for very long."

Emma nodded. "I have the same problem. But I'm not sure it's a problem."

That didn't make any sense. "How can it not be?"

"I think our connection keeps slipping away because she's paying more attention to Someone Else."

Ra'anan gasped. "You mean... you mean she's dying?"

"It doesn't sound like it." Emma smiled. "Esam said they heard voices coming from inside the mountain. It was Lileela and Kughurrrro singing praise songs." She chuckled. "And apparently Kughurrrro's musical abilities leave something to be desired."

Standing knee-deep in the flowing water, Daviyd bent and lifted one of the rocks that held down the ayal pelt. He tossed the rock onto the bank then rubbed one edge of the folded skin. Much of the hair sloughed off and swirled away in the current, but some still clung.

THE LAST TOQEPH

He removed another rock, unwrapped the skin a little more, and tested other sections. It was coming along nicely, but it should soak another day or so yet.

He refolded the skin, weighted it down again, and clambered up the bank.

"Ho!" His em approached, her bare, brown feet silent on the smooth trail. "I come to see the progress of my skin only to find thee disturbing it."

Daviyd plucked a piece of clinging water weed from his leg. "It needeth more time. No need to trouble thyself with it today."

Her violet eyes narrowed as she peered up at him. "Thou art not oft so solicitous. Why show thine old em such concern now?" Her meah caressed his, feeling for a way to his innermost thoughts.

He wasn't ready to give her access. "I have always loved thee, Emma. As it shall ever be."

Her expression softened and her meah ceased its probing. "Yea, thou art the best of sons. And shalt make a fine husband to Nechama."

Daviyd's good humor fled before it had quite appeared. "Thou knowest my thoughts on that." He braced for an argument.

But she didn't take up the challenge. Instead, she nodded toward the stream. "Is that a *tsab* trap I see?"

Relief at the change of subject animated his gestures. "Yea. I saw a tsab disappear into that hollow on yonder shore."

"A tsab liveth in that hollow beneath the bank?"

"Perhaps. If so, I dare not breach the treaty and invade its home. But in open water, it is at my mercy." He made a slashing motion across his throat. "And I shall show it none. It is the largest tsab I have ever seen." He made arcs with his arms to form a circle too wide for his hands to meet. "Near four stone in weight. It be covered with moss but seemeth to be a tri-color beneath the green. Its casing shall yield the most beautiful tsabshell, and that in abundance."

"A tri-color, thou sayeth? And that big?" She stared at the hole as if willing the beast to emerge. "With so much meat, I shall make a stew to feed the whole village twice over. And can render much oil, and—"

"And Mattaniah can use the claws to make a lahab."

Emma turned to him, brows raised. "Yea? That can be done?"

"He said he heard of it. His ab hath said that in the old days, lahabs were oft made of a tsabshell case with claws for blades."

THE LAST TOQEPH

She nodded, her expression thoughtful. "That could be."

"He hath made one of wood for his new babe, without blades. But his daughter must needs have a true lahab when she is older."

"Yea. Unless one of us should die first and have no more need of ours." She sighed, and the old familiar bitterness returned to harden her face. "The Great Wave took all our lives. It washed away all we had, all we were, and dropped us here to live as beasts, fighting for every bite and breath." When she gazed up at him again, her mouth curved an angry talon above her stern chin. "And thou refuseth to do thy duty? To marry and replenish Gannah?"

The words came too close to truth and cut him deeply. "Refuse? Nay. But I cannot wed yet."

Once again, she didn't push when usually she would have. "We must speak, my son. But of other things. Let us pick chophen fruit." She pulled two pouches from her belt and handed him one. "We can talk as we work."

He followed her as she struck out away from the path. "What wouldst thou speak of?"

Not here, her meah told him. "It is nothing," her words said. *Nothing I would have others overhear.*

Beyond that, her meah was closed on the subject.

Which was only fair. He kept things from her too.

Adam filled his lungs with air then dove for the patch of *mallach* growing on the ocean floor. Roasted, the bulb just above the root would make a good meal.

He swam through the thicket of tall stalks to the murky bottom, then grasped a thick shoot at the base and tugged. It wouldn't budge. Feeling with his fingers, he found the bulb wedged between rocks just below the silt.

He tried another plant, and then another. None of them wanted to let go. Finally, when his lungs were nearly bursting, a stalk loosened. One last yank uprooted it, and he shot to the surface with his trophy.

His head broke through and he sucked in air, eyes closed against the glare of the overhead sun. Holding the long mallach parallel with his body with one hand, he stroked with the other as he kicked toward the shore.

His ears roared—and not from water in them. An unusual sound assaulted them.

THE LAST TOQEPH

Something blocked the sun's glare for a moment then continued on, casting a rippling shadow across the water. Squinting, he looked up.

A small plane glittered in the sky.

He'd been found! His quest was over. He dropped the mallach and swam unencumbered toward shore.

The plane circled then returned, lowering as it drew near. He'd expected a toppeller for the pick-up. Good thing the plane had pontoons. Was Jax flying it?

Adam waded out of the water and stood on the grass to wait while the plane descended. The sea was calm, but the landing couldn't have been bumpier if it had been on the shore. Adam chuckled. Yep, that was Jax.

The plane finally settled and slowed as it moved toward Adam. It drew close enough that he could see Jax behind the controls. Once it came to a stop, Adam waded out and climbed onto the nearer pontoon.

Jax powered down the engines and lowered the anchor, then shouted out the window. "If you were trying to swim to the point, you were headed the wrong way."

Adam didn't understand. "But if you were trying to shake the wings off this thing, sir, you were on the right course."

Jax grinned. "Yeah, I need a little more practice on the landings. But seriously, man, I'm supposed to pick you up on the Point. This ain't it."

The plane rocked on the waves, and Adam wrapped his arm through a hand-stirrup to keep from falling. He still wasn't sure what Jax was talking about. "The Point of Chen is under water. This is as far as I could get."

Jax pointed out to sea. "It's still there, but it's an island now. About fourteen kilometers due west."

Adam's foot slipped and he took a better grip on the stirrup. "What are you saying?"

"I'm sayin' I'm supposed to pick you up on Chen. Today. So you'd better get going, or you'll miss your pick-up."

The Point was still there? A wave of unaccountable rage washed over him, and he flung away the stirrup and jumped from the pontoon into the shallow water. Anger building, he stared in the direction Jax had pointed. How was he supposed to know Chen was out there?

He'd be disqualified. Have to do the whole thing all over again. But on a different part of the planet. Some other place that would look nothing like it did on the maps.

THE LAST TOQEPH

He was probably disqualified anyway, since he'd stopped to talk to that Natsach person. He shouldn't have stopped. If Natsach hadn't told him the Point was under water, he might have swum out looking for it.

But no, he'd have done the same thing. Come to the sea, found the whole region of Dedan under water, and stopped traveling.

Still, he couldn't shake the idea that Natsach had somehow ruined everything.

While he fumed, Jax exited the plane and splashed down beside him. "I'll grab your clothes. I see 'em layin' over there on the beach. Ain't nothing in the rules sayin' I can't do that for you."

Adam glared down at Jax. "Whose brilliant idea was it to pick me up at the Point of Chen anyway?"

Jax shook his head, frowning, his lips pressed together. "You've got eight hours. The tide's in your favor." Without waiting for a response, he turned away, wading. After a few steps, he dove in and swam toward the shore.

With the waves lapping at his waist, Adam fought down his roiling frustration. He'd completed his quest! And now he had to swim fourteen kilometers? Toward an island he couldn't see?

His mind reviewed everything he knew about Nasi quests, and his conscience stabbed him. Jax was bound to the ancient ways with no discretion to change the rules. Strictly speaking, he probably should have flown to the Point of Chen to wait for Adam without stopping to advise him.

His anger drained, and chagrin rose to take its place. What was a quest, anyway, if not a test of resilience and resourcefulness? He was out of line for speaking to his superior the way he had.

He turned toward Jax, who'd reached water too shallow for swimming and now splashed toward the small pile of Adam's clothes at the edge of the grass. Adam cupped his hands around his mouth and shouted. "Mr. Jax, sir!"

Jax turned.

"Thank you, sir!" Adam bowed as deeply as he could in the water. "And I apologize. I was out of line."

Jax didn't respond. Did he even hear him?

Adam shouted again. "I'll see you at Chen!"

Jax waved at that, then turned back toward the shore.

THE LAST TOQEPH

Adam took off swimming.

Had Jax accepted his apology? Would he disqualify Adam? Punish him for questioning orders? This quest could be disallowed for multiple reasons. But whatever happened from now on, Adam would perform to the best of his ability and be wiser for the experience.

Maybe that's what this was all about. To prepare him to lead Gannah. That was no doubt the case. As toqeph, he'd have to deal with unexpected circumstances. Yes, there was a purpose to all this.

His smooth stroke faltered as the image of Natsach's angry face flashed across his mind, but he quickly recovered his rhythm. He'd deal with that issue after he reached Chen.

He lifted his head, checked his bearings, and swam west.

THE LAST TOQEPH

14

Lileela preferred to keep her eyes closed. Most of the time, she couldn't see anyway, as Kughurrrro seldom lit the lamp. But when he did, the sight that met her dry, burning eyes was too depressing to endure.

She was trapped in a hole in the bowels of Gannah, where she'd no doubt spend the rest of her short, pointless life.

What had she accomplished in her twenty-two years? Caused her family grief, and nothing more. She hadn't even contributed to Gannah by procreating, which was something anyone could do. Something every Gannahan *should* do. She wept for Faris, and the tears turned to mud on her face.

How wrong she'd been about Kughurrrro. She'd first resented him for his anti-Gannahan activities. When he seemed to have a change of heart, she distrusted his motives. And when he married Aunt Skiskii, she'd been deeply offended. Never mind that he'd been a comfort to Auntie in her grief. He even gave her the child she'd always wanted.

Perhaps she resented him for that very reason. He'd done what she'd never been able to do: rise above his Outworld breeding to become a good, productive Gannahan.

One who loved the Yasha, no less.

Lileela floated between waking and unconsciousness. But whenever she awoke, he was there. Both were there, the Yasha and Uncle Kughie. One to comfort her spirit, the other to hold her hand, or share his meager supply of water, or help her forget her pain through conversation. Conversation that grew increasingly centered on the Yasha and His truth.

Lileela had much Scripture memorized, and she sometimes shared it with Kughie through those interminable, indistinguishable dark days and nights. He saw things from a thoroughly Karkar perspective, but his insights illuminated the Scriptures' universal truth and deepened her understanding.

THE LAST TOQEPH

They sometimes made up songs, putting the Yasha's words to Karkar melodies. Until, one time as they sang, a strange sound invaded their sanctuary.

Uncle Kughie stopped singing and squeezed her hand. A tremor rippled from his body to hers.

"What is it?" she asked. Then she heard the sound for herself.

A voice. Neither Kughurrrro's nor the Yasha's. Muffled, as if coming out of the surrounding rock. "I hear them! They're alive!"

Kughie suddenly released her hand and turned on the light. Then he called in answer, his voice thin and crackly. "We are here! We are alive!"

Lileela moaned in annoyance. "It's no use, Uncle. They don't speak Karkar." As they both listened for more sounds from beyond, she slipped into sleep, dreaming Faris came through the wall and cradled her face in his hands.

She awoke to find that what she felt was dried mud peeling from her cheeks. But a different noise assaulted her ears. An awful drilling sound. She had the impression that was a good thing. But as she considered it, the vibration of the floor beneath her sent a wave of pain through her legs that flung her back into unconsciousness.

Adam swam through burning muscles, exhaustion, hunger, and doubt until he arrived at a place of rhythmic strokes independent from thought. All he had to do was breathe, and his arms and legs moved of their own accord, a tireless machine of sinewy flesh and bone.

The sun lowered in the sky. When it drew level with the horizon, he closed his eyes to the blinding glare, only peeking from time to time to make sure he continued in the right direction.

Then it sank into the sea, taking the light with it. Panic seized his heart for a second. Once the residual glow died away, how would he navigate? What if he missed the island? If he didn't arrive by the designated time, Jax would fly off and leave him.

Or would he?

Adam didn't want to find out.

Gradually the moons rose, the stars flickered to life. He was still on course. Relief gave him a burst of energy, but he didn't break his rhythm.

Nothing existed but the infinite water, the infinite heavens, and his ceaseless breaths. The rest of the universe revolved around him, held

THE LAST TOQEPH

together by a gasping inhale followed by a controlled, bubbling exhale, repeated, and repeated, and repeated.

Not long before the night passed from Blue to the hours of Black Slumber, he caught sight of a new light due west. It wasn't a star.

He swam on, glancing at it from time to time. Not a light; a cluster of them, flickering on the water. He noted it, but his mind was too numb to wonder.

Inhale. Breathe out. Inhale. Breathe out.

The vision took shape. A small plane, resting on pontoons, lights blazing.

Inhale. Breathe out. Inhale. Breathe out.

Beside the lights, something black loomed out of the sea, blocking the stars.

Inhale. Breathe out. Inhale. Breathe out.

It was Chen. The now-island of Chen rising from the sea, with the plane at its point like a beacon.

Inhale. Breathe out. Inhale. Breathe out.

Adam made for the shadow instead of the light. His destination was the Isle of Chen, not the aircraft.

Inhale. Breathe out. Inhale. Breathe out.

It had been so long since he'd seen anything but water and sky, the land looked foreign, the plane out of place.

Inhale. Breathe out. Inhale. His leg brushed against something rough and solid. He lowered his feet and touched bottom. He rose from the water, but found the weight of his body too great for his strength. He fell, to swim and crawl the rest of the way to shore, where he lay gasping, arms and legs twitching.

Strong hands grasped his arms. "Good to see you, man. You made great time. Almost an hour to spare." A water bottle was thrust into his hands. "Here, drink. Spring water, not salt."

Adam's hands shook as he lifted it to his mouth, and he rammed the bottle into his nose. Jax steadied his hands, and Adam drank. Paused to take a couple of gasping breaths, then drank again. By the time the bottle was empty, his hands had stopped shaking, though his legs still felt quivery. "Thanks."

Jax chuckled. "That was quite a swim. Didn't know you were a fish."

THE LAST TOQEPH

Natsach's mocking words rang in Adam's mind: *Thou lookest not like a fish.* He chuckled, though he saw no humor in it. "I've been told that before." He rose, with Jax's help.

Jax's eyes glittered in the plane's light. "You've been told what before? That you swim like a fish?"

"That I don't look like one." He stared at the plane. Did he have the strength to get up into it?

Jax supported him as he walked. "Maybe you didn't then, but you do now. Like a flopping fish out of water. But you're in luck. We have to swim from here."

Adam looked at his feet. What they stood on must be a small bump on the cliff face, and they'd come to the end of it in three steps.

A moment later, Jax dove in and swam for the plane. Adam followed, reaching it in four breaths. A rope ladder hung from the plane's open door. In the circle of light surrounding the plane, he grabbed the ladder, planted his foot on a rung, and pulled his heavy body out of the water.

Standing on the pontoon above him, Jax watched. Just as Adam's head rose to shoulder level, Jax pulled his arm back. "I hate to do this, kid, but I have to."

A ball of pain slammed into Adam's face like a rock, and he fell backward, seeing stars. Another splash told him Jax had fallen in too.

Had Jax punched him? Jax had punched him! He foundered in the water, trying to catch his breath. The shock ebbed away, and a new wave of shame rolled in. He'd earned that blow, but he'd never been physically punished before, and the pain of it surprised him.

Vision blurry, he floated on his back outside the reach of the plane's lights and looked at Jax, who'd wrapped one arm around the ladder and hung there, rubbing his hand. "That skull of yours is harder than I expected. I think I broke my hand."

Adam felt above his eye. It was already swelling.

Jax flexed his fingers. Apparently nothing was broken after all. "You know why I did that?"

Adam's head hurt too much to nod. But the facts hurt even more. "Yes. Yes, sir. Because of the way I spoke to you, sir."

"That's right." Jax turned and lifted himself onto the pontoon. "The way you spoke, and the way you thought." He extended his hand, not the sore one. "Come on up here."

THE LAST TOQEPH

Adam's stomach churned as if preparing to spill its watery contents into the sea, but he obeyed. He swam to the ladder and grabbed hold.

Jax grabbed his other hand and hauled him up, while Adam's feet clawed the pontoon for a foothold. Jax's tone was uncharacteristically stern. "You will never do that again."

Adam found his footing. Then, hoping he wouldn't slide off into the ocean, he prostrated himself on the pontoon. "No, sir. I will not. I was in error, and you are wise to correct me."

Jax nudged him with his foot. "Get up before you fall." He waited until Adam had risen clumsily, then moved close and jabbed him in the chest with a finger. "That's right. You will not. And do you know *why* you'll never do it again, kid?"

Adam was too sore, ashamed, and weary to know how to respond. "Ah… because a Nasi always obeys."

Jax's nod was vehement. "Even an ordinary Gannahan does that. But you're not ordinary. You're training to be a Nasi. Don't even think about whether your orders seem fair. You will obey without question. And if you ever—and I mean *ever*—show me, or Jerry, or anyone else on the face of this planet the slightest bit of disrespect again, you're done. No more chances. Is that understood?"

Bowing, Adam swayed and clung to the plane's open door. "Yes, sir. I understand, sir. It won't happen again." He wanted to slip away from Jax's glare and sink to the bottom of the sea.

Jax's face was grim in the harsh artificial light. "See that it doesn't."

Adam's head reeled. All his life, he'd excelled at everything he put his hand to. He'd considered becoming a Nasi a given, a simple matter of taking advantage of the opportunity. Was it possible he could fail?

The lumpy chophen fruits glittered like stars on a deep green, leafy background.

Daviyd popped a berry into his mouth then plucked another handful for the bag at his waist. "We shall need more than these two sacks."

Emma didn't look up from her work. "While her children nap, Timna will harvest what we cannot carry."

Daviyd pulled down a high branch to reach the fruit, taking care not to break the slender cane. "So if you and I are to speak before she arrives, mayhap we should do so."

THE LAST TOQEPH

She'd said they needed to talk in private, but now that they were alone, he sensed a reticence to begin the discussion. It wasn't like Emma to keep her thoughts to herself, and he was curious.

She moved over a few steps, and the bush blocked her from view. "Yea. Verily."

Daviyd released the high branch he'd stripped of its berries and strained upward for another.

Emma picked in silence for a moment or two then spoke again. "I heard the Voice."

The branch slipped from his startled fingers and whipped upward, sending a nosy *rakiyl* bird fluttering away in a panic.

He must have misunderstood. "What voice?"

She sighed. "It was no voice that is heard with the ear. More like a knowing in the heart."

He stared through the bush, though he could barely discern his em on the other side. "Abba's voice?"

"'Twas not my husband, but it mayhap have been the Voice he heard."

From the sound, she continued picking fruit as she spoke. But Daviyd stood in stunned amazement, unable to move or think.

"And he told me to ask thee—" She took a deep breath. "To ask thee what thou didst see and to whom thou didst speak the day thou brought me that ayal skin."

Daviyd found his feet, and they took him, unbidden, around the chophen patch to approach his em. "*He* didst tell thee? Who might *he* be?"

"I know not. But he spake in my meah as if he had known me all my life. As, indeed, I feel he has." She turned to face Daviyd. "What didst thou see, my son? And why hast thou said naught about it to me?" She sighed, took a few steps back, and sank to the ground as if too weary to stand. "I know the answer to the last. Thou hast said naught for fear of my scorn."

He squatted before her. "Mine em, I revere thee as ever a good son doth. What I have seen—" He lowered his gaze to the stony ground then lifted his eyes to meet hers. "I cannot explain what I cannot understand. But, yea. I did see something."

Emma took his hand. "Tell me, my son. I believe it is of great import."

He sat cross-legged on the ground beside her. "Yea. As do I. But I know not what it might mean."

THE LAST TOQEPH

He told her how he had seen the young man across the river, tall as a tree and standing in the prism's light. Her face and meah registered amazement as he described their meeting and conversation. She appeared as confused as he at the talk of truth and redemption.

He wished he found more in her, though, than surprise. He needed more wisdom. More direction.

"And thus I crossed back over the river and returned to my kill," he concluded. "The Outsider hath not contacted my meah since."

She pressed her lips together, and he knew she digested this bizarre tale.

After a moment, she spoke. "If he is, in fact, on quest for the Nasihood, he would not contact thee until his quest were complete."

"Truth, mine em."

"And if your meahs met—" She reached his with hers to complete the thought. —*he cannot be an Outsider. For only we of Gannah possess the meah.*

She spoke aloud again. "If he be true, he shall return."

Daviyd nodded. "And if not?"

She sat silent a moment, then spoke with conviction. "He shall. The Voice guided thine ab aright, and so it spake truth to me. The young man shall return. Moreover, he shall ask thee to go with him."

Daviyd sat up in surprise. "He what—How knoweth thee this?"

"Though certain I am as the sun shineth above, I cannot tell from whence cometh this knowledge. But the man shall ask thee. And thou shalt go."

Every fiber of his being rebelled at the thought. Go where? Go how? Into what danger? With that mongrel aberration?

"Nay, my son." Emma knew his thoughts. And understood them. But her mind remained firm. "Thou shalt not refuse. I have declined to require thee to marry against thy will, but I do most certainly command this. When that man returneth, thou shalt go with him whithersoever he may ask." Her face grew long with sorrow as she gazed at him. "Even if thou returnest not."

His stomach lurched. "What sayest thou, mine em? Dost thou think...?" He couldn't voice the question.

She answered anyway. "I cannot know the future. But clearly, the Voice knoweth what we cannot. And do not true Gannahans obey?"

THE LAST TOQEPH

15

Adam awoke, sneezing. His head hammered, and he half-rose in his bedroll, still sneezing, ears ringing.

No, it wasn't his ears. It was the aphaph birds. And the insistent tickle in his nose—he sneezed again—was from ednats flying into it.

A third sneeze made him groan. His entire body screamed with pain, as if he'd been beaten all over with a club. But he had to stand, or the singing birds whizzing just above his head would drive him mad. He clambered to his feet and yelped as an aphaph slammed against the cut above his eye. The throbbing eye. The one that was swollen shut and was no doubt as purple as a Nasi's tongue. He fingered the shiner and winced.

"Good morning." Jax stood by the fire in the pale gray morning, knee-deep in swirling aphaph. "Nice place you've got here. How long did you camp on this spot before I made you go swimming yesterday?"

Adam sneezed again. "Three days. Yes, it is nice here."

Jax chewed as he spoke. "I made you some fish for breakfast, and over there's some of Gillian's trailfriend." He swallowed his mouthful. "My wife makes the best, you know." He gestured toward a seaweed-wrapped packet keeping warm by the fire. A jar stood beside it, the colorful contents of which he'd no doubt been munching.

Head and limbs aching, Adam stumbled through the cloud of birds toward a nearby bucket of water standing on a rock. "With all due respect, sir—" He stopped and bowed toward Jax, as deeply as possible without being thwacked by the aphaph. "But *my* wife makes the best trailfriend." He turned back to the bucket, took a ladleful of water, and drank deeply.

THE LAST TOQEPH

Jax laughed. "That's the right answer, kid." He approached and took the ladle when Adam had finished with it. "Sleep well?"

Adam grunted, stretching his limbs. Other than his eye, he was feeling better already despite having had only a couple hours of sleep. His Gannahan physiology was a blessing.

But Jax? Though Earthish by birth and breeding, he looked more Gannahan than Adam as he slurped from the ladle, water trickling down his black beard. His short frame was thick with muscle, and his hair, unbound, fell to his elbows as he bent.

The longer Adam watched him, the more Jax looked like Natsach. Adam rubbed his good eye then turned toward the fire and breakfast.

Behind him, Jax dropped the ladle back in the bucket with a clunk. "When you're through, we'll get going."

Adam picked up the seaweed-wrapped fish. "I won't be long." Then he lifted his hands and sang a morning praise to the Yasha.

Jax waited until the song ended before resuming the conversation. "Take your time. I've got some things to do meanwhile. But hey, do you figure these birds'll be a problem? Or should we wait for them to leave before we take off?"

"They seem pretty good at getting out of the way." Adam ate the fish — seaweed wrapping, bones, and all. "I figure once you start up the plane, they'll steer clear of it. Not like the *gazal* birds that get in the engines."

The aphaphs had risen higher, and Jax watched them with fascination while Adam ate. "This isn't an unusual phenomenon then? You've seen them do this before?"

"Every morning since I've been on Yereq."

"They're crazy. I can't figure how they don't run into each other."

Adam ate the last bite of the fish then licked the juice from his hands. "They're quick, that's for sure." He shook out a handful of trail friend then extended the jar toward Jax. "Want some more?"

"Sure." Jax strode over, took the jar, and poured a little into his hand.

Did Natsach eat trailfriend? Probably; it was an Old Gannahan recipe. Or, he'd eat it if his people could find a variety of nuts, seeds, and fruits to cover each of the nutritional color groups. Adam chewed the sweet mix. Oh, yes, and honey to hold it all together. He didn't recall having seen any bees on Yereq.

THE LAST TOQEPH

Jax had updated him on news of the settlement the night before, and he'd communicated with his family through his meah. Now, as he munched trailfriend to the rising music of the birds, he connected with his family again briefly. No changes there. How he longed to be able to connect with Elise.

Jax pulled his hair back and fastened it as he glanced up at Adam. "Looking forward to seeing the wife?"

Adam wondered what kind of expression he'd let Jax see. Probably none, since he'd developed the habit of keeping his face as expressionless as a Karkar's.

He made himself smile. "Yes, sir. I sure am." And it was no lie.

Neither was it untrue that Elise's trailfriend was better than Gillian's.

Faris's fingertips were raw where the gloves had worn away. But there were no more gloves to be had, so he bled on the rocks where he gripped them.

He'd long since lost track of time. One of the men drilled, then he and Safiy tore away the rubble while others hauled it out of the tunnel. Still others shored up the growing opening with timbers in an effort to keep the hole from collapsing.

During the drilling, Faris and Safiy exited the mine to take in the clean, Gannahan air. Except for their eyes glowing with determination, every part of their bodies not covered by filter masks wore a thick coating of reddish dust. Everyone else worked in shifts, six hours digging and six hours resting. But Faris and Safiy—cut from the same cloth, a significant portion of which was native Gannahan fabric—seldom took a break for more than an hour.

Last night, the men had broken through into a relatively undamaged part of the mine. Faris's heart leapt with hope as he widened the opening as much as he could, calling, "Anyone in there?"

The others had gathered around. "What is it? What did you find? Is it them?"

He held up his hand for quiet, then called through the hole, "Lileela? Kughurrrro?"

A hoarse affirmative reply from Kughurrrro was all it took to spur Faris and Safiy to frenetic action. Before long, they'd widened the entrance until Faris could slither through.

THE LAST TOQEPH

Against the wall opposite the opening, Kughurrrro crouched beside a pile of rubble. He was so camouflaged by dried blood and dust that Faris might have missed him if he hadn't spoken.

"Never thought I'd be glad to see you, little man." Or at least, that's what Faris thought he said in a croaking, impeded Standard Language.

Safiy squeezed through the narrow entrance after him. Next came Rocco Stein, the medipeller pilot, who was bigger and almost didn't make it through. But Faris paid them no mind. "Nor I you, you big oaf. Glad to see you're alive."

"Your lovely wife is also living." Despite Kughurrrro's clumsy pronunciation, Faris had never heard more beautiful words. "But she is asleep inside the wall." He gestured toward a jagged hole beside him.

Faris let Safiy and Rocco worry about Kughurrrro. All he could see was that black hole, barely big enough for a Karkar's arm to fit through.

He shone a light in. A good distance down the shaft, a shapeless lump darkened the shadows. Nearer the opening lay something that looked like a limp, filthy hand. "Lileela!"

The hand twitched.

He reached his arm into the hole and stretched, squeezing his shoulder until he thought it would dislocate. But all he could feel was the same grime and rock he'd handled day and night for days and nights on end.

He pulled his arm out and peered in again. "Lileela!"

He could hardly hear for the pounding of his heart, but she did answer, weakly. "Faris?"

All this time, all this digging, and he still couldn't reach her? How badly was she injured? He needed to touch her, to hold her, to get her out of there, to —

A hand gripped his other shoulder. "Faris." It was Safiy. "Faris. Did you hear?"

Furious at the interruption, Faris spun around. "What? Did I hear what? I heard my wife dying inside that wall. What else is there to hear?"

Safiy reacted calmly. "Kughurrrro just spoke to her a few minutes ago. She drifts in and out of consciousness, but when she's awake, she's lucid. We'll get her out in one piece."

His words sank in slowly, and Faris relaxed his aggressive stance.

THE LAST TOQEPH

"But you're right, brother, it's got to be soon. That's what we're here for." In the eerie light of their torches, Safiy's eyes glowed with an inner fire. "First, we have to get Kughie out of here."

Faris shifted his gaze toward the battered Karkar. His eyes looked sunken. One of his ears was torn, and a furrow of dust-caked blood carved a crease down the side of his head and neck. His filthy clothes looked like they were a size too big, except for where part of one grotesquely swollen knee seeped through a hole in his pants like a purple growth.

And Lileela was in worse shape than this?

Faris turned toward the hole, but Safiy grabbed him. "We can't open that passage until we get Kughie out. And he's too big to fit." Safiy gestured toward the hole they'd just squeezed through. "We've got to open that up first. Then we can work on reaching Lileela."

Faris stared dumbly at the entrance gaping blackly in the shifting shadows, trying to envision fitting the Karkar through it. Safiy was right; first things first.

He nodded. "Thanks, brother. For bringing me back."

Safiy patted his back, loosening dust. "Let's get this oversized lout out of here."

He made no objection when Faris bent again to speak into the hole. "I'm coming for you, Lileela. I'll be there soon."

And so they dug and dug some more.

Pik told Faris to be in the group that carried Kughurrrro out and to stay above ground to rest before going back in. It grated on him to leave Lileela behind, but Faris didn't argue.

In another few hours, Rocco got a stretcher through, and he and Faris helped Kughurrrro onto it. Once he was secured, they half pushed, half dragged until there was more room to maneuver. Then two more men joined them, each taking a corner of the stretcher, and, staggering, carried him out of the mine.

At the first breath of fresh air, Kughie said something unintelligible. Sharing the load of the head-end of the stretcher with Faris, Rocco answered. "We've got a medipeller out here, Kughurrrro. We'll get you fixed up as well as we can. But we're going to have to wait until we get Lileela out before we get you to the hospital. We're running out of power and will only be able to make one trip."

THE LAST TOQEPH

Faris's mind and heart were back in that dark hole with Lileela, and he moved through a haze of weariness toward the medipeller. It was as dark outside the cave as in, so it must be nighttime. Last time he'd come out, the sun had blazed hot and bright, but now the air had a damp chill to it. The only light came from the men's headlamps and the waiting 'peller, which Rocco had powered up before bringing the stretcher for Kughurrrro.

Faris could barely feel his hands, and he struggled to keep his grip. To prevent stumbling, he considered each step. Even with the weight shared with three others, the Karkar was heavy. Must be 140 kilos. And that was after being trapped in the mine for days on end.

What could be left of little Lileela? He hadn't heard a sound out of her for quite some time, though he'd strained to listen as they dug.

Near the 'peller, Pik came to greet them and help get Kughie into it. But was that really Pik? He was an ancient thing, stooped and wan. He and Rocco spoke as he examined the Karkar on the stretcher. In this light, the patient looked even worse than he had in the cave. When Pik cut the pants away from Kughurrrro's knee and revealed the injury in all its swollen, green-and-purple glory, Faris wondered again what shape Lileela was in.

Kughie said something in a hoarse, croaking Karkar, and Pik bent closer. Whatever his words, they made Pik look up and cast his gaze around at the men standing nearby until he lit on Faris. He motioned him into the 'peller.

Heart pounding, Faris climbed in. "What is it?"

In the bright lights of the examining area, Pik's pale face looked ghostly. He was almost as thin as the patient, and his amber eyes were sunken and bloodshot. "Kughurrrro says to tell you Lileela was still in good spirits a short time ago. She called to you, but he doesn't think you could hear over all the work that was going on."

Faris almost cried at the thought he hadn't heard her voice. "That's good news."

"Yes. You'll want to be there when they reach her, of course."

"Of course."

"But for now, I want you to get something to eat. Drink as much water as you can hold. Then find an empty tent and sleep until you're called for. We'll waken you when the excavation is wide enough to reach Lileela."

Faris stared. He couldn't sleep now. He had to open that hole and get her out of there.

THE LAST TOQEPH

Before he could voice his thoughts, Pik continued. "You've been going too hard for too long, and I want there to be something left of you for Lileela. She'll need you to be whole."

Faris was too well trained to argue. Besides, Pik was right. He wouldn't be of any use to Lileela in his present state.

He bowed. "I'll do that."

Pik turned back to his patient, and Faris started for the camp. On a second thought, he made a detour for the tidal basin, where he waded out a short distance and then plunged in, bobbing and rolling in the water to rinse away some of the grit. When he waded out, he was cold, but somewhat refreshed.

He hardly knew what he did after that. He'd been ordered to eat and drink, so he must have done so. And he knew he'd entered a tent and lain on a sleeping mat, because that's where he was when Adil shook him from sleep. "Wake up, Faris! We've reached her!"

16

The first thing Adam was aware of when he awoke was the scent of Elise beside him.

He opened his eyes. Her copper-colored hair lay across the pillow, and the corners of her sleeping mouth were drawn up in a near smile. He smiled back.

Behind her, light filtered through the bed curtain. They must have slept almost into Yellow Morning. He yawned. What luxury to lie in a real bed. With his beautiful wife.

His eyes took in her sleeping form silhouetted in the dim light. When his gaze rested on the pregnant abdomen, it shifted as his son within it moved. She made a little moan, and her dainty five-fingered hand moved from where it had rested on her hip and spread to span her belly. She murmured a sleepy something that sounded like, "Settle down in there, would you?"

Chuckling, Adam lifted a section of silky hair from her face then kissed her. "Is he eager to see his abba?"

She moaned again as her belly lurched. "He's a monster. I have no idea what he wants."

Adam laid his hand over hers on her abdomen and felt the movement. "I think he wants out. But I'm glad he waited for me to come home."

She opened her eyes and fixed her gaze on his face. "Do you think I can't do it alone? Because where childbirth is concerned, you're really not much help, you know."

He kissed her. "Just try making a baby without me."

"Making it's no problem." She wrapped her arms around him and pulled herself close. "It's getting it out that's the lonely job."

Several kisses later, she spoke again. "What do you hear from Lileela?"

THE LAST TOQEPH

His mind was busy with other things. "Mmmm?"

"Lileela." She pulled away. "Now that you're through with your quest, you can communicate with her. I've been worried sick, and we don't get much news. How is she?"

He rolled onto his back and reached in his meah for his sister. He'd been worried about her too, earlier. Was it wrong of him to put her out of his thoughts for a few minutes?

He connected. "She's weak, but hanging in there. Ra'anan's in touch with her almost constantly, and the Yasha is so real to her it's almost like He's right there with her. I get the impression the rescuers are getting close."

Turning, he propped himself on his elbow and gazed at Elise. "Satisfied? Can we get back to what we were doing?" He moved in without waiting for a reply, and she offered no objection.

Oh, yes, this was good. He'd missed Elise more than he'd realized. He simply hadn't allowed himself to think about it. Now he wasn't thinking, either. Just responding to his feelings. What a delight, almost unbearably so, to lie snug and safe in this little nest with the most beautiful woman in—

He tensed at the sound of the bedroom door sliding open. Little feet pattered across the floor. "Emma?"

Elise closed her eyes as if willing away the interruption.

Adam glared first at the shadowy form on the other side of the curtain and then at his wife. "Did you allow him in here when I was gone?" His voice sounded gruffer than he'd intended—but not more than he felt.

Her eyes filled with tears. "We both missed you…"

"Emma?" Everett's voice quivered. "Who's in there with you?"

Adam reached across Elise and yanked back the curtain. "I'm your father. Who did you think would be in here?"

Everett burst into tears, and Elise reached for him. "It's okay, baby."

Adam scowled, which made his swollen eye hurt. "No, baby, it's not okay. You're not allowed in your parents' bedroom." If Elise weren't in his way, Adam would have jumped out of the bed and escorted Everett from the room. But in her condition, she presented quite an obstacle.

At the moment, she was an immobile one, and tearful. "Don't yell at him like that, he's just a little guy. I let him come in because I was lonely. We both were."

THE LAST TOQEPH

The way Everett screamed at the sight of him, Adam couldn't believe the kid had missed him in the slightest. "You can't change the rules just because you're lonely. How's he going to learn to behave if you tell him *No* one day and the next day it's okay?"

Adam managed to get out of the bed without crushing her, and when he rose to his full height, Everett screamed even louder and dove into Elise's outstretched arms. Tossing Adam a jagged glare, she dragged the boy into the bed with her and yanked the curtain closed. Everett's sobbing was muffled, and she crooned to him. "It's okay, baby. Abba's happy to see you, but he's still tired from his long walk. It's okay."

Adam gritted his teeth. If he'd ever come into his parents' bedroom as a kid, he'd have found himself sitting in the Grey Room before he could finish a yawn.

"Elise, what are you doing?" He opened the curtain again. "He's not allowed in here and you know it."

Holding Everett protectively, she struggled to rise. "What am I doing?" She had to let go of the clinging child to pull herself up. "What am *I* doing? Look what *you're* doing, you ogre." Finally out of the bed, she took Everett into her arms and glowered up at Adam, her face red and blotchy. "How'd you say you got that black eye?"

"I didn't say." He couldn't say. No aspect of the Nasi training was discussed, not even with wives. Not that he'd want to tell her anyway.

"Well, I'd like to give you another one. You're a big brute, you know that?" Carrying Everett and the unborn child at the same time though both were unusually large, she lumbered away, radiating anger.

Adam stood in bewilderment as they disappeared into Everett's room. A moment later, the little bed curtain closed with an irritable swish, and Elise's cries and the boy's became nearly indistinguishable.

Adam ran his hands across his head. This was not the way it was supposed to work. But if he went in there and pulled them both out of bed, he truly *would* be an ogre.

What was it Abba used to say when the kids carried on? *Tears can't hear.* True enough, apparently. With women as well as children.

He'd wait for them to calm down. But once she was rational, Elise was going to get an earful. Pregnant or not.

A glance at the timedial told him that would have to wait. He was to appear at Gullach at half past the second hour of Yellow for his audience

THE LAST TOQEPH

with the toqeph. He grabbed his clothes and headed for the bathroom. Maybe the crying would be over by the time he got out of the shower. He turned on the water.

Yesterday, Jax had debriefed him and seemed satisfied with all his answers. Adam's moment of insubordination was a factor for consideration, but it was still possible Jerry might rule the quest complete and allow him to move on to the next stage of his training.

"There's just one thing, sir," Adam had said.

Jax raised his brows. "What's that? Didn't I cover everything?"

"You did. But there's a matter I need to discuss with the toqeph. Directly. I think she'd want it that way."

Jax shrugged. "Okay, kid. The toqeph's door's always open, as you know. Jerry and I are meeting with her tomorrow morning, and I'll let her know this decision is on hold until she's heard you out. Does that work for you?"

Adam bowed. "Perfectly, sir. Thank you."

Now as he showered, fixed his hair, and trimmed his beard, he had to decide what he would say. There didn't seem any good way to break the news that she'd somehow managed to overlook the existence of a number of Plague survivors all these years.

When he exited the bathroom, the house was quiet. He stealthily entered Everett's room and peeked behind the curtain. They both slept, Everett in Elise's arms. Shaking his head, he tiptoed out then entered his bedroom—his and Elise's, their private space—and pulled the red collar from the drawer. In the kitchen, he wrote her a note. "Have audience with the toqeph @ Yellow Morn half past 2nd hr. Put this on. We will talk later. Love you both. Truly. A." He laid the collar on top of the note then left the apartment.

His stomach was too unsettled for breakfast.

Lileela couldn't stand the drilling. The mechanical shriek tore through her head, growing more intolerable as it worked its way nearer. But the vibrations were even worse. They made her pain ratchet to such heights she'd have vomited if she hadn't been dehydrated.

Instead of puking, she fainted. But awake or asleep, the drilling noise throbbed in her ears.

THE LAST TOQEPH

She didn't even have Uncle Kughie to talk to anymore. They'd taken him away. And was that a dream, or had she heard Faris's voice? She preferred to think it was true. That he'd be there when they pulled her out of this hole, if they ever got here.

What would she have done without the Yasha's continual presence? She couldn't have endured it, she was certain. Sweet Ra'anan was a comfort, too. Always thinking of her. And Emma, Tamah, and the boys. The farther she drifted from reality, the more tangible was their presence.

How long could a person go without water? A Gannahan could outlast an Earther or a Karkar, but which of her genes would dominate? Kughie had shared what little he'd had when they'd first become trapped. When rainwater had filtered through the roof, he'd captured it in a bottle. But even that was long gone.

If not for the love of her family, she'd truly rather die here. She'd never be able to walk again. She'd be a burden to dear Faris. He'd never complain, but the thought that he'd have her dragging him down the rest of his life broke her heart. Whenever she started to plead with the Yasha to take her home to Him, though, He reassured her. *It is not time, my child. Thou shalt yet walk on Gannah.*

Walk? Would she really? She didn't want to doubt the Yasha, but it didn't seem possible. She thought of her mother's arm, broken in the shuttle crash all those years back. Without proper treatment, it had healed badly, and Emma still couldn't extend it fully. How could Lileela's legs be repaired after all this time?

She drifted between the meahs of her family and an occasional agonizing consciousness. She basked in the Yasha's comfort and longed to join Him forever, only to awaken to an awareness of her pain again, and darkness, and noise.

It was during one of those awful awake times that an unusual brightness appeared beyond her closed eyelids, and it seemed the walls didn't press in so closely around her. It was such a surprising change in her environment, she was afraid to open her eyes. Then someone touched her. Though alarmed, she was too weak to do more than twitch in response. She heard words and recognized them as familiar, but couldn't put meaning to them.

The voice was not Faris's. Hands lifted her body. The pain! She fainted again.

THE LAST TOQEPH

When Adam had to travel between the second chatsr and the rest of the settlement, he usually went by foot. Or, if he were in a hurry, rode a biwheel. He liked the exercise. It helped him think, gave him an opportunity to meditate. Made him feel connected with Gannah.

Today, he had neither time nor energy. He took the tube.

His legs stretched across the aisle to the seat opposite, and the tunnel's walls raced past in a blur. Much like his life. He'd thought he knew where he was, where he was going. But meeting that man in the meadow had sent everything out of control. Furrowing his brow made his bruised face throb, so he stared blank-faced out the window at the fast-flying nothingness, contemplating.

When the tube slowed to a gentle stop beneath Gullach, he pulled his feet to the floor and groaned. Why did he ache so? That long swim had taken more out of him than it should have.

Another pod was at the station. A cart stood on the platform beside it, piled high with wooden crates, and Daniel Lucas emerged from the car backward lugging another box.

He glanced up as Adam exited his pod. "Hey, Adam! Back in one piece, I see. So your quest was a success?"

Adam's ears tilted back. Daniel presumed upon their old friendship. He knew a Nasi trainee couldn't discuss these things. "I've returned, yes."

Daniel found a place on the cart for the last crate. "Do you have a minute? I could use a hand moving these. Last week, Zuri Ayo took inventory of the store here in Gullach and made a list of things to restock. We've been too busy managing the place at First Town to keep up with it lately."

The request was a welcome distraction. "Glad to."

"And I'm glad you came along just now. I wasn't looking forward to getting this up the ramp alone."

"I'll push." Adam approached the cart. "You can pull and lead the way."

Daniel watched him, a smiling twitching the corner of his mouth. "Nice shiner."

Adam shrugged. "Want one of your own?" He grasped the handles at the back of the cart.

Daniel laughed as he took the bar at the front. "Guess not, thanks."

120

THE LAST TOQEPH

Together, they got the heavy load rolling. Daniel would, indeed, have had a hard time managing it alone. "What do you have here, anyway?"

"Mostly hardware. The store's out of fabric, too, but we can't restock that until we get new goods."

Adam helped Daniel manhandle the cart up the ramp toward the next level. "I hear the factory start-up's on hold for now, with so many people working on the rescue out at Orville's mine."

"I hear the same." Daniel's voice, sounding distant because of the crates between them, echoed off the tunnel walls. "But no one's complaining. Lives are more important than fabric."

Adam envisioned Natsach in his leather skirt and thought of his own patched and threadbare wardrobe. Would they soon be forced to wear animal skins in Periy, too? "Yes. Life is more important." But why must one thing die in order for another to live?

He concentrated on the task at hand, being careful not to push too hard and run over Daniel behind the stacks, and also to not let his feet slip out from under him on the sloped floor.

They were nearly at the top of the curving ramp when a sudden wave of emotion flooded through Adam's meah, nearly causing him to let go of the handles. He kept his grip but fell forward against the crates, scraping the side of his face as he turned his head to avoid smashing his nose.

"Hey!" Daniel yelped. "What's going on? You okay?"

Adam readjusted his position and kept pushing. "Yeah." He tried to understand what that rush of feeling was, though he knew it came from Lileela. "I think… I think they've just reached my sister."

"No kidding? That meah thing must be something else." They brought the cart to a stop on the flat at the end of the ramp. Daniel stepped away to stare at Adam, wide-eyed. "She told you that?"

"She didn't tell me, exactly." A little lightheaded, Adam let go of the handles and flexed his fingers. "It's just a feeling. But it's a good feeling." If it was so good, why did he want to cry? "Kind of euphoric and exhausted at the same time."

Daniel grinned. "She's gonna make it? For sure?"

"Not for sure. But I think so." He paused, staring at the floor while he analyzed the sensations flowing through him. Simultaneous communications with each of his meah-possessing family, all relieved and rejoicing.

THE LAST TOQEPH

How he wished he could commune with Abba as well.

And then Natsach chimed in. Not with the family celebration, but in a separate touch. *The time for thy quest has past. Wilt thou return as promised?*

Adam sensed doubt in the little man's mind. As if he considered Adam untrustworthy. *Yea. I must speak with the toqeph. Should she permit, I shall join thee, and we shall speak at greater length.*

Come to the place we first met, but on the south side of the river. By the rock in the meadow. Sixthday, the third hour of Yellow Morning.

Day after tomorrow. What if he had no way to get there?

What if Emma forbade him to go?

But he had a promise to keep. Once he explained, she would make sure he kept his word. *Sixthday. The third hour of Yellow Morning, thou shalt find me beside the rock in the meadow beside the waterfall.*

He sensed grimness in the reply. *Until then.*

Adam had every reason to dislike Natsach. But why would the little man have such a low opinion of Adam?

Daniel put his hand on Adam's arm, awakening him to his surroundings. "You sure you're okay?"

"Verily." Why was he speaking Old Gannahan? He shook his head and answered again in the Standard Speech. "I'm fine. Just a little tired, I guess." He forced a smile. "Let me help you deliver this to the store. Then I need to get to my meeting with the toqeph."

THE LAST TOQEPH

17

When Adam entered the toqeph's residence, the dining room door was closed. Muffled voices on the other side told him the meeting with Jerry and Jax had not yet ended. He took a chair in the sitting room to wait.

It smelled old in here. Just like the rail tube. He stared at the sagging sofa opposite. Abba had ordered it custom made on Earth before the settlers left for Gannah more than thirty years ago, as no furniture on this planet suited his Karkar stature. Now, it looked more ancient than the 300-year-old timedial on the sideboard across the room. More dilapidated than the sideboard, too, and all the other original Gannahan furniture. The Old Gannahans made things to last.

Emma said it was all about money. On Earth, when things wore out, people threw them away and bought new ones, which kept the manufacturers in business. The Old Gannahan ways made more sense. Their concern had been with quality, and the only monetary unit in their society was pride in their contribution.

Adam smoothed down a frayed area on the arm of his chair. At least the toqeph had furniture. And a palace that, if not pristine, was mostly in decent repair. What sort of conditions did Natsach and the rest of those people live in? They must have escaped the disaster with nothing more than the clothes they wore.

How had no one been aware of their existence? Emma said she'd done everything in her power to look for survivors during the Plague. Just seven years ago, the satellites surrounding the planet were fully functional, able to see every inch of the globe in clear detail. Moreover, orbiting League ships had scanned for human life and found no other inhabitants.

THE LAST TOQEPH

True, the world was a big place. But if people were there, they should have been detected.

The dining room door opened. Adam rose and turned toward the sound.

Jerry emerged with Jax behind him. Both looked trim and grim and every bit like the Nasi knights they were. Like Adam had always hoped to be.

He bowed, they nodded.

As Adam passed on his way to the dining room, Jax pointed at Adam's eye. "I do good work, don't I?" His noble-knight expression melted into a smile and a wink.

Adam bowed again and spoke in Old Gannahan. "Thy punishment was just."

When Adam straightened, Jax's brows were raised. "That was no punishment. Just a warning. You don't want to know what a Nasi punishment's like."

Jerry put his hand on Adam's shoulder. "He's right. And now that you've passed your second quest, the last third of your training will be tougher than the first two combined."

Adam heard the words, but wasn't sure he understood. "I've passed?" He thought the decision hadn't been made yet.

Jax's grin broadened. "You have indeed."

"Yes." Jerry removed his hand from Adam's shoulder. "But now, the pressure increases. From this day on, you'll feel locked in a vise. And the pressure will hurt."

Adam met Jerry's pale blue gaze, and his mouth went dry. How could it be tougher than it already was? He bowed. "I am at thy service, sir. I wish only the good of Gannah."

It was the prescribed response. He'd been saying it with pride since his training began. But this time, it filled him with dread.

Though Adam had hoped for a little encouragement, Jerry's expression remained sober as he gave the usual reply. "As do we all."

Even Jax sounded serious. "As do we all."

What did they plan for him? The records of Nasi training methods and rituals were sealed to all but those who had passed through the ordeal. Adam hadn't been able to find a single story or anecdote about what went on in the old days. He only knew that an inductee went into it with

THE LAST TOQEPH

trepidation and emerged a changed man, stern and strong and well-nigh invincible.

Such a transformation couldn't come easily.

Giving a final nod, the knights strode out, and Adam turned to the dining room doorway. He straightened his shoulders and entered.

Emma sat at the head of the table.

The toqeph. Every son revered his em, but in this case, she ruled not only him but the whole planet. She was mother of the world.

All he'd been through recently suddenly overwhelmed him. When she looked up and smiled, he prostrated himself like a penitent. Words failed him.

"Rise." He heard puzzlement in her voice. Felt concern in his meah. Motherly concern.

He rose, wondering if the tears that threatened to overcome him finally would. He kept his head lowered, but still didn't know what to say.

"Jax told me how you got that black eye, and why. Are you concerned that your insubordination should have disqualified you?"

Why was he surprised when she spoke in the Standard Language? "Yes, in part."

She paused. "To be frank, it might have, were this the old days. But the native Gannahan's rigid obedience does not come naturally to those of Earthish or Karkar blood. It must be learned. I knew from the beginning that I could not expect any of the settlers to be thoroughly Gannahan. That's why you get a second chance."

Though his head remained bowed, he felt her studying him as she continued. "You've completed your second quest. A difficult accomplishment in the extreme. You're reunited with your family, and we've just now learned that our Lileela is safe. That's a lot to be thankful for."

"Yea, verily." He lifted his gaze and allowed a smile to relax his face. "I am thankful, mine em. My heart overfloweth."

Though he spoke the old language, she replied in Standard. "But you have something to tell me." The way those green eyes bored into him, it seemed she already knew everything. "I want to hear it. But please, sit."

He made a small bow then pulled out a chair.

"Adam."

He looked up again.

THE LAST TOQEPH

"First, let me get this out of the way: as the toqeph, I'm pleased with your progress. I can't express the comfort it gives me to see how well you conduct yourself. To see how you hold the good of Gannah above any personal agenda. I feel secure in the thought you'll be ready to reign when I must pass on and sit in the Hall of the King."

Adam swallowed hard. He bowed his head. "I will do my best to not disappoint."

"I have no reason to expect you to fail. But if something should happen and you don't complete your task? I'm still your mother. You can never do anything to make me love you less."

He didn't look up. "Yes, Emma. I know."

"I know you do. Now, tell me something I don't know. I see it weighs heavy on you."

The love in her brilliant green eyes leapt across the distance between them, and he smiled back. "Emma." He swallowed. "In Yereq, I..." He took a deep breath.

The only way to do this was to plunge in. He leaned forward in his chair. "Standing beside a river, I saw an ayal fall on the other side. Its throat had been slit by a well-thrown lahab."

He felt her confusion, but she didn't say a word, and he continued. "Then a man stepped out from behind the rock that had concealed him. He saw me. He came over the river to me, and we spoke. His name is Natsach. I promised him when my quest was done, I would return."

At the name *Natsach*, her face blanched.

Feeling nothing from her meah, Adam went on. "He's asked me to return on the morning of Sixthday, and I've agreed."

The green of her eyes faded to a dull jade color, and she said nothing.

Adam had known Emma to be speechless only one other time. When Abba brought her home after she'd been lost on the other side of the planet, she'd had that same look. Like she'd been walking with the dead.

He wet his lips with his tongue. "I don't know how it's possible, but we are not alone in this world, Emma. Some of the Old survive."

She covered her face in her hands and bent forward to rest her forehead on the table. Still without a word.

Adam's skin prickled. Her silence was more eerie than a wail would have been.

THE LAST TOQEPH

What had he said to cause such a reaction? True, it must be a shock to learn Old Gannahans survived, but there had to be more to it than that.

He raised his hand to touch her shoulder but lowered it again. "My apologies. If my speaking to him disqualifies me from passing my quest, I understand."

She shook her head, barely. He understood her intent through his meah, though she still didn't speak. *This was an unusual situation. You would have been remiss to pass him by without stopping.*

He shifted in his chair and studied the top of her head, trying to reach her meah more clearly. Instead of clarity, he met a dizzying swirl of thoughts and feelings. He'd thought her mind more ordered than that. It was almost as muddled as he expected Elise's would be if she had a meah to read. Surprising that a person with such strong emotions could behave in such a controlled manner. The force of each individual thought reminded him of…

Of Natsach. Funny how he'd never noticed before. Undiluted, as his was, by Earthish and Karkar blood, her Gannah-ness put him in awe. She was the heir of Atarah the king. True royalty, the genuine article. When Adam took the throne, he'd be a pretender. A pale imitation.

She lifted her head and removed her hands from her ashen face. No spark flashed from those green eyes. Instead, they seemed to look inward even as she turned her gaze to Adam.

"Tell me again." She cleared her throat. "Tell me all you saw, every word you both said."

Adam did. Related every action, every syllable. Including his communication with Natsach that morning.

She listened with all her ears and meah, not speaking until he had finished. "His eyes are violet, like a ripe *peret* in autumn?"

Adam shook his head. "More like the *achlamah* stones in the timedial in the sitting room."

"Of course." She nodded. "His eyes looked like achlamah when he was upset."

Before he could phrase his *how do you know that* question, she went on. "And his hair. Looser curls than mine? His face longer, less round. His nose less broad?"

THE LAST TOQEPH

Had she gotten all that from reading his meah? Adam nodded. "Yes. And he is quite short. Barely above one and three quarter meters, I would guess."

"I would guess." She almost smiled. "Those are the classic Natsach traits. Was his voice deep and strong as thunder but smooth as a flower petal?"

Adam's ears stiffened in amazement. "You might say that. Though I heard no trace of flowers."

Her gaze still looked inward, and he felt no probing of his meah. Wherever her mind was, it was not in this room. He felt it best to wait for her to break the silence.

After a moment, she did. "You shall meet him on Sixthday as he said. I think it would be appropriate for you to take the Hatita. You know the basics of flying, and that's a simple craft to operate. I'll have Jarol Dudte go out with you this afternoon to make sure you're ready to take it alone."

Adam blinked. Fly alone? A third of the way around the planet? In the most amazing aircraft on Gannah? He wanted to prostrate himself, but instead bowed in his seat. "I would be honored. Do you think I'm capable?"

"That's for Jarol to decide. If he's not completely comfortable with it, I'll have him fly you there. But I hear you're competent behind the controls, so you should have no trouble with the Hatita. I've flown it myself, you know."

He nodded. Everybody knew about the time Emma and Abba, before they were married, found the aircraft that a man named Hatita had made for their use years before. It was one of Adam's favorite stories.

"I don't expect you'll have any trouble with it. I hope not, because it's a little small for two passengers."

Adam lifted his brows but lowered them again as the pain in his eye reminded him of his shame. "Two passengers? Who will be there besides Jarol and me?"

"Natsach Daviyd, of course. I wish to speak with him. Here."

Was he delirious with exhaustion, or relief? Faris wasn't sure. But he certainly wasn't in his right mind.

First, it had taken all Rocco's and Roshan's strength to hold him back when, wanting Lileela all to himself, he'd shoved Pik away as he tried to examine her. Then, once she was stable and being loaded into the

THE LAST TOQEPH

medipeller, he couldn't restrain himself from hugging everyone in sight, hindering their task. He watched his behavior, as if from a distance, with a mixture of wonder and embarrassment.

And gratitude that so few remained to see him make a fool of himself. Most of the others, including Orville, had gone in the other topeller back to Chabbassa.

As if Faris's delirium weren't enough distraction, Kughie's sedation wore off as the team prepared to depart. The Karkar let loose with a caterwauling that would shatter glass if the only glass in the vicinity weren't of the unbreakable Gannahan kind.

To Faris, it was just noise, but Pik thought it intelligible speech. The doc's subsequent conversation with the giant in Karkar resembled a combination of grinding gears and a donkey's agonized bray.

While Faris helped Roshan and Rocco perform a pre-takeoff inspection, Pik quieted the big guy with what looked like reassurances but sounded like a malfunctioning popcorn machine. Then Pik rose and, bent like an old man, turned to stand in the craft's entrance, holding on as if too weary to stand without support. "He wants his bag."

Faris and the others groaned. "What bag?" "You're kidding, right?" "We got what we came for, so let's get out of here. Lileela needs a hospital."

That last comment was Faris's. But Pik shook his head. "She does, and soon. But the bag contains what *he* came for. The whole point of this trip to begin with." He directed his bloodshot gaze to Faris. "He says it's leaning against the wall where he was sitting. The sooner you get it, the sooner we can leave."

There was a certain logic to that. Without another word, Faris sprinted back the way they'd just come. The tide was rising, the basin filling with puddles, but he splashed through them.

At the too-familiar tunnel entrance, he located one of the lanterns the rescuers had left behind, turned it on, and hurried in. He thought he'd seen the last of this place. But then he knew he never would; he'd see it and smell it in his dreams the rest of his life.

He made his hurried way to the room where they'd found Kughie and shined the light along the back wall. At first he thought there was nothing but the usual rubble, but a closer look revealed a strap curving up from a pile of rock. The bag had been buried when they widened the tunnel to get Lileela out.

THE LAST TOQEPH

What's a little more rock when you've already moved half a mountain? He tossed the mess right and left until the massive bag was exposed.

He grabbed and pulled, but it didn't move. He cleared away more rubble and tried again. What in the world was in that thing? He was finally able to lift it out, but it was the size of a two-man tent and weighed as much as he did. Or so it seemed, in his exhausted state.

By the time he'd lugged it back to the tidal basin, his every pore ran with sweat and his legs wobbled with weakness. He set the bag down to rest a moment before trying to carry it through the mud across the flat.

Roshan saw him and came to help. He and Faris lifted it together, and Roshan groaned. "This'll never work." They set it down again. "A stretcher will help distribute the weight."

Faris nodded, glad someone could still think clearly. He sat on the bag and waited while Roshan slogged back to the medipeller and returned with a stretcher.

Together they hefted it onto the center then toted it through the ankle-deep water to the 'peller. Pik helped them load it, Roshan replaced the stretcher, and finally, Faris collapsed into the seat beside Lileela, who lay in a blissful, drug-induced oblivion.

Pik laid a weary hand on his shoulder. "Thank you. When he said *bag*, I'd envisioned something smaller."

"Me too." Faris buckled up and affixed his headphones. "Will we be able to take off with all that extra weight?"

Rocco's voice came through the headset. "We've each dropped so many kilos the past few days, it shouldn't take us over the limit." After a pause, during which he probably checked the numbers, he added, "We're fine. Everybody ready?"

Faris took Lileela's hand and traced her pain-pinched profile with his finger. "More than ready."

Pik's voice sounded beyond weary. "Take us home, Rocco."

18

Dawn bleached the star-studded sky when Adam, standing outside the clinic, spied the blinking lights of the approaching medipeller. Its distant rotors strummed the air with a faint heartbeat. His own thumped in rhythm.

Jane, beside him, pointed to the sky. "I see them!" On his other side, Emma watched in silence, her tension palpable.

Adam tore his eyes from the 'peller long enough to glance around. "Where are Lucian and Dale?"

"They're inside, getting things ready." Jane tossed him a reassuring smile. "That was a good idea you had, calling on the boys to help. With two wounded coming in and your father exhausted, we could use their assistance, and this will be valuable experience for them."

He nodded. "After tonight, they'll have a better idea of what a medical career involves."

Emma glanced back at the clinic behind them, its lights ablaze. "I suspect in Lucian's case, it'll confirm that this is his niche. And Dale will probably find the opposite."

Jane spoke above the throb of the incoming medipeller. "Why do you say that, Madam Toqeph? Dale's got a quick mind, and he's enthusiastic. Lucian is a little withdrawn, more apt to hold back and wait to be asked."

Emma shrugged. "I could be wrong."

Adam doubted it. She was seldom wrong.

The 'peller loomed nearer. He imagined Elise and Everett stirring in their beds at the sound, perhaps putting their pillows over their heads. Maybe Everett would cry for his emma.

But she wouldn't bring him into her bed, would she? No. They'd discussed it yesterday. At length. Elise wouldn't make that mistake again.

THE LAST TOQEPH

Adam pulled his thoughts from his home and directed them to the patients within the lowering vehicle. Turbulence whipped his clothing and he mentally reviewed Safiy's report of their condition. Both severely dehydrated and starved as well as filthy. Those problems were easily remedied. In fact, hydration and nutrition were being addressed en route.

Kughurrrro's wounds would require thorough cleaning and stitching. Adam was concerned about the dangling ear. Would he be able to reaffix it properly, or would the geologist's appearance be lopsided the rest of his life?

But Lileela was his greatest concern. Safiy said her legs were terribly mangled, and Adam had only the most basic of training in orthopedics. Abba's experience was greater, but as Jane had said, he was done in. A man in his seventies needed more than a nap to bounce back from this sort of ordeal.

The 'peller touched down beside the fountain. Lucian and Dale ran out of the clinic as Rocco powered down. When the door opened, Adam and Jane hastened toward it. Emma, probably wanting to avoid getting in the way, watched from a distance.

The odor that poured out almost made him take a step back. It was a powerful combination of unwashed humanity and something Adam had never smelled before. He tried not to wonder how long it would take to get that stink out of his clinic, for they'd certainly bring it in with them.

A man met them at the door. "We'll get Lileela out first." Adam didn't recognize him at first, and he stared into the vehicle, confused. Everyone in the 'peller looked the same, with their skin, beards, hair, and clothing a uniform reddish-brown color.

There wasn't much room in there. Adam waited until the man, whom he determined from voice and manner to be Roshan Tewodros, brought Lileela's gurney within reach. Then he helped Roshan maneuver it out the door and into the pool of illumination the 'peller's lights spilled onto the courtyard.

Faris, hollow-eyed and scruffy, was identifiable by his stature, short hair, and the fact that he stuck to Lileela as securely as the intravenous tube. "She's sedated. I can't talk to her. She's going to make it, isn't she?" His azure eyes glowed up at Adam from a darkly grimed face. "Can you reach her with your meah? Does she know I'm here?"

THE LAST TOQEPH

Emma stepped over to stand beside Faris. "She knows. And it comforts her."

Adam couldn't see much through the filth, but Lileela's legs were, in fact, a mess of dried blood and mud. They appeared to be straight, however, not bent at the unnatural angles he'd expected. And her vitals were good. "She's strong as Gannahan glass." He saw the relief in Faris's expression. "Let's get her in where we can get a better look."

Jane took over then, and Adam turned back to the 'peller to see to the other patient.

Kughurrrro was sedated too—in order to keep him quiet, according to Roshan. His weight was more than twice Lileela's, and his lower legs extended a good half meter off the end of the gurney. It took the combined efforts of Rocco and Roshan inside and Lucian and Dale outside to unload him.

It occurred to Adam that he hadn't seen Abba. "Where's my father?"

Rocco grinned. "Sound asleep."

Adam's stomach plummeted. "He's injured?"

"No." Rocco shook his head. "Just overextended. A couple days' rest should fix him up. He's quite a guy, your ab."

Adam ducked into the medipeller. The stench was only slightly diminished with most of the sweaty people now outside. Shaggy and filthy as the rest of them, Abba sprawled across a too-small seat, more out of it than in. He'd be mighty stiff when he woke up.

Adam turned toward the doorway and called to Rocco and Roshan outside. "What did you do, drug him?"

Rocco chuckled. "No need to."

Adam exited the 'peller and spoke to Lucian. "I'll let him sleep until we get Kughie situated then I'll come back out for him."

"I'll handle it." Emma appeared from the early-morning gloom. "Between Jane and Faris, there's nothing for me to do for Lileela at the moment. Did I hear you say he's asleep in there?"

Adam nodded. "Snoring like a luglit."

She smiled and walked toward the medipeller.

Adam approached Dale, who watched over the unconscious Kughurrrro. "How's he doing?"

Dale shrugged. "He stinks. What is that smell, anyway?"

Adam's ears twitched in annoyance. "I meant, how are his vitals?"

THE LAST TOQEPH

"Good, I guess. For a Karkar. It looks like his ear's about torn off. It's kind of gross."

Adam tended to agree, though it would have been unprofessional to say so. "Let's get him inside and see what we're looking at."

In the clinic, he had Dale and Lucian take Kughurrrro into the bathing area and told Rocco and Roshan to take showers before going home. "Your wives will never let you in the door smelling like that." Then he checked on Lileela. Still unconscious, she lay on a metal table with Jane and Faris on either side, washing her. "Oh, good, you're making progress. I'll be right back."

In Kughie's room, Dale and Lucian had the patient's boots and socks off and were creating a cloud of dust as they tried to peel his blood-crusted shirt from his body.

Adam hurried toward them. "What are you doing? You can't just yank it off like that. Look at how bloody it is. You don't know what kind of wounds are under there."

Both of the younger men flushed. "Sorry," Lucian said. "We thought..."

Adam pushed the gurney to the shower table. "I'm going to need help moving him."

It was a struggle for the three of them, but they managed to slide him from the gurney onto the metal table.

Adam coughed on the dust. "If we wet his shirt, we can loosen the crud and see what it's stuck to. The pants are already cut away from the injured knee, so there's no point trying to save them. Just cut them the rest of the way off. We'll need scissors."

The boys looked at one another a moment, then Dale said, "I'll get them," and hurried out.

Adam grabbed the sprayer. "Let's start at the top." He directed the stream toward the crown of Kughie's head, and the water flowed off in muddy rivulets.

When Dale returned with the scissors, Adam instructed him and Lucian to cut and remove the pants. Then he showed them how to continue washing the body, making sure they didn't tear off any scabs with the clothing. "Use plenty of cleanselotion and rinse it well. Be careful around the wounds. I'll be back after I look in on Lileela."

Finally.

THE LAST TOQEPH

It wasn't that he didn't care about Kughurrrro, but Lileela was his sister.

He entered her room. Her wild curls were loose and wet. A towel covered her torso, and what skin he could see was already clean. Her eyes were closed, but she was awake, holding onto one of Faris's hands while he cleansed one of her legs with the other hand. Adam swallowed a lump when he saw Faris's eyes streaming tears.

No one looked up, but Jane, working on the other leg, spoke. "She's got a bump on her head, and there's hardly any part of her that's not bruised, scraped, or both. We'll have to do a scan to see for sure, of course, but it looks like her only serious injuries are here."

The legs did look serious.

Gannah's population was small, and Adam hadn't seen a lot of trauma injuries. The sight of the exposed bone made his stomach churn.

He steeled himself to think like a doctor instead of the patient's brother. "You're doing a good job."

She glanced up. "Faris missed his calling. He'd make a wonderful nurse."

Faris didn't respond, but Lileela opened her eyes and looked at her husband with an expression of adoration.

Adam drew a deep breath to brace himself before taking a closer look at the wounds. Jane and Faris had made good progress cleaning them. Just a scattering of grit left, which they removed with a combination of forceps and irrigation.

Lileela's injuries gave the phrase "rubbed raw" new and horrific meaning. He was glad for the skin grafting experience he'd had when Henry Gazlo suffered burns two years ago.

The bones, in places clearly visible, showed many cracks but seemed perfectly aligned. His ears frowned. From the extent of the external damage, they should be every which-way. Why were they straight as a *taqan* limb?

"I'm going to do a whole-body scan." Feeling Lileela's gaze, he raised his eyes to meet it. The pain etching her face made his breath catch. "I can put you to sleep again. The scan won't hurt, but what I'll have to do later certainly will."

Faris put down his forceps and grasped her hand with both of his. "Yes. Give her relief, please." He kissed her hand.

THE LAST TOQEPH

She gave him a weak smile then shifted her dull gaze back to Adam. "Whatever you say. You're the doctor."

In theory, yes. Less so in practice. He needed his father's expertise. But he couldn't go running to Abba like a little boy. This responsibility was his.

"I'll get the scanner. And a sedative." As he exited, a loud clatter next door and Lucian's shout hastened his steps toward Kughurrrro's shower room.

"Doctor! Dale just fainted!"

19

Sitting in the limbs of the ancient elah tree in the palace courtyard, Ra'anan heard footsteps approach across the pavement below.

Great. She didn't need an audience. She looked down at Tamah, who waved to someone. A moment later, Mrs. Dengel appeared, eyeing Ra'anan in the tree. "Is that a new species of bird I see?"

Tamah's giggle filtered through the leaves. "That's not a bird, it's my sister."

Mrs. Dengel and her younger daughter, Priscilla, flashed white-toothed grins her way as Ra'anan flushed hot with embarrassment. "Tamah kicked the ball up here."

Mrs. Dengel shielded her eyes. "Did she, now?"

Priscilla glanced at the multi-colored ball in Tamah's hands and then up at Ra'anan. "The ball's down here."

"I know." Ra'anan shifted on the branch. "I just unsnagged it. And I'm coming down too. Once I figure out how." She eyed the distance between her perch and the ground. "I guess — I guess I just do it."

Lips pursed with resolve, she eased herself over the limb, hanging on with her arms, then let go and landed on her hands and knees with a tooth-jarring thud.

Tamah giggled. "You did look kind of like a bird up there. Or maybe a great big arnebeth. But without the fluffy tail."

"And less graceful." Rising, Ra'anan brushed off her knees and glanced at Mrs. Dengel. "I'm sorry, I'm a bit of a mess."

"You'll wash." Mrs. Dengel turned to Tamah. "Were you going to Shua's tea party, hon?"

THE LAST TOQEPH

Tamah's eyes widened. "Oh, I forgot!" She turned to Priscilla, who stood about Tamah's height though she was three years older. "Are you going too?"

Priscilla nodded. "I came to get you. Come on."

Ra'anan picked a tiny insect out of her ear as she answered Tamah's questioning look. "Go ahead. But you need to be home by the second hour of Green Afternoon, like Emma said."

"Okay!" Tamah and Priscilla ran off.

Hands still stinging from her hard landing, Ra'anan pulled a twig from her hair. She hoped to distract Mrs. Dengel from the awkward scene she'd just performed. "When the ladies came to pick up their kids a little bit ago, they were talking about how good the Bible study is every week. They say you're a wonderful teacher."

Mrs. Dengel gave a shy smile. "Why, thank you, child. But they exaggerate."

Ra'anan gave her tunic a final brush-up. "I'm looking forward to when I'm an adult, so I can come too." As an afterthought, she added, "It's not that I don't enjoy watching the kids for the ladies, but—"

Mrs. Dengel put a hand on her shoulder. "I understand, dear. I'll be happy to have you join us." She paused. "But I have a request."

"What is it, ma'am?" What could a wise woman like Mrs. Dengel want from a girl like her?

Mrs. Dengel led her to a nearby bench. "I love your planet, Ra'anan. It's a beautiful place. And I'm thankful to the toqeph for granting my daughters and me asylum six years ago."

"Yes, ma'am." Ra'anan sat beside Mrs. Dengel.

The woman took a deep breath. "Any word on your sister and Mr. Kughu— Ku— your uncle?"

"They arrived at the clinic in the second chatsr early this morning." Ra'anan focused her meah on the people in question. "Adam is working on Lileela's legs. Kughurrrro's knee is injured, but it will heal. Abba is exhausted, but unhurt. Emma is taking care of him." She pulled herself out of her meah-reverie and smiled at Mrs. Dengel. "Thank you for asking. We all appreciate your concern."

Mrs. Dengel's smile looked pinched. "The Yasha answers our prayers." She sighed. "I don't wish to bother the toqeph at such a time, but—but as

THE LAST TOQEPH

you know, I've petitioned for an order to repair the communication satellites."

Ra'anan's brain hummed. How would she know that? "I'm sorry, ma'am, but I don't know any more about what's going on than any other citizen. The toqeph doesn't discuss these things with the family."

Mrs. Dengel's dark complexion deepened. "Oh. I suppose that's true. I just thought—" She shifted her position and clasped her hands in her lap. "You're a good girl. Your em relies on you to help with things at home. But I suppose it doesn't follow that you would be involved in official matters as well."

The woman looked forlorn and uncomfortable, and Ra'anan's heart went out to her. "I'd be happy to help if I can, though. What about the satellites?"

"When my girls and I arrived—" Mrs. Dengel cleared her throat. "The satellite system surrounding your planet had been damaged just prior to our arrival." She shifted her position. "It's been six years, and still they go unrepaired. Do we not have the means to fix them? Or is there some other reason why the toqeph has made no effort to bring us back online? I only ask because—" Her eyes filled with tears. "Your uncle and Lileela are home. The toqeph's husband? And the other men who went out to bring back the injured? They're all back safely. But I remain apart from my husband. My daughters grow up without their father. And we have no means of communicating with him. We can't even know if he's still alive." Her voice broke.

Ra'anan took both Mrs. Dengel's hands in hers. "It must be terrible." She swallowed a lump.

Mrs. Dengel shook her head. "You've all been wonderfully kind. Taking us in and treating us as if we were your own. But this separation? This uncertainty? Yes." She nodded and averted her gaze. "It is difficult."

Ra'anan bit her lip. "You say you've petitioned for Em—I mean, the toqeph—to do something about it?"

Not lifting her head, Mrs. Dengel nodded again. "Two years ago. I have not mentioned it again, other than to ask your ab to verify that she did, in fact, receive the request. He assured me she did, and is considering it." She looked up at Ra'anan. "But how long? I lie in bed alone at night praying for Philip, and my heart cries for him. I see my girls growing into women without their father to teach them, and I can scarcely bear it." She lowered

THE LAST TOQEPH

her head, and her voice grew husky. "I do not fault the toqeph, mind you. I would only like to know."

Uncertain how else to reply, Ra'anan repeated the platitude she'd heard her father say when a settler asked about a pending request. "The toqeph takes each petition seriously and prays over it before making a decision. She will act when the Yasha gives her clear direction."

Mrs. Dengel pulled her hands away and fumbled in her pocket for a handkerchief.

Ra'anan wished she could be of more help. "If Ab told you the petition was received, then Em is praying over it every day. When the Yasha reveals the action He wants her to take, you can be sure she will take it." Ra'anan gave her what she hoped was a reassuring smile. "And I expect you'll be the first to know."

Mrs. Dengel blew her nose. "Thank you, child. Your words confirm what the Yasha has been telling me—when I quiet my heart enough to listen." She gave her nose a final wipe then put away the handkerchief. "I shouldn't have questioned the toqeph's intent."

Though Mrs. Dengel had no meah, Ra'anan could feel the woman's frustration almost as if it were her own. "I don't think either the Yasha or the toqeph would blame you."

She couldn't help but wonder, though, about Mrs. Dengel's question. Surely they had the ability to restore the damaged technology. Why did Emma seem determined that they continue to live without it?

In the second hour of Blue Night, Adam climbed the spiral staircase to his apartment. When he opened the door at the top, the vestibule's baseboard glowlights activated. Leaning his hip against the wall for balance, he unzipped his shoes, pulled them off, and laid them on the mat. Then he made his quiet way through the dark house.

In Everett's room, he pulled back the bed curtain just enough to see his son sleeping like a cherub. He smiled.

Elise lay in bed in their room, snoring. The curtain was open as if to welcome him. He undressed and slipped in beside her. Her small, lumpy body tipped on the mattress as his weight compressed it.

He brushed her cheek with a feathery kiss.

Her eyes fluttered open, and she smiled. "I wasn't sleeping."

THE LAST TOQEPH

"Could have fooled me." He closed the curtain. "But if you weren't, you should be. A woman in your condition needs her rest."

She snuggled close. "It's you who should be tired, working in the clinic since before sun-up."

"Perhaps, but I'm not." He nuzzled her neck.

"Of course not." She giggled as his attentions became more insistent. "You're never *that* tired."

Sitting on the floor, Hushai studied the game board on the low table. Across from him, Ittai yawned. Ra'anan reclined on a sofa, reading aloud to Tamah, who snuggled beside her.

Emma had called to say they could stay up until she and Abba came home. Hushai knew the others shared his excitement. Once Abba came through that door, everything would be right again.

Hushai examined the playing pieces' positions. Three more moves, and he'd have Ittai as good as dead. Unless Ittai tried to—

The front door slid open, and Hushai sprang up, bumping the board and knocking off the pieces. "Abba!" Ittai and Tamah were on their feet and rushing to Abba within a second. Ra'anan followed with only slightly more dignity.

Emma gasped. "Children, don't knock your poor ab down!"

For once, no one heeded Emma's command, but she allowed it to slide. Despite their enthusiastic welcome, Abba kept his feet and embraced all four in one long-armed hug.

He felt hard and bony and smelled strangely. "Glad to see you, kids. But your mother's right. I'm a little wobbly. Let me come in and sit down."

Ra'anan and Tamah each took a hand and dragged him into the sitting room, with the boys pushing. Emma laughed. "I'll make tea, and you can tell them all about it."

Abba sank onto the sofa. "I missed you all." He kissed them each in turn.

Tamah and Ittai shared his lap, while Ra'anan and Hushai each snuggled under one arm.

Ra'anan started the questions. "How are Lileela and Uncle Kughurrrro?"

Hushai knew as well as Ra'anan they were both fine. He'd rather hear about the rescuer's adventures. "What took you so long to find them?"

141

THE LAST TOQEPH

"Was it dark in the mine?" asked Ittai.

Tamah said what they'd all probably been thinking. "You smell funny."

Abba chuckled. "You should have smelled me this morning when I got off the medipeller. I've bathed twice, but your mother tells me the mine odor still lingers."

Hushai fingered the fabric of Abba's shirt. He recognized it as being borrowed from Adam. "I didn't know it smelled inside a mine."

"Neither did I," said Abba. "But that one did. Our noses got so full of it we didn't notice it anymore. Not smelling it was a blessing." He leaned back and gave a contented sigh. "The Yasha has blessed us in many ways."

He shifted into story mode. Nobody could tell a tale like Abba. He always included just the right mix of detail, suspense, and humor, and he was in perfect form tonight. While he talked, Emma brought tea for everyone then sat in a nearby chair and listened.

He paused to refill his cup, and she took over the narrative. "When the medipeller arrived in the courtyard outside the clinic, I watched as the people stumbled out, so covered with dust I couldn't tell one from another. But Abba didn't come out. He was asleep in the 'peller. So while Adam and Dr. Jane dealt with the injured, I went in to find him.

Emma smiled. "I had a hard time waking him. And once I did, he was so stiff and sore, he could hardly move. It seemed to take half the morning to get him up and out of the medipeller. Once he was moving, he smelled so bad, getting him cleaned up was my first priority."

Abba shifted his position. "You'll never guess what your em did next."

"Tell us," Hushai and Ittai answered together, and Tamah asked, "What did she do, Abba?"

"She led me to the fountain. I was so groggy I hardly knew where we were going until we reached the edge of it. Then, to my surprise, she stepped in."

Hushai directed wide eyes to Emma. "You waded in the fountain?"

From her expression as well as the feeling emanating from her meah, it was plain she was embarrassed as she nodded. "And I invited your ab to join me."

Abba chuckled. "It woke me up rather abruptly. We stayed there, splashing each other and standing under the flow, until the water had rinsed away most of the grime."

THE LAST TOQEPH

Ittai sat up and gasped. "You played in the fountain? You said me and Hushai are too old for that, but you're lots older than us."

"I did say that." Emma turned her green gaze to Abba and smiled. "But I was in error."

Adam laid his six-fingered hand on Elise's bulging abdomen, reveling in the vigorous movement beneath the surface. "What's my boy doing in there?"

She giggled. "We'll have to ask him when we see him."

"I'm anxious for that." Adam kissed her belly then lay back down beside her.

She shifted her position, groaning. "Me too. It'll be a relief to be able to put him in his cradle." She ran her hand along Adam's cheek and down his beard. "You were right, you know. It's best if children don't come into their parents' beds."

"Of course I'm right."

"It happens. More than I like to admit." She kissed him. "I can't believe that about Lileela. Are her legs really healed?"

"Not healed. Healing. What I can't figure is how, as badly as they were injured, the bones are perfectly aligned. It's as if someone had already done an expert job of reducing the fractures before she ever got to me."

"You mean the Yasha?"

"I have no other explanation." Adam shook his head. "Lileela was in no shape to question about it. I asked Kughurrrro what happened, but he didn't know what I was talking about. When I reached out to Lileela's meah, I felt something about her body being jostled around in an aftershock. Like she was in one position when her legs were broken, then the tremors moved her around and left her legs in the proper alignment. I don't know what to think except that it was a miracle."

Elise yawned. "Seems like if the Yasha was going to heal her miraculously, He'd have healed her completely. I mean, didn't you say you had to do skin grafts or something?"

"I started them, yes. Most of the rest of the work, she'll accomplish with no help from me. All bodies have an amazing ability to heal themselves, but her Gannahan genes will accelerate the process. Her own skin tissue should grow over the temporary webbing in short order."

THE LAST TOQEPH

Elise yawned again. And that's the last thing Adam remembered before his bedside timedial rolled into the last hour of Gray Dawn and woke him with its music.

He reached over and shut off the sound, orienting himself.

It took all of a second for him to remember. This was the day he must bring Natsach Daviyd to the toqeph.

Daviyd stared upward through the night gloom. Across the hut, Emma's breathing rasped in deep slumber.

In three or four hours, the aphaph birds would sing to the Gray Dawn and a new day would begin.

A new day indeed.

Daviyd thought of the Voice that had spoken to Abba, and again to his em. Whose voice was it?

A great weariness came over him. He knew so little. He lived like an animal. His people's far-reaching knowledge had been swept away in a flood and lost forever.

The weight of his helplessness pressed down on him. One harsh winter — one severe drought or crop failure — it would take but one calamity, and his people would be no more. There was nothing he could do to prevent it.

Or was there?

If the pale giant asked him to go with him, he would go. The Voice and his em had commanded it, and he would obey.

THE LAST TOQEPH

20

Half an hour into his flight, Adam tried to find a more comfortable position in the cramped cockpit. No luck. The best he could do was sit at an angle and extend his legs to the side.

Though uncomfortable for a man his size, the strange little plane flew swift and smooth, operating as easily as Emma had said. He ran his hand along the sleek instrument panel encased in gleaming blue *tekeleth* wood, appreciating the delicate inlay of leafy vines twining along the edges of each gauge.

When the Yasha told Hatita, the craftsman of old who'd built it, to deliver this plane to the airport at Yabbasha at the height of the Plague, had the dying man longed to know the purpose for the command? Adam certainly wished to know why he was flying it to Yereq and what that day would bring. Had Hatita, like Adam, asked the Yasha for explanation but heard only silence in reply?

Daviyd heard it before he emerged from the scrubby trees. A monstrous hum, as from a gigantic insect. Distant, but tainting the air with its alien vibration.

No ayal grazed by the river this gloomy morning as Daviyd waded through tall grass wet from recent rain. He lifted his eyes to the heavy clouds. The sound grew louder but still took no form.

His gaze shifted to the Tebah shrouded in mist beneath the falls. No sun crept out to splatter the spray with color. The rainbow always infused him with hope. Its absence now filled him with dread.

Searching the sky once again, he shivered. This was a dark day indeed.

THE LAST TOQEPH

Adam located the river and followed it to where, according to his instruments, it dropped off the cliff to the meadow below.

Since he was to meet Daviyd on the west side of the river, he banked that direction and reduced altitude. When he emerged from the cloud cover, the spray of the falls rose from the left, and the green meadow, bisected by the river, spread out before him. He spotted the rock on the other side of the water and calculated his approach. If Daviyd was there, Adam couldn't see him.

But he was there, Adam was certain. A Gannahan always kept his word. And no one could argue Daviyd's Gannahan-ness.

Standing beside the rock, Daviyd searched the roaring sky with a mixture of fascination and dread.

Then, like a bird diving toward its prey, a machine parted the gray vapor and came into view, louder and larger by the minute.

The sound and size and power of it overwhelmed him. He wanted to throw himself flat and cover his head.

He resisted the urge. Planted his feet and watched the creature's approach. The sound reverberated in his chest and the wind made him narrow his eyes, but he didn't take even one step back.

The monstrous conveyance bounced along the uneven ground for a short distance on round, rolling feet. The huge circular blurs on the front of its wings slowed and revealed themselves to be fantastic blades that spun at a great rate. Behind the clear glass of the thing's huge face, the pale stranger sat, his expression as blank as a bird's, doing whatever was required to control the machine.

Even after it came to a stop, Daviyd remained motionless. He waited for the man to look up. When their eyes met, Daviyd nodded as they exchanged cordial greetings in their meahs. A few moments later, a piece of the giant bird's skin opened, and the long-legged man climbed out, hanging onto the door as he slowly straightened and flexed his limbs. Apparently, large as the beast was, the interior was too cramped for its operator's comfort.

Ah. So the machine was not made by the murderous Karkar, but by native Gannahans. How that made a difference, Daviyd wasn't sure, but he found the thought somewhat comforting.

THE LAST TOQEPH

When the outlandish man walked toward him, Daviyd went to meet him, and his fate, head-on.

Adam strode toward Natsach, the wet grass soaking his pant legs and making them cold against his skin. The savage little Gannahan closed the gap between them, his expression fiercer than ever. Shoulders hunched and head forward, he reminded Adam of a growling *keleb* with glowing violet eyes.

They met at an invisible midway point. Holding Adam's gaze required the shorter man to straighten and tip his head back, but the action did not soften his scowl.

They each bowed but came up eyeing one another with distrust.

Adam swallowed. "I have returned as promised."

Natsach stood like a pillar of stone. "I have met thee as agreed."

Now what? "The toqeph doth send thee greeting."

The black eyebrows rose. "The toqeph who is thine em?"

At the mention of the toqeph, Natsach should have bowed again, not looked askance. Adam kept his expression blank, but his ears jerked with annoyance at the rudeness. "The daughter of Atarah Degel Jachin. Heir to the throne since her father's death in the Plague." He wet his lips. Might as well be blunt. "She believed she was the only survivor of that dread scourge. How hast thou…" His knowledge of the ancient language seemed insufficient to express his thoughts. "She sought others who lived, but found none. How have thy people remained unknown to us?"

"If my fathers had wanted to be found, they would have been."

His mother's shock at learning of Natsach's existence still haunted him. She'd never explained her reaction. Just ordered him to bring the wild man to her. Until now, seeing Natsach's belligerence, it hadn't occurred to Adam to wonder if the man might be unwilling to come.

But the toqeph commanded it. Could Adam persuade him? Or would he have to take him by force? Though a student of the arts of combat, Adam had no practical experience. He wasn't ready to tangle with a wild Gannahan who meant business.

It might be preferable to gain his trust. If that were possible. He sought the Yasha's guidance, and a trickle of confidence seeped into his mind. *He will go with you, but he needs reassurance.*

So Natsach's bravado stemmed from fear, then?

THE LAST TOQEPH

"Why would thy people not want to be found? Were they criminals?" Adam tightened his jaw in frustration at his stupidity. He'd make no friends with questions like that.

Natsach's face darkened, and the anger in his meah flared hotter. "We? Nay. We are the True Ones. It was the toqephs who stole what was ours."

The toqephs stole from the Natsachs? Though Adam didn't know the history behind the words, they rang true in his meah. Would Emma know what Natsach was talking about?

Since his brain refused to form a conscious thought, he responded by instinct with a deep bow. "My apologies." Feeling as if he watched himself from a distance, he sank into the rain-soaked grass and sat crosslegged. "We have somewhat to discuss."

Taken aback, Daviyd sat too and studied the pale giant's placid features, probing deeper into the Toqephite's meah. He found confusion, but a quick human intelligence and complete lack of animal guile.

Daviyd offered the prescribed reply, though the words nearly choked him. "Yea, brother. Speak thy piece."

The man hesitated a moment then spoke the right words. "I would hear thee first, brother, for I know not where I stand."

His voice grated, like the sound one makes whistling on a blade of grass. Nevertheless, he used the correct words. Daviyd stiffened and his eyes narrowed. "Thou art not Dathan."

The man's meah flowed with confusion. "Dathan?"

"Yea. The True Ones who embrace not the perversions of the Toqephites. The descendants, at heart if not in blood, of our father Natsach, the true heir of Atarah."

For such a huge thing, the man's mouth was small in proportion as it gaped in speechless amazement. Then the jaw snapped shut and opened again to speak, though the rest of his face remained placid. "I know nothing of Dathan, nor have I heard the name before this moment. Thy words are as strange to my mind and heart as thy image is to my eyes."

Daviyd struggled with the impossibility of sitting at parlay with a man who had never heard of the people whose tradition he followed. "I might say the same of thee."

They stared at one another a long moment. Then the stranger spoke. "I am as I have told thee, a man of mixed race but born on Gannah. My father

THE LAST TOQEPH

is half Karkar, half Earthish." He gestured toward the sky, as if that explained everything. "My mother was near death of the Plague when she was rescued by a man from the League of Planets and taken to Earth to recover from her illness. She and the man, my father, later married and returned with some thousand Earthers to establish a settlement on Gannah. Many of us have since been born here."

Daviyd pursed his lips. "Have not ye newcomers been instructed in the history of your world?"

The Toqephite hesitated, as if sorting his memories. "Yea, we value education. But I have read nothing about a people called Dathan."

"Thou hast read?" Daviyd sat up straighter. "Ye have books? They were not all swept away in the wave?"

"The flood six years past?"

Daviyd nodded.

"The storms ravaged much, all across Gannah. But by the Yasha's grace, our settlement was spared."

The Yasha? Daviyd couldn't connect with the meah-meaning.

The man continued without explanation. "We lost no lives, and our homes and farms remained whole." He paused. "I regret your people fared not as well."

"Nay. We have not fared well." Daviyd scowled.

"Tell me of the Dathan. I would learn from thee."

Daviyd couldn't shake his suspicions. "Thy education is the domain of thine em. If thou wouldst learn, ask her."

The way those dull amber eyes examined Daviyd's face made him burn as if touched by the slime of a fire-frog. But when the man spoke, his words were not what Daviyd expected.

"Thou dost advise well. I shall ask her to instruct me. But why thinkest thou that I must already know this?"

How could such a dense one bring the promised deliverance? "If thou art ignorant of Dathan ways, how didst thou know how to call for a parlay?"

The man's blank face looked even blanker.

"A parlay." Was he really that stupid? "A meeting to settle disputes."

When the stranger merely blinked, Daviyd's voice rose with frustration. "When thy suggestion that my people are criminals offended me, thou didst call for a parlay to settle the matter with civility." Daviyd

THE LAST TOQEPH

gestured with broad sweeps of his arms. "Thy actions then were proper and wise. Why dost thou now play the fool?"

Comprehension filtered across the man's meah. "When I sat in the grass and asked to discuss the matter? I knew not what I did. I merely obeyed the Yasha's instruction."

"And where is this so-called redeemer? I see no one, nor did I hear—" Daviyd's heart nearly stopped. "The Voice? Thou hast heard it?"

The stranger hesitated. "The Yasha speaketh to all who know Him. But I know not for certain what thou meanest."

They fell silent for a moment, staring at one another and communing on a level that transcended speech.

His truth shall lead to your redemption. That was the promise. Daviyd clung to it with the ferocity of a mad keleb. Heart pounding with an intensity he didn't understand, he broke the silence. "Tell me of this Yasha."

21

When Lileela heard her name, she opened her eyes. Once she could focus, she saw her friend Lynne Lucas standing by the bed. Then her gaze moved to the empty chair beside Lynne. Where was Faris?

"Your handsome hubby asked me to come sit with you." Lynne read her reaction correctly. "He had to go home to get some things done and didn't want you to be alone. Ra'anan will be here in a little bit, but in the meantime, you're stuck with me." She tried, with little success, to smooth Lileela's corkscrew hair away from her face. "But he neglected to warn me you look like a pile of old dung."

Lileela almost smiled. "That's better than fresh dung, I suppose." Her lip cracked as she spoke, and she licked it. "Could you hand me my water?"

Lynne glanced around then reached toward the bedside table. "Here you go. It's pretty warm, though. Would you like me to get some fresh?"

Lileela shook her head. "Don't need it cold. Just wet."

She took the bottle and drank as deeply as she could through the straw. Though they'd been hydrating her intravenously for hours, her mouth was still parched. The room-temperature water felt like sheer luxury.

Lynn helped herself to the bedside chair. "Seriously, I'm glad you're back."

"So am I. I thought sure I'd die down there with—" She lifted her head from the pillow. "I don't hear Kughie. Is he okay?"

Lynne chuckled. "He's fine. You must have almost gone deaf, spending all that time underground with His Noisiness."

"We were separated by a wall." Lileela's stomach felt queasy, and she burped. Apparently there was a reason Faris had been making her take it easy on the water. "Otherwise I might have. But where is he now? Last I knew, he was yelling from the next room. Then I fell asleep."

"They're moving him to the clinic at Gullach so he'll be closer to his family. Just for a day or two, and then he can go home. In the meantime, he

THE LAST TOQEPH

has to keep moving his knee so it doesn't seize up. They've got it in some sort of a contraption that flexes it every few minutes, and he lets out a shriek every time it moves." Lynne gestured toward the equipment hovering above Lileela's lower legs. "What's all this for?"

"They explained, but I only half-heard what they said." She burped again, and the water came up into her throat. She swallowed. "It's supposed to make the skin grow back faster or something, like grow lights. If I were a real Gannahan, I'd just go to sleep and my body would heal itself. When I was stuck in the mine, I was afraid to sleep deeply for fear I'd never wake up. Now I'd like to, but I can't figure out how."

Lynne stood to examine the glowing equipment and peer beneath it at Lileela's legs. "Yuck!" She shuddered and hurried back to her chair. "Makes me want to barf. That's gotta hurt like—I don't know what."

"It does. But not as much as it used—" Lileela stretched her arm toward a basin on the bedside table but couldn't quite reach it. "I feel sick."

Lynne grabbed the bowl and thrust it into her hands. "Great grunting grompkins, girl! You look green."

"Sorry." Suddenly hot all over, Lileela put her face over the bowl and breathed slowly, trying to calm her seizing stomach. "I think I drank that water too fast."

Lynne turned away. "Don't you dare puke, or I probably will too. I can't look."

The distress passed after a few moments, and Lileela laid the bowl back on the tray. "Never mind, I think I'm okay."

Lynne turned and faced her again. "You sure? No surprises?"

"I'm sure. You can sit down." This convalescence business was a pain. How did the Old Gannahans do that coma thing? She imagined going to sleep and waking up almost good as new. How nice that would be. She let out a sigh and relaxed into the mattress.

Lynne sat in the chair beside the bed, eyeing the apparatus over Lileela's legs. "This room gives me the creeps. But, hey." She pulled a small herb jar from a tunic pocket. "I have a gift for you." She opened the lid and waved the bottle under Lileela's nose. "Take a whiff."

Lileela sniffed. "Smells nice. What is it?" She took the jar.

"Audrey made it. You know how she's so interested in chemistry and things. She's working on a line of scented lotions and skin creams so we can

THE LAST TOQEPH

have moisturizers that smell better than those plain old vegetable oils we've been using." Lynne wrinkled her nose.

Lileela dipped her finger into the cream and rubbed a little onto her hand.

Lynn watched her. "So what do you think?"

Lileela's dry skin drank it up and begged for more while a fresh fragrance, grassy-green and faintly floral, filled the air. "I love it." She took another dollop and rubbed it into her hands, wrists, and lower arms. "Your little sister made this? How did she do it?"

Lynne shrugged. "I have no idea. Pendo Sayami taught her some of the basics a few years ago and helped her set up a lab to play in. She's been experimenting ever since, and this is her latest result. Pretty nice, isn't it?"

"Your sister's a genius. Will this stuff be available at your parents' store?"

"As soon as she gets enough made to supply the demand we expect." Lynne helped herself to a dab of the cream. "This is just a sample." She rubbed it into her hands, her expression dreamy. "I swear, it makes you feel good body and soul." She glanced at Lileela's face. "Tummy okay now?"

Lileela nodded. "I just drank too much too fast. You should have stopped me."

"Do I look like Faris? He's the only one you've ever listened to." Lynne leaned back in the chair. "Before your sister gets here, tell me about being stuck in Orville's mine. I want to hear everything." She paused. "Except the disgusting parts."

Lileela licked her split lip. "Not much to tell, other than what you don't want to hear."

Once she got started, though, she had no trouble finding the words to relate the high points of the story.

She found it gratifying that Lynne made exclamations in all the right places, but she noticed her friend's comments and questions focused on the romantic aspect.

When she got to the place where she was finally rescued, Lynne sighed. "Faris would move heaven and Gannah for you, you know."

"I know. He and the others moved too much of Gannah for me as it was. For me and Kughurrrro, that is."

"Kughurrrro? Humph." Lynne scowled. "Why would Faris care about him? It's you he just about killed himself for, not that big jerk."

THE LAST TOQEPH

Lileela frowned. "He's really not such a bad guy, you know. Just a little loud."

"Have you forgotten what he did six years ago? Bringing a warship here to blow up the whole settlement? He planned to wipe out everyone on Gannah so Karkar could take our planet."

"It wasn't a warship, it was—"

Lynne cut off the words with a wave of her hand. "You know I'm right. He wanted to kill us all. I don't want to hear about how—" She wrinkled her nose and repeated Lileela's words in a sneering voice— "*He's not such a bad guy, you know.*"

Lileela's eyes filled. "He's loud and obnoxious, but he has a good heart. You ever wonder why he stayed here instead of going back to Karkar with the rest of them?" All this conversation wearied her. But she felt she had to defend her uncle.

"Yeah, I've wondered plenty." Lynne's eyes narrowed. "And whatever he told you, it's got to be a lie. I don't trust him as far as I can hear him." She leaned forward. "But I don't want to talk about Kughie. Have you heard what your brother was working on before he left on his quest?"

Brother? Quest? That's right, Adam had been on his Second Quest when she left for Orville's camp. Had he returned safely? Yes, of course. He was treating her injuries. "No. I have no idea."

"I don't know for sure, either, but—" Lynne leaned closer and lowered her voice. "It's got something to do with, um, fertility issues. Adam's been experimenting on Esam. Sammi's got his eye on Zuri Amo, you know, and he'd like to be able to give her children."

A wave of weariness flowed through Lileela's mind and came out her mouth in a yawn. "He can't. He's like Faris and the other Special Starforces guys."

"I know." Lynne put her face near Lileela's ear and whispered. "That's why he's working on him. But he's being real quiet about it so you don't get your hopes up."

Lileela turned her head to stare. Lynne's eyes were wide and her expression eager. What on Gannah was she talking about?

Whatever it was, Lynne seemed to think Lileela understood, because she leaned back with a satisfied expression. "Remember when we went camping that time a little while after you got back from Karkar? I'd just turned sixteen."

154

THE LAST TOQEPH

Still trying to follow her friend's thread of thought, Lileela gave a slow nod. "Yeah. The big storms were over, but it started raining again."

"That's right. And while we waited in the tent for it to quit, you asked what it was like now that I was an adult, when I was going to marry Dale, and all that."

Lileela bit her split lip, surprised Lynne would bring up that subject. Ever since they were kids, Lynne and Dale assumed they'd marry when they were of age. But a couple years ago, when his mother finally gave permission, he changed his mind. Lynne had never gotten over the hurt. Lileela yawned. "Sure. What about it?"

"Remember what you said then? That you couldn't see yourself ever marrying?"

Lileela felt herself drifting off, but she remembered the conversation word for word. "Sure. I said if I ever married, it would have to be to a man who didn't have a mother. I didn't like the thought of a mother-in-law dictating everything that went on in my marriage."

"Exactly! And then Faris and his men came along—and you married a guy with no mother."

Lileela yawned so wide she almost split her face. "Maybe I can do that Gannahan healing sleep thing after all."

"It would probably be good for you." Lynne took her hand and squeezed it. "I hope you can. And I hope your brother figures out how to help Sammi, so then he and Zuri will get married, maybe. And if that works, Safiy says he's going to let Adam do the same to him, so— Lileela?"

Lileela opened her eyes. "Yeah?"

"That was a good idea you had, about marrying a man who doesn't have a mother." Lynne bent close again. "Safiy doesn't have a mother either. And he's as good-looking as Faris."

Lileela was barely conscious, but that prompted a snort. "His nose is too big."

"I could live with it. Especially if Adam can fix things so we could have children. Wouldn't it be great if—"

If Lynne ever finished the sentence, Lileela didn't hear it.

Adam studied Natsach's earnest face. Tell him about the Yasha? How could he explain? It was like telling someone about breathing.

THE LAST TOQEPH

A light drizzle began as if urging Adam to rouse himself and answer. He cleared his throat. "We sometimes call Him the Bara."

"The creator?" Natsach made a puzzled frown. "Creator of what?"

"Of everything. The heavens above and the ground beneath. The seas and the sky and everything in them. Everything that is created."

The little man snorted. "Everything? Hath the one who created the stars also made thy flying machine? And my skirt? The water that doth flow over the cliff? The rain that now falleth, and that bee on the flower?" He gestured at each as he spoke. "A busy person, thy Bara must be."

Adam's ears tilted back with irritation. "The things man hath made—" he fingered his tunic— "the Bara hath not. But when we make things, it is with the minds and hands and resources the Bara hath given us. All that we have is a gift from Him."

Natsach's meah probed. Adam tried to make him understand his meaning, but it seemed he looked past it, unseeing.

Then the connection closed with an almost palpable snap, and the little man leapt to his feet with catlike agility. "Come."

Adam rose as Natsach continued. "I shall show thee what thy great gift-giver hath bequeathed to my people." He waved toward the waterfall. "Seest thou the Tebah?"

Adam sheltered his eyes from the rain with his hand, wishing he'd worn a hat. "Tebah?"

"That which riseth from the river beneath the falls. 'Twas built by the Toqephites many years past, at Arawts atop the cliffs. People came to see this thing for amusement and education. It was said to be made like a famous one in the book from Earth that the Toqephites so revered."

Adam stared back and forth between Daviyd's angry gesticulations and the strange object under the falls. The book from Earth?

"In the story, Earthers found deliverance from a flood on a boat filled with animals."

Of course. Adam was more familiar with the word in the Standard tongue. "The tebah of Noah?" When Emma was young, she'd visited a life-sized replica of Noah's Ark that had been built based on its description in the Bible. Inside the structure was a theater where people could see, on a screen surrounding the audience, a film depicting the story of the Flood. She said it had frightened her as a child, and she had never liked the story of Noah's Ark since.

THE LAST TOQEPH

Natsach studied Adam's face. "Thou knowest the legend, then?"

Adam nodded. "Yea. But what hath it to do with this?" He gestured toward the waterfall.

A cloud of sorrow floated across Natsach's face. "The Voice told mine ab to take the people and go to the Tebah at Arawts, where they would be safe. But he knew not what endangered us."

Perhaps the rain was hampering his hearing, for Adam wasn't sure he understood correctly. "What sayest thee?"

Natsach continued as if Adam hadn't spoken. "Mine ab told the rest of the elders. They decreed that anyone who wished might go with him, but commanded none to go if it went against their better judgment. Mine em disagreed, but she obeyed her husband. Most of the other families went as well. Only a few thought him mad and remained behind."

While Natsach spoke, Adam studied the thing standing up from the water. Could that have been a boat at one time?

"We traveled to Arawts and found the Tebah. As we stood in the rain gazing upon it, a roaring sound was heard. 'Get ye in, get in, and quickly!' mine ab did cry, and all did, though none knew what danger they fled. Then one of the other men shouted, 'A great wave cometh! It rolleth like a wall of water, higher than the cliffs!' The people hastened their steps, and the roaring grew ever louder. The very ground thundered.

"No sooner had the last man entered than the door slid down with a boom that made our ears ring. Some tried to open it, but their pounding was to no avail. As they labored, the Tebah rocked and nearly tipped over, throwing us about inside. Then it seemed to lift up off the ground and righted itself.

"One window there was, on an upper level, and mine ab and two of the elders climbed the ladder to look. They told us we were afloat in a sea of foaming water and debris."

Natsach turned and looked up at Adam, violet eyes flashing as if in accusation. "We had naught but what we'd had with us when we entered. The wave carried us swiftly. We tossed and spun. We heard things strike the hull with great force, as if to break through and sink us. We rode it for days, though I know not how many. Those who had food and water shared it, but it was little enough at first, and all was consumed before our journey ceased.

THE LAST TOQEPH

"At last the Tebah came to a sudden stop with a grinding sound, listing to the side and throwing us about. The hull was damaged, and water poured in. Our journey ended there." Natsach gestured toward the top of the cliff. "Water filled the lower levels, and we climbed the ladders to escape it. The men looked out the window but saw nothing but sea.

"As the water entered, the Tebah sat lower until even on the top level our feet were wet, and outside, the water almost reached the window. We tore wood from the ship for rafts, and Ab sent everyone out the window before the Tebah went under."

The rain fell in earnest now, as if to illustrate the story. Natsach closed his eyes, and his shoulders slumped. "We were all out but Abba, floating on boards or hanging onto whatever we could get our hands on. He was within, trying to loosen a wide board for his own use. Then we heard a sound like that of rushing water. A sudden current grabbed hold of us and sucked us downward. Always down, ever roaring. Some were flung against boulders, others were impaled on broken trees."

Natsach opened his eyes and shook his wet hair away from his face. "Those of us who survived were swept a distance until the waters threw us against a mound of debris. We climbed up to escape the flood, which still raged around us." He gestured toward the southwest, where a bluff loomed gray in the distance through the sheeting rain.

"The whole ridge here—" Natsach turned and indicated the near cliff— "had broken away and carried us down with it. The Tebah remained at the top. We could see it afar off. But we saw not mine ab.

"We knew in our meahs that he was still within the vessel. He'd fallen into the bottom of the boat and swum to regain the upper level. As mine Em and I communed with him, the Tebah became dislodged from the rocks where it had been wedged. The Tebah went over the cliff. Abba died in the fall.

"We watched it tip and plunge. Bit by bit, the wood frame was broken by the force of the falling water, and the pieces were swept away, mine ab's body with them. What remains now is the metal core that the frame once surrounded. There were machines inside that inner body that performed some function long since forgotten."

Thanks in part to the meah connection, Adam could visualize the scene almost as if he'd been there. He felt the terror, the wrenching sorrow, the helplessness of plunging through the boulder-filled water. He and Elise had

158

THE LAST TOQEPH

experienced a drama of their own during those worldwide storms, but nothing to compare with what Natsach related.

"I am sorry." It was the only thing he could think of to say. "I cannot imagine how awful that was."

"Nay. Thou cannot." Natsach lifted his head and speared him with a furious violet glare. "That is the legacy thy Bara hath given us. Now come with me to my village. I shall further show thee how thy gracious one hath gifted us." He turned and strode off through the rain.

Adam followed, speechless.

THE LAST TOQEPH

22

Adam kept up with Natsach's vigorous pace without difficulty for nearly an hour before the village emerged from the mist before them.

It would have been a grim sight even in the sunshine.

The conical, thatch-roofed dwellings comprising the single chatsr were constructed of a collusion of mud, sticks, and scraps of whatever the builders could find. Most had one window and one door with a makeshift cover that could be rolled up and tied, or opened on a flapping leather hinge. Several had thatched canopies in front to form little porches. Cut grasses laid on the ground beneath the canopies formed a barrier against mud.

The wall that connected the buildings to enclose the circle was built of a similar hodgepodge. Too rickety to withstand even a half-hearted animal attack, it was no more than a symbol declaring the area off-limits to beasts.

As Natsach led Adam toward the open gate, a voice cried, "They come! Daviyd doth bring the tall man!" People, as if arising from the ground itself, appeared from under the canopies or out of dark doorways. Or, as Adam saw as he drew nearer, from the open pavilion in the chatsr's center. The air smelled of sewage, decaying vegetation, and Gannahan sweat.

The villagers stared in grave silence. Though a few of the men were clad in skirts like Daviyd's, most wore nothing but loincloths with lahab pockets, and the small boys wore less. Women and girls were more modestly covered with patches and triangles of assorted materials. Male and female alike, bodies were small and compact, with thick muscles rippling beneath brown skin.

Hair was secured with bone or sticks. The mud that paved the chatsr courtyard splattered feet and lower legs. Wide eyes bored into Adam like hundreds of probing violet lights. Strange meahs fingered his with an unnerving mix of revulsion and fear. He clenched his jaw against a rising terror, and every hair follicle stiffened.

THE LAST TOQEPH

These were the fabled wild Gannahans come to life. Each had a lahab and was skilled in its use. If Adam were to reach toward his pocket now, his throat would be sliced by fifty blades before his hand moved two centimeters.

Still unspeaking, Natsach led him through the courtyard to the central pavilion where a woman stood waiting, surrounded by several villagers. They all stared at Adam as if unable to loosen their gazes.

Natsach stopped before the woman and bowed. "Mine em. May I introduce to thee the stranger the Voice hath promised." He rose and turned to Adam.

Adam made a deep bow and held it for a respectful duration. Staring at his boots, it occurred to him they were the only pair in this part of the world. And they were freakishly large.

He straightened. "I am Pik Adam Atarah. It is my honor to meet thee, madam."

She lifted her head high to study his face, and a tremor ran through him.

"Natsach Naomi Aman Natsach. My son hath spoken of thee." She ran her gaze down the length of his body and back up again, exaggerating the effort. "Thou art as he hath said: tall as a tree. Doth it not make thee dizzy to hold thine head at such height?"

The villagers' stern expressions melted and several of the people chuckled. Adam flushed. But his em had raised him to be courteous.

He bowed again. "Nay, madam. On the contrary. The elevation affordeth a clear view."

His meah told him she approved of his response, as did the hint of the smile in the crinkled corners of her bright violet eyes. "And what, pray tell, dost thou see from thy lofty perspective?"

He paused in indecision until the Yasha whispered in his meah. "I see brave and faithful Gannahans who have waited long for that which is theirs."

The villagers caught their collective breath.

Plainly, that statement meant more to them than Adam comprehended. He continued without need for further prompting. "The toqeph would speak with thy son, Natsach Daviyd Natsach, and hath commanded me to deliver him into her presence. With thy permission, madam, I would obey that command."

THE LAST TOQEPH

The corners of her mouth caught the smile in her eyes. "One who claims to be heir of Atarah would meet with a Natsach? I have heard many strange things, but never such as this." She turned to Daviyd. "Wilt thou go with this man tall as a tree?"

For an instant, mixed feelings wrestled across Natsach's face, but he disciplined them quickly and bowed. "Yea, mine em. The toqeph of Gannah hath summoned me. And thou hast commanded that I obey."

The woman's smile faded as she gazed at her son, and Adam felt her concern. She had already lost so very much, and he was about to take all she had left.

"I shall do everything in my power to bring him home to thee safely, madam." As Adam bent before her, the gaze of every eye in the village riddled him with holes. The shiver that shot through him had nothing to do with his wet clothing.

He stood upright. "If I may." He turned and faced the crowd. "I would ask for men to accompany us back to the meadow. The toqeph hath sent gifts to all ye who dwell in Yereq. It will require a dozen strong backs to convey the goods to the chatsr."

After a pause during which Adam got the impression the people communed in their meahs, one of the young men spoke up. "We shall all go."

The rest of the village nodded, murmuring variations of, "Yea. Many hands turn work to play."

His em often said that. How odd to hear the familiar words coming from such an outlandish source.

No, it was he who was the Outlander. These were the true Gannahans.

His ears twitched in annoyance. How was any of this possible?

Daviyd found comfort in the presence of his people as they accompanied him to the meadow. He'd be alone with the giant throughout the flight in the plane, but for now, friends surrounded him. Among them, he knew who and what he was. Once he entered that giant metal bird, he would lose himself.

He fell toward the back of the procession. Jether walked beside him, closer than a brother. His nieces and nephews, as he called all the children of the village, dashed about, chattering with excitement until shushed by their elders.

THE LAST TOQEPH

No one spoke to the stranger who strode in their midst, neck and shoulders above the tallest, a ridiculous height for a human. But the Toqephite seemed undismayed. Was he listening and observing, learning something to use against them? No, Daviyd felt no wickedness about him. Just an awful strangeness. An assumption of superiority that extended beyond his greater size.

And a knowledge of something Daviyd craved to understand.

Jether jostled his arm. "Methinks Nechama findeth thy new friend an item of interest."

Daviyd glanced in the direction Jether indicated with a bob of his head. Nechama walked hand in hand with her little sister, Na'arah, but couldn't seem to keep her eyes off the tall stranger for long.

"Shouldst thou be jealous?" Jether chuckled.

Daviyd snorted. "She is free to pursue whomever she will. But did I not see a brand behind his left ear?"

"Yea. He is at least betrothed."

"So then. Nechama must be disappointed."

The Toqephite's meah was closed to Daviyd, so it was anyone's guess what went on in that mind.

Clouds still purpled the distant northern sky, but a few white wisps were all that remained overhead when the flow of wild Gannahans engulfing Adam reached the meadow. The Hatita glinted in the sun, representing home and safety. The sight sent relief coursing through Adam all the way to his boots.

The ragtag band of eerie impossibles seemed reluctant to draw very near the metal monster. Even a person familiar with aircraft would be amazed. This creation was no doubt the only one of its kind on any planet, giving its pilot the choice of using the retractable wings or the collapsible top propeller, depending on his needs.

As the people hung back, staring at the Hatita, Adam passed through their midst and approached the craft. Behind him, he sensed some of the others moving forward. He lifted the hatch and heard a few gasps.

He turned. Daviyd stood a meter or so back. The girl who'd been eyeing Adam with unmistakable interest since they'd left the village was among those who'd drawn nearest.

THE LAST TOQEPH

"I shall enter and move the toqeph's gifts near the opening." He directed his next words to Daviyd. "If thou and some others would lift the boxes to the ground, we can unload quickly."

Daviyd nodded, and Adam climbed into the plane, bending double in the small space. He dragged the first wooden crate to the doorway then turned back inside. When he returned to the doorway with the next crate, the first was gone.

The villagers jabbered with excitement. A tremor ran through Adam as he realized that in their eyes, the wood of the crates was a rare commodity. And there were twelve in all. Even if the boxes had been empty, they'd be a treasure.

He couldn't begin to anticipate their reaction when they saw what they held. Emma had given the Lucas family a detailed list of what she wanted to send with Adam, and they had spent hours collecting everything on the list, building the crates, packing them, and hauling them to the airport. He wished they could see the recipients' delight.

Once the last was unloaded, he picked up a crowbar, jumped from the plane, and approached the nearest container. The people who stood nearby, touching it with reverence and discussing the things they could do with it, stepped aside.

Adam pried up the lid, careful to not splinter the wood so it could be reused. He lifted the cover, leaned it against the crate, and stepped to the next box to repeat the procedure, leaving the villagers to crowd around the open crate to see what it held.

That one contained bolts of fabric. When the New Gannahans had tested the machinery on the old textile mill at Chabassa, their first experimental run had numerous imperfections. Though Emma had been reluctant to send Daviyd's people flawed goods, she was certain they needed fabric, and the settlers had no perfect cloth to give them. She needn't have worried. The gift was gratefully received.

But that wasn't all. The toqeph had included in this shipment needles, threads, scissors, and pins, as well as ribbons, laces, and various trims. Other crates contained tools like hammers and saws, brand-new nails, shovels and hoes, buckets and brushes. Another box held handy items like fire strikers and lahab sharpeners, as well a tall stack of small collapsible stoves such as campers used. One of the older women gave a cry of delight

THE LAST TOQEPH

when she saw them, then pulled one off the stack and set it up to demonstrate for the younger ones how it worked.

There were crocks of parched sheber, powlroot pasta, beet sweetener, and *kuccemeth* flour. Jars of cooking oils and tins of various teas. Glass canisters filled with fresh-baked rolls. A mammoth sack of hard candies. Two crates held New Gannah's best blend. The last box to be opened contained books.

Watching their inexpressible delight as they examined these mundane items, Adam's legs felt weak. He flushed with shame at the thought that other people in the world were in desperate need of the things he took so for granted.

The children appeared too awestruck to know how to respond. Having never seen such things before, they'd probably been unaware that they lacked them. The women showed joy through the brightening of their somber expressions, the animation of their movements, and their squeals. But it was the men who broke down in tears as they handled the tools, showed their children a picture book, or savored a piece of candy.

Their emotional response surprised him, though it shouldn't have. Hadn't Emma told him about the Old Gannahan ways?

After Abba had found her alone on the other side of the planet and brought her home, she'd cried for days. And she confessed to the eleven-year-old Adam that she was ashamed of her tears. Among her people, she said, only men showed such weakness; no decent woman would be so frivolous.

Adam had wondered about that ever since. Her people? Hadn't Abba brought her back to her people? And what was so frivolous about crying?

The scene before him answered the first of those questions. A short distance away, a scarred, near-naked man draped cloth around a wide-eyed girl who looked about twelve. "This shall make thee a beautiful tunic, my daughter. Thine em would have rejoiced to see this day."

These were what Emma had meant by "my people." These, and not the Earth-born settlers. Not the mixed-breed Adam.

That question was answered definitively. But not the other. For when the man drew his daughter into his arms, the tears that coursed down his worn, brown cheeks into his beard did not seem the least bit frivolous.

23

Daviyd's seat in the flying machine was the most comfortable thing he'd ever sat in. The massive Toqephite, on the other hand, barely fit in his.

In his cramped position, the grim giant went through some preliminary checks and manipulations before the vehicle coughed and then settled into a deep rumbling. The villagers standing nearby jumped at its first sounds. Daviyd's stomach did flips.

The Toqephite spoke in a language Daviyd didn't recognize, but he understood the meaning through his meah: it was a prayer to that Yasha of his for safe travels. The man did something with the devices in front of him, and the bird lurched into motion.

Pulse racing, Daviyd leaned toward the window and waved at his people's awed, upturned faces as they ran along beside the plane until they couldn't keep up. The ground raced past with jaw-rattling thumps at a terrifying speed. Then the vehicle lifted, and the bouncing gave way to smooth flight.

Daviyd leaned back and tried to calm the pounding of his heart. The Tebah and the river grew small beneath him, and then the view was obscured by clouds. How amazing they were from up here! It looked like you could step out and walk on them.

The big man shifted in his seat, trying to reposition himself in the small space. Daviyd thought he looked ridiculous. "Thou doest not appear to be comfortable. Will the journey be long?"

His companion nodded. "Yea. Very long. Might I extend my legs thy way? Would that inconvenience thee?"

THE LAST TOQEPH

"Please do." He made as much room as he could for the other man's ungainly limbs.

"Thou mayest unfasten the restraints." The man unbuckled his own as he spoke. "They are only needful when the going is rough, as upon take-off and landing."

Daviyd was happy to comply. Then he pulled his feet up and sat cross-legged, leaving more room for the other man. "I have heard of flying vehicles, though ne'er did I expect to travel in one."

"This is a fine machine. It was built before the Plague by a man named Hatita. He was told the toqeph would have need of it, and so he flew it to Yabbasha and there died."

"Who told him the toqeph would have need of it?"

The man rubbed the back of his neck with a grotesque, six-fingered hand. "The Yasha."

Something within Daviyd tightened. "We True Ones have no use for the Outsiders' Yasha, nor He for us."

The big man spoke slowly in that strange, reedy voice of his. "Methinks the Yasha doth care for you very much. If not, why did He warn thine ab of the Flood? Why did He tell him of a man tall as a tree who would stand in the prism's light? And why arrange for me and thee to meet in the meadow that day?" He shook his head. "Nay, thou art mistaken. The Yasha hath done all this for good purpose."

Daviyd hated to admit it, but there was some sense to that. "Didst thy Yasha also instruct the Toqeph what gifts to send?"

His massive companion shifted in his seat. "I know not. But, many years past, she lived in the wilderness after becoming separated from the rest of us. She might know from experience what things thy people would have need of."

"Truly?" Daviyd remembered his father saying he'd seen a woman traveling alone. "How long since that occurred?"

The man made an adjustment on one of the instruments before him. "Sixteen, seventeen years. I was a boy." He glanced at Daviyd, meah probing for what lay behind the question. "Why?"

"I was also a boy. We lived then in Adummin. It was in the spring when mine ab came home from a hunt with a report that he had seen someone on a snowsled. The hunting party stayed out of sight and shielded their meahs as the sled passed by near enough for mine ab to see the driver.

167

THE LAST TOQEPH

He said it was a woman. She was the first person anyone had seen apart from the Dathan since the plague. Until then, we had thought none survived."

The strange man's face showed no expression, and his cold, colorless gaze set Daviyd's teeth on edge. This unnatural creature called itself a Gannahan? Pah!

Daviyd clenched his jaw against an upwelling queasiness. Until a moment ago, delight in the gifts, fascination with the marvelous machine, and the excitement of soaring through the air had made him forget his revulsion. But now it returned in a boil and churned his gut sour.

The feeling intensified when the man spoke again in that unnatural voice, too high-pitched for a man of such size. "Mine em thought the same. That none had survived, that is."

Daviyd's meah told him the giant felt the full force of his resentment. Yet there was no change in the man's expression when he spoke again. "I fail to understand why I am such an offense to thee. Thou refusest even to acknowledge my name."

Daviyd crossed his arms and stared straight ahead. Raindrops struck the window and fled in fear before the rushing wind.

The man's beady stare struck Daviyd, but unlike the rain on the glass, it clung. "I have a name. It is Adam. And I am a man even as thou."

"So thou sayeth." Other than the movement of his lips, Daviyd remained motionless.

"Had we known of you, we would have sought you sooner."

Did he really think that was the problem?

"If that not be the reason for thy anger, what is?"

His meah was sharp. His questions relentless. But his ignorance was perplexing. Daviyd uncrossed his arms and met the man's—all right, Adam's—gaze. "Why should I not abhor thee? Thou art the unnatural offspring of the toqeph. Even the word *toqeph* is an abomination. It doth represent everything we Dathan despise: from the deceit of the usurper to the contamination of the true Gannah."

He felt Adam's surprise and confusion but didn't stop to explain. He couldn't have staunched the outpouring of bitterness had he wished to. "Every true Gannahan, few though there be, doth hold you Toqephites in well-deserved contempt. Had not Degel, twisted Toqephite spawn of the bloody Hoseh, not unleashed the Great Death, the Dathan would have

THE LAST TOQEPH

retaken that which was theirs in the space of a half-century. The only good thing to come of the Plague was that the Toqeph killed all his own as well. Or so we thought, until thine em was spotted."

His spittle flew in his fury. "And now she, heir to the murderous Degel and usurper to the throne, hath somehow caused the flood in an attempt to drown us, while all ye with her did sit high and safe, with food and clothing and tools to spare. But as thou canst see, she hath not succeeded in killing us. Gannah still liveth. And so Gannah shall continue, whithersoever thou doest carry me in this Toqephite machine, for whatsoever unsavory purpose."

A slight movement distracted Daviyd's attention away from Adam's gaze. Were those ears twitching? Yes. The movements were slight, but agitated. How could they move independently from the rest of his face, which remained as blank as ever?

Ah. That was how this strange being expressed emotion—not with his face, like a real person, but through subtle ear movements. How bizarre. Based on the speed of the tiny twitchings, those emotions must be frenzied.

Daviyd opened his mouth, but Adam spoke first. "Mine em is no usurper. She is the rightful heir of Atarah. She completed her Final Quest and her father pronounced her a Nasi. He placed his ring on her finger just before breathing his last." His voice turned cold and grating. "None can invalidate her claim."

"Nay, it is void, for the title was not his to give. The throne was stolen from Natsach long before the day of Hoseh. Why think ye the filthy Fueraqi were able to invade? Gannah was weak, for our king was a pretender. If evil had not then reigned, no Others could have touched us. It was only through the wisdom of the Natsachs that the attack was finally repelled. But then, instead of rewarding us with what was rightfully ours, the bloody upstarts shamed Gannah further by spreading their wickedness across the galaxy."

Daviyd's rage made him tremble. "Thine em's people, through their murderous deceit against Natsach of old, caused all the destruction that has besieged Gannah for thousands of years. Thou thinkest I have no cause for anger?"

The only visible sign of Adam's agitation were those ears, which gave one last quiver then stiffened. "Why, then, hast thou come? Why didst thou not slit my throat at the first?"

THE LAST TOQEPH

David expelled a lungful of air along with the bulk of his fury. "At our first meeting? Because my lahab lay with the fallen ayal." His fingers itched with desire to reach for it even now. "And this day?" A rueful chuckle escaped him. "Because mine em hath commanded me."

Adam's rigid face seemed to soften. "Ach. I am here for the same reason." He studied the panel in front of him and made some adjustments of the controls as he spoke. "What of the voice thou didst speak of? Did its words not have somewhat to do with thy restraint?"

For an ignorant, the Toqephite was discerning. Daviyd shrugged. "Mayhap the Voice's words are the reason behind mine em's command."

"Fulfilled prophecy is hard to ignore."

Daviyd leaned back and watched the rain. "Yea. It cannot be ignored. But I would like to know what it means."

Adam wished he'd never met this angry little man.

Sometimes Abba called Emma *the mad Gannahan* when she was in a mood, but her temper was benign compared to this guy's.

Adam's head hurt. Not just from the way it kept bumping into things in this tiny aircraft, but also from the questions his fiery companion posed. They were too many and too deep to sort out, let alone answer. He had little choice but to leave it up to the Yasha.

And to the toqeph. She'd sent for Natsach for a reason. Presumably she knew what she was doing. In the meantime, he wished his passenger would shut up.

As the giant had said, it was a very long journey. Daviyd's bladder was full nearly to bursting long before the big bird finally swooped down in the dark and came to a painful, bouncing stop on an unnaturally flat field lit by artificial lights.

Daviyd couldn't imagine how uncomfortable Adam must be by now. After positioning his over-long limbs in various arrangements throughout the flight, he'd recently pulled his legs back to his own side of the plane. This required him to rest his arms on his upright knees in order to do whatever it was he did with the various mechanisms that brought the bird to the ground.

THE LAST TOQEPH

In the semi-dark, Daviyd pawed the wall beside him, seeking some sort of knob or lever that might open the door, until Adam said, "We are depressurizing. The hatch will open in a moment."

Depressurizing. Whatever that was, it meant having to wait even longer to escape this thing. While Daviyd waited, he peered through the glass.

The vehicle sat on a paved area. He'd forgotten there was such a thing. Electric lamps embedded in it made it glow, and a building off to the right was brightly lit. A lump formed in his throat. This wasn't a dream.

The humming and roaring within the machine changed pitch and faded away, and the glass at David's right gave a gasp and then lifted upward. Cool, damp air flowed in, smelling of hot pavement—why was that a familiar scent?—and machinery and nighttime and a heady concoction of unknown smells.

But he had no time to analyze it. He scrambled out of the vehicle, which made strange little clicks and hisses as it sat, and hurried out of range of the lights, where he relieved himself at long last.

He'd nearly finished when Adam's squawk reverberated in that alien language. Strange as the words sounded, the meaning was plain. "What are you doing?" He switched to the civilized tongue. "We have a place for that!" His bulk moved toward Daviyd.

Daviyd let his skirt drop and turned to face him. "My need was great. Is not thine?"

"Yea. But I have the decency to not defile the tarmac."

Daviyd glanced down at the puddle he'd just made. "The next rain will wash it away." And from the feel of things, the next rain was soon coming. As for defilement, the man's huge feet on Gannah were a greater, as was the foul air he expelled from his lungs.

"I shall show thee the proper place for these functions." Adam turned on his heel and headed for the building, carrying that bag of belongings he'd carried with him all day. "We do not relieve ourselves in public."

Daviyd turned in a circle to scan their surroundings. "Public? Thou and I are alone."

Adam made a choking sound, and Daviyd hurried to follow him toward the building.

A real, solid building. Lights inside shone through the broad glass front and illuminated the world in the near vicinity, drawing moths and other

THE LAST TOQEPH

insects that beat against the window. Brown-striped birds hopped about, picking up the insects that lay stunned on the ground or nabbing those that crawled on the lower part of the glass. As Adam neared the building, the birds skittered away, emitting whistles that sounded like a stick whipping the air.

The little creatures ran hunched over, eyes to the ground as if afraid to look at the approaching men. Daviyd had never seen anything like them. "What birds be these?"

"They are called *yacar*."

Daviyd understood the meaning of the name, *chastised*, even before Adam explained.

"They wear brown stripes. They hide from the daylight as if ashamed to be seen."

Daviyd nodded. "And their cry doth sound like a switch in the hand of an angry em. But without the bitter smite."

"Yea." Adam had reached the building, and the door opened for him. "And when provoked, they wail like a child."

Daviyd considered putting that to the test, but instead followed Adam through the door. "What have they done to deserve such shame?"

"It be not shame to them, but the way the Bara made them."

Daviyd would have snorted at that, but the beauty of the building they entered changed his derision to awe. The ceiling rose high in graceful arches supported by round pillars of polished stone. The smooth floors, inlaid with a mosaic design of ripe grain, gleamed with a brilliant sheen, cool and hard beneath his feet. Up and down the cavernous room, comfortable-looking furniture clustered in groupings on round carpets, with sufficient open space that a herd of ayal could have passed between the arrangements. Light glowed from numerous locations overhead and on the walls, bathing the entire place with a soft radiance.

Walking across the width of the hall, Adam's booted feet thumped out crisp echoes, reminding Daviyd of his own rustic appearance. "What is this place?"

Adam slowed his stride and turned to look down at Daviyd, his expression blank as ever. "My apologies. We are at the airport at Periy City." He pointed to an indentation on the far wall. "Our first stop is what is known as a restroom. That is the proper place for doing what you did on the pavement."

THE LAST TOQEPH

A flush heated Daviyd's face, though he wasn't sure what he should be embarrassed about. "The entire city uses one room?"

Adam's ears lifted ever so slightly. Was that a sign of amusement? "Nay. It is used by people when they are at the airport. This one for men, and that one for women." He gestured toward another alcove beside the one they made for. "Other public buildings have their own restrooms, and private homes have them as well."

As Daviyd followed Adam into the alcove and then around a sharply curving hall, he gaped. At home, one refuse hut served the needs of all the village, though there were several pits within it. Whenever it was practical, though, the people left the chatsr to do what needed to be done beyond its walls, so the pits would require less frequent emptying.

"Of course." David bit his lip. "I remember now. We had indoor plumbing at Adummin when I was a boy." How could he have forgotten?

While Adam conducted his business, Daviyd gazed about the room, which had been dark until they'd entered. Apparently some mechanism turned on the lights when they passed a certain point, though he couldn't see what had caused that to happen. He hesitated before peeking into a stall, but nothing happened when he did.

The metal fixture at the back of it had a seat, unlike the receptacle Adam stood in front of. In that bowl, a stream of clear water flowed through as Adam added his, and the fluids mingled as they disappeared down a hole at the bottom of it. Daviyd wondered if the larger, lower bowl in the stall would flow with its own water too. Too bad he had no need to try it out.

He backed out of the enclosure as Adam crossed to another wall and thrust his hands beneath a pipe that jutted out over yet another bowl. Water flowed from the pipe, and Adam washed his hands.

Daviyd sniffed. "The water here hath a different smell."

Adam seemed to consider a moment then nodded. "Yea. It is wash water. Not water to drink, but to wash with only. Before it comes out of the pipe, it flows through a steristone."

Daviyd's expression must have betrayed his confusion, because Adam explained. "A porous stone that's filled with... I know not the Gannahan word. In the Standard Language we would say *organisms*. Small creatures, too small to be seen, which eat any other *germs* they come in contact with. Germs are also organisms. They —" Adam stopped. "It is a way of cleaning

THE LAST TOQEPH

hands more efficiently than with water alone. But as thou observed, it doth have somewhat of an odor."

"The odor is pleasanter than that of our refuse hut."

Adam almost smiled. "Verily. But ye must put your waste somewhere, and it is no fault of yours that it smelleth."

Daviyd felt utterly filthy. He glanced at the line of bowls with their pipes. A smooth glass above them reflected a clear, unblemished image of the two men. "Might I wash as well?"

Adam nodded. "Thou mayest indeed." He seemed pleased at the suggestion.

Daviyd thrust his arms below the pipe Adam had used, and warm water poured out. Imitating what Adam had done, he rubbed his arms and his hands beneath the water but wondered about plunging his head under the flow as well.

"Arms and hands," said Adam, "should be sufficient. Later, thou canst shower."

Daviyd paused and studied Adam's reflection, seeking clarification.

"We have a place where thou mightest stand beneath the water and cleanse the whole body."

"Just one place? Or—" Daviyd grinned. "Or be there many such places?"

Adam nodded. "There be many." He laid his hand upon an empty shelf. "There once were towels here, but I see they are no more. It would appear thou must air-dry." He waved his grotesque hands to demonstrate.

Daviyd shook his hands, splattering droplets across the reflective glass. He sensed Adam's displeasure at that, but all the big man said was, "I shall have it cleaned. But now, I must take thee to the toqeph. She awaiteth thee at the palace."

He gestured toward the doorway, and Daviyd exited around the tight curving passageway. Back in the wide hall, he waited for Adam to take the lead.

He tried to recall the geography he'd learned as a child, before everything had changed. Adam had said this was Periy City. "The palace? Doest thou speak of Gib'ah, the toqeph's provincial palace in Periy?"

Heading across the vast room, Adam shook his head. "That was the old name. Gib'ah, the Hill. It doth look like a hill, but it hath a new name. It is now Gullach."

174

THE LAST TOQEPH

Beside him, Daviyd scowled. Gullach. The Redeemed. These people tainted everything. "Redeemed. Did ye call it that because of thy Yasha? Or because of thy ambition to restore a dead world?"

Adam's meah registered surprise. "Both. We settlers are, most of us, redeemed by the Yasha. And all of us are here to restore Gannah."

What could these polluted Outsiders know of Gannah's need for restoration? But it had been a long day, and he was too weary to sort it out. Moreover, the thought of standing before the wrongful one made his legs feel weak. "This airport, as thou didst call it, is very large, and the palace must be a very long way. Will we be there before Gray Dawn?"

"I shall deliver thee before the dial rolls into the next hour, for we shall take the tube."

Daviyd couldn't believe his ears. "Truly? The tunnels still exist?"

"Though many have collapsed or are filled with water, in this region they still function."

Daviyd shook his head. "Thou dost live in a land of wonders."

Adam seemed to ponder that statement as his booted footsteps made the walls ring. "Yea. But I have seen nothing fill the toqeph with amazement as did my telling her of thy existence. She would say thou art the greatest wonder of all."

Though Daviyd's steps didn't falter, his heart did. Did she know he was the rightful king? To what lengths would she go to maintain her throne?

THE LAST TOQEPH

24

Ra'anan flipped over her pillow in hopes the other side would be cooler.

It was, and it brought relief. But before she could slip back into sleep, her eyes flew open at the sound of her parents' bedroom door opening. A dim gleam beneath her own door told her the glowlights in the hall had been activated.

She heard nothing further, so it must be Emma. Abba was too big to move so quietly.

The indicator on the glowing timedial fell halfway across the band of Black Slumber. Ra'anan closed her eyes again and tried to relax. Whenever something important was going on, she felt the tension, and it disturbed her sleep even when she didn't know what was happening.

Like now.

Though Lileela had been rescued from the mine and was on the road to recovery, Emma had been edgy all day. Anticipating something. And despite the fact that Elise was due to have her baby any second, Adam had taken off again early in the morning, flying the Hatita.

Contrary to what Mrs. Dengel may think, there was no advantage to living in the toqeph's household. You always knew when something was happening, but you never knew what it was.

Sounds of activity in the bathroom were followed by light footfalls on the stairs.

Ra'anan sat up. She'd never sleep until she knew more.

She slipped from behind the bed curtain and grabbed her threadbare robe. Her attempts to reach Emma with her meah were fruitless, but a

THE LAST TOQEPH

verbal question might yield results. As Abba always said, you can't have what you don't reach for.

Wrapping her robe about her like a cloak of invisibility, Ra'anan stood in the doorway and peered toward the stairs. Emma was nowhere in sight.

Ra'anan stepped into the hall. Drat. The glowlights came on. She hopped back into her room. Should she risk angering Emma by following her? Yes. She had to know what was going on.

Winding up the spiral stairs without a sound, Ra'anan strained her ears. If the tower was Emma's destination, Ra'anan would hear that door open.

Which is just what she heard as she reached the main floor. She peered down the dark hall and across the sitting room. The door to the tower stairs closed with a sound of finality.

Ra'anan couldn't follow. No one climbed to the tower without an invitation.

She entered the kitchen. A cup of *deshe* tea was Emma's usual antidote for sleeplessness, so the toqeph could scarcely object to Ra'anan resorting to it.

The glowlights in this room had quit working long ago, and no one had seen the need to fix them. But Ra'anan knew where the tea things were, and her Gannahan breeding gave her good night vision, so she made the tea without turning on the overhead light. She'd sit in the dark and sip slowly. By the time the tea was gone, she should be relaxed enough to sleep.

As she sat, she listened to the subtle night sounds around her. Nothing could be heard from the tower above, but the usual creakings within the apartment played across her ears, along with the calls of night creatures outside and the whisper of a breeze fingering a vine near the window.

She started at the sound of the front door sliding open and blinked when the entry light came on.

This must be why Emma was up; she'd summoned someone to meet with her. But who? And why at this hour?

Adam spoke, answering one of those questions. "The toqeph doth live here."

Why was he speaking in Old Gannahan? And who would he be talking to? Everyone knew where the toqeph lived. Ra'anan set down her cup and rose silently.

"The throne room is in the tower."

THE LAST TOQEPH

She slipped from the kitchen and, hugging the wall, watched from the sitting room doorway. The musky odor of a body overdue for a bath wafted toward her as two men's movements stirred the air. Adam was the tall one, but the other? She'd never seen him before. The stranger's skin was as dark as a roasted shaqued nut, and he stood only as high as Adam's shoulder. His black hair was unkempt and tightly curled, and a braided beard jutted from his chin. His chest was broad, his limbs thick and powerful, and he wore nothing but a ragged leather skirt around narrow muscular hips. In the light of the entryway, his eyes gleamed a brilliant violet.

A tremor ran through Ra'anan, and she pulled back into the shadows. Who or what this man was, she couldn't fathom. But he made her hot and cold all over.

The tower door opened. Her brother's heavy footfalls covered any sound the stranger's bare feet may have made padding up the long staircase.

Once the thudding told her they were nearly to the top, she crept across the sitting room and into the entryway. Adam had left the light on. She breathed in deeply and extended her hands, searching for some lingering sense of the man's brief presence there. Nothing remained but a faint feral scent and the memory of the sight of him.

At the top of the stairs, Adam led the wild man along the curving passage to the throne room. He paused at the gleaming doors, carved with the symbol of Atarah hovering above the Tree of Life. Should he brief him on the proper protocol? No, he seemed to already understand, and it would be insulting for Adam to instruct him.

A glance at his expressive face, as well as a brush with his meah, told him Natsach was steeling himself to commit an act he dreaded. To the wild man's credit, it was plain he appreciated the gravity of receiving a summons by the ruler of all Gannah.

Adam pressed the button in the wall, announcing their presence and requesting permission to enter. A moment later, the doors slid back into their pockets. The room was well lit, not by lamps, but by the walls themselves, which glowed with a soft white glow.

If it had been daytime, the round skylight in the ceiling to the right of the doors would have cast a column of sun on the golden circle on the floor beneath. That fateful execution site, Adam expected to see. What surprised

THE LAST TOQEPH

him were the room's new additions: two comfortable chairs positioned off to the left with a small table between them. Two steaming teapots stood on the table.

Otherwise, the room was empty as usual except for the throne on a low platform opposite the door. There toqeph sat, her eyes devouring Adam's companion.

Adam approached and prostrated himself. Natsach did the same.

They both kept their foreheads to the floor until the toqeph spoke. "Pik Adam Atarah, arise."

"My toqeph." He obeyed. "I present to you Natsach Daviyd Natsach, of… the chatsr in Yereq." It occurred to Adam he didn't know the name the wild people had given their town.

Emma's attention never left the visitor. "Natsach Daviyd Natsach." Her voice sounded hoarse and pinched, her pronunciation much like that of the muddy man before her. "Arise. Welcome to Gullach."

She turned her green eyes, bright with emotion, toward Adam for the first time. "Thank you, Adam. Well done. You are dismissed."

The finality of her statement stung like a slap, but, obedient servant that he was, he bowed deeply. "Thank you, Madam Toqeph." He took three steps backwards before turning and leaving the room.

Behind him, the doors slipped shut with the sound of rejection.

25

At the woman's command, Daviyd rose and lifted his gaze.

"Natsach Daviyd Natsach." Her pronunciation was better than Adam's, and, from the tightly braided hair, embroidered tunic, and bluegray trousers to the proper high-laced shoes, she looked every whit the ruler of Gannah.

He bowed. "Madam Toqeph. I am here at thy command."

She rose. "Please sit. Have some tea." She gestured toward the small table.

"I accept with thanks." He waited for her to step down from the dais then followed her across the smooth, cool floor.

Table and chairs. Proper tea things. None of this seemed real.

She sat, and he did the same, watching for his next cue.

She lifted the lid from the teapot on the tray nearest her, fitted the strainer into the matching cup then replaced the lid. "Thou art Dathan."

Though Adam didn't seem to know what that meant, the toqeph plainly did. He nodded. "Yea, Madam."

She poured her tea. "Who is thine ab?" After removing the strainer from the cup and laying it on the tray, she dribbled in a small amount of pink honey from a jar beside the teapot.

The forgotten tea ritual brought back memories of his childhood. He was almost afraid to join her in it for fear the fragile illusion would vanish.

But when he poured the steaming tea from the pot beside him, the fragrance was real. "Mine ab is dead these six years past." That vision, he wished he could wake from.

"My condolences." Her meah was weak, but it seemed her sorrow was genuine.

THE LAST TOQEPH

"His name was Natsach Rosh Emeth, son of Natsach Etsbon Marrah."

Her green eyes widened for the briefest of moments when she glanced up. "Natsach Etsbon Marrah? Was he truly thine own ab's ab? I knew him. He was a good man."

If he'd been swallowing tea at that moment, he would have choked on it. "Madam?"

"Etsbon was the cousin of my first husband, Natsach Rosh Gershon."

Daviyd laid the strainer on his tea tray with careful deliberation, concentrating on keeping his hands from trembling. "I... I understand not, Madam."

"Thine ab, Rosh. Was he named for his father's cousin? Had thy grandfather and that cousin grown up together like brothers, along with Rosh's twin sister Ra'anan, in Nagad City north of Har?"

Daviyd stared. "Yea, Madam. To the best of my belief, that is the Rosh mine ab was named for. Mine ab used to say..." Daviyd clenched his jaw. It would be unthinkable to repeat the Dathan dogma to the very toqeph herself.

Her meah pressed against his with a gentle pressure. "I know how painful it can be to bring up memories of loved ones."

Her words sounded fair, but what was her intent? Was she trying to seduce him to let down his guard and share Dathan secrets?

"I would that we understood one another." She took a sip of her tea, holding her cup with a steady hand and his gaze with a steadier eye.

"How so, Madam?" He made no polite attempt to keep his distrust from his voice.

She nodded toward his tea tray. "It is not poisoned. Thou mayest drink without harm."

He glanced down at his untouched cup with its steam rising in beckoning waves. The thought of poisoning had never occurred to him. Such was the difference between the honest Dathan and the shifty Toqephites.

He picked up the cup and sipped. It tasted as good as it smelled. No, better.

"I know somewhat of the Dathan." She set down her tea.

When he opened his mouth to speak, she raised her hand to stop him and addressed the question he'd been about to ask. "Nay, thine ab Etsbon shared naught with me. He would not break trust with his people. Nor did

THE LAST TOQEPH

mine husband Rosh instruct me in your ways. Though he followed the Yasha while Etsbon followed the way of his fathers, he would not betray his family."

Daviyd took another sip of tea while he tried to sort it all out.

She leaned forward, hands clasped on the table. They were small and brown like Emma's, though not work-worn. The creases in the corners of her earnest eyes showed she'd seen many years and born much care.

"Hath Adam told thee I was separated from the settlement for a time?"

He nodded. "He did say something of that."

She fingered the honey bowl. "I was called off the planet for a short time to visit an orbiting starship. I did not wish to leave, but mine husband did think it was best."

Daviyd knew nothing about orbiting starships, but a woman's obedience to her husband was a familiar truth. "Then thou hadst no choice, Madam."

She freshened her tea with some from the pot. "When my errand there was done, I returned in a shuttle —" She paused, apparently seeing he didn't understand. "One of the men from the starship flew me home in a small vessel designed to go between the big starship and the ground. But an electrical problem caused him to lose control, and we crashed in Adunnim, near the rim of Ruwach Gorge. The man was killed, and I was injured."

She lifted her right arm and attempted to extend it. Daviyd saw then that the elbow was misshapen. The arm was thinner than the other, and permanently bent. "My arm was broken, and my head was injured." She touched the base of her skull. "The meah, specifically. Both are now healed, but I have not recovered full use of either."

He nodded. That explained why he found it difficult to make a connection.

"It was autumn, at the beginning of the snows."

His brows lifted. Surely she didn't expect him to believe she'd survived the harsh winter of Adunnim. "What didst thou do?"

"I took refuge in the canyon, where I wandered for some days before I stumbled upon Ga'ayown."

He froze. Ga'ayown. The most sacred site of the ancient Dathan. "How couldst thou — Didst thou —" The idea of a Toqephite setting foot in that secret place of refuge was almost enough to make him spit his tea. He started to rise.

THE LAST TOQEPH

She raised her hand. "Be seated and hear me out."

Not realizing he'd tried to stand until she stopped him, he sank into his chair, head buzzing. "Thou didst not enter Ga'ayown!"

She gave him a moment to collect himself. When she spoke again, her voice was low and gentle. "Ga'ayown gave me my life back. There, I found safety from the *zeeb* that hunted me, for I had lost my lahab and had no weapon. There I found clothing and shoes, grain to eat, and blend to drink. And thy grandfather Etsbon met me at the door."

Daviyd's jaw dropped, but before any of the questions spinning in his mind found their way out of his mouth, she continued. "He died as a warrior. On his feet, guarding the front entrance. Though he could not keep me out, I was no threat to him or his people. I identified him by his lahab, but I returned it to him. When I left, the only weapon I took with me was a knife from the kitchen."

"Didst thou see them? They were all dead?"

She nodded, her eyes dull with grief. "They all died. All Gannah died." She fixed him with a look of intense interest. "During the Plague, I searched for survivors but found none. The medical ship that rescued me searched from above and found no one living but me. How did your people not die with the others, and how did they hide from scanners?"

David swallowed. He'd always been taught that they mustn't be found. It seemed wrong to speak of this.

Yet he could not defy her, for all authority was hers until it was returned to the rightful ruler by the one who had taken it. This was the Dathan credo, instilled in him all his life.

He rose only to prostrate himself as he had at first. "Madam, I beg thy forgiveness on behalf of my people. If we have offended thee, we will accept whatever—"

"Nay!"

Her loud interruption made him cringe.

"Rise, Natsach Daviyd. Your people have not offended me."

He rose but remained standing, head bowed.

"Sit. Please."

Her voice choked, and after he sat, when he dared look her in the face, her green eyes glimmered with tears.

THE LAST TOQEPH

"Your people have not offended me." She swallowed. "Tell me, please. How is it that I never learned of you until my son came upon thee during his quest?"

"Before the Plague, my grandfather Etsbon, who was then leader of the Dathan, did learn—that the evil toq—" His heart nearly stopped along with his speech. "Forgive me, Madam."

To his surprise, her face softened in a near-smile. "Allow me to help. The Dathan learned that mine ab, the toqeph Atarah Degal Jachin, prepared to raise the ancient airships that had been buried in the seas by that spawn of beasts, Atarah Hoseh, centuries before."

Daviyd gaped. "Madam?" How could she speak about her ancestors like that? Then he flushed, embarrassed at the realization that she mocked him. But no, she didn't mock. She cleared the air. Wanted him to know she understood.

She nodded, apparently sensing that he grasped her intent. "I know how thy training has taught thee to believe, and I commend thy obedience to thy teachers. When I visited Ga'ayown, I did much reading in the training center. My heart and mind were forever changed."

"Madam?" Never in his wildest dreams had he expected his meeting with the toqeph to take this direction. "Art thou—"

She shook her head. "I am no Dathan. I do not shun Outside technologies nor the Earthish beliefs you have been taught to disdain. We shall speak of that later. Now, I would know how your small group survived the Plague."

He could hardly think of the words to explain it, so surprised was he at her understanding. "I was not yet born, but I shall tell thee what mine ab and em told me."

She nodded. "That is all I expect."

He took a sip of tea to fortify himself. "When they heard of the toqeph's plan, they knew no good would come of it. So they made preparations. All who could come were summoned to Ga'ayown. Of those, some were chosen to remain and others to hide in the oldest tunnels. These had no ventilation shafts as the newer ones did. Supplies were stored of sufficient quantity to feed the people for two years. When the people in Ga'ayown received word that the first ship was raised, those who were chosen to go into the tunnels were sent there and sealed in. They were able to communicate with those who remained in Ga'ayown, and they did so for

THE LAST TOQEPH

some days. One of the last communications stated that the air had been poisoned. There was death in the skies, in the snow that fell, in the lungs of those who were the last to seek refuge at Ga'ayown. None were turned away. But those in the tunnels were warned to remain underground and not come out until they were told it was safe."

The toqeph's face sagged with grief. "But that word never came."

"Nay. I am told that the last words they heard were, 'The death hath come. Remain where you are, so that Gannah might live.'"

The toqeph sighed. "When I searched, when I sent out calls on all the communication lines, they were not able to hear the signal. And I was not able to pick up their images so deep underground."

Daviyd shook his head. "That, I know not. Only that they believed everyone had died. They remained underground for nearly the two years. Then, five men re-entered Ga'ayown. They found the people dead, much as—" He gave the toqeph a sideways glance, hating the thought that she had been in that place. "Much as thou must have found them. They then went into the canyon, and there they stayed for a month, not willing to return to the rest of the people until they knew the death had not attached to them. When they remained well, they carried food and blend from Ga'ayown into the tunnels. The palace was never entered again, and those who were last there vowed it would remain a shrine forever to our fallen faithful, slain by the—"

The toqeph nodded, her face ashen. "Slain by the sin of my ab. He had no excuse. And I have no remedy." She paused, as if summoning the strength to continue. "They are gone. Gannah as we knew it is gone. What you see here today, this tower and this palace—" She waved her good arm to gesture at the room. "It is but a shadow of what was. We can no more revive the true Gannah than we can make the sun go backward."

It occurred to Daviyd that as much as his people had lost, she had lost more.

They sat in silence for many minutes, communing through their meahs as much as possible considering her crippled condition.

Their tea had grown cold before she spoke again. "I cannot undo what mine ab hath done. But what I can do, I shall do." She fixed her penetrating gaze upon him. "I would bring thy people here to Periy.

26

Adam clattered down the tower steps and exited the stairwell into the foyer.

"Adam?"

It was Ra'anan in her nightclothes. "What are you doing up?" His voice sounded harsh as a Karkar's.

She moved closer, her bare feet making no more noise than Natsach's. "I couldn't sleep, so I went to make some deshe tea. And then I heard you come in." She peered up at him. "What happened to your eye?"

He fingered the half-healed cut on his brow. "You should be in bed."

She took a step nearer and spoke in a near-whisper. "Who was that man with you? And why is he up there with Emma?"

A cauldren of anger bubbled up within him. He grabbed his sister by the shoulders. "Go back to bed." Ignoring her look of hurt dismay and the prick of his conscience, he spun her around and gave her a push. "Now do as you're told."

She skittered off with a stifled cry. He didn't watch to make sure she obeyed, but stormed through the foyer and out the door.

In the passage outside, he paused; he'd forgotten to turn out the light. No matter. It was nearly morning. Abba would get up and tend to it soon.

After two more steps, he turned and went back. If he left the light on, it would burn in his mind and give him no rest.

When he re-entered the suite, Ra'anan was nowhere in sight. Probably crying into her pillow by now. She deserved it; a child had no business wandering the house at night, sticking her nose where it didn't belong.

He stiffened his jaw, shut off the light, and went home.

THE LAST TOQEPH

From the fading of the starry black above the skylight in the tower room, Daviyd figured it to be about the second hour of Gray Dawn when a tinkling chime came from the vicinity of the door.

The toqeph rose. "Ah. Mr. Maddox is here." She spoke toward the doorway. "Enter."

Daviyd stood when the toqeph did and turned to see what sort of pseudo-Gannahan would come through.

At first glance, the man who stepped in and did obeisance could have passed for the real thing. But when he rose at the toqeph's command, Daviyd saw his blue eyes lacked the Gannahan glow. His build was slighter than most, and his hair and beard were brown streaked with gray, not black. Nevertheless, he had the confident bearing of a True One, and he studied Daviyd with intelligent intensity.

When the man opened his mouth to answer the toqeph's greeting, Daviyd caught his breath. His tongue was purple.

A Nasi?

Daviyd brought his thoughts back to the toqeph, who was speaking.

"Mr. Maddox, my Chief Nasi. Please meet Natsach Daviyd Natsach, newly arrived in Gullach."

Daviyd bowed deeply. "Mr. Maddox."

The man made a small bow in return, as was fitting. "Mr. Natsach. An unexpected pleasure. Very unexpected." He smiled. "And very much a pleasure. My only regret is that we have not had occasion to meet sooner." He bowed again. "The Yasha's blessings be upon thee and all thy family."

The man's speech was so thickly accented Daviyd struggled to understand. However, he'd once heard that if a Nasi bowed to you a second time, it was a sign of great respect. Though the speech was unclear, the gesture wasn't, and Daviyd was therefore obligated to return the blessing.

But he couldn't speak the name of the Yasha. Instead, he bowed all the more deeply. "I thank thee, sir. Thou art a fair speaker indeed."

The Nasi's mouth twitched with a near-smile. "Thou art generous."

The toqeph stepped away from the table. "And weary, I am sure. Mr. Maddox doth offer thee a bed, clean clothes, and food from his table. We have other things to discuss, but they can wait. Wilt thou join me for dinner this even? It is the night the children celebrate Wormfest, and we have entertainment planned."

THE LAST TOQEPH

Wormfest? That wasn't one of the four seasonal festivals Gannah traditionally celebrated, and he wasn't familiar with it. But the tone of the toqeph's invitation made it sound like a command. "Of course, Madam. I look forward to it."

His empty stomach gurgled. Her comment about Maddox sharing food from his table was heartening, though he hoped the repast wouldn't include worms.

Maddox extended a hand. "If thou art ready, let us go." He cast a glance the toqeph's direction.

She nodded. "We are finished for now. Thank you, Mr. Maddox." She turned to Daviyd. "Mr. Natsach. We shall speak again."

He bowed. "Thank you, Madam." As Adam had done earlier and Maddox did now, Daviyd stepped backward three paces before turning, then followed Maddox out the door.

The Purpletongue walked beside Daviyd toward the stairs. "I spake with all truth. It is a great pleasure to meet thee." He formed his words slowly and with evident care. "I fear my skill in speaking your language is not great. I hope we shall be able to communicate."

At the stairway, Maddox gestured for Daviyd to go first. Daviyd kept his gaze downward as he descended. "It may be difficult. My people communicate through their meahs as well as through words. But thou hast not that ability."

"Nay, I have no meah. I hope thou wilt be patient with my lack."

Daviyd nodded. "Patience is an admirable trait. I have not mastered it as yet, but I shall endeavor to practice it with thee."

He stepped aside at the bottom of the steps to make room for Maddox, who rounded the last curl of the stairway.

The Outsider paused. "Wouldst thou consider it too forward of me to call thee by thy given name?"

"If thou wisheth. I am Daviyd."

"I would be pleased if thou wouldst call me Jerry. Though I am a Nasi of Gannah, I am Earther born and find old Earthish ways still linger." He extended his hand. "In that world, when men meet or come to an agreement, one doth shake the other's hand."

Daviyd glanced at Jerry's hand then lifted his gaze to the man's pale blue eyes. "I follow no Outside customs." He raised both hands, palms facing Maddox, offering the Gannahan version of a similar gesture.

THE LAST TOQEPH

The man's brows lifted, then he bumped the heels of his hands against Daviyd's. "Well said. I like a man with solid principles."

Daviyd followed him into the richly furnished room he'd passed through earlier with Adam. It would be difficult to respect an Outsider in Gannahan clothing. Particularly one who dared to wear the purple tongue. But in the case of this man, it might be possible.

Hushai woke to the sound of Ittai snoring in the bed alcove beside him. His internal clock told him it was time to get up, and the light from the windows beyond the bed curtain confirmed it.

He flung open the curtain. "Morning, 'Tai! You gonna sleep all day?"

Ittai sniffed and rolled over. Hushai slipped from the bed, collected clothes for the day, and hurried off to the bathroom.

Drat. The door was closed. He knocked.

Ra'anan's voice sounded annoyed. "I'm in here."

"I know. When're you coming out?"

"In a minute."

Upstairs, Abba's heavy tread creaked in the kitchen. A glance into the girls' room revealed the bed curtain open and the alcove empty; everyone was up but Ittai. Tamah was probably upstairs with Abba. After a minute or two, the tower door opened and closed, and light footsteps crossed the foyer. How long had Emma been up there?

And how long would Ra'anan be in the bathroom? He raised his hand to knock again but the door opened.

Ra'anan wore her best clothes, her hair twisted in a formal style, and an uncharacteristic scowl as she glared at him. "No need to knock again. I told you I was almost done."

Something wasn't right. He narrowed his eyes. "How come you look nice? But your face doesn't?"

She blushed and her scowl deepened. "What do you mean? I just spent a long time working at it, so I'd better look nice."

"Then maybe you shouldn't work so long, 'cause it's not helping." He brushed past her into the bathroom.

She uttered a growl before stomping off.

Hushai growled back as he shut the door. It would be wonderful to be a married man. Then you could tell a woman what to do instead of obeying one all the time.

THE LAST TOQEPH

True, Adam still had to listen to Emma. But everyone had to listen to Emma. And every man had to obey his mother.

Unless you were like Faris, and had no mother. Imagine never having to obey a girl your whole life. Except for Emma, of course.

But if you didn't have a mother, and the toqeph was a man as would be the case when Adam was toqeph, that would be glorious.

The smile that started at the idea faded instantly at the thought of what would have to happen before Adam could be toqeph: Emma would have to die.

No, not die. Ordinary people died, but as long as she remained faithful to the Yasha and led the people rightly, the toqeph would go bodily into the presence of the Yasha, to sit at His table with the toqephs who had gone before.

Except for her father, the one who'd caused the Plague. His soul was redeemed, but he'd forfeited the toqeph's privilege through his disobedience.

Hushai put his head in his hands. He didn't understand what most of that meant. He just knew what he'd been told.

After dressing, he carried his nightclothes back to his room as Ittai clambered out of the bed alcove. Hushai tossed his nightclothes onto the mattress and pulled the curtain closed. "Hurry up. Everyone else is already at breakfast."

Ittai yawned. "Yeah, yeah, I'm comin'. Save me some micken."

"Not likely." Hushai left Ittai to his stretching. He needn't worry. Emma always made plenty.

Good thing, too, because he'd slept up an appetite. He scampered up the spiral stairs and into the kitchen where Abba and Tamah sat at the table, reading. Emma stood at the counter separating plump cerecfruit into sections.

She gave him a smile as she handed him the bowl. "Did you see your sister?"

He carried the fruit to the table and set it down. "Ra'anan? She was in the bathroom before I went in. I figured she'd be up here by now. Oh—" He heard her climbing the stairs. "She's coming."

A moment later she entered the kitchen, smelling like Aunt Skiskii. Hushai made a face.

THE LAST TOQEPH

Tamah waved her hand in front of her nose. "Ew. Ra'anan, what did you spill?"

Abba looked up, and Emma turned from the sink where she'd been rinsing her hands.

"Whoa," Abba said. "What's the occasion?"

Ra'anan blushed. "It's Wormfest."

Abba's only reply was an expressionless blink. Tamah made a show of coughing, and Hushai's eyes watered.

Emma dried her hands on the dishtowel. "Wormfest is this evening."

"True, but it's a special event, and —"

"And it's informal. We don't dress up for it. And we certainly don't dowse ourselves in Auntie's cologne."

Ra'anan's green eyes filled with tears. "But Emma, I —"

"Go change your clothes, sweet. And wash off that scent."

Open-mouthed, Abba, Tamah, and Hushai stared back and forth between Ra'anan and Emma. Any child foolish enough to start up with a "But Emma" was cut off with a sharp word, sent to the Grey Room, or both. For Emma to respond to backtalk with a "sweet" was unheard-of.

It wasn't until her daughter hesitated that Emma became stern. "Ra'anan."

Face flushed and eyes brimming, Ra'anan bowed deeply then fled.

Emma crossed the room and opened a window.

Abba rose. "What was that all about?"

"I thought I heard your daughter get up last night shortly before our visitor arrived." Emma poured a cup of tea.

Visitor? Hushai and Tamah, wide-eyed, searched one another's meahs. Neither had any idea what Emma was talking about.

Abba took the tea Emma handed him. "*My* daughter, you say?"

Emma's face softened. "Where affairs of the heart are concerned, my husband, she is yours to educate."

His ears twitched. "You mean she…"

"I believe so, yes."

"But she's only fourteen."

Emma gave him a pointed look. "Yes. Fourteen. That is why, my husband, I respectfully suggest that you speak with her."

Exasperated, Tamah spread her arms out on the table. "Will someone please tell me what's going *on*?"

THE LAST TOQEPH

Before anyone could answer, Ittai came in. "Phew, it smells like Auntie's here. Is she downstairs? 'Cause it stinks down there, too."

Hushai was tired of waiting for answers. "That was Ra'anan. She musta borrowed some of Auntie's smelly stuff, but Emma told her to go wash it off so we could eat. But what visitor? Is there someone else here?" He addressed his questions to Abba, who was more apt to answer them.

It was Emma who spoke. "We have a visitor in Gullach, yes. He was here with me for a short time early this morning, but for now, he's staying with the Maddoxes. I'll explain it at breakfast, and you'll all get to meet him soon." She turned to Tamah. "Put your book away, hon. Once your sister comes back, we'll sing the blessing and eat."

While they waited, Emma set out bowls and scrapers, and Abba distributed plates of wet finger cloths. By the time Emma had set the pot of micken on the table, Ra'anan returned in everyday clothes. Her expression was sober and her eyes were red-rimmed. Hushai couldn't figure out what was the matter with her, and she didn't seem inclined to communicate through her meah.

They stood behind their chairs while Abba led the morning blessing. Hushai was glad he chose the short version of the song, because he was anxious to hear about the visitor.

After taking their seats, they launched into the juicy cerecfruit while Abba scooped steaming micken into their bowls. He'd just handed the first to Tamah when Hushai sat bolt upright. So did everyone else around the table but Abba, who stared from one to another. "What?"

Beaming, Emma announced to her meah-less husband what the others had just learned from Adam. "Elise is having her baby!"

27

Much as he longed for his cozy bed alcove, Adam knew he'd never be able to sleep. And in Elise's advanced stage of pregnancy, she didn't need him tossing beside her. Better to unwind before going home.

While considering going for a run, he remembered the Hatita sitting on the tarmac. Perfect. He'd run to the airport, clean the plane, and put it away. That would help him unwind and accomplish a useful purpose beside.

After spending half the day coiled in the cockpit like a spring under tension, the eight-kilometer run was just what he needed. The night was cool and the humidity low enough that he perspired only lightly. In almost no time, the airport terminal came into view. A black lump on a black plain beneath a star-sprinkled sky, it loomed ahead like a threat on the near horizon.

Odd that he'd think of it in such terms. He searched his surroundings with all his senses for subliminal signs of danger. He saw nothing but the fields asleep in the dark. Heard only the usual night insects, the rhythmic thud of his feet on the pavement, the swish of his clothing, and his steady respirations.

But something pressed against his meah. A wrong crying to be righted, perhaps. A sin hiding from confession, or a crime on the cusp of commission. What was it, and who did it involve? He couldn't tell. But the impression spurred his pace.

An hour and a half later, Adam's tension had ebbed. He'd washed the Hatita and cleaned the interior with painstaking thoroughness. Then he started it up and taxied it to the hangar. After removing the fuel

THE LAST TOQEPH

cells and plugging them into their ports, he wrote up a report of his trip, including statistics from the onboard computers.

As groggy as he was by the time he'd finished, he knew he'd have no trouble falling asleep. He made his way into the terminal and then the rail station below ground. His eyelids were heavy as he settled into the tube and directed it to take him home.

When the pod pulled to a stop at its destination beneath the second chatsr, he woke with a start. The stirring air from the opening doors tickled his nose with his own unwashed odor.

He couldn't go home in this condition.

Adam exited the rail station on heavy legs and climbed to ground level. But instead of going to his apartment, he went to the clinic. He should check on his patient before he went to bed. But first, he showered and changed, which revived him a little.

In the rehab section, he found Lileela asleep with her husband sitting nearby, head bowed.

Faris looked up when Adam entered. "Good morning."

Adam nodded. "Morning." He scanned the data on the monitor then took a closer look. What was he seeing? He forced his mind to concentrate.

Faris chuckled. "From the way your ears are twitching, you must be surprised. I think she's in a Gannahan healing sleep."

That explained the readings. He'd heard of the phenomenon, of course, but had never seen it. Intriguing.

After manually checking her vitals, Adam moved the equipment out of the way to examine her injuries, taking care not to disturb her. But she was no more responsive to his touch than if she'd been Tamah's doll. When he brushed her with his meah, he felt a deep peace.

Faris never took his eyes off him, as if trying to read his thoughts. "If not for that monitor, I'd think she was dead."

"She nearly is. In this deep sleep process, the body focuses all its energy on healing and spares very little for staying alive. It's dangerous. Astonishing how effective it is, though. If I hadn't seen it for myself, I'd never believe the skin growth already."

Faris rose and came near to examine her legs. "I can see the change myself. It's like a miracle. Medical science couldn't do that."

THE LAST TOQEPH

"Medical science can't heal injuries anyway. The body heals itself using the resources the Creator gives it. All doctors can do is create conditions to facilitate that."

"I guess that's true."

Adam shut off the lights that had been shedding their healing glow on her legs. "Let's see how the regeneration progresses without our help." He folded up the contraption and moved it against the wall.

When he turned back to the bed, Faris held Lileela's limp hand. "So just how dangerous is this coma?"

Adam understood his fear. Shared it, in fact. "I don't know. If there are records of the percentage of people who succumbed to it, I've never seen them. Even if there were, we couldn't know how many of those would have died from their injuries regardless."

Faris nodded but kept his gaze on Lileela's face.

"My mother was in a coma for weeks while she recovered from the effects of the Plague. She says the Yasha awakened her when she'd reached the end of her strength. So I'm trusting Him to do the same with Lileela, if it comes to that."

Faris lifted his head and met Adam's gaze. "The toqeph suffered no ill effects from the experience?"

Adam bit his lip. "Nothing immediate. But it... it shortens the lifespan."

"What?" Faris's brilliant eyes flashed.

"The longer a person sleeps like this, the shorter his life will be. For Lileela, it should make little difference. She'll linger only a couple days in this state. Provided this is the only occurrence, it's not likely to take more than a year or two from her."

Faris's voice softened. "But the toqeph..."

"She has little hope of seeing her ninetieth birthday." Adam felt sick as he said the words. A native Gannahan would ordinarily expect to surpass his hundredth year by a decade or two.

"But she's already... how old?"

"If she were an Earther, her hair would be white and her back bent with age."

Faris took Lileela's hand in both of his. "I am sorry. She seems ageless."

"That she does." Adam nodded. "But she's as mortal as the rest of us."

THE LAST TOQEPH

He lifted his gaze from Lileela and gave Faris his full attention. "Once things settle down around here, I'll get back to my research. My findings have been promising. A little more testing, and we should have some definitive answers. But..."

Faris raised his hand as if to ward off the rest of the statement. "One thing at a time, brother. First, we get Lileela back on her feet."

Adam nodded. "Looks like that won't be long, the Yasha be praised." He gave the monitors another once-over. "Anything I can get you? Have you had breakfast, or..."

Faris shook his head. "Katarina will be here shortly to spell me. I'll go get washed up, something to eat." He smiled. "We're fine. It's you who looks like you need something."

Adam smiled. "Yeah. It's been a long couple of days." He gave a weary wave as he exited the room. "I'll check in on her later."

The laboratory above the clinic had a passage that connected to his apartment, so he went upstairs. As he passed through the lab, it seemed forlorn and abandoned. He sighed. Between his absence and Abba's, the work here had fallen behind schedule. But it couldn't be helped.

Almost sleepwalking, he made his way through the passage to the adjoining building and into the hall outside his door. Then he slipped off his shoes and entered.

The smell that greeted him was not breakfast. "Elise!" He hurried to the bedroom.

The bed curtain was pulled back. Wet, bloody sheets lay in a pile on the floor. Elise reclined on the bed, upper body propped up by pillows, her face strained and framed with sweat-darkened hair. "About time you... got here," she gasped. "Ice chips. I'm parched."

He ran to the kitchen and scooped up some ice. He returned to the bedroom, where he dropped to his knees beside the bed. "Elise! Wh—how long—where's Everett?"

He had to wait before she could answer. "The contractions started a little before Black Slumber. Once I knew it was the real thing, I called my mom and she came and took Everett home with her. We figured you'd be here any minute." She opened her mouth for ice, and Adam gave her a piece.

"Sorry. I wish you had a meah, or I'd have come sooner."

THE LAST TOQEPH

He watched the progress of another contraction. "You're seven centimeters. Sorry I wasn't here, but you've been getting the job done without me."

"Yeah." She panted. "Tell me about it. What were you doing, anyway? Mom said she saw you flying into the airport when she came here. That was hours ago." Another contraction took her.

"Long story. For now, this is more important." He waited for the contraction to end, wishing he could take over for her. Childbirth was so one-sided.

She relaxed into her pillows, breathing hard.

He gave her more ice. "Are you okay here? Would you like to move somewhere else? How can I make you more comfortable?"

"Ha!" She closed her eyes. "Comfortable." From her breathing, he thought she was ready to go into another contraction, but then she spoke again. "I'm fine, really." Then she gasped at a new onslaught.

He gathered up the soiled sheets to put them in the laundry pile. Not much else he could do at this point.

As soon as he left the room, she let out a prolonged, "Aghhhhhhhh."

He wanted to cry.

As a boy in Adunnim before the Flood, Daviyd never gave thought to material things. No one went hungry or was in any great need, and from his point of view, life was good.

But if his people had been well off in those days, these at Gullach were fabulously wealthy.

He walked with Jerry along the broad, curving balcony that overlooked the magnificent room below. Beneath his feet, a soft, smooth padding stretched the length and breadth of the balcony's floor. Luscious to walk on, it bore a design that resembled a rippling field of grain bordered by various fruits on interweaving branches and vines. Periy means fruitful. Of course the toqeph's palace here would reflect that.

The hall below loomed huge in the semi-dark. Above, the domed ceiling rose like the sky and glittered with what appeared to be large glass windows. During the day, this whole room must be lit by the sun.

It smelled of age and use and — he hated to admit it — nobility. The place was clean and well cared for. The people loved and respected what

THE LAST TOQEPH

their predecessors had built. They had not come to destroy, but to plant, nurture, and grow.

His head hurt with the clamor of thoughts jostling for his attention.

Jerry led him down a short passage and stopped at the first door they came to. "This is my home. I hope thou shalt find comfort here."

How could he ever be comfortable in such a foreign place?

Jerry pressed a button, the door slid open, and he passed through before Daviyd. "Come in, please."

But it wasn't foreign. This was Gannah. And Daviyd had more right to be here than Jerry. He stepped through the doorway.

This dwelling, though spacious, was smaller than the toqeph's. The only furniture was of a comfortable sort for sitting, along with three small tables. One entire wall was comprised of bookshelves.

At their entering, a woman rose from one of the chairs and approached, smiling. She wore the traditional Gannahan tunic and loose trousers as well as the collar of a married woman. Her pale Earthish eyes and complexion twisted the image askew.

She honored her husband with a deep bow, keeping proper silence until Jerry spoke first. Despite her alien appearance, it was plain she'd had proper training.

Smiling, Jerry favored her with a gesture to come near. "My wife, Katarina, and a worthy one." He put an arm around her. "Please meet our guest, Natsach Daviyd Natsach, of whom the toqeph spoke."

"Thy visit doth fill us with joy." She bowed.

He returned it. Though her wording was clumsy, he got the impression of sincerity, and he responded with reciprocity. "Your hospitality is well appreciated."

"Hast thou eaten this day?" She gestured toward a doorway, and he noted a table and chairs in room beyond. "I put on a pot of micken yesterday eve. Wouldst thou have tea? Some blend, perhaps?"

Ah. So they ate in a separate room. "I shall eat with gratitude whatever thou dost wish to set before me." His stomach gurgled.

Jerry and his wife ushered him across a narrow hall and into the room with the table. Its walls held many cabinets. In their midst stood a deep bowl with water pipes, similar to the one in the airport restroom but with no reflective glass above. There were other fixtures as well that held a dimly familiar feel, as if he'd seen such things in Adunnim.

THE LAST TOQEPH

Katarina went to what must have been the cooking appliance and picked up the pot that sat upon it. "I hope thou dost take no offense at breaking thy fast in the kitchen?"

"Nay. Why should I?" It seemed the perfect place to eat.

"We have a dining room," Jerry said, "but I use it as my office. My work is spread across the table, leaving no room to eat."

A room exclusively for dining? "The kitchen is quite suitable."

The table was set with three bowls and scrapers, finger cloths, glasses and blend, a pitcher of water, and a bouquet of mintsticks. The three chairs, of sturdy manufacture and graceful design, all matched. The floor was smooth and spotless.

Katarina set the pot on the table and removed the lid, releasing a nutty aroma that made Daviyd's mouth water.

"Thank you, Kat," Jerry said, "it doth smell wonderful, as ever." He glanced at Daviyd. "'Ere we sit, let us sing the morning blessing."

Daviyd had put his hand on the nearest chair to pull it out, but paused.

His hosts lifted hands and faces upward. Daviyd glanced toward the ceiling but saw nothing unusual. Then he noticed their eyes were closed. What was this?

Next moment, Jerry broke into song, and after the first line, his wife joined in. They sang in the Gannahan language.

> We thank thee, our ab, faithful and true,
> For thy love and thy favor, for all that ye do.
> Thou hast blessed us with food, with oceans of love,
> Thou giveth us wisdom and grace from above.
> We give thee our thanks and pledge that this day
> Thy will and thy word we with joy will obey.
> Amen and amen and amen again.

Daviyd watched their rapt faces, struggling to understand.

He was Gannah. But these people, and this ritual? It was alien. A defilement.

Why, then, did it seem to fit so well here?

Since first entering the giant bird, he'd maintained contact periodically with his em and Jether and others in the village. He'd let them know he was

THE LAST TOQEPH

well, had landed safely. Had met the toqeph, who spoke well and treated him with respect.

Now his meah message was short and succinct. *The people so far are civilized and hospitable. But mad.*

28

The cerecfruit was ripe and juicy, but Ra'anan could only eat one piece. Her first slurp of micken stuck in her throat. The blend, diluted with water in the usual ratio for breakfast, tasted more like water than blend.

She set her glass down and stared into her micken bowl. Why had Abba given her so much? She'd never be able to get all that down.

Abba scraped the remainder of the thick porridge into his own bowl, set the empty pot in the sink, then returned to his seat. "So tell us, please, Emma. What's this about a visitor?"

Ra'anan's head snapped up. The younger children bounced in their chairs. "Yes, Emma, tell us!"

"Is he from another planet, like Faris?" Hushai asked the questions that had been on Ra'anan's mind all morning. "Is he going to live here now?"

"Or is it a she?" Tamah smirked, as if proud of herself for thinking of something no one else had considered. "You just said stranger. You didn't say he or she."

Emma set her micken bowl on the table then wiped her mouth on the damp cloth. "It is a man. And he is not from another planet. Your brother met him while on his quest in Yereq."

The children's meahs all foundered in confusion, but it was Ra'anan who put the roiling thoughts into words. "That's not possible. Nobody lives in Yereq."

"Yeah," said Husha. "Nobody lives anywhere on Gannah but us settlers." He frowned and looked back and forth between his parents. "Right?"

Emma sighed. "That is what I believed. What we all believed."

THE LAST TOQEPH

"We had no reason to think otherwise." Abba eyed Emma. "During the Plague, when I came here aboard the hospital ship *Barton* in response to the distress signal, the ship scanners showed only one human life form. Yours. When we left with you aboard, there was no sign of any other survivor. The *Promontory* found no one else either. How could you have known there were others?"

Emma frowned. "The *Promontory* didn't look for anyone else."

Abba's ears tilted back. "They scanned for you when the shuttle went down. If there had been—"

"They searched for the landing craft's location beacon, not human life."

The children stopped eating. She'd interrupted Abba! Ra'anan's brows lifted at the breach of domestic rules.

Emma went on without a hint of remorse. "Once they found it, they looked for crash survivors in the immediate vicinity. Neither they, nor the orbiting Karkar ship six years ago, nor the *Photuris* that brought Faris and his men, undertook a thorough search."

Abba's expression remained unchanged. "They had no reason to. As you said yourself."

"Because I told them there was no one to look for. I should have asked them to search further." Emma's eyes filled and her voice broke. "How could I have given up so soon?"

As Emma spoke, Tamah rose, her face contorted in a struggle to hold back tears. She scurried to Abba and climbed into his lap as Hushai and Ittai stared at Emma with wide eyes. Ra'anan had never seen her mother like this. The sorrow and guilt emanating from her meah made Ra'anan want to join Tamah in Abba's arms.

But Emma went on, shifting into Old Gannahan as she sometimes did when upset. "How could I have been so arrogant as to think I alone could survive? I have betrayed my own—"

Abba's voice, despite its sudden gentleness, cut through her words. "Hadassah."

Ra'anan caught her breath. He never called her by her full given name.

Tamah buried her face in his shirt. Wide-eyed, Ra'anan and the boys clung to one another in their meahs.

"You're upsetting the children." Abba peeled Tamah from his chest and set her on the floor. "It's all right, sweet. Go sit in your own chair."

She obeyed, gaze downward and lip quivering.

THE LAST TOQEPH

Ra'anan's whole body quivered. Whatever was happening, it was unprecedented. And it felt very, very bad.

"Children." Abba's quiet command drew their eyes to his blank face. "Your mother is upset, as you can see. But it has nothing to do with any of you."

Emma started to say something, but he broke in before she'd gotten a word out. "I will explain it to them."

Her mouth hung open, and Ra'anan could feel her struggle with obedience.

"You are wise to correct me, my husband. I accept whatever—"

"Oh, for goodness sake, stop apologizing."

Emma flushed but didn't look up. Was she crying? She cleared her throat. "I am sorry, my husband."

He expelled a Karkar snort. "What am I supposed to do with her, children? I tell her to stop apologizing, so what does she do? She apologizes."

Ittai's giggle sounded more nervous than amused. But it seemed to encourage Tamah, whose lip quit trembling and curled up in a grin. "Send her to the greyroom, Abba. She disobeyed you."

Abba stroked his beard. "That's true. She did."

Emma sat, eyes downcast and hands in her lap, awaiting her fate. The children held their breaths.

Abba gazed at her. "But the greyroom is for disobedient children, and your em is no child. She is a wise woman with the weight of a planet on her shoulders." His ears lifted, ever so slightly. "I will forgive your outburst, my wife, the love of my life. Provided you sit quietly and allow me to tell our curious children what is going on without interrupting me again."

When she lifted her head, he raised a finger. "Don't speak. Bless me with your silence."

She smiled. And the children let out their breaths.

Abba took a sip of blend. "Better eat while I'm talking, kids, or your breakfasts will get cold."

They picked up their bowls at almost the same time.

While they ate, Abba talked. "As your em said, Adam met a man in Yereq when he was on quest, and it shocked your brother as much as it would have any of us. From his and Adam's conversations as well as his discussion with the toqeph this morning, we know he is one of a group of

THE LAST TOQEPH

people who escaped the Plague by hiding in sealed underground passageways. They were not picked up on the scanners because their hiding place was too deep underground. And they did not make themselves known because they did not wish to be found. Your mother did, in fact, do everything possible to locate any survivors. She not only conducted searches by air and by satellite, but she also broadcast requests for any survivors to contact her. The visitor's own statement confirms this. They were not overlooked. They intentionally stayed out of sight."

Ra'anan frowned. "Why would they not want help?"

"They had their reasons. It may not make sense from our point of view, but they believed they did the right thing. It doesn't matter. The point is that now they've been found. Your mother would like him to get to know us a little. To see that, although we are Outsiders by breeding, we are not a threat to his people."

Hushai scraped the last bits from his bowl. "Are those people gonna live in Yereq? Or are we gonna get to visit them?"

"Can we take the train there?" Ittai wiped cerec juice from his chin.

Tamah's face was the picture of concentration. "Were they trapped in a mine or something, like Lileela? How'd they get out?"

Abba shook his head. "They were not trapped, Tamah. They hid in tunnels like what the rail cars run through, but with all the outside air vents sealed up so the plague virus couldn't reach them." He took a breath. "And Hushai, we don't know the answer to your question yet. All that is still to be decided."

He nodded at Ra'anan. "You haven't said a word. Do you have a question too?"

She blushed. "What's his name?"

Abba turned to Emma. "I will let you answer that, my dear, because my pronunciation of your language is impossible."

She turned her gaze to Ra'anan. "His name is Natsach Daviyd Natsach." Then she smiled—and her meah emitted a tangled, aching combination of joy and longing and love and grief.

Ra'anan almost choked when Emma silently conveyed to her through her meah, *I was not much older than thee when I, too, fell in love with a Natsach.*

Daviyd pulled back the bed curtain and looked inside. He compressed the mattress with his hand. Drew down the blanket to reveal soft

THE LAST TOQEPH

sheets. Picked up the pillow and buried his face in it. Soft and clean. What was it filled with, that it bore no animal smell and no sharp ends of straw stuffing poked through?

Everything here was so different—but it had a scent of familiarity nevertheless. Had he slept in an alcove as a boy? He sat on the bed and closed his eyes. Yes. The memory seeped back into his brain. But his childhood room had walls of stone, not like these, which were padded and fabric-covered. That apartment had been smaller, the bed bigger, and he'd shared it with other children. But yes. This was Gannah.

The way Gannah should be.

He hated the thought even as it came to him, but he couldn't deny it. These Outsiders were living like Gannahans, while his people lived like beasts.

He closed the curtain and lay down. Cozy. He pulled up the covers. Comfortable. His taut muscles relaxed as he stared at the alcove's ceiling. He reached, but couldn't quite touch it without sitting up. With arms outstretched to either side, his right fingertips brushed the curtain but his left couldn't quite reach the padded wall.

A real bed, with real sheets. But it was the middle of the morning. He doubted he'd be able to sleep, wound up as he was.

The bed was comfortable, though.

He reached for Emma in his meah. *The Nasi and his wife suggested I shower and rest. "Shower" is to bathe in warm water that doth fall from a pipe in the wall then flow out through a hole in the floor. I dried myself on clean, soft towels in a blast of warm air. I trimmed my beard with sharp metal tools and put on clothing such as I remember from when I was young. And now I lie in a bed alcove. A real bed alcove! Though wide awake, I almost think I dream.*

Emma's meah beamed pleasure though her verbal communication expressed concern. *Beware, my son, that the Outsiders bewitch thee not with their subtle enticements.*

But Daviyd was aware only of her pleasure, for her words didn't penetrate his slumber.

Grinning like an Earther, Adam recorded his new son's weight then lifted him from the scale. A solid four point four nine kilograms. The boy was perfect. In every way. The lack of the Karkar's sixth digit on hands and feet, though a little disappointing, was not disfiguring.

THE LAST TOQEPH

"A beautiful little man. Thou hast done wonderfully, my beloved."

Elise smiled. "Just give him to me. And why can't you speak plain Standard like a normal new father?" Her hair lay tousled on the pillow and her blue eyes glowed almost Gannahan-like.

He inspected the infant once more before wrapping him in the softest towel he'd been able to find. "I am not a normal new father. I am — or will be, once I achieve Nasihood — heir to the throne of all Gannah. The birth of the son of such a one is too proud an occasion for the Standard Language."

"Yeah, sure. But I did all the work. Would you give him here already?"

Adam grinned all the more. His son was perfect — both sons were. And his wife was a marvel. A beautiful little dynamo, with as much spunk as a native Gannahan.

"And you do magnificent work." He ran his finger along the side of the tiny face, and the child turned toward it, mouth seeking. Adam chuckled. "He doth ask for thee as well, my beloved." He handed the baby to Elise.

Tears overflowed her eyes as she cradled her new son. "Joseph. Pik Joseph Finnegan. What a handsome boy you are." She adjusted his position until he could nurse, and he took to it like a pro. She giggled. "What a hungry boy you are!"

Adam gazed down at them. "He knows what he wants, and he knows how to get it. You'll have to be firm with this one, Em."

Her face darkened in a deep scowl. "He's five minutes old, for crying out loud. Give me a break."

Adam laughed and reached for his messenger. "I'll give your parents the good news. But I'll ask them not to bring Everett around until tomorrow."

Finished with his prayer, Faris rose and went to Lileela's bedside. The only signs of life came from the monitor, and from what he could make out, the indicators were weak. He studied her face, wishing he had a meah.

Perhaps he had one but hadn't yet discovered how to use it. He concentrated on her forehead, trying to will his mind to enter hers. Nope. He sighed and went back to his chair. He'd tried countless times, but whether Lileela was awake or asleep, he never met with success. Apparently he didn't have the capabilities.

THE LAST TOQEPH

He glanced at the timedial on the wall. Here it was halfway through Yellow Morning, and he hadn't checked the update from the Information Ministry. They weren't likely to have anything important to report, and he didn't care about the mundane details of the settlers' everyday lives. But he liked to check every morning and evening anyway.

He picked up the remote and turned on the screen in the wall across the room, then selected "Ministry of Information Dissemination – Latest Update." When the page came up, the banner across the top made his eyes widen. "IMPORTANT INFORMATION FROM THE TOQEPH." What was going on?

He opened the article and read, eyes widening in surprise. Before he finished the third paragraph, his jaw hung open. Then he rose and walked closer to the screen to make sure he was reading it correctly.

"This afternoon, the Council will meet with a visitor from the province of Yereq.

"We understand this statement will cause considerable confusion, so please read on.

"While traveling on his Second Quest, Pik Adam Atarah met a stranger on a plain in Yereq. Upon further investigation, Adam discovered the man to be one of a hundred or so native Gannahans who survived the Plague and the Great Disaster. We are endeavoring to ascertain the details of how they accomplished this, but it was unquestionably the will of the Yasha that they are alive and were undiscovered until now.

"Upon completion of his quest, Adam returned to Yereq and invited the man, whose name is Natsach Daviyd Natsach, to visit our settlement and meet with the toqeph. Our guest arrived early this morning.

"Because this is the evening of Wormfest, we will extend the celebration to include a feast in his welcome. Those who are involved in the preparations for the festival, please see your team leader for any changes in plan.

"Invited guests are welcome to meet with our visitor during the feast. However, we ask that those who are not on the guest list refrain from approaching Mr. Natsach at this time to prevent his being overwhelmed.

"More details will be forthcoming as they are available."

Faris read it through twice—enough to imbed it permanently in his mind. A sense of great significance swept through him. How he wished he could be in on that Council meeting!

THE LAST TOQEPH

When he and his men had arrived shortly after the Great Disaster, they had scanned the planet and found no signs of human life except at the settlement. But how closely had they looked? On his way back to his chair, he replayed that day in his memory then sank into his seat with a gasp. They *hadn't* looked. They'd surveyed the topography, focusing on the physical changes—the breaking up of the single landmass into three continents, the changes in the seas and water courses, and the destruction of the orbiting satellites. They'd ascertained that the Karkar ship hanging above the planet was crippled and empty, and that, despite all the damage elsewhere, the settlement was still intact. But they had not searched for human life, as they believed the entire population was in Periy. This visitor and his people would have been discovered years ago had Faris taken the time to look.

Faris turned his attention to the screen again. A second banner announced "Important Information from The Ministry of Education." Nasi Jerry Maddox, Education Minister, would be revealing upcoming revisions to the requirements, including changes to the history curriculum.

Faris muttered, "I should say so," and continued reading. "Gannahan language proficiency requirements will also be added incrementally, beginning with Level 1. The Ministry will release detailed explanations early next week."

Faris leaned back in his chair. Old Gannahans in the flesh. Speaking the language, living the life. Communicating with meahs, fighting with lahabs. The real thing.

His gaze moved to the sleeping Lileela. "What news, my love. You'll think you're waking into a whole new world."

29

A knock invaded Daviyd's dreams, along with an oddly accented voice. "I regret having to wake thee."

Another knock. The sound of a door sliding open.

Daviyd sat up, eyes wide. He was in a cave of fabric. No, it was —

Someone moved on the other side of the curtain. (Curtain?) "Daviyd?"

His racing heart slowed. He was in a bed alcove. In the Maddox home. On the other side of the world. "Jerry?"

"Yea. It is the second hour of Green."

Daviyd pushed the curtain aside and swung his legs out of the alcove. "I did not wish to sleep so long." Embarrassment burned his face. Ordinarily he had no difficulty waking at the time he wanted.

Holding an armload of clothes, Jerry nodded. "No doubt the difference in time zone hath disoriented thee."

"Time zone?" Daviyd rose and ran his hands through his hair. It had never felt so clean. The air on this side of the curtain felt cool against his skin, bare except for the garment he'd put on after his shower, which Jerry had said was the settlers' version of a breechclout. *Underwear*, he'd called it. To be worn, for cleanliness and modesty, under skirt or trousers.

Like so many of the new things he saw here, it seemed right and familiar.

"Yea." Jerry nodded. "Yereq is far to the west, and the sun doth cross its skies later than here. In thy village, it is yet Yellow Morning, perhaps nearly High Day. Thy mind is yet in that time."

"Ah. A zone of time. Indeed." Daviyd yawned.

"I have found these for thee." Jerry laid the clothes on a piece of furniture. "They were made by the Old Gannahans before the Plague. But

THE LAST TOQEPH

they are still whole and should fit thee well, for thou art the size and shape of their makers."

Daviyd picked up a shirt. "I thank thee." It was of sturdy construction, though it looked as if it had seen some wear. The embroidery couldn't have been original, for it was inexpertly stitched.

He pulled it over his head. How could he, a man who hadn't owned a shirt in years, be so critical? He straightened it on his torso and extended his arms. He caught a glimpse of his reflection in a glass across the room, and it surprised him.

"Thou dost look like a different man."

Daviyd picked up the trousers. The fabric was heavy but soft. Not at all like his leather skirt.

"If thou wouldst prefer a dress or a skirt, I could possibly —"

Daviyd shook his head. "Nay, this is more than adequate."

Jerry smiled. "If thou shouldst have any additional needs, please tell us. We would like thy visit to be as pleasant and comfortable as possible."

"Thou and thy wife are exemplary hosts." Daviyd put on the trousers.

Jerry pointed to the objects that remained. "Those, if you have not guessed, go on thy feet. I also have some shoes for thee, but they are not worn in the apartment. I shall leave thee now to prepare thyself. The toqeph would see thee in a quarter hour." He stepped from the room.

Daviyd picked up the socks—for he knew what they were. He knew how they'd feel before he slipped them on. What he didn't understand was why the memory of these things was so dim. He'd been nearly fifteen when the wave had washed away his world. It had not been so long ago that he should have forgotten.

A short time later, he walked with Jerry along the balcony to the toqeph's residence, reversing their route of the early morning. Now, in Green Afternoon, the sun shining through the skylights above brought clarity to the great hall below, much as Daviyd's recent experiences shed light on remembrances that had, until now, lain in the shadows.

Yes. Coming here to Gullach was like a sunrise after a six-year night.

The clothes, even the shoes that had initially seemed so confining, suddenly seemed as natural as hair to his head or beard to his chin.

Ahead, a sunbeam slanted down at the spot where the corridor branched off toward the toqeph's suite. They reached it and made the turn,

THE LAST TOQEPH

Daviyd squinting as he passed through the rays. Would the new light of these experiences dazzle his mind as the sunbeam did his eyes?

Then, out of the glare, the toqeph's ornate door towered at the end of the hall, the mark of Atarah emblazoned upon it in glittering gold.

Daviyd's jaw tightened. It was he who should dwell behind that door. He was the rightful heir of Atarah. Had the green-eyed woman brought him here to return that which her forefathers had taken?

Or to crush the noble Natsachs once and for all?

In the toqeph's suite, Daviyd followed Jerry through a sumptuous, irregularly-shaped room filled with oversized furniture.

They headed for another wide doorway with narrow windows on either side. Daviyd straightened his shoulders and entered behind his guide.

The toqeph sat at a long oval table with three men. One of them, huge and pale and drawn with age, was plainly her husband.

All of them, including the toqeph, rose when Daviyd entered.

Jerry bowed. "Madam Toqeph." Then he turned to the rest. "Gentlemen of the council. Please greet Natsach Daviyd Natsach, our honored visitor from the land of Yereq."

The men bowed, and Daviyd returned the gesture as Jerry introduced them. "Dr. Pik, husband of our toqeph. Jacksonville Florida, who is Second Nasi and Minister of Domestic Peace. And Rip Tischtuch, mayor of the city of Qatsyr. These, along with myself, make up the Ruling Council of Gannah."

Such outlandish names. Daviyd's every muscle tensed. "Ye are Earthers." He leveled his gaze at the toqeph's monstrous husband. "And a Karkar."

The toqeph took her seat, and Jerry answered as he motioned Daviyd to a chair. "We each have chosen to leave our homes to come here and rebuild Gannah. Dost thou not see this as an honor to your people and culture, that we would give our all so that Gannah might continue?"

Daviyd frowned. The argument almost seemed reasonable, but he wouldn't accept it. Settling into his seat, he stared at the old blond giant.

The toqeph spoke at last. "I understand thy resentment against the Karkar. Thou shouldst know, however, that this man—" She put her hand on her husband's arm. "—is the staunchest defender of Gannahan law and tradition. In my absence some years back, he made no compromises and

THE LAST TOQEPH

held the settlement together. Where wast thou then, or thy people? Hiding, I daresay. Allowing this Karkar to stand, without your help, against those who would corrupt all that is good and Gannahan."

Daviyd flushed. He should have an answer to that, but his mind and mouth were empty. He bowed his head in acquiescence.

The toqeph's voice was firm. "I shall entertain no criticism of my husband. He hath proven himself many times over. Thou must now do the same."

Feeling her cold, green stare, he lifted his gaze to meet it. "I am at thy disposal, Madam Toqeph." He hoped her weak meah could detect the true meaning behind his words, that he considered himself something less than a willing guest here.

He sensed she understood, and her expression softened a little. "We know thou art not responsible for the actions of thy fathers. None here accuseth thee of a crime. But I would like the council to know the things thou didst tell me earlier. Because they lack meahs, thy speech is difficult for them to understand. I will, then, tell the tale on thy behalf. If I err, please speak up. I would like the report to be wholly accurate."

He nodded. "Yea, Madam."

The toqeph then, in clear and precise Gannahan, gave an accurate recital of the story he'd told her. No one interrupted with questions until the part where Daviyd's father had seen her pass by on a motorsled during the months of her separation from the settlement.

The man named Florida spoke up then, with speech almost as perfect as the toqeph's. "Why did he not reveal himself? Why did he allow her to go on alone?"

Daviyd cleared his throat. "He recognized her not. He said only that he saw a person on a motorsled."

The one described as the mayor frowned. His speech was unintelligible, but almost the instant he spoke, a mechanical-sounding voice emanated from his direction, translating his speech into the Gannahan tongue. "Why, if your people believed themselves to be the only living on the planet, were they not more curious at seeing another? Why would thine ab allow the toqeph to pass without making himself known?"

When the man shifted his position, Daviyd caught a glimpse of a small device snaking around his neck. Then the mayor lifted his right arm from

THE LAST TOQEPH

where it had lain in his lap, and Daviyd stared. The man's hand was missing, replaced by an unnatural-looking imitation.

While Daviyd pondered his response, Florida's dark eyes scoured Daviyd's face, though he had no way to probe with his mind. "If my understanding of history be true, in the old days, everyone recognized Atarah. Even the animals. Thine ab must have known who it was he saw." Florida held Daviyd's gaze. "What had he to hide?"

The Karkar spoke then, in a high, reedy voice that seemed wholly unsuitable for a giant. Not surprisingly, he spoke gibberish, but he also wore a device that translated. "It would seem we all have the same question. The toqeph has told us of the Dathan, of their origins and their purpose. But we would understand better if our information came from thou, who art thyself a Dathan. For, wise though the toqeph be, she hath not thy depth of knowledge as regards this subject."

Jerry nodded. "Indeed. We would know more perfectly who thy people are, and why they have hidden themselves for so long."

Daviyd's mouth went dry. His father's words echoed in his memory. *Would that I might stand before Atarah and plead our case.* And now Daviyd was asked to do just that. What a gift!

He felt inadequate to the task. How much did these people know? They were Outsiders. Only the toqeph had any part in this, and she, like Daviyd, had merely inherited the situation, not created it.

All eyes were upon him. But he ignored the others and locked his gaze with the toqeph's. "I am honored, madam, to speak on this matter. Long has it been the desire of my people to see justice done, such justice as only Atarah hath the power to grant."

A faint longing emanated from her meah. Longing for what? Her expression contemplative, she repeated his statement for the others, then turned back to Daviyd. "Is it possible, Mr. Natsach, to pronounce thy words more clearly? The electronic translators cannot manage thy slurred speech." She smiled, as if fingering a fond memory. "You Northerners always did have an unusual way of speaking."

He nodded, though he wasn't sure he could comply to her satisfaction. "I shall make every effort, madam, to be clear." He tried to enunciate each syllable. "Wouldst thou have me begin with the story of Natsach and Charash?"

THE LAST TOQEPH

"That is, as I understand it, the beginning of these events." She addressed the Council. "If you any have questions, let us wait until Mr. Natsach doth finish his tale." Then she turned her green eyes upon Daviyd.

He took a deep breath and began.

He told of how, in antiquity, the twin brothers Natsach and Charach strove for the throne upon the death of their father, the king. How Charach, contrary to all that was good and Gannahan, cheated his brother and banished him to the far northern reaches of the world. He explained that many of Natsach's friends, as well as others who were appalled at Charach's treachery, fled Ayin, which was the center of civilization at that time, and joined Natsach in his banishment. Charach decreed that there would henceforth be no communication between the faithful who stayed and the rebels, as he called them, who left. Those who rallied to Natsach called their group the Rahab, which meant the Proud.

The remainder of the Gannahans were of the dull, unimaginative sort, and over the next several generations, their civilization made little progress. The Rahab, however, thrived despite the inhospitable northern climes in which they were forced to dwell. It was they who developed the sophisticated underground tunnel system. Science blossomed, and while the Charachites continued to live in primitive conditions, the Rahab enjoyed beautiful architecture, modern conveniences, and advances their southern cousins would have considered magical had they known of them.

Until finally, they did learn of them. And in a horrific act of genocide hitherto unknown on Gannah, one of the descendants of Charach tried to wipe out the Rahab by diverting the river and flooding their stronghold in the Ruwach Gorge. Many died, but not all. Those who survived believed the event to have been a natural disaster; it wasn't until many years passed that they discovered that Atarah's heir, Naphtali, had engineered it with cruel craftiness.

The Charachites adopted the Rahab technologies as their own. To their credit, they learned quickly, and many of the Rahab survivors, no longer anathema provided they lived and worked among the rest of Gannah, helped in their training.

And then the Fueraqis came, with their starships and their weapons and their intention to subjugate Gannah, ravage the planet's resources, and enslave the people. It took decades, but, largely through the ingenuity of the Natsachs, Gannah fought off the invaders, chased them back to Fueraq

THE LAST TOQEPH

using the enemy's own warships, and annihilated the populace, leaving that planet little more than a smoking cinder.

Drunk on blood, the Gannahans then launched their own rampage through the galaxy, absorbing new ideas and technologies even as they destroyed civilizations. The debacle ended at Karkar, when those oversized people fought back with a specially engineered plague that attacked Gannahan muscle tissue.

Atarah Hoseh, the king at the time, returned to Gannah after his warships of dead warriors had limped home under automatic piloting and gathered around the planet. When the plague was introduced into the ships above Karkar, Hoseh and a few of his men had been away, exploring their next intended target, Earth. While searching out terrestrial riches and vulnerabilities, they had picked up a different sort of contamination: the Earthish religion known as Christianity. Hoseh commanded that the plague-ridden vessels be brought to the planet surface, weighted down, and sunken into the sea, never to be raised again. But even though he attempted to protect his people from the Karkar's disease, he did his level best to spread the Earthish contamination of religion to all of Gannah. He even went so far as to say the Earthish God, whom he called Jehovah, was the true King, and changed his own title to toqeph, or steward.

The Natsachs refused to accept the new, off-world ways. If a technology or philosophy did not originate on Gannah, they would have none of it, and that included Christianity. Hoseh allowed the Natsachs to practice the old ways without prosecution. Nevertheless, over the tumultuous years that followed, many of the Natsachs migrated north once again, preferring to retain their autonomy from the Toqephites, as they called the majority who embraced the new religion of Hoseh. They gradually opened up the ancient Rahab palace of Ga'ayown in Ruwach Gorge and rebuilt the ruins, establishing a stronghold there and calling themselves the Dathan, the People of Tradition.

For generations, they were content to retain their identity as traditional Gannahans, and they were accepted by the Toqephites as eccentric but harmless wrinkles in the orderly scheme of things. After a time, however, the Dathan leadership, which descended directly from the original Natsach, began to talk about how they might arrange to have the throne returned to Natsach's heir. A plan was devised. Daviyd didn't know the details, but it involved a takeover through strategic marriages, education of the populace

THE LAST TOQEPH

to teach them of the wrong that had been committed by Charach those many ages past, and, if necessary, subtle assassination.

It was this last that met with resistance. Whether Dathan or Toqephite, Gannahans were law-abiding at heart, and the idea of a violent takeover of any authority was unpopular at best. Those who proposed that extreme course pointed to the fact that Charach had been the original perpetrator, and Natsach would only be taking back that which was rightfully his. Others argued that Charach was long dead, the current Atarah was guiltless of any wrongdoing, and it would not be just to punish him and his family for his forefather's errors. It was finally decided that the change must be accomplished gradually and through nonviolent means. They drew up a plan that was agreeable to all, and moved forward with it.

Daviyd reiterated that he knew only what he was told. His grandfather, Natsach Etsbon Marrah, had been the leader of the Dathan headquartered in the old palace of Ga'ayown. It was he who had chosen which of his people would seek refuge in the tunnels and who would remain above ground to die in the plague. He sent his wife and children underground, as well as many others, but he himself remained in Ga'ayown.

Daviyd had been taught that the Plague was the result of the toqeph's attempt to wipe out the Dathan once and for all. Daviyd's family remained hidden because they believed they were being hunted. They didn't know how it had been accomplished, but they also believed the flood that destroyed their homes and carried them to Yereq was created by the toqeph for the same end, for hadn't the toqeph's ancestor Naphtali tried wiping them out through similar means generations ago?

It appeared Daviyd was able to make himself understood, because the toqeph seldom had to clarify anything, and the Council sat in rapt attention as he finished his speech. He turned at last to the toqeph. "Madam, I bear thee no ill will. Thou hast treated me with kindness, and I perceive thou art just and fair. I honor thee as Atarah's heir and as the one who doth sit on the throne of Gannah." He moistened his lips. This is why he had been brought here, was it not? Why the voice had spoken to his father? "But in truth, thou dost hold that place unrightly." He swallowed. "If thou wouldst do justly and deal with thy people in truth, thou shalt return the throne to Natsach. Of whom I am rightful heir."

THE LAST TOQEPH

The only man at the table who didn't look ready to leap at Daviyd's throat was the Karkar, whose pale, impassive face was matched by an overall calm that almost looked like slumber. The others half rose from their seats, their exclamations silenced when the toqeph raised her hand.

After the council settled down, the toqeph addressed Daviyd. "The tale thou tellest is much the same as what I read for the first time some years ago. As a child, I heard a different version of the story of the brothers Natsach and Charach. I was told the Rahab never existed and Ga'ayown but a fairy tale. I believed a Gannahan was incapable of deceit or cruelty to his fellow Gannahans.

"But then I stumbled upon Ga'ayown. There I discovered compelling evidence that not all I'd been told was true. Thy story, Mr. Natsach, compliments what I learned in that place. But I believe even this version of the events is flawed and incomplete."

Daviyd scowled. She would declare his words untrue? He shouldn't be surprised. Her forefathers had been denying the truth for centuries.

He made no attempt to conceal his thoughts, and she caught them, he could tell. But rather than respond, she continued as if she hadn't.

"The truth of our fathers Natsach and Charach — for I have no doubt that we both, as thou sayest, descend from these brothers — has long since faded into legend. One side tells one story, the other side another. But who can say with certainty what happened? We only know that in their day, Gannah was divided.

"I claim no innocence on the part of my father Charach. It is possible his brother, and likely those who followed him, are guilty of crimes against Gannah as well. It is beyond my power today to right the wrongs that were committed in ages past, or even to know with certainty what those wrongs were. Nor canst thou, as heir of Natsach. The best we can do, thou and I, Natsach and Charach, is come to terms with what we have before us today."

Daviyd struggled to follow. What was she proposing?

She turned her gaze upon each man at the table. "Gentlemen of the Ruling Council, ye have heard the testimony of Natsach Daviyd Natsach. Have ye any reason to think he doth not speak the truth as he doth verily believe?"

The Councilmembers glanced at one another, but the Karkar spoke first. "I believe his testimony, as I know thou dost as well."

The others murmured their agreement.

THE LAST TOQEPH

The toqeph directed her gaze to Daviyd. "I see thee as a true Gannahan. One who would not willingly deceive. Who desireth above all else to see justice done and goodness prevail for all Gannah."

Daviyd's heart leaped in his chest.

Her brows lifted, and he flushed with embarrassment that she could see his excitement. The corners of her eyes crinkled with a gentle smile as she continued. "As I have said, we cannot know the truth concerning what occurred in ancient times. Memories and written records alike can be distorted, and not always with deliberate intent. However, a few things I know to be true.

"First, thou art here before us today. This was accomplished through the direct intervention of the Bara, the Creator of all things. Thy people have not wished to acknowledge Him. But do ye not stand on the Gannah He created, and breathe the air, eat the food, and drink the water He hath provided? For reasons He alone knoweth, He created all things but chose to reveal Himself only to the people of Earth. It is through them that we learn of Him and can read His book. Didst thou know, Mr. Natsach, that He gave the early Earthers a book that told of Him, written in our own Gannahan language?"

Daviyd gasped. The woman was as much a liar as her father Charach! But before a word could escape his lips, he knew in his meah she spoke the truth, unbelievable though it was.

The men around the table nodded in agreement. They had seen it. They knew this book. He glanced about at their faces. They knew this Bara she spoke of. The one Adam had called the Redeemer.

He shook his head. "Nay, madam. How can that be?"

"We do not know the how. We only know what is. The Bara gave a race of Earthdwellers His book so they might know Him. Later, He came to Earth and lived among them. Even then, most did not believe in Him, for the Earthers are a proud and foolish people, willing to die rather than bow the knee to the One Who gave them life.

"Later still, Atarah Hoseh visited the planet. There he learned of the Bara and His book. And he was never the same again. I shall tell thee the whole of it, Mr. Natsach, when we have more time. Now, however, this meeting doth grow wearisome. We must press on."

A glance at the Karkar revealed the truth of the "wearisome" part. His massive head was bowed and amber eyes were closed.

THE LAST TOQEPH

The toqeph continued. "It is certain that the Bara hath brought thy people to our attention at last. That, we can know without doubt. Dost thou not agree?"

Daviyd's head ached. This talk of the Bara should be an offense to all that was good and Gannahan, but it made too much sense for him to be offended. He needed more time to consider it. "As far as I understand thy saying, madam, I cannot argue. But I would know more of the business before I give full agreement."

She smiled. "Well said. Thou shalt indeed know more. For now, let us agree on this: Gannah should be divided no longer. It is not sensible that thy people live in poverty when ample provisions exist for all of us. Thou sayest thou art the heir of Natsach of old. Art thou, then, the leader of thy people?"

"We have no ruler, as such. Decisions are made by agreement of the village based on the laws and traditions of Gannah and what is best for all."

"The laws and traditions of Gannah, thou sayest? Would, then, thy people acknowledge the authority of the toqeph?"

He hesitated. "I should think they would, Madam."

"Yea. If they be true Gannahans, they would indeed." She cast her glance around the table once again. "Gentlemen of the Council of Gannah, I propose that we extend to Mr. Natsach's people the invitation to live among us. Mr. Tischtuch, ample housing can be prepared for their numbers?"

The man with the artificial hand nodded. "Yea, Madam Toqeph. As thou knowest, Qatsyr was once a great city, and only a small part of its space is now used."

"All our services are equally expandable?" She raised her brows as she glanced at each man.

"Yea, Madam," they answered in turn. The ministries concerned with food and other provision, oversight of the people's education, and civil and domestic order could all deal with the newcomers. The Karkar roused himself to add, "I would anticipate a problem initially with the supply of clothing and other textile goods. However, provided our factories begin production as planned, those needs can be met in a timely manner."

"The first practical challenge," the toqeph said, "will be transporting them here. But we need not resolve it today. If we have no further questions for our guest or additional business to discuss?" No one indicated there were any, so she finished. "Let us adjourn."

THE LAST TOQEPH

30

Hushai spent the better part of the day helping set up for the festival. By the time his work group completed all the duties assigned them, he was ready to relax and play Situation Solver. He didn't often get a chance to play undisturbed.

But what if the council meeting wasn't over? He frowned as he neared home. He'd been itching all morning to get back to his game, but no one was allowed in the apartment while official business was being conducted in the dining room.

He tiptoed into the suite and paused in the foyer. The dining room door was open and the light was off. But the apartment wasn't empty. He sensed someone in the sitting room—someone with a scent similar to Emma's, but more masculine.

A few steps later, he found the answer to the puzzle standing before the bookcase. The man turned, black brows raised in a question above bright violet eyes.

Hushai grinned. "Hey, you're that guy Adam found in Yereq." To his surprise, he met the man on a meah level, an experience he'd never had with anyone other than his immediate family.

From the man's perplexed response, it was plain he didn't speak the Standard language. Hushai summoned his best Old Gannahan. "Thou art the man my brother did find in Yereq."

The stranger stood about Faris's height, with broad chest and thick-muscled arms. He studied Hushai from head to foot. "Adam is thy brother?"

THE LAST TOQEPH

Hushai's grin broadened. Though what the man said sounded like "Admsdybruthr?" Hushai understood it perfectly—not with his ears, but in his meah.

"Yea. He is the eldest. I have a younger brother as well, and three sisters."

"How old art thou?"

Hushai pulled himself up to his full height. "Almost twelve years."

The hard face softened a little beneath the curly black beard. "Thou dost take after thine em in size." He glanced at Hushai's hands. "And thou hast the proper number of fingers."

Hushai nodded. "Adam doth look the most like Abba. Save, perhaps, for our youngest sister, Tamah. She is only six but is tall as I and hath the Karkar hands." He wondered why the man was in the sitting room alone. "Wilt thou be seated at our table for Wormfest?"

"The toqeph hath invited me, and I cannot say nay."

Hushai wondered why he would want to. It was an honor to sit at the toqeph's table. Before he could ask, the man offered a question of his own.

"What is Wormfest? We do not celebrate it in our village."

Hushai frowned. "No Wormfest? What do you do with all the powlworms?"

"I have not seen one since we arrived in Yereq. We had them in Adunnim before the Flood, but we had no festival for them."

"Truly? It be an Old Gannahan tradition. Mine em hath memories of it as a child." Recalling the things she'd told the family, Hushai pursed his lips. "But I believe it was only celebrated in Periy. Her family would travel here sometimes so they might take part."

The man's mustache edged upward in a near-smile. "Tell me of this festival. You entertain powlworms?"

Hushai chuckled. "Nay! We eat them."

The man's eyes widened. "Truly?"

Hushai could sense the man searching his meah to see if he were joking. "I jest not. Beginning in Ebmonth, we pluck them weekly and put them in a—" He gestured the width and depth with his hands. "An enclosure. We put it in a root cellar where they lie in the cool and dark but have no need for food. We let the worms sleep in the dark 'til the first week of Rabmonth. Then we have a party. It is like any party, with food and music and dancing. But when the dial rolls over into Blue Night, we go

THE LAST TOQEPH

outside and roast the worms in an open fire. They bounce around in the pan, and then, in a flash, they pop open." He hopped up to demonstrate. "And I do mean flash. A yellow spark doth fly out, and they become soft and chewy and delicious."

The man watched with evident amusement. "I remember powl beetles and their orange larvae. But I believed them good for naught."

"Oh, but they are good for much. The roots cannot grow properly without them."

"Truly?" The man zoomed in on that statement like a hawk on an arnebeth.

Hushai rubbed his jaw. "I know not how it doth work, but somehow, the worms' eating of the foliage causeth the roots to grow long and fat. That is why we can collect them only weekly. We must leave some to reproduce, and we must allow them to eat. Only, we cannot allow them to eat enough to kill the plant."

The man's expression was thoughtful. "We had thought our roots small because of poor soil. No one in the village doth know this about the worms."

Proud of his knowledge, Hushai felt seven feet tall. "The first and second year, the worms are not needed. They are only necessary when the roots develop."

"That is why our plants produce many leaves and healthy pods, but our root crop is ever disappointing." The man nodded. "I am happy to have learned this." He smiled at Hushai. "Thank you, Mr. Pik."

Hushai laughed. "It be more than four years before I am Mister. But thou art welcome, Mr. Natsach." He bowed.

The man lifted an eyebrow. "I have never told thee my name."

"Nor have I told thee mine. But thou dost know it."

"I know only thine ab's name and thine em's. I cannot say what goeth between the Pik and the Atarah."

Hushai bowed. "I am Hushai. Pik Hushai Atarah."

His expression amused, the man did the same. "Natsach Daviyd Natsach."

They both looked up at the sound of Emma's voice. "Ah, so ye have met. But I am surprised to see thee here, Hushai. Hath Mr. Makris no work for thee?"

"We're finished, so he sent us home."

222

THE LAST TOQEPH

Though he answered in the Standard tongue, as it was more comfortable for him, she replied in Old Gannahan. "That is good. While thine ab doth rest, thou mayest help me conduct our guest on a tour, if thou wisheth."

Hushai beamed. "For real? Sure! Thanks, Emma!"

The insistent whistling of Adam's messenger worked its way through the curtain of his slumber.

Despite being on the sofa to allow Elise to rest undisturbed, he'd had no trouble falling asleep. Now, hours later, the noise jarred him.

He fumbled for the device on the floor then hooked it over his ear. "Yes?"

"Yes, *sir*, to you, Trainee." Jax's voice pulled Adam into full wakefulness.

He sat up straight and nodded a bow. "Yes, sir. I'm sorry, sir. I was sleeping." He clenched his jaw against a yawn. "Didn't realize who was calling." The yawn broke through anyway.

"I'm glad you got some rest, man. But enough of that. The toqeph requests the presence of all Nasis and novices at her table this evening."

"All three of us, huh?" Adam's bleary eyes sought the timedial across the room. "At the second half of the first hour of Violet Evening?" The dial was now rolling into the last hour of Green Afternoon. He'd planned on staying home tonight, but since that wasn't going to happen, he appreciated Jax giving him time to get ready.

"That's correct. And wives, but not kids. They—" Jax's manner suddenly turned jovial. "Hey, congratulations, by the way. How are Elise and that new boy of yours?"

Adam's ears lifted and he glanced toward the bedroom. "They're wonderful, thank you."

"How would you know? You've been sleeping. Better go check on them." Jax's smile was audible.

"Yes, sir, that was my plan."

"Good. Meet me at Maddox's at the top of Violet to discuss the next aspect of your training. Then we'll make our entrance together."

Adam nodded. "Yes, sir. I'll be there."

"Yes, you will." Jax disconnected.

THE LAST TOQEPH

Adam rose to indulge in a luxurious stretch-and-yawn exercise. Considering everything his body had been through recently, he didn't feel too bad.

He padded into the bedroom and pulled back the bed curtain just enough to peek in. Elise slept soundly. Probably for the first time in several weeks.

He turned and gazed at the infant, also asleep, and swelled with pride. A perfect boy, pink and healthy. And big. He glanced between the baby and Elise, marveling that her Earthish body had been able to contain such a marvelous creature.

Moving quietly, he found some clean clothes—not an easy task, since the laundry hamper was overflowing—and carried them into the bathroom, then closed the door to avoid waking the sleepers before activating his messenger.

Riana Groenewald answered with a cheerful, "Hello, Adam. Congratulations!"

He grinned. "Thank you, Mrs. Groenewald. I'm sorry to bother you, but you said if we needed any help, you'd—"

"No bother at all, dear. What do you need?" She'd lived on the African continent of Earth for her first twenty years, and her Standard language was still quaintly accented.

"Would you be able to come and stay for a while this evening? Everett is with Elise's parents—"

"Yes, I know. I've just been visiting with them. Such a dear boy. And so very clever."

He imagined her beaming expression. "Thank you. He is a fine boy. I trust he's behaving himself for his grandparents?"

"Oh, my, yes. He kept us all entertained." She chuckled.

"They'll have him with them at Wormfest, so that's all taken care of. I'd thought to stay here with Elise and Joseph, but the toqeph requires my presence at her table this evening. So if you could—"

"Come to your place? Of course, dear, I'd be glad to."

"I appreciate it. I expect I'll be home rather late, so would you mind spending the night?"

"Oh, no, hon. I'll just head for home whenever you get back. If I take the tube, I'll never have to go outside the chatsr walls, so no nasty beasties will get me."

THE LAST TOQEPH

"If you're sure. Because you could sleep in Everett's bed if you'd like."

"Oh, no, dear. I can't sleep unless I have my own dear Ben beside me. I'm sure you know how it is."

Adam didn't—he could sleep anywhere. But he knew not everyone had that ability. "If you'd like to go home, you certainly may. As you said, the traveling is safe provided you stay within the walls. But if you decide to stay, I've changed Everett's bed, so the sheets are clean."

Which meant he needed to do the laundry. Every scrap of cloth in the house was dirty.

"You needn't have gone to all that trouble for me, dear. I hope you didn't cook, too, because, I'm bringing dinner. I baked some sheber pasta with powlcurd cheese for the festival, a veritable vat of the stuff. I'll bring a little of that, along with—"

"Thank you, Mrs. Groenewald." Adam hated to interrupt, but he didn't have all evening. "You're a thoughtful woman. Elise is sleeping now, but I expect she'll be hungry as a zeeb when she wakes up."

"Very good, dear. I can't wait to see that baby! I suppose you expect me to keep my hands off of him and let him sleep."

Adam chuckled. "I'll defer to his mother. She'll let you know her thoughts on the subject when you arrive. See you in a little while, Mrs. Groenewald. And thank you again."

After his shower, he returned to the bedroom, where Elise was stirring. He sat on the edge of the bed and kissed her.

Her face melted into a contented smile. "That was a really good sleep. Did Joseph wake up?"

Adam kissed her again. "He's starting to come around now. I checked on him a minute ago, and he's still as handsome and healthy as when you last saw him." He smiled at the soft baby noises coming from the cradle nearby. "Maybe even handsomer."

Elise wrapped her hands around the back of Adam's neck. "He's his abba's son, alright. But why is his abba dressed up in his finest?"

Adam looked down at his embroidered tunic. "What, this old thing?"

"Of course it's old. All our clothes are old. When's someone going to get that textile factory running, anyway? They've been talking about it for years."

"Soon, my dear. The workers dropped everything to dig my sister and Kughie out of the ground, you know."

THE LAST TOQEPH

Elise pushed herself up to sit. "I know. How's she doing?"

"In a coma." At her look of alarm, he hasted to explain. "That is, the Gannahan healing sleep. And it's working. If I hadn't seen it for myself, I wouldn't have believed how fast that skin is growing." He paused. "Hmm. I should stop in and see her before I leave."

Elise narrowed her eyes. "Leave?"

Whether from the sharpness of her voice, or because he was hungry, Joseph let out a cry of his own.

Adam kissed her again. "The toqeph requires the Nasi and their trainee to sit at her table at Wormfest. Riana Groenewald's on her way here so you won't be alone with this terrible monster." He rose and bent to pick up Joseph, who had found his voice and was trying it out with enthusiasm.

"Gimme him. Poor thing, sleeping over there all by himself. He misses me."

Adam carried him to the bed, but Elise threw up a hand and shook her tousled head. "Wait. I need to use the bathroom."

Holding the squalling child in one arm, he assisted Elise out of the bed with the other hand. "Are you okay? Do you need help?"

She took a careful step and shook her head. "I'll be okay, thanks."

He kept his hand on her elbow to support her anyway. "You look a little wobbly. Don't fall, now, because I won't be able to catch you. I have my hands full."

"I'm not going to fall." She batted his hand away. "I'm fine."

"Okay, but give me a call if you need me."

She gave a wave as she disappeared into the bathroom. "Yeah, yeah. Like you'd hear me over that racket." The door closed behind her.

Adam directed his attention to the noisemaker nestled in the crook of his arm. "My son, you have a way with words. Just like your Karkar relatives." He rubbed the infant's cheek with the tip of his sixth finger, and the child turned his head and latched on with a strong suck.

The door buzzer brought him into the sitting room. With the baby occupying both hands, he called, "Come in, Mrs. Groenewald."

"Sorry, hon, but my hands are full. Could I trouble you to get the door?"

"Of course." He strode across the room and pushed the button with his elbow. "I wasn't thinking."

THE LAST TOQEPH

The door slid back and Mrs. Groenewald came through like a sunbeam, bearing gifts of food fragrant enough to remind Adam he hadn't eaten since his snack in the plane last night. His hunger made him look forward to Wormfest with the sort of eagerness Joseph showed in the way he worked on Adam's finger.

She exclaimed about the baby as he led her to the kitchen. But at the doorway, he stopped, appalled at the clutter there. "Put them wherever you find a place, Mrs. Groenewald. I should have straightened up a bit before you came." He flushed with shame. Yes, Elise had been tired lately, but how hard could it be to clear the table and load the dishwasher?

Though gracious enough to make no comment, Mrs. Groenewald couldn't find a place to set her dishes. To free a hand to help her clear a spot on the table, Adam removed his finger from Joseph's mouth, and the baby made his feelings known about that immediately. Adam soon offered his finger again, but it held no sustenance, and Joseph alternately sucked and fussed.

"Thank you, Mrs. Groenewald." Adam twisted back and forth in an attempt to calm the baby. "I appreciate your coming. Truly. Elise is in the bathroom, but when she's free, I'm sure she'll be able to give him what he's looking for."

"I'm sure. In the meantime, though—" She extended her hands, wiggling her fingers. "I'll take the lad."

He handed the baby to her. Joseph didn't like having the finger withdrawn again, but the change in scenery distracted him, and he paused in his fussing to stare at the new face smiling down at him.

"Thank you. You're a good Gannahan."

He went to the bathroom door but didn't open it. "You okay, love?" He heard water running.

"Yeah, all good."

"Mrs. Groenewald is here. She has the baby. And she's brought food. I'm sure you'll both appreciate a good meal."

"I sure will. I'm starved. And I'm leaking colostrum all over the place, so I'm glad the baby's hungry too. I'll be out in a minute."

"Okay. I'm going now. See you tonight."

He turned to go.

"Wait!" The door opened, and the sight of his near-naked wife, beautiful even in her sagging, post-partum mess, nearly stopped his heart.

THE LAST TOQEPH

"You're not going anywhere without a kiss."

He leaned into the bathroom and willingly obliged. "You are an amazing woman. Thank you."

Her pale coppery brows rose. "For what?"

"For the children you give me. And for being so understanding about my leaving you alone so often. You know I'd rather be here with you than anywhere in the galaxy."

She took his beard in both hands and pulled the rest of him into the room, where she whispered in his ear. "I know. But why do you suppose I'm so understanding?"

His tickling ears lifted in a smile. "Because you're an amazing woman?"

She giggled. "Of course. But also, because one day, it will be *thou*, my royal husband, who doth summon others to the table of Atarah."

31

Outside the pavilion, Ra'anan waved a fly from her face and lifted her eyes to the brilliant blue sky. A few white clouds drifted above in an unhurried way, and the warm air breathed no threats.

Beside her, Fidelity Heusen gave the table a final wipe with her drying cloth. "Looks like the weather will be perfect."

Ra'anan dipped her scrub brush in the bucket of cleaning solution and attacked the next table. "It does. And I'm glad. After all this work, it would be terrible if a storm messed things up."

"We've got, what, four more to go?" Fidelity set her two-sectioned bucket on the other end of the table Ra'anan worked on. "And then we're finished?"

"Washing them, yes. Then we must put a vase of mintsticks on each one and set fingerbowls at every place. We've got chorus practice third hour of Green, and after that, there will be more things to be done than we'll have time for." She rinsed her section with a rag that looked like it had once been a piece of floral-print wall covering. "What's Hushai doing tagging along with Emma, I'd like to know? She should make him help like everyone else."

"Hush!" Fidelity tossed a glance at two girls cleaning tables under the pavilion then went back to scrubbing, as if trying to wash away the words. "We don't criticize the toqeph."

Ra'anan bit her lip. "I apologize." Instinctively, she bobbed a little bow. "But I'm not, really. I'm criticizing my brother. I can't figure how he convinced her to let him take the afternoon off when there's so much work to be done."

Fidelity lifted her cloth from the bucket's rinse water section and squeezed it out. "I think you're jealous."

THE LAST TOQEPH

Ra'anan snorted. "Of what?"

"I saw the way you looked at that man when the toqeph brought him by. You wish you were the one taking him on a tour instead of Hushai."

The girl was pretty insightful for a person without a meah. "That's what you think."

"Yes. That's what I think." She smirked. "And you know what else I think?"

"Hmph." With quick motions, Ra'anan polished the center of the table though Fidelity had already done it.

"I don't blame you." Fidelity gave Ra'anan a sidewise glance. "He looks like he stepped out of an old movie. He's the real thing, Ray. A real Gannahan. A real man." She picked up her bucket and carried it to the next table, whispering as she passed, "How many more like him are there in Yereq, do you think?"

"You're crazy, girl." Ra'anan joined her friend at the next table. "You know how the Old Gannahans treated their wives, don't you?"

"The right way, that's how. The way your brother treats Elise and my ab treats my em. We're all Gannahans, you know. It's mostly the ones like your parents, who were married before they came here, who don't follow the traditional ways."

"I suppose you're right." Ra'anan scraped off a crusty spot with her fingernail.

"Of course I am. Stern as Gannahan men can be toward their wives, most of the time, they're sweeter than sweet. Look at Faris, how he adores your sister. Like now, for instance. Even though she doesn't even know he's there, he hardly leaves her side. He's totally devoted." She gave a dreamy sigh. "How could you not want a man like that?"

Ra'anan pictured Natsach Daviyd Natsach gazing at her the way Faris looked at Lileela and felt another surge like she'd experienced this morning. Heat in her belly despite an all-over chill. "I don't know, Delly. The whole thing scares me." She scrubbed harder. "I almost wish Adam had never met that man."

Adam rang the bell at the Maddox apartment, and Katarina met him at the door with her ready smile.

"Hi, Adam. Jerry's in the dining room. Go on in."

THE LAST TOQEPH

He bowed. "Thank you, ma'am." He passed through to the dining room, but not without noting that the kitchen was immaculate.

His ears jerked with annoyance. The state of a man's house was a reflection on the man, and at the moment, Adam's didn't project the image of one worthy of the Nasihood. He'd do a thorough cleaning tomorrow. Thereafter, though, he'd have to impress upon Elise the need to keep up with the housework. In his position, he couldn't afford to do otherwise.

He paused outside the dining room, where Jerry sat at a computer, surrounded by papers and books.

"Mr. Maddox, sir."

Jerry looked up. "Oh, Adam! Is it Violet already?" He made several more keystrokes.

"A few minutes of, sir."

"Well, come in. Have a seat. And congratulations on the birth of your son. All's well with em and child?"

Adam entered, bowed, and sat as instructed. "Yes, sir. Both are healthy and hungry."

Jerry rose and moved a few boxes to the floor to make room on the table. "I apologize for the mess. While my office is being renovated, I've had to move all this in here. As you can see, it's not the most convenient solution."

"I'm sure it's just temporary, sir." As, he reminded himself, was the mess throughout his own house. Very temporary.

"Thankfully, yes." He sat. "With the toqeph's new educational standards, I have to revamp all the level requirements, revise the examinations, completely redo everything. The new standards are needed, for we certainly want our people to learn an accurate history. And if we're to be Gannahans, it makes sense that we should speak the language. But rewriting everything will take time. I've postponed all the level exams until we decide what the requirements should be." He tossed Adam a weary smile. "I hope to have the reorganization finished long before your older son wants to take his Level One exam."

Adam returned his smile. "I'm sure you will, sir."

While they spoke, Katarina had again answered the door buzzer, and now Jax entered the dining room. Adam rose and bowed. "Mr. Florida."

Jax grinned. "Good to see you, Adam. Did you check on that baby like I told you to?"

THE LAST TOQEPH

"Yes, sir, and it was good advice. If I hadn't, I'd have missed him getting cuter by the second."

Jerry laughed. "Get the door, would you please, Jax?"

While Jax closed the door, Jerry moved to a chair at Adam's end of the table. "Well, then. Your training is progressing satisfactorily. Your recent quest, in particular, yielded some unexpected results, one might say."

Adam nodded. "Thank you, sir. And yes, sir. Unexpected is one word for it."

"Because of the chain of authority, you erred in not reporting your findings to Jax at the first. Withholding that information from us and taking it to the toqeph directly was not the proper procedure. I've noted that in the record, along with your—" He touched his brow, reminding Adam of his black eye— "questioning of a command."

Adam's empty stomach tightened. He bobbed in a small bow. "Yes, sir. I understand, sir."

"I hope you do." Jerry's steady blue stare couldn't match a true Gannahan's searing glare, but it was enough to chill the blood if not the bone. "Because a trainee cannot afford to be lax. And we cannot afford to overlook lapses in your behavior. Being son of the toqeph does not exempt you from discipline. If anything, it raises the standard, for of all the Nasi, the heir of Atarah especially must be purged of his weakness."

Adam slipped from his chair and prostrated himself on the floor. "Your judgment is wise."

"Rise, Trainee."

Keeping his gaze on the floor, Adam took his seat, and Jerry continued. "I have every expectation that you will hereafter perform well. From your next assignment onward."

Adam looked up at him. "Yes, sir. I will, sir." The reprimand was deserved. Sick at heart as it made him, though, Adam relished the opportunity to redeem himself. Whatever assignment he was given, he would carry it out to the detailed perfection worthy of Atarah's heir.

Jerry seemed to relax a bit then, as if signaling a change in subject. "I don't need to tell you that your discovery of the Old Gannahans changes everything."

Adam knew that all too well, but didn't interrupt.

THE LAST TOQEPH

"The toqeph and Mr. Natsach have discussed bringing the others from Yereq and assimilating them into our settlement. The survivors have not yet agreed, but the toqeph has reason to expect they will see the wisdom of it."

Adam swallowed hard. That uncouth Natsach bunch didn't belong here.

Jerry picked up a remote and activated a viewing screen embedded in the far wall. A topographical map appeared, contoured to suggest the spherical shape of the planet. He enlarged the center section, with Yereq at the top left, Periy at the bottom right, and the remaining provinces curving away into the margins.

"Based on your recent quest and information we've received from other travelers, we've updated our map." Jerry rose and walked to the screen. "This was just completed yesterday, so you don't have this version yet. I'm sending you the file so you'll be able to access it."

He found a pointer amongst the clutter on the table. "As you know, these represent the underground rail lines that still function." He indicated the markings. "Those we know of, anyway." The lines spidered away from Gullach and Qatsyr but ended where earthquakes and floods had destroyed them.

"We believe there may be other functional sections in Ayin." Jerry indicated the area northwest of Periy. "But it is certain that the system no longer exists in its entirety between here and Yereq." He tapped the province in question, separated from Ayin and Periy by the Nazal Sea.

"Air travel is still possible, of course. But the only plane able to go the distance is the Hatita. You're aware of its limited size, so I don't need to point out how impractical it would be for transporting an entire village."

Adam nodded. "Yes, sir." His limbs ached at the memory of being crammed into that cockpit for hours on end.

"So this is the situation. We must be prepared to move approximately one hundred men, women, and children from here to here—" He indicated Yereq and Periy—"across some five-and-a-half thousand kilometers of land and sea. And the toqeph would like it to be accomplished by the middle of Harvestmonth."

Jerry lowered the pointer and turned to face Adam. "You may transport them by any combination of air, land, sea, and/or underground means. You may enlist the expertise and labor of anyone you choose. But the task must be carried out with maximum efficiency of power, as our

THE LAST TOQEPH

energy resources are not unlimited. We must treat those being transported with courtesy and comfort, for they are people, not cargo. And we'll have only three months to do it. The toqeph would like to see your plan Secondday morning next week."

Adam kept his face Karkar-blank, but he couldn't prevent it from flushing. This was to be *his* responsibility? What Jerry asked was impossible.

No, it was the toqeph's request, not Jerry's. But it was impossible nevertheless. It wasn't Adam's fault she'd overlooked the existence of those people all this time. Why was it now up to him to fetch them?

Perhaps they wouldn't want to come, though. Maybe they'd refuse to be tainted by contact with all these Outsiders.

An image flashed in his mind of the near-naked people in their muddy little village with its squalor and stench. Their joy at the gifts. Natsach's intense interest in everything he saw at Gullach. No, they would not turn their backs on this.

Moreover, it was the toqeph's intent that they come. And a Gannahan did not say no to Atarah.

His mouth went dry and his stomach soured.

"Do you have any questions, Trainee?"

Adam's head buzzed. "None, sir."

"Very good. Draw up a plan and get it to Mr. Florida no later than the first hour of Blue Night on Firstday, so he can present it to the toqeph the next morning."

Adam glanced at Jax, who gave him an enigmatic smile.

"Certainly, sir." Adam's voice croaked, and he cleared his throat.

"We only need a proposal at first," Jerry added. "Outline how you envision the move to be conducted. The transportation methods, equipment, and materials you expect to use, the people whose help you plan to enlist, and the schedule you intend to implement. After the general plan is approved, the finer points can be worked out."

Adam tried to work up enough saliva to speak. "Yes, sir. I understand."

"I look forward to seeing what you come up with." Jerry set down the pointer and picked up the remote. "And you will, of course, be in charge of implementing the plan when the time comes."

"Yes, sir." Adam's brain went numb.

THE LAST TOQEPH

Jerry shut off the view screen. "Excellent. Katarina had something she wanted to drop off at the ministry office before the festival, so she's already left. She'll join us at the back courtyard before we enter the pavilion." He turned to Jax, who rose. "Will Jillian be joining us there as well?"

"Yes. She'll sit with us at the toqeph's table." Jax glanced at Adam. "Is Elise home alone with the baby?"

Adam stood, trying to force his stunned mind to function. "Yes, sir. I mean, no. Riana Groenewald is staying with her this evening. And Everett is with my in-laws. They'll bring him home tomorrow afternoon."

"Good." Jax exited the room after Jerry, with Adam following. "You know, man, you keep adding these arrows to your quiver, you're going to need a bigger quiver."

Adam nodded. "The apartment will be crowded with the four of us. But we'll take things one step at a time."

He and Elise had discussed expanding their quarters, but they'd never come to an agreement. She'd hinted about moving to First Town to be near her parents. But with his work at the medical center, he wasn't willing to leave the second chatsr.

It was hard enough balancing his responsibilities as doctor and researcher with the demands of his Nasi training. Now, this new, overwhelming task of transporting the Old Gannahans to Periy would take every bit of his time and attention. How could he possibly manage his obligation to his family as well?

Standing in the courtyard at the rear of the palace, Ra'anan watched as Mr. and Mrs. Maddox and then Mr. and Mrs. Florida passed through the gate and down the path to the festival grounds. Adam followed.

Her brother was a head taller than the rest. Ra'anan had often thought that if rank were determined by height, Abba would rule, not Emma. Now she applied that to Adam. Despite his superior size, her brother was as carefully submissive to the Nasi as a woman to her husband, and she could feel his tension in that role through her meah.

The happy sounds of the crowd outside the wall quieted as the Nasis and their wives came into view. Their entrance signaled the impending arrival of the toqeph. And that meant the festival would begin.

The distinguished couples—and Adam—stood behind their seats around the table. In the courtyard, Abba gave the go-ahead, and the family

THE LAST TOQEPH

passed through the gate. First Emma on Abba's arm, followed by Mr. Natsach, and then the children in order of age.

They would be seated at the oval table oldest to youngest. That meant Ra'anan would be next to Mr. Natsach—a prospect that made her stomach flutter.

The sun hung low west of the palace, casting a mountain-sized shadow across the grounds. In the pavilion, the toqeph's table was out of the weather. But the evening promised to be pleasant, so even the people at the tables in the grass should be comfortable. Torches placed at frequent intervals throughout the area kept bothersome insects at bay. As the night deepened, electric lights would be lit as well.

All who were seated rose when Emma and Abba reached the grounds, and all talk ceased as the royal family entered the pavilion and arranged themselves behind their seats. Only a few birds and the slightest of breezes stirred.

Kote Kotila, Overseer of the Festival, climbed the three steps to the stage at the edge of the pavilion. He lifted his hands and head, eyes closed, and everyone joined him as he sang the evening blessing.

Ra'anan loved hearing the voices swelling around her, from Mr. Kotila's strong tenor coming through the speakers to the resonant bass of Baako Ayo from somewhere under the pavilion roof. Two thousand voices, old and young, thin and full, wove together in harmonious praise and gratitude to the Yasha. Despite the warm temperatures, goosebumps skittered up and down her arms.

It wasn't until they'd begun the third verse that she noticed Mr. Natsach wasn't singing. The realization jarred her from worship, and she opened an eye to look. He stood still, arms crossed, scowling at the rapt, uplifted faces around him.

Scowling? Could it be... Yes, that was it; he didn't understand. He didn't know the Yasha. Had never met Him in his meah. Had never had the opportunity to worship Him, to commune with Him, to revel in His favor.

The tragedy of his condition stabbed her heart. Despite his animal masculinity, he wasn't all man, as Lissy had said; with no living spirit, he was but half a man.

How was it possible? Hadn't all the Old Gannahans known the Yasha?

THE LAST TOQEPH

His vibrant violet glance swung her way, and she jumped, closed her eye and her meah, and stretched her hands higher. Her face burned as she imagined the wild man's scorching glare sweeping across it.

She felt sick. The man was foreign. Frightening. A bit of breeze wafted his scent her way, and she envisioned herself clinging to the Yasha's hands to steady herself as she stood on wobbly legs.

32

When Daviyd felt Ra'anan's eye upon him, he glanced her way. She closed up in an instant, as if horrified by the touch of his eye.

Such a strange child. Her revulsion was much like Adam's. The young giant towered on his right, haughty and distant, too wrapped up in himself this evening to give Daviyd more than a cursory greeting.

The little brother, on the other hand, was different. Of all the people Daviyd had met so far, he felt most comfortable with young Hushai. But the boy entered into the song to the Yasha wholeheartedly, arms raised and meah directed to some mysterious Outlandish deity that no true Gannahan would have anything to do with. Even the toqeph admitted the Yasha focused his attention on Earth. So why did her ancestor, Hoseh the Wicked, bring him here? And why did the toqephites flock to him?

And why did he speak to thine ab? The thought seemed to float on the song. And it was a lovely song. The Natsachs were better singers—a wave of homesickness swept over him at the thought of their music around the fire in the evenings being sung without him—but for a gathering of Outsiders, it was strangely moving. It must have been their corporate emotion that sucked him in and carried him with it.

The song ended, and for a moment, no one spoke, as if the people reveled in the afterglow of the experience. Then the bald-topped, rotund man on the stage smiled and cast his gaze around the pavilion. Though he spoke that Outsider language, Daviyd was able to follow the drift. These people had no meahs, but their faces and body language were as expressive as a Gannahan's, and it was possible to make an imperfect connection with their minds.

THE LAST TOQEPH

Best as Daviyd could tell, the man welcomed everyone to the party and gave permission to begin the meal, which had already been placed on each table in covered tureens. After delivering his short bit of gibberish, the smiling man stepped down and went to his seat.

At about the same time, a woman and a man approached. Mumbling something that sounded apologetic, the man reached across the table to pick up a bottle of blend. He then opened it and filled the old Karkar's glass. Meanwhile, the woman stood between the youngest girl's seat and the littlest brother's — Tamah and Ittai, if he recalled correctly — and lifted the lid of the tureen.

The aroma wafting up in the steam made Daviyd's mouth water. The woman ladled a scoop of rich, red stew into a bowl and set it in front of Tamah.

"Ummm!" Tamah inhaled the steam and grinned, and the woman filled another bowl for Ittai.

Conversation had started all around. Daviyd glanced about the pavilion and saw that only at the toqeph's table were there people serving. Elsewhere, people poured their own blend and dished up their own stew.

When the woman placed the steaming bowl in front of him, Daviyd noted her earring, upon which was stamped the *aleph* character. He glanced at the man distributing the blend. He wore the same hoop with the aleph on a flattened area.

Daviyd picked up his bowl and sipped the sauce. It was even tastier than it smelled. With his fingers, he pulled a chunk of something out of it and tasted. It burst in his mouth with a spicy fruitiness. The next chunk proved to be a small bit of tender meat. Fruit and meat in a spicy-sweet sauce.

He glanced again at the earring on the serving man, now on the other side of the table. He'd seen no jewelry like it anywhere else in the settlement. It had to mean something. Consumed with curiosity, he turned to Adam. "The man who doth pour the blend. He weareth an earring. Why?"

The question seemed to jar Adam from his thoughts. "Hm? Oh. The hoop with the aleph insignia doth indicate they are the property of the house of Atarah."

The man emptied his bottle into a glass then picked up a fresh bottle from the table. These people were owned? Daviyd tried to recall his history

THE LAST TOQEPH

lessons from before the Flood. Something about this seemed familiar. Why couldn't he remember?

The toqeph had been in conversation with the children, but now she turned toward Daviyd. "How dost thou find the red course, Mr. Natsach? The stew is called *naziyd*. It's one of mine em's favorite recipes."

He licked his lips. "She was not a Natsach, was she? For this is truly delicious."

Emma chuckled. "Nay. She was of the Chen family in the province of Am. This stew is typical of that region's cuisine."

Katarina joined in the topic of recipes and seasonings, while Jerry, Jax, and Jillian discussed child rearing and education with Adam. On the other end of the table, the toqeph's husband spoke with Hushai, gesturing with his hands and drawing invisible diagrams with a finger on the table. Daviyd thought it had something to do with agriculture, but he couldn't follow it.

The whole pavilion rang with the sound of eating and conversations, punctuated by scattered laughter.

The heavyset man rose from his table near the stage then mounted the steps. What he said sounded like a call to give thanks to those who prepared the food. Immediately, the festival ground erupted with shouts of "Thank you!" along with hands pounding on tables and feet stomping the pavilion floor. The people in the grass shouted and pounded as well, but they couldn't make much noise with their feet.

Daviyd joined them, but he wondered that so much preparation would go into a festival in which only one dish was served. The stew had been delicious, but he'd only had a small amount, and the tureens sat forlorn and empty on the table. Even Adam and his father, whose size would indicate huge appetites, didn't ask for more.

When the appreciation died down, Mr. Kotila spoke again. Something about partaking of the rest of the meal. Ah, so there was more to come. That was reassuring. But the man said something else as well.

Beside Daviyd, Ra'anan stiffened. Then she rose, patting her mouth, and laid her napkin on the table before heading for the stage. She'd hardly touched her food.

With the spot between them vacated, Daviyd turned to Hushai. "What doth transpire next?"

THE LAST TOQEPH

Hushai slid to Ra'anan's empty seat. "Music. Ra'anan is in a group of girls called the Fourblers, because they are all in the Fourth Level of education."

Daviyd nodded. "Do they warble like birds?"

"Some birds shriek." Hushai grinned. "But the Fourblers are not bad to listen to. Mrs. Ayo—that is, Bisa Ayo. She is married to Baako. They went not with the Bushatites."

Daviyd didn't know what any of that meant but didn't wish to interrupt, and Hushai went on without pause. "All the Ayos are fine singers. Abba saith they could have been professional entertainers in other worlds. Mrs. Ayo is instructor to the Fourblers, so they always give a good performance."

While the boy spoke, one of the servants approached. She called the boy "Master Hushai" and apparently asked if he'd like her to remove the girl's bowl from the table.

Hushai answered with a shake of his head and a gesture toward the empty bowl at his own place.

The woman nodded and picked up his bowl, then continued around the table removing empty dishes.

Hushai set to work on the abandoned stew. "If Ra'anan wanteth it not, I shall be happy to dispose of it for her."

Twenty or so girls assembled on the platform. As Hushai had promised, the girls did well despite there being no Natsach among them. But rather than sit and listen, the people talked among themselves and moved about. It was good the music was somehow amplified and distributed throughout the grounds, or only those nearest the stage could have heard it.

Again, it was only the toqeph's table that was cleared by servants. Elsewhere, two or three people from each table removed the used dishes. They stacked them in bins on the ground then picked up the next course from long tables off to the sides of the pavilion. This course consisted of pale green leaves on a platter and bowls containing something else, Daviyd wasn't sure what.

The girls sang three songs, all of them enjoyable. Though the people didn't seem to be listening, they stomped and pounded their appreciation when the singers left the stage. The servants were distributing the next course when Ra'anan returned.

241

THE LAST TOQEPH

"Your music was lovely," Daviyd told her as she sat beside him.

She flushed, refusing to look at him. "I thank thee."

The girl was as unwilling to speak as Adam. Daviyd felt as if he sat between two grunting beasts.

This time, the food was served in the reverse from last time, eldest to youngest. Daviyd watched Jerry across the table as he laid a generous pinch of some minced material from the bowl into the center of a curving green leaf. He then rolled the leaf around the filling and took a bite, paying little heed to the juice dripping from the other end. At the end of the table, the toqeph and the old Karkar did the same.

Interesting. When Daviyd's portion came, he found it a succulent, if messy, treat.

One course followed another, with a variety of music filling in the gaps. The next two courses were both in the blue food group: slices of a deep purple vegetable pickled in a sweet-sour brine, and blue powlroot sliced and fried. The white selections were a flaky fish and sheber pasta baked with powlcurd cheese.

People carried away the bins of dirty dishes and brought in a supply of clean ones. Some stopped by to speak with the toqeph, her husband, or the Nasi. Many appeared to hope for an introduction to Daviyd, but the toqeph didn't always accommodate them. The children scampered off to visit friends at other tables. It seemed disorganized, but in a relaxed and happy way.

The musical number that interested him the most, and the one that captured the full attention of most of the partiers, was a *machowl*. The ancient art form was a beautiful combination of poetry and dance wherein a performer recited a poem while a chorus danced to the music of their own wordless song, enacting the story related by the poet. The legend told by this machowl was an ancient Natsach tale of love and devotion against all odds. When it ended and the artists took their bows, Daviyd hooted his appreciation and pounded the table until his hands felt bruised.

The Karkar was off somewhere, and the toqeph summoned Daviyd to sit beside her. "Dost thou know the children's song 'One-Two-Three'?"

He thought he knew the one she meant but wasn't sure. When he hesitated, she sang the first part. "One, two, three, me and thee. Ab and son, one and one."

"Of course." Every child knew that song.

THE LAST TOQEPH

"And the dance?"

Daviyd nodded. "Yea, if it be the one in the song that concludes the Festival of Voices."

Her smile transformed her face. "Thou knowest the Festival song?"

"A Gannahan doth always learn it in childhood."

"That was true at one time." Her expression turned to one of regret. "Though I have considered doing so, I have not taught it to the settlers. It is so much to learn. And..." She sighed. "The Festival of Voices cannot be held except at the Cliffs of Arawts. Thou hast been there? Thou and thy people have sung in that valley?"

Her longing touched him. "Yea. Before the Flood, we kept the Festival." Strange, though, how his memory of the event was so dim.

She sighed. "It was the best day of the year." Were those tears in her eyes? She blinked, and they were gone. "The people do not know the whole Festival song, but the children know the one part, One-Two-Three. They will perform it next. Would you like to join them? I would love to see it danced by—" She smiled. "By a real Gannahan."

Their meah connection nearly crackled with intensity, and her sorrow and longing for all she had lost made him light-headed. He stroked his beard, willing the tactile sensation to ground him in the immediate reality and keep him from being swept away with her memories.

"There?" He nodded toward the stage. "For all the people to see?"

"Yea. All the children will dance. Then they will go to the bonfire, roast the powlworms, and play until Black Slumber. We adults will continue our celebration here." She leaned forward, brows lifted. "Wilt thou dance with them?"

He grinned. "I shall, if the toqeph wouldst as well."

She moved back as if to avoid being struck by the suggestion, then chuckled. "Very well, then. We shall show these Earthers how a Gannahan doth dance."

Holding Everett in his lap, Adam sat at the table with his in-laws when the call came for the children aged five and older to come to the stage to sing. As his children were too young to participate, he didn't pay much attention but continued telling Elise's parents and Everett about baby Joseph's arrival.

THE LAST TOQEPH

"She came through it like a Gannahan. Three pushes, and there he was. And then she laughed and said, 'Whew! That wasn't so bad.'"

Everett pulled on his beard. "Where's Emma now? Why can't I see her?"

"She's resting, sweet. Having a baby is hard work, and she was up all night doing it. But your mamaw and pawpaw will bring you home tomorrow afternoon. All my side of the family will be there too. We'll have a little party of our own."

Everett put one hand on each side of Adam's face and pressed his nose to Adam's, crossing his eyes. "You look funny up close, Abba."

Adam leaned into him, widening his eyes. "No, *you* look funny up close."

His father-in-law gasped. "Take a look at that!"

"What?" Adam's beard was in Everett's grip and he couldn't turn his head.

His mother-in-law looked where her husband pointed. "Oh, my. Did you know they were doing that, Adam?"

He pulled his son's hands from his face and turned toward the stage where the children were gathering. Everett stood and pointed, yelling in his ear, "There's Grandma!"

Adam lifted the boy off his lap and set him on the bench beside him. "Yes, it certainly is."

"What's the toqeph doing up there?" his mother-in-law asked. "She's never danced with the children before."

His father-in-law watched the singers. "And look. The visitor, too."

Adam gaped. "I have no idea..."

It was Emma who had taught the children the song when he was young. It was her idea that they perform it at festivals, though others had taken over the task of teaching and directing them. When Adam was little, he used to beg her to perform it with them. But she always refused. "Nobody wants to see me up there. People want to hear their children sing, not an old woman." So who had persuaded her to get up there now?

The song began. All the children on stage sang and danced, though the voices of the older ones in the back contributed the most and their movements were more precise. But Adam doubted the audience, save possibly a few doting parents, had eyes for anyone except the two dancers on either side. Emma and Natsach. They moved with precision and graceful

THE LAST TOQEPH

energy. They sang as they danced, their clear voices rising above the others and ringing throughout the pavilion. Their faces glowed, their animation speaking of a joy of life, a delight in their Gannahan-ness.

All conversation stopped and all eyes turned toward the stage. As if fueled by Emma and Natsach's vigor, the children performed as never before. Many in the audience sang and danced by their tables. Before it was over, most in the crowd were on their feet joining in the song.

At the end, the hooting and pounding lasted for several minutes. On stage, the children hugged each other, jumping and laughing, before climbing down and running to their parents. Emma and Natsach slipped back to their table. Abba wrapped his arms around Emma and spoke in her ear. Grinning, Jerry and Jax butted the heels of their hands against Natsach's.

Everett pounded Adam's leg. "Why aren't you applauding, Abba? Didn't you like it?"

33

Lileela drifted into a dull, fuzzy wakefulness. Peering through unfocused eyes, she saw Faris nearby working on a computer. She tried to speak, but all she could do was croak.

He looked up with a start then smiled. "Welcome back! How do you feel?" He rose and moved to her bed.

Her mouth was so dry she could hardly get words through it. "Where have I been?"

He held her hand and kissed her forehead. "In a Gannahan healing sleep. You've been out for three days."

His breath on her face revived her a little, but his answer made no sense. "Who was?"

"You were." He chuckled. "Adam was just here to check on you. He said the wounds are closed and you should be waking soon."

"I think—I think I knew that." She yawned, and her dry lip split. "Or maybe I dreamed it."

His gentle touch smoothed back her hair. "Do you dream in a healing sleep? What's it like?"

She yawned again. "I don't know. I slept through the whole thing." She giggled. "I don't remember a bit of it. Last I knew, Lynne was here, and now I wake up to your handsome face." His image blurred.

He kissed the tears away. "But you said you dreamed about Adam."

"It wasn't a dream, really." She licked her lip. "I think I knew he was here."

Were those horribly battered legs really healed? She lifted her head to try to see, but a sheet covered them. "And he was worried about me. But didn't you say the wounds are closed?"

THE LAST TOQEPH

"Yes, completely. He was very pleased. Want to see? I'll help you sit."

She tried to lift her upper body a little then sank back down, shaking her head. "No. Not yet. Let me wake up more first."

"That's fine. But you'll be impressed. Adam says the new skin is thin and tender, so you'll have to be careful to not bump it. But the fractures are knitting, and the bones are straight."

"Then what's he so worried about?"

Faris squeezed her hand then kissed it. "The coma concerned him. He's never seen the Gannahan healing sleep before, and I think he was a little afraid you were in too deep. But your father assured him everything was completely normal." He shook his head. "I agree with Adam, though. It was pretty scary."

She smiled. "I didn't think you were afraid of anything."

"Not of much." His voice broke, and he kissed her lips.

His emotion roused her from the remaining languor. Wrapping her arms around his neck, she returned his kiss. "I think I'm ready to sit up now."

He put his arm behind her and raised her as if she weighed nothing.

She relished the feel of his strong arm at her back. "Have you been here the whole time?"

"Mostly."

Her head spun, and she was glad he was there to hang onto. "How sweet of you! But there was no need. I didn't care if you were here or not, I was dead to the world."

"Yeah." He propped a pillow behind her for support. "That's what we were afraid of. How're you doing? Comfy?"

She nodded. "How's Uncle Kughie?"

"Driving your aunt crazy, no doubt. But he's recovering. Should be no permanent damage to the knee."

"The Yasha be praised."

Faris gently pulled down the sheet. She flexed her feet at the ankles. "Wow. I feel a little stiff, but I wouldn't call it painful." She leaned forward. "I can't really see. What do they look like?"

"Pink and new. The skin has a funny texture to it, but Adam says that will clear up as you grow additional layers."

She giggled. "I wish I could see them, but I'm afraid to move too much. What did he say about using them?"

THE LAST TOQEPH

"Nothing. And I didn't think to ask. But he did tell me to give him a call when you woke up." He reached for his messenger. "Hungry?"

It suddenly occurred to her that she was. "Famished. But mostly thirsty. Is there any water around here?"

"I'll get you some." Faris spoke into his messenger. "Hi. She just woke up. Yes, she looks great. Says she's hungry."

"Famished," she corrected.

"Famished. And thirsty too. It's okay to give her some water, isn't it?" He listened, nodding. "Oh, and she was asking about moving around." Another pause. "How much is too much? Really? Okay. Great. Thanks." When he disconnected the call, he looked unusually happy.

"What did he say? And where's my water?"

"Out here." He left the room, raising his voice to be heard as he walked. "He said he put some food in the chillbox for when you wake up. You should take it easy at first. Give your stomach a chance to get used to working again." He returned with a bottle of water and a glass. "I'll give you a few sips to start out."

Lileela's stomach felt beyond hollow as she eyed the water. "I don't see the food."

"Let's see how you handle this first." He poured a centimeter into the glass and handed it to her. "And he said you can move around. He wants to look you over before you put any weight on your legs, but if all goes as expected, he'll kick you out of here today. He seems to think we'll both be better off at home."

She drained the glass and extended it toward him. "Home? I like the sound of that."

"So do I. A lot."

When he didn't take the glass, she shook it at him. "More! More!"

"We'll give it a minute." He took the glass but made no move to put anything in it.

"Okay. But just one minute and not a second longer. I feel like I could drink a river."

He chuckled and poured two centimeters. "Let's try this."

He insisted she drink in small increments, resting between each, before he agreed to give her food. Her stomach was gurgling loudly by the time he finally brought her a small bowl of micken he'd warmed in a quickheater.

THE LAST TOQEPH

She took it from him and inhaled the savory scent. "Is there any blend around here?"

He shook his head. "I didn't see any. I had to thin it with water."

"No problem. Just asking."

While she ate, he sat in the chair and watched her every move. "Oh, by the way. We had a little excitement while you were sleeping."

"Hmph." Her gnawing hunger made it hard to eat slowly. In an attempt to not overdo it, she lowered the bowl and wiped her mouth on the back of her hand. "Elise have her baby?"

He gave her a napkin. "Yesterday morning. Mother and baby are both doing fine."

"Good." She slurped more micken, trying not to wish that one day she'd be the mother in that cliché.

He leaned back in his chair and laid one leg across his knee. "But that's not the big news."

"Don't know that I want to hear the rest." She took another slurp. Even without the blend, this micken was indescribably good. "I've had enough excitement to last a lifetime."

"Oh, but you'll want to hear this."

Something in his manner made her lower her bowl and give him her full attention.

In the kitchen, Daviyd turned the handle on the faucet. Water burst from the spigot into the micken bowl, splashing the front of his shirt. He shut off the faucet immediately, but it was too late. His tunic was splattered with water and the remainder of the breakfast that had clung to the bowl.

Lifting his shirt, Daviyd nibbled off the bits of gruel. The idea of rinsing food down the sink had bothered him to begin with. Since the remnants had come to him like this, he'd make use of them.

Once he'd eaten every trace of the grains, he smoothed out the crinkled fabric and resumed rinsing the dishes.

Jerry and Katarina were truly hospitable. Cleaning up after breakfast in their absence seemed the only reasonable thing to do. Katarina had duties that took her away early. She was gone before Daviyd had gotten up, and Jerry excused himself immediately after breakfast.

THE LAST TOQEPH

"Hushai will be along in a little while," Jerry had told him. "He shall take thee to Mayor Tischtuch in First Town. While thou dost wait, please make thyself comfortable. Wouldst thou like to peruse the news?"

He showed Daviyd how to make the window in the sitting room wall light up. An *open* symbol, a dot within a circle, floated across the window, and he demonstrated how to make it hover over an item of interest and then make that item fill the whole window. Creating this perplexing display was what Jerry said Katarina did when she left the house every night toward the end of Black Slumber. It gave access to the information she shared with the settlers as Minister of Information Dissemination.

After Daviyd arranged the dishes in a cabinet called a dishwasher—which made no sense, since Daviyd had just washed them, hadn't he?—he went to the sitting room and picked up the device Jerry had used to make the window light up.

Pressing the same button Jerry had pressed produced the same result. Daviyd smiled.

But the writing was foreign. How had Jerry changed it to the civilized language? Daviyd didn't remember, and studying the device yielded no clue. He pushed several buttons one by one, but nothing made the view through the window look right. His frustration mounted. When one of the buttons made the window go dark again, he left it that way and dropped the device onto the sofa.

Jerry had said to make himself at home. This place was nothing like Daviyd's home, but he might as well explore and see more of what an Outsider's home looked like. Starting by the front door, he examined everything he found, whether lights or buttons or furniture or loose objects, either sitting around or in drawers and cabinets.

Some of the things made sense and others were perplexing, and he didn't know how to distinguish what was of true Gannahan origin, what had been brought here from Outside, and what had been made on Gannah but inspired by Outside influences.

When he removed things from boxes or drawers, he wasn't always able to make them fit back in the way he'd found them. No matter. Jerry or Katarina would know how they should be arranged. In the dining room, the boxes stacked everywhere were all marked with the *locked* symbol, a dot in a triangle. He left those alone, for one didn't open a locked container.

THE LAST TOQEPH

He was in Jerry and Katarina's bedroom when he heard the front door open and Hushai's voice call, "Mr. Natsach?"

He dropped the small, frilly item of clothing he'd been puzzling over back in the drawer and went toward the sitting room. "Good morning. Mr. Maddox hath told me thou wouldst come, but he did not say at what time on the dial."

He was surprised to see two boys in the sitting room, Hushai and Ittai. Both gave him curious looks. Hushai said, "Wert thou — is that not Mr. and Mrs. Maddox's bedchamber?"

"Yea. He hath said thou wouldst take me to the man with the false hand, but said not why. What is my business with him?"

Hushai gave another glance toward the bedroom before answering. "He will show thee First Town, where most of the people live and all the shops are. Thou wilt see many things there. My brother wished to come with us. Emma hath granted her permission, provided thou hast no objection."

Ittai gazed up at Daviyd, hope in his face and his meah.

Daviyd smiled. "Why should I object?"

"Then let us go!" Hushai took a step toward the door then glanced down at Daviyd's feet. "Dost thou wish to put on shoes?"

He shook his head. "Nay. My feet were imprisoned all yesterday. I prefer to let them breathe this morn."

Ittai sat on the floor and tugged off his shoes without untying them. "Goody! I shall go barefoot too."

Hushai removed his as well, then hopped up and took Daviyd's hand. "Come! We have no need for haste, so we can walk instead of taking the tube."

"Or run," Ittai said. "Emma seldom rideth the rail. Only when she must be somewhere quickly. She doth ever say it be better for the health to stand than sit, to walk than stand, to run than walk."

Daviyd let Hushai lead him out of the apartment and into the hall. "She doth speak truly. Shall we run?"

Hushai pulled back on Daviyd's hand as if to stop him. "We may not run indoors."

"But once we are outside we can!" Ittai took off at a fast walk.

Hushai dropped Daviyd's hand and hurried to catch up.

Cute kids. Too bad they weren't real Gannahans.

251

THE LAST TOQEPH

Adam set a bowl of micken on the table in front of Elise. "Would you like that thinned with a little blend?"

She wrinkled her freckled nose. "No, thanks. It's your family that does that, not mine." She picked up the bowl. "I'd take a little blend in a glass, though, if you offered me one."

Adam picked up the bottle. "Diluted, as usual?"

"Definitely." She slurped a little micken but pulled away. "Ooh, that's hot!" She fanned her mouth then sipped the watered blend he handed her. "Guess I'll let it cool a bit."

Adam thinned his own breakfast with blend then sat at the table with her. "Mrs. Groenewald is a gem. When I got home last night, the whole house was clean as a luglit's whiskers."

Elise dipped her scraper in the micken and licked the thick porridge off the tip. "Yeah. She made a racket doing it, too. I couldn't sleep until she finally finished."

Adam's ears twitched. He'd been hoping for something like, *Yes, wasn't that sweet?* "We should do something to thank her."

"What did you have in mind?"

"Nothing in particular." Adam shrugged. "Maybe when you make *tappuwach* butter you could give her a few jars. She always says how she loves that stuff."

He got the idea from Elise's demeanor she was about to object. Probably say something like *How am I going to make tappuwach butter with two little boys underfoot?* But she gave a shrug of her own. "Sure, she'd like that." She slurped her breakfast. "So Mom and Dad are bringing Everett this afternoon?"

Adam nodded as he ate.

"Good. I'm a little jealous that you got to see him last night and I didn't. Does he miss me, do you think?"

"Of course. All us boys are very attached to our emmas."

She smiled then lifted her bowl to her lips. "I can hardly wait to introduce him to his little brother."

"And my family will be here for lunch."

Above the bowl, her blue eyes widened. "All of them?"

"Don't worry." He chuckled. "They're bringing the food. They just want to see you and the baby. They won't be here for long."

THE LAST TOQEPH

"I guess it's a good thing Mrs. Groenewald picked things up around here, then." She set down her bowl and took a sip of blend. "How's Lileela? Still in that Gannahan coma-thing?"

He nodded. "It's strange, but effective. What I can't figure out is how she can survive with no food or water. Now that the wounds are healed over, I hope she'll be waking soon. I wouldn't think she could go much longer."

Elise scraped the remaining porridge into a puddle on the bowl's edge. "Your mother was in a sleep like that for weeks, wasn't she? When she was recovering from the Plague?"

"Yes, she was." He pursed his lips. "And it takes its toll." He could still hear the sorrow in his father's voice as he described the expected long-term effect of such a suspended animation. But before she could ask for an explanation, his messenger buzzed.

He snapped it up. "Faris! Oh, good. How does she seem?" Faris's answer sent joy coursing through Adam's veins. He watched Elise eat while he listened to Faris and gave instruction. "Let me finish up here and then I'll be in to take a look. See you in a bit."

By the time he ended the conversation, Elise had finished her micken and begun to plow through a bowl of shaqorberries.

Adam's ears smiled. "Still eating for two? That's fine. You'll need your strength keeping up with my boys."

She smiled back. "So Lileela's awake? You're going back to the clinic?"

He scarfed down the rest of his breakfast. "Yes, and yes. You'll be okay while I'm gone?"

"Of course, my darling. Why wouldn't I be?"

Adam rose, leaned across the table, and kissed her. "You're an amazing woman."

THE LAST TOQEPH

34

Ra'anan held Joseph in her arms—a solid, warm, somewhat frightening bundle. Like a doll, but too easily damaged. When Mrs. Finnegan reached for him, Ra'anan was happy to hand him over—carefully.

Abba cleared his throat. "We should be going. We're taking up too much space."

It was true. The Pik family filled the sitting room, leaving Mr. and Mrs. Finnegan hardly a cranny to call their own.

Beaming, Emma put her finger in the baby's hand, and his tiny fingers curled around it. "It's been wonderful meeting you, Joseph. We'll see you again soon." She kissed him, gently slid her finger from the infant's grip then gave Elise a hug. "He's beautiful."

Ra'anan wove her way through the crowd to the kitchen where she picked up the empty food containers. After farewells all around, the family filed out the door, onto the landing, down the corkscrew stairway, and into the courtyard.

Abba scanned the sky. "Glad to see it clouding up. The sheber crop could use some rain."

The boys ran toward the fountain, Tamah following. Emma called after them. "Hushai, Ittai! You've already splashed in there once today. We don't have time for it again."

They slowed to a stop and turned to face her, but Tamah kept running.

Emma frowned. "Tamah, you too."

The child froze like a statue, giggling.

Emma motioned the children toward her. "Come back, all three of you. If you want to run, we can run home. And if you want to get wet, I think Gannah will grant your wish before we reach Gullach."

THE LAST TOQEPH

"Abba, will you run with us?" Tamah scampered back with the boys.

He shook his head. "No, I'm past the age for that. Anyway, I'm going to the lab, not home. We've fallen behind on our research schedule." He bent and kissed Emma. "Don't look for me until after the dinner hour."

Ra'anan watched him head for the clinic. "Can we go see Lileela again?"

Emma shook her head. "She needs to build up her strength, which she can't do with us underfoot." She herded the children down the lane that tunneled through the clinic building on its way to the chatsr gate. "Perhaps we can visit tomorrow after she's settled in at home." Emma's voice echoed as they passed under the arch.

Ra'anan expelled a happy sigh. "I'm so thankful she's going to be okay. Her and Uncle Kughurrrro both. And that Elise had her baby, and Adam got home from his quest, and everything's working out. The Yasha's so good."

Emma nodded. "Yes, He most certainly is. But you know, He's good even when it seems like everything's falling apart."

"What do you mean?"

"He's not good only because He gives us what we want. He was good when the storms tore all Gannah apart six years ago. He was good when all the people died from the Plague. He was good when His own Son was tortured to death on Earth."

Ra'anan wasn't sure what to think about that, so she said nothing. By that time, they'd reached the gate, and the boys unlatched the two heavy wooden doors. The hinges worked smoothly and the doors opened without difficulty. But the road beyond had aged with less grace. The pavement had crumbled to gravel and the grass encroached on either side, leaving a rustic track only wide enough for two to walk abreast.

The main road it led to, which ran between First Town and Gullach, was in no better condition. In the old photos, the Qatsyr Road was wide and bustling, with paved branches passing through well-tended gardens to each chatsr. Now, the regions beyond the walls were wild, the domain of beasts. Travel during daylight hours was usually safe, especially in a group. But only the brave—and those well able to defend themselves—traveled abroad at night.

The boys closed the gates then scampered to catch up. Turning onto the main road toward home, Ra'anan's skin prickled as if someone or

THE LAST TOQEPH

something were watching them. She turned in a slow circle as she walked, but saw nothing out of the ordinary.

"I thought we were going to run," Ittai said.

Emma nodded. "Everybody willing?"

Ra'anan liked to run as much as anyone, and Tamah, though only six, was long-legged enough that she could keep up. Without speaking but sensing agreement in their meahs, they took off at the same instant.

It always felt good to use her muscles, and pulling all that sweet Gannahan air into her lungs made Ra'anan feel alive. But today, she welcomed the speed even more. The lowering sky promised to fulfill Emma's prediction of rain any minute. A run through a shower would be fun, but now that they were outside the chatsr walls, the breeze grew stronger and the temperature dropped. She saw the run as a lively competition with the storm to see who could reach Gullach first.

They ran hard, wordlessly communing in their meahs about their enjoyment of the activity, the scenery's beauty, their love of Gannah. It must be sad to be part of a family that had to speak aloud to be understood.

But all the while, Emma kept glancing at the sky. The dark clouds covered the landscape, so there was no need to look upward to check the weather. When she fixed her attention on something high above and slowed to a stop, the others straggled back to see what was going on.

Tamah reached her first. "What is it, Emma?"

Craning her neck, Emma didn't speak, and her meah seemed focused elsewhere.

Ra'anan and the others stared in the direction she looked. The sky was so dark the stars were visible.

No, those weren't stars. They were lights, high in the sky. And moving. Ra'anan gasped. "Emma! What is that?"

The others stared upward, and Ra'anan sensed their growing fear. "It's nothing to be worried about, is it?" But even as she spoke, hoping to reassure the younger ones, she knew the answer.

Lifting a "wait a minute" finger, Emma reached for her messenger. "Jerry." Her steady voice held an urgency that wouldn't take a meah to detect. "Drop whatever you're doing and meet me at the airport. You and Jax both. Also, Järn Hand and Faris's old team, Safiy, Esam, Adil, and Binya. But don't bother Faris. Have everyone gather at the terminal as quickly as they can." She closed her eyes and took a deep breath. "I need Pik."

THE LAST TOQEPH

Ra'anan knew that last statement was merely Emma wishing to have her husband by her side, and she was surprised Emma would speak it aloud. Jerry wouldn't understand. He'd summon Abba along with the others. But Ra'anan said nothing. Emma was disturbed, and that made Ra'anan's world seem to heave. The toqeph of Gannah, afraid and uncertain?

Emma nodded at whatever Mr. Maddox said in reply. "Yes, that's correct. We have company. And I have no idea who it might be." She disconnected and looked at the children standing around her.

Tamah's lip quivered, and Emma bent and took the child's face in her hands. "No need to fear. The Yasha is good, remember?"

All the children nodded. Ra'anan guessed she looked as scared as the others, with their faces pale and their eyes wide.

Emma stood upright and gave them each a determined smile. "Go on home. The men and I will meet the visitors to see what they want. The Yasha will be with us all."

Ra'anan wondered why Emma wasn't coming with them. She could take the tube from Gullach. Wasn't that the best way to get to the airport?

Emma answered her unspoken question. "Go. I can get there faster if I cut across the field."

Of course. It was a straight shot from here. Ra'anan nodded, and the boys and Tamah each gave a quick bow. "Yes, Emma." Then together they turned and ran toward home.

Tamah slipped her hand in Ra'anan's as they went. The boys ran ahead, but not very far. The four shared their concerns through their meahs. Tamah wasn't old enough to remember, but she'd heard about the difficulties that ensued when the Karkar ship came. Not all visitors brought trouble; the last one had brought Faris and his men, and that was a good thing. But when Emma's heart quailed, it didn't bode well for Gannah.

The clouds to the west opened their floodgates over the sheber fields, and the rain chased the children as they ran. It reached them before they'd gotten to the palace gardens, and despite a last burst of speed, they were drenched before they made it to the gates. They ran beneath the trellis of flowering *gaph* vines overarching the main road through the courtyard, the broad leaves above them flapping madly in the wind.

Ra'anan brushed dripping hair from her eyes as they approached the doors. "She was right. Gannah gave us a wetting before we got home."

THE LAST TOQEPH

Tamah's lip quivered. "I want Emma."

Ra'anan agreed with all her heart.

She remembered how preoccupied Emma had been when the Karkar threatened to attack. She'd spent night and day in her tower office, when she wasn't in meetings and negotiations. It was as if her own family didn't matter to her. And now she was absent again when they needed her. In the vacuum, the younger ones looked to Ra'anan for guidance, but she had none to offer.

The doors slid back and they entered the vestibule. "Take your shoes off." She bent and unlaced her own.

Hushai said, "We aren't wearing any."

"Well, you are, Tamah."

Tamah quit hugging herself to keep warm and obeyed.

Removing their shoes, of course, didn't prevent the rest of their clothes from dripping. Ra'anan was glad there weren't many people in this part of the palace to see them as they hurried to their apartment. Two or three people smiled as they passed, or made some obvious remark about their being caught in the rain. But no one seemed concerned. They had no idea Gannah was likely to be under attack at any minute.

The apartment was empty and forlorn. Miami and Faye had been cleaning when the family left, but they were finished by now and performed other chores about the palace. The only welcome the children received was the cold glowlights turning on when they came through the door.

They stood in the entry, each wishing for Emma. Ra'anan tried not to sound scared. "We should change clothes. Put your wet things in the bathtub, and then I'll take them down to the laundry and dry them."

Hushai glared at her. "Emma wants us to stay here."

Emma hadn't verbalized it, but her command to go home did, in fact, carry that connotation. "Well, then, hang them on the little laundry rack in the bathroom. And when we run out of space there, on towel rods." She ushered them through the sitting room. "We'll find places for them."

Ittai asked, "After we're changed, what do we do then?"

Ra'anan had only been Tamah's age the last time the planet was threatened, but she remembered one aspect of how Abba and Emma had handled it. "We'll pray."

THE LAST TOQEPH

Daviyd followed the mayor around First Town that morning, with Hushai helping to translate and Ittai grinning alongside him. Most of the buildings held residences, particularly on the upper levels. But on the street level, the chatsr was home to a number of shops and businesses.

Everything a person could want could be found there, whether at Lucas's drygoods, the grocery, bakery, or meat market. There was a woodcrafter, a place called the tech shop, and an herbalist, whose building was overwhelmingly fragrant.

In addition to mobile carts selling food, two establishments called restaurants contained tables and chairs where a person could sit down and be served a fully prepared meal for the asking. The marvels seemed to have no end, and Hushai assured him there was still plenty more to be seen.

Shortly after the timedial rolled into orange High Day, Hushai and his brother left to meet their family at Adam's for the midday meal, and Jax joined Daviyd and the mayor at one of the restaurants. After a meal of stir-fried vegetables in sauce over tender sheber grains, they thanked the proprietors of the restaurant and headed for the machine shop.

The entrance was off an alley at the far side of the chatsr. As they crossed the courtyard, children playing in the green at the foot of the timedial tower paused in their game to wave. Daviyd waved back and tried to connect with their meahs. Which, of course, they didn't have. Such a strange feeling to find a windowless wall when trying to communicate with these people. How could they stand living in such isolation? He reached for his mother and the others in Yereq and was reassured when they connected. No, he was not alone. He would never be alone, as long as his people lived.

A chill made him clench his teeth at a sudden thought. What must it have been like for the toqeph in the grip of the plague, to reach for others in her meah and find no answer? She'd been alone in the universe for decades, or however long it took her to find a mate and birth children. Daviyd couldn't have endured it. He almost understood how she could lower herself to marry a half-Karkar. Appalling as that relationship was, it must have been better than the deep loneliness.

The mayor led the way through the shop entrance into a wonderland of metallic, oily smells.

The floor was unfinished wood, gouged here and there but worn smooth by generations of booted feet. Metal shelving about the room held a variety of objects whose uses Daviyd couldn't imagine. No one was in sight,

THE LAST TOQEPH

but deep-throated machinery noises punctuated by a sharp whine indicated someone was at work nearby.

One of the roaring sounds diminished in volume and pitch until it settled into a contented, rumbling purr. A moment later, the shop's proprietor appeared. A little taller than the average settler, Matthias Craig wore a long white ponytail, and his skin was reddish and freckled. As he approached, he wiped his hands on a filthy rag. "Jax. Mayor." He made a small, polite bow to each then turned to Daviyd and said something that sounded vaguely like, "Mr. Natsach. Pleased to see you again."

They'd met at the festival the evening before, when Craig's clothes had been considerably cleaner than what he wore today. Last night, Daviyd had noticed the man's hands and forearms were darkened with a ground-in grime that scrubbing had apparently been unable to remove. It made the Outsiders' strange custom of shaking hands particularly unappealing, and Daviyd was glad he'd decided right from the first to not participate in it.

He nodded. "Thank you. They tell me thou wouldst like to show me thy shop."

Craig looked puzzled until Jax translated. Then he smiled. Giving up his valiant attempt at speaking the civilized language, he rattled off something in gibberish as he led them through the door he'd appeared from earlier. They entered a cavernous room that was uncomfortably warm despite the high ceilings. Translating Craig's chatter, Jax explained that whenever a metal part was needed for any purpose, Matthias Craig and his son Ari, who worked at a machine two rows down, were able to repair or produce it using the resources in this room.

He demonstrated the workings of some of the machines, but Jax didn't know the proper translation for much of the terminology, and everything was too far beyond Daviyd's experience for him to figure out half of what he was seeing.

When Jax's messenger went off, he asked Craig to shut down the machine he was showing them then answered the call.

"Yes, sir." He bowed. Must have been speaking to Jerry. "Yes? Yes, sir." Something in his voice made Daviyd's breath catch in his throat. "Right away. Of course sir."

He disconnected the call and turned to Daviyd and the mayor, his expression serious. "I must go." He apparently forgot to speak in Gannahan,

260

THE LAST TOQEPH

but Daviyd got the drift anyway. "We'll have to continue the tour another time."

The mayor's brows rose. "Something wrong?"

Jax didn't answer but turned to Craig. "We'll let you get back to your work. Thank you for taking the time to show us around."

The machine man shrugged and gave a dismissive wave, though Daviyd couldn't guess what he said.

Jax waved back and headed for the door. "We'll see ourselves out."

Daviyd followed, with the mayor hurrying to keep up. When they were out of the back room and breezing through the display area toward the main entrance, Tischtuch spoke again, louder. Sounded like he was demanding to know what was happening. He, too, must have felt the tension that seemed to have electrified Jax since the call.

"The toqeph has summoned the Nasi to the airport. You are not included in the summons."

Daviyd reached for the toqeph in his meah. Though the connection was weak, what he understood from the exchange made his mouth go dry.

Jax continued speaking as they passed into the alley. "If you would escort our guest back to Gullach, it would—"

Daviyd interrupted, speaking the best gibberish he could manage in order to spare Jax having to translate for the mayor. "No. I come with you."

Jax paused, his dark eyes boring into Daviyd. "Doth the toqeph approve?"

"She doth not say nay."

Jax paused then nodded. "Very well." He took off at a fast jog, and Daviyd followed.

He wasn't sure why he wanted to come. But the toqeph was alarmed. She'd called for men to stand with her to face some possible danger. He was no toqephite, but answering her call seemed the appropriate thing to do. She'd stood alone far too long.

35

Pete Finnegan slapped Adam on the back. "Great job, son! He looks like a champ."

Adam gazed down at the infant in his mother-in-law's arms. "Thank you. But your daughter is mostly responsible." He put his arm around Elise. "She delivered him like it was a walk in the park."

Elise snorted. "A walk in Nightmare Park, maybe. It wasn't as easy as it looked, you know."

Adam pulled Elise close and kissed the top of her head. "It didn't look easy. Not even a little bit. The fact that you were up and walking around right away is a marvel."

Fern stroked Joseph's tuft of curly fuzz. "He's a bruiser. What did you say he weighed? Almost five kilos?"

"Four point nine seven three. Tiny, for a Karkar."

Fern smiled. "But huge for a Finnegan. My babies were only seven, seven-and-a-half pounds. Joseph here looks like he's two months old already."

Everett, who had been clinging to Elise's legs, reached up. "Hold me, Emma!"

"Let me sit down first." She went to the sofa and sat beside her mother. He climbed into her lap and she wrapped her arms around him and squeezed. "I missed my big boy!"

"I'm bigger'n Joseph!"

She hugged him tighter. "Oh, yes. Lots."

Adam's ears smiled at the scene. No one had ever been prouder. He'd like to offer Elise more support and pay more attention to his boys, but after this sweet afternoon, every minute on the timedial would be scheduled with

THE LAST TOQEPH

other duties. "Can I offer anyone tea?" He gazed down at Everett. "With lots of honey?"

The adults agreed, but Everett shook his head. His grandmother explained. "He didn't want any breakfast, either, and I couldn't get him to eat much lunch. I think he's still full from last night."

He nodded in his mother's lap. "I love Wormfest. I ate all! Night! Long!"

"So did I." Adam offered Everett his hand. "Want to come to the kitchen with me and help with the tea? Your em's not the only one who missed you."

"I'll stay here." Everett snuggled against Elise.

Adam remembered his own insecurities every time Emma had a baby. Which happened often. "Okay, kiddo. I'll try to manage without you."

In the kitchen—which his family had left gleaming and in order—he filled the teapot at the sink then opened the tea canister. As he measured the fragrant leaves into a strainer, a wave rolling over his meah made him drop the scoop and grab a cabinet to keep from swaying.

It was a surge of communications between Emma and Daviyd, and it ran across his mind because he was on theirs. But, after briefly considering, they chose to block him.

Something big was happening. Something that could affect all of Gannah. It had to do with an incoming starship. Emma had summoned the Nasi. She'd included Natsach.

But she didn't want Adam.

Hot with cold fury, he gripped the edge of the sink, knuckles whitening.

When they entered the rail station beneath First Town, Daviyd and Jax met a giant of a man waiting for the tube. A little shorter than Adam but broader, Järn Hand had been introduced to Daviyd last night as the town magistrate. He nodded in greeting now, but before he spoke, lights flashed and an alarm sounded to signal the arrival of the tube bound for the airport.

It rushed up and slowed, and the magistrate grabbed the door handle the instant it came to a stop. The door slid back to reveal Jerry and two other men already seated inside.

THE LAST TOQEPH

The three in the tube greeted Jax and Järn as they climbed in and found seats but gave Daviyd questioning looks. Except for Jerry, who frowned.

Daviyd didn't wait for them to voice their queries. "The toqeph doth know of my coming."

Jax closed the door. As the pod started forward, Jerry let out a noisy sigh and leaned back in his seat.

Though the others remained silent, Daviyd could surmise what was on their minds and answered their question. "If Gannah be in danger, I must do what I can to defend. I am Gannah. More than any of you."

The others exchanged glances. One of them, who, except for the fullness of his beard would look barely of age, spoke to the others in passably clear speech. "He hath a point, doth he not?"

Jerry's frown now seemed more from thought than displeasure. "Mayhap." He eyed Daviyd critically. "Thou art a Gannahan, to be sure. More than we. But we are trained warriors." He gestured toward the men with him. "Ishaq and Binyamin have not purple tongues, but were raised from the cradle for war. We will be joined by three of their brethren, equally capable. And as thou canst see, the magistrate is mighty as a dowb."

"And as hairy." Daviyd ran his gaze from Järn's head nearly grazing the ceiling to his expansive chest to his massive, booted feet. "I was but fifteen when I leapt upon the back of a dowb and slit its throat."

The magistrate grunted and shifted his boot to make it bump against Daviyd's bare foot. "It is well he did not step on thee first."

The others chuckled.

Though Ishaq and Binyamin might lack purple tongues, they had Gannahan eyes—an unexpected aspect Daviyd wondered about. With their nut-brown coloring and stocky, muscular build, he might have taken them for native Gannahans except for their lack of meahs. Those Gannah-bright eyes surveyed him now with curiosity.

His gaze went back and forth between them. "Magistrate Hand doth look like a dowb. But your appearance is much like my kinsmen. How can that be?"

They glanced at Jerry. If anything, his frown had deepened, and he didn't answer. Instead, he turned on Daviyd his Earthish version of a hard glare. "Didst thou find what thou sought?"

Daviyd blinked. "What I sought?"

THE LAST TOQEPH

"In my home. Katarina was quite upset to return and find thee gone and everything in disarray. It appeared thou had searched for something with desperation."

Daviyd beetled his brow, trying to understand. "Nay. Thy provision hast been most generous. I had need of nothing."

"How, then, didst thou occupy thyself after I departed?"

"Only as thou didst bid me. If I were to consider thy home as mine, I should see what lay within the many doors and drawers. How could I enjoy thy hospitality if I knew not what it offered?"

Jerry lowered his eyes and raised a hand to his face then slowly smoothed first his mustache then his beard. "I see." He stroked his beard again. "I see."

The others watched, their expressions varying from confusion to amusement. What had Daviyd done to cause such a response? A mental review of the morning's activities yielded no clue.

Jerry lifted his gaze, his face settled, as if coming to a satisfactory decision. "And the small shoes on the floor just inside the door? They belong to the toqeph's boys?"

"Yea. When Hushai and his brother saw I wore none, they removed theirs as well."

The younger of the bright-eyed warriors seemed to fight with a grin. "Why dost thou not wear shoes? Because thy feet are not comfortable in them?"

"That is so!" Daviyd experienced a swell of gratitude for the man's understanding. "They are such confining contrivances. I thought their protection would not be needed for touring your lovely town."

"I am sure that is true." Jerry let out a long sigh. "So now, shod or not, thou dost join us in this mission. If thou canst cut the throat of the mighty dowb, thou art properly adept in the use of the lahab, I take it?"

"If I could not hunt, I would not eat." Daviyd's natural honesty compelled him to continue. "But I am seldom challenged. Predators are scarcely seen in Yereq. And the dowb I killed as a youth?" He turned to the magistrate with a rueful smile. "When I leapt upon its back, I knocked it to the ground. It was but a cub, and too small to bear my weight."

They all laughed, even Jerry, as Daviyd concluded, "But it is a good tale for the telling."

THE LAST TOQEPH

Jerry quickly sobered. "We know not what we shall find at the airport. But it is well to have a good Gannahan like thee beside us."

Daviyd nodded. "Methinks I, too, am in good company." They were Outsiders by birth, yes. But Gannahan by choice. He had to respect them for it.

From a chair in their second-floor sitting room, Lileela watched the rain sweep across the courtyard below. It seemed one of the most beautiful sights imaginable.

The swarm of neighbors who'd welcomed her home had scattered before the downpour. Though she appreciated their concern, their questions were exhausting. Especially when they scarcely listened to her answers before launching into excited reports of the Old Gannahan visitor. It was a relief when Faris finally intervened. "Thank you all for coming to visit, but I need to get Lileela inside. It looks like rain."

He'd lifted her from the wheelchair and spoken to the two O'Dell boys who hovered nearby. "If one of you gentlemen could carry the chair up the stairs for me, I'd be most obliged."

The boys wrestled it up together behind Faris, who carried Lileela. He set her gently in the sitting room then took the wheelchair from the boys. "Thank you. I appreciate your help. But you'd better head for home." He gestured toward the dark clouds swirling ever closer, and the boys scampered back down the steps with shouts of, "Goodbye! Get better soon, Mrs. Faris!"

Finally alone, Faris kissed her. "Comfy?"

She nodded. "It's good to be home." The words scarcely expressed the feeling behind them.

Faris left the room, and she listened to him moving around in the kitchen as the rain scoured the courtyard. With it came the usual thunder and lightning. After a childhood in a domed city on Karkar, and then enduring the Great Disaster shortly after her return to Gannah, storms used to make her nervous. This one merely lent a cozy ambiance to the dimly lit sitting room.

After a few moments, Faris returned with a bottle and two glasses.

She glanced up at him. "Look at me. Sitting here by the window watching the storm and not the least bit edgy."

THE LAST TOQEPH

He opened the bottle. "No wonder. You've just survived far worse." He poured her a glass and handed it to her. "Let's celebrate."

She made sure their hands touched when she took the glass. "The trip from the hospital pretty well wore me out. Let me rest a bit first."

He gave her a quizzical look then laughed. "I meant celebrate with a good blend." He bent and kissed her. "You can rest as long as you want before we celebrate further."

She sipped, gazing up at him. "I did just sleep for three days, you know."

The tube exited the tunnel into the artificial light of the depot. Daviyd recognized it from when he'd first arrived here with Adam. It had seemed so strange then.

The pod slowed to a stop, and Jax, nearest the door, grabbed the handle to open it. They filed out, the magistrate yelping as he bumped his head on the doorway.

Jerry led the way. "We are to meet the toqeph in the main lobby."

Daviyd assumed Jerry spoke the civilized tongue for his benefit, and young Ishaq answered in the same language as they left the platform. "Know we what sort of ship it is? How large? How many are aboard?"

Jerry shook his head. "We know only that one cometh."

An echoing alarm caused them all to turn toward the rail, where a new pod appeared from the gloom, slowing until it stopped behind the one they had just exited. The door slid open and three men climbed out. None had to duck to avoid hitting their heads. When they turned toward Daviyd and the others, he saw that they, too, had Gannahan eyes. No Natsach purple, but some azure, some green.

Very curious.

Jerry motioned for them to follow. "To the lobby, gentlemen." The whole group took off at a brisk trot. In the middle of the pack, Daviyd could feel the eyes of the newcomers on him.

The sound of their boots echoed heavy and threatening as the men jogged through the depot. The long, straight stairway that led to the ground floor went into motion at their approach. Dashing up the moving steps two at a time, they made it to the top in remarkable time.

Though the men had no meahs, Daviyd caught their tension and shared their anxiety. According to what he'd heard, traffic between Gannah

THE LAST TOQEPH

and the rest of the galaxy had never been frequent even before the Plague, when Gannah had the capacity to travel through space and to communicate with the Outside. What were their capabilities now?

He had many other questions, but they'd all have to wait.

Jerry led the group through the wide halls toward the main entrance where Adam had instructed him in the use of restrooms. A ripple of embarrassment at his earlier ignorance added to his discomfort.

Beyond the pounding boots, heavy breathing, and rustling clothes, another sound could be heard. Drumming. Then a rumble. After a moment Daviyd realized it was a thunderstorm. Though it was right over them, the sturdy building kept it at a safe distance.

Just before they reached the lobby, the toqeph intercepted them, hair and clothing spotted from the rain.

The men stopped and bowed deeply. She gestured toward an open doorway and spoke in the Outsiders' language, saying something about the ship descending. Apparently, however, they had time to arm themselves with something other than lahabs before the ship's occupants disembarked.

When Jerry led the men into the room she'd indicated, she summoned Daviyd before he could follow.

He stepped out of the flow and approached, bowing again. "Madam Toqeph."

"I assume thou art not familiar with the use of an electrodart."

Electro what? "Nay, madam."

"Then thy only weapons shall be thy lahab and thy wits."

"They are at thy service."

"Communication with the visitors, whoever they may be, will be in the Standard Speech. Thou art able to make out much of what is said in that language?"

"Yea, madam. The general meaning."

"Keep thy meah open to me, in case I must communicate with thee. I know not what may transpire here."

"I am at thy command."

She almost smiled. "And I am thankful for that."

The others emerged, fastening belts around their waists. Heavy pockets hanging from the belts held some sort of implement that appeared to be somewhat larger than a man's hand, but not particularly weapon-like. At

THE LAST TOQEPH

least, it appeared to have no blade. Nor were any darts visible, despite the fact that these must be what the toqeph called electrodarts.

A deeper rumble covered the roar of the storm. More prolonged than thunder, and it grew ever louder. The lightning that accompanied it, as seen through the glass front of the building, flashed with an unnatural, pulsating rhythm.

The toqeph turned to Jerry. "While we await our guests' arrival, we should pray."

The men nodded, answering in the affirmative.

"Let us go by the windows." She gestured to the front of the building. "We can kneel there."

Kneel?

Without another word, they followed her to the glass. The roar grew louder and the lights brighter, and Daviyd followed at a distance. What were they doing?

Furious winds, seeming to come from every direction at once, slammed the rain against the glass where it ran down, stunned and bleeding, to lie in helpless puddles on the pavement below. The powerful roar of the descending vessel assaulted Daviyd's head and made his very teeth ache. He put his hands over his ears and squinted against the lights that flashed through swirling clouds of rain and smoke. The combination of the strobing lights and violent sounds made his gut clench in distress.

His jaw dropped at the sight that greeted him next. The two Nasis, along with the big magistrate and the smaller, Gannahan-eyed men, joined the toqeph in kneeling before the windows and reaching toward the savage sky. Their reflections in the glass showed their eyes were closed and their mouths were moving, though nothing could be heard above that infernal roar.

These were Nasis of Gannah? Trained warriors? Defending the settlement on their knees?

He barely made it to the restroom before losing his lunch, while the whole world trembled under the roar of the invading vessel.

36

Ra'anan combed out Tamah's tangled curls. A towel around the little girl's shoulders caught most of the water, but a few drips found their way to the floor.

"Ouch!" Tamah jerked away. "Don't pull it out by the roots."

"Hold still, I'm almost done." Ra'anan grabbed her by the shoulders. "It's you who's pulling, not me." She tackled the tangle again.

"That's what you—ow! That's what you think." Tamah's reflection in the bathroom mirror wore a pout. "Emma doesn't pull this bad. Even Aunt Skiskii does it better than you. OW!" Tamah turned around, scowling deeply. "Let me do it myself!"

"Fine." Ra'anan shook the comb at her. "Suit yourself. But your hair had better be fixed by the time Emma gets home."

Tamah snatched the comb and went to work—tugging harder than Ra'anan ever had.

Ra'anan wanted to slap her. Or cry. Or both. Mostly, she wanted Emma to come home and tell them everything was all right. And why did Abba have to choose this afternoon to go to the lab?

"There!" Triumphant, Tamah ran the comb through her hair. "Now you can braid it for me."

The door buzzer sounded. "Braid it yourself." Ra'anan stomped from the room and trotted up the spiral stairs. Too late, she remembered that running up them so fast made her dizzy. At the top, she struggled to walk without staggering on her way to the front room.

Mrs. Maddox stood in the foyer holding two pairs of shoes that looked like Hushai's and Ittai's. "When I didn't see anyone, I went back out and rang the buzzer."

THE LAST TOQEPH

Ra'anan bobbed a polite bow. "Yes, ma'am. We were downstairs. We got caught in the rain." She lifted her wet, freshly braided hair to demonstrate. "Is there... something I can help you with?"

Mrs. Maddox's brow was wrinkled, her eyes narrow. "I don't know." Mrs. Maddox pressed her lips together and raised the shoes, one pair in each hand. "Can you explain why I tripped over these when I came in my door this morning?"

Because you're clumsy? was the first response that came to mind, but Ra'anan had the sense to keep it to herself. "Umm... no, ma'am. Were they on the floor?"

"I wouldn't have tripped over them otherwise, would I? The question is, what were they doing there?" She set them with trembling hands on an end table. Ra'anan got the impression she would have preferred to throw them at her.

"I'm sorry, Mrs. Maddox, is something wrong?"

"Are those your brothers' shoes? And if so, what were they doing in my house?"

Ra'anan bit her lip, praying for one of her parents to walk through the door in the next two seconds. She eyed the shoes. "They look like theirs, yes. Now that you mention it, the boys did go to your apartment this morning to get Mr. Natsach. Emma asked Hushai to take him to meet Mr. Tischtuch at First Town, and Ittai wanted to go along. But I don't know why their shoes would have been at your place." *Nor why you should be so upset about it.*

When Ra'anan mentioned Emma, Mrs. Maddox's expression darkened. "Oh, is she here? Your mother, I mean."

"No, ma'am." *I wish she were!* "She had to—she told us to go on home while she went—" How much should she tell her? "She called Mr. Maddox and asked him and—and some others—to meet her at the airport." She tried to keep her chin from quivering.

Mrs. Maddox gave her a sharp look—but now it was laced with uncertainty as well as anger. "Very well, then, it can wait. I'm afraid I came at a bad time."

Yes, you did. Now please leave. Ra'anan stared at the floor, not trusting herself to speak and thankful Mrs. Maddox couldn't read her thoughts.

Downstairs, Tamah let out a howl, making Ra'anan look up.

Mrs. Maddox's brows rose. "Is everything all right?"

"We're fine, ma'am. It's just—"

271

THE LAST TOQEPH

"I'm telling Emma when she gets home!" Tamah pounded up the stairs, shrieking like a scalded Karkar. "Ra'anan! Ittai was mean to me! He—" Seeing their visitor, she came to an abrupt stop. At least she remembered her manners enough to bow. "Oh, hello, Mrs. Maddox."

Mrs. Maddox looked back and forth between the girls. "I'm sorry to intrude, but someone ransacked our home this morning, and I intend to find out who."

Ra'anan put her arm around the sniffling Tamah. "Ransacked? What do you mean?"

"Someone went through like a cyclone, pulling things from cabinets and drawers, tearing the whole place up." Her tone turned threatening. "Even our bedroom." She inserted a chilling pause. "And the only clues I found as to the culprit—or culprits—were those." She pointed to the shoes. "Which belong to your brothers. Should we call them here to explain themselves?" Her eyebrows arched. "Or should I tell your mother about this?"

Tamah sniffled. "Emma and the Nasi went to fight off the invaders from space."

Ra'anan gasped, but Tamah was on a roll. "When she gets back you can tell her, though. I want her to beat Ittai with a stick."

"Tamah, you do not!" Ra'anan wanted to throttle the child.

But Mrs. Maddox didn't seem to have heard anything after *invaders from space*. "She and the Nasi went *where*?"

The terrible noise had dulled, though Daviyd's ears still rang as he washed off his face at the restroom sink and dried his beard with his sleeve.

Determined to face whatever awaited, he returned to the lobby.

The toqeph and the men hadn't moved. But the starship had landed, and Jerry's voice could be heard above its rumble. It stood beyond the window, a smooth, elongated mass of scorched metal steaming in the rain. It reminded him of the Tebah, except that it stretched parallel with the ground instead of pointing to the sky. The sight of the smoking monster outside and the warriors kneeling before it turned his blood to ice.

As Daviyd made his way toward the windows, Jerry called upon that invisible Yasha they were always talking about, asking for things like

THE LAST TOQEPH

wisdom and protection. Claiming Gannah was safe in the Yasha's hands today just as it had been six years ago.

Six years ago. Did he mean the time of the Flood? How could he call a disaster of that magnitude safety? Oh, but here at the settlement, they were safe, weren't they? The whole world was swept away except for this little corner of Periy. But what did that have to do with a visiting starship?

Other than a gradual lessening of the rain, nothing happened outside; the vessel just sat there, blinking and steaming. Here in the huge empty room, the people prayed, apparently taking turns. They seemed to think the imaginary Yasha heard them. What a fantasy.

What would these "warriors" do when Outsiders came pouring out of that ship? Close their eyes and wish them to go back in? Daviyd's fingers touched the solid flatness of his lahab in its pocket. His blade was sharp, as was his skill in using it. That was protection. Not prayer.

After several minutes, they concluded the nonsensical ritual by uttering the Gannahan word for *verily, so be it* in unison—strange, since their prayer was in the foreign tongue—and then rising.

"The Yasha is good," the toqeph said in the barbaric speech, and all the men repeated the Gannahan word, *amen*. Daviyd shook his head as he approached them. There wasn't a whit of sense to any of this.

Beyond the windows, the sun pushed a cloud aside and shot out a ray, wreathing the steaming ship in a glimmering rainbow. Daviyd's breath caught in his throat. A moment later, the clouds swallowed the sunbeam and the rainbow was only a memory.

But the vision seared in his brain. It meant something. It had to mean something. The Tebah. The rainbow. His skin prickled.

And then came the Voice. *I speak only to those who listen.*

Daviyd's breath caught. "What sayest thou?"

The nearest of the men—one of the new arrivals whom Daviyd didn't know—turned, eyebrows raised in question.

Daviyd stared at him. "That voice. Didst thou hear it?"

The man took something from his ears. "I heard nothing. But I had forgotten to remove my earplugs."

"Earplugs?"

"They protect against the terrible roar. Where are thine?" His expression went from surprise to understanding. "Ah. We obtained them

THE LAST TOQEPH

from the weapons room, which thou did not enter. Thy ears must ring from the clamor."

So that's how the others could bear the noise without covering their ears with their hands. "Verily. Perhaps the voice I heard was nothing. Just the ringing."

"I wish thine ears a speedy recovery." He smiled and extended his hand. "Thou must be the one everyone speaks of. I am Esam."

Daviyd scowled at the waiting hand. The man might look like a Gannahan, but he acted like an Earther.

Esam withdrew his hand. "My apologies. I forget myself." He bowed. "I am pleased to make thy acquaintance."

Daviyd returned the bow. "Natsach Daviyd Natsach. And I thine."

Before they could bump the heels of their hands together, the toqeph interrupted. "There will be time for that later. For now, Mr. Natsach, I would like you to come with me." She then instructed the men how she wanted them to receive the visitors on her behalf. Daviyd followed the gist of the gibberish and understood that the others would take the intruders prisoner and bring them to her.

Assuming they weren't killed first.

The men bowed then turned toward the lobby's entrance, taking their positions as instructed. Beyond them, the sun glinted off the metallic beast and raised steam from the pavement.

At a gesture by the toqeph, Daviyd followed her out of the room—though it went against his grain to turn his back on the enemy crouched out there behind them.

Adam exchanged kisses with Everett. "Be a good boy for your mamaw, big guy. She'll need your help taking care of Emma and Joseph."

The little boy's curls jiggled as he nodded. "Uh-huh."

As soon as Adam set him on the floor, he ran to Fern and bounced in front of her. "C'mon, Mamaw, let's play shuffaball."

"That would wake the baby. How about we do some puzzles instead?"

"Don't wanna do puzzles. I wanna play shuffaball." He tugged her hand. "We'll go outside."

Pete chuckled and pushed himself up from the chair. "We can do that, since the rain's over. We can make all the racket we want out there."

THE LAST TOQEPH

Adam managed what he hoped were appropriate words of thanks and farewell as he left the apartment to his in-laws. With all that was on his mind, it was difficult to go through the motions of being a good father and son-in-law. But he must, because that's what a Nasi did. And if Fern was kind enough to stay with Elise and the kids for a few days, he didn't want to appear ungrateful.

Once he passed through the front door, though, he put all else aside he mentally organized the rest of his day.

As soon as he got to his office, he'd review his reading list. Though Nasi training involved as much or more bookwork as his medical training, he was a fast reader and retentive. Keeping up with the requirements was rather like keeping up with housework. That is, it took some effort, but wasn't difficult unless you fell behind.

Also, thanks to the recent interruptions, his lab work was going nowhere. It irked him to be stalled at the very cusp of a breakthrough.

A wonderful breakthrough. His thoughts flashed back to Joseph and Everett, and his ears smiled. If things went as planned, Faris and Lileela would know the joy of parenthood.

He was glad Abba was at work on the project again. It seemed a little soon after his return from helping dig out Lileela, suffering from exhaustion as he was, but he should be okay as long as he didn't overextend himself.

Adam's first priority, however, was coming up with a plan for moving the Old Gannahans to Yereq. So Natsach and all the stinking Rahab villagers could be permanent residents.

The euphoria of new fatherhood burst with an almost audible pop.

He passed through the passageway connecting the residence building to the clinic, trying not to hate Natsach. And not succeeding.

Forcing his mind off the subject, he decided his first act upon entering the lab would be to check in with Abba for an update. If the cells they'd been growing hadn't survived, he and Abba would have to start over with a new culture.

He reached the lab, but what was this? The lights were off. Adam opened the door.

No one was there. Where was Abba?

He hadn't forgotten that flash of meah communication he'd picked up between Emma and Natsach. Apparently she'd summoned Abba as well. Probably Jerry and Jax, too.

THE LAST TOQEPH

But not Adam.

He stood motionless, his intellect struggling to bring his emotions under control. After several moments, he turned and strode into his office. He had work to do.

But just inside the doorway, he paused. In one rapid-fire motion, he pulled out his lahab, spun around, and flung his weapon. The blade whizzed across the lab. It stuck fast in a cabinet door—throat-high to a Gannahan—on the far side of the room with a deadly thunk.

Take that, Natsach.

THE LAST TOQEPH

37

The toqeph led Daviyd through echoing halls and areas of the airport he'd never seen before. Neither of them spoke.

Had his people survived the Fueraquis, Outside cultural contamination, plague, and flood, only to perish in this invasion? If the so-called Redeemer existed, why would he toy with them like this? Why not just wipe them out once and for all instead of torturing them like a predator with its helpless prey?

They turned at a doorway marked "Conference Room" in the Gannahan language. The squiggles beneath the words probably designated the same meaning in the Outside tongue.

Lights came on when they entered. The oblong table filling most of the room stood surrounded by more than a dozen chairs. As he counted them—there were fourteen: two sevens, a good Gannahan number—the toqeph ran her hand across the table, leaving streaks in the dust.

"Hmmph." She frowned, rubbing her fingers together, then went to a row of cabinets along one wall. "I expect there are cleaning supplies here somewhere."

She pulled out a box containing several soft cloths, took one out, and extended it to him. When he unfolded it, it crackled with static.

She took another and unfolded it as she walked toward the table. "The static draws the dust into the cloth." She ran the cloth in a broad swipe across the table, leaving a clean, shining surface behind.

He joined in, and soon the entire table gleamed. All the while, he listened for signs of conflict elsewhere in the airport but heard nothing.

THE LAST TOQEPH

When they'd finished, the cloths were gray. She deposited her dirty rag in a slot in the back of the cabinet. Daviyd stuffed his in the same opening, and it disappeared from sight. "Where do they go?"

"Into the laundry bin. When the airport had regular use, the bins were emptied daily. Now, though, we only send someone to collect the laundry when we happen to think of it."

"I did notice there are no towels in the restroom."

Her brows rose. "Didst thou? We must send one of the servants to take care of it."

Daviyd remembered the people serving the toqeph's table at the festival. "Those who are owned by the house of Atarah?"

"Thou did see the earrings?"

He nodded. "And Adam explained."

She went to the far side of the table and took a seat facing the door. "Knowest thou why Atarah would claim ownership of people, like objects?"

"I think perhaps..." He frowned. "I may have known once, but it doth now escape me."

She leaned back and studied him, probing with her meah. "It would seem numerous things escape thee."

That was true, but how could she know?

"Such as the laws of Gannah under which freedom is forfeited by the commission of certain criminal acts."

"Is that the case with those people? They are criminals?"

She steepled her fingers. "Of the worst kind. Conspirators against the Gannahan good. Thieves. Deceivers. Rebels against Atarah."

Daviyd frowned. The people with the earrings were meek and respectful. What had the toqeph done to break their spirits so completely? Was he — were all the Dathan — in danger of suffering the same fate?

"Gannah deals with rebellion in its own way." She lowered her hands to the chair arms. "They left the settlement in arrogance but returned with changed hearts. Their guilt, however, left me no choice. If I had failed to punish them as prescribed by the law, I would have been in rebellion as well. And no good can come of that." She fixed him with a steady green gaze. "There is an authority above the crown of Atarah."

His head felt light. "Madam?"

"The One who gave Atarah the rule at the beginning."

THE LAST TOQEPH

He didn't know how to respond. He was spared having to answer, though, by the sound of footsteps in the hall.

It sounded like ten or more pairs of feet in heavy footwear. No one spoke, but the steps drew steadily closer. Understanding from her gesture and her meah that he was to take a position behind her chair, Daviyd hurried to his place. Together, they watched the entrance.

He discerned no fear in her. Only curiosity. Also, a longing for someone or something. He couldn't tell what, but she seemed to hope someone in particular would come through the door.

As the footsteps neared, Daviyd's tension mounted, and his hand hovered over his lahab pocket. Then Jerry—whole and unbloodied—entered, followed by eleven men. The five settlers with the Gannahan eyes each accompanied a stranger, and Jax brought up the rear. The so-called warriors' expressions revealed nothing.

It was a strange group they herded in. All wore Outlandish clothing. One man had dark skin. Two appeared to be pale-skinned Earthers. But that tall one...

Daviyd bristled at the sight of the giant with his face painted with bizarre designs and his hands sporting one extra finger each. A full-blooded Karkar. Daviyd had neither seen nor imagined a person with such short, straight hair standing up evenly around his head, nor a face decorated with sparkling colors and intricate designs drawn in black around the eyes.

The fifth man was the strangest of all. Though similar in size and build to the Earthers, he was utterly hairless, and the skin of his head and neck were decorated with colorful pictures. The artwork did not appear to be paint, for it was smooth as his skin.

Daviyd had no idea what world produced this fellow, but he gritted his teeth at the thought of such an abomination sharing his pure Gannahan air. He felt duty-bound to sever that unnatural head from its neck.

Only the quiet presence of the toqeph nearby kept him from pulling out his lahab. But at the slightest nod from her... He strained his meah for a sign, but when she gave none, he reluctantly lowered his hand.

Jerry bowed. "Madam Toqeph. The visitors come from the starship *DeLaCruz*, escaping Station 27 before its demolition."

Or at least, that's what Daviyd understood him to say in that Outworld language, though he had no idea what was meant by "Station 27."

THE LAST TOQEPH

Jerry bowed again and stepped back then nodded toward one of the newcomers.

The pale, beardless Earther stepped forward. His appearance was neat and clean, and he held himself erect, as one with authority. When he spoke, his accent was different from that of the settlers, and Daviyd struggled to discern the meaning of his gibberish. "Madam Toqeph. I am Captain Daniel Bennett of the vessel *DeLaCruz*. On behalf of my passengers and crew, I thank you for agreeing to this meeting. Please allow me to introduce my companions."

He gestured toward the others as he spoke their names. The other light-skinned Earther was John Weiss, who seemed to be there as the traveling companion of the dark one, Philip Dengel.

At Dengel's introduction, the toqeph's meah exuded delighted recognition. She must have heard of him but hadn't recognized his face. The Karkar's name, too—Kohz—seemed to strike a familiar chord with her, though Daviyd got the impression she was more curious than pleased.

When the captain introduced the hairless man as The Second Hegigar Hool, her intense surprise aroused Daviyd's curiosity. Who were these people with the ridiculous names? How did the toqeph know them?

The captain explained the purpose for their visit. Something Daviyd couldn't quite grasp about Dengel reuniting with his family, and the Karkar's past relationship with Dr. Pik, and the hairless aberration having heard of the toqeph all his life. The visit was precipitated by their having to leave Station 27 in a big hurry. It seems the League—whatever that was—ordered the Station—whatever that was—dismantled because it had become a breeding place for vermin. But the vermin were something the captain called Christians, which were apparently people, including those who now stood before the toqeph.

It was easy to see the Karkar and the bald man were vermin. The others, though, except for their peculiar appearance, seemed much like the average New Gannahan. Had the settlers come here because they were expelled as vermin also? Was Gannah to become a human trash dump, with wave after wave of assorted vile Outsiders invading Daviyd's beautiful world?

Perhaps he didn't understand the situation. His comprehension of the language was limited, after all. He focused his attention more sharply on the conversation.

THE LAST TOQEPH

The toqeph thanked the captain and addressed the dark-skinned man. As she spoke, she allowed Daviyd to understand her meaning through their meahs. "Mr. Dengel, also called Philip the Evangelist. It is a pleasure to make your acquaintance at last. Your wife and daughters are well and have been a blessing to our settlement these past six years. You might also be interested to know that your spiritual son, Faris, is now my son-in-law."

Smiling, the man bowed and expressed pleasure at the report.

"I'm sure you're eager to see your family, and we will arrange that as soon as we can." She turned her gaze to the Karkar. "Mr. Kohz. I expected Dr. Pik would be here as well, but he must have been delayed."

Ah. That was what the toqeph had been longing for. She was disappointed her husband hadn't come.

"But I'm surprised to see you here. We didn't realize you were interested in either Gannah or the Earthish religion."

The Karkar bowed deeply, but he didn't speak. The man named Bennett answered for him. "I'm sorry, Madam Toqeph, but we can't get our translator to work here. Unless you understand the Karkar language—"

"We have devices that will suit the purpose, and we also have people who speak the language. You should be able to communicate with us shortly, Mr. Kohz."

She turned to the hairless man and addressed him with a tone of amusement. "The Second Hegigar Hool, is it?"

He bowed, giving a clear view of an image of his own grinning face portrayed on the top of his head. "It is, Madam Toqeph. And I am at your service." Unlike the others, who bowed in the manner of the Gannahans as they'd probably been instructed, this slug made a jaunty flourish with his hand on the way down. Daviyd clenched his jaw. Disrespectful, to say the least.

But the toqeph didn't seem to care. "And was your father The First Hegigar Hool, by any chance? Captain of the Cephargian vessel *Death Knell*?"

"One and the same, Madam." Looking up from his bow, he flashed a toothy grin. "You remember him, do you?" He straightened to his full height.

"The experience was unforgettable." Her meah revealed a memory of violence, fear, and oppressive loneliness. Whatever circumstances she

THE LAST TOQEPH

recalled, they were unpleasant in the extreme. Yet the man stood there grinning. Daviyd's hand poised ready to grab his lahab.

She continued. "And how is your father these days?"

"Long gone, Madam. And flopping in his grave at what his boy's come to." He shook his colorful head. "If he weren't already dead, it would kill him to see me turn my back on the pirate trade to become a different kind of rebel." He chuckled. "But he'd probably approve of the *vermin* label."

"I would like to know more, from all of you. But first, Captain Bennett. Are there others aboard ship who would come to the surface as well? What is your plan? How long do you hope to stay?"

Bennett stepped forward. He said something about there being others aboard the *DeLaCruz*, but they had no desire to set foot on Gannah. The toqeph seemed to understand why without explanation. Daviyd didn't, but he was relieved to hear it. The fewer Outsiders defiling the world, the better.

The captain went on to say something to the effect that they would remain for only a couple of days. But in midsentence, he paused and lifted his eyebrows.

Daviyd had heard the sound before Bennett spoke, and from the expressions of the others in the room, they were also aware of it. Heavy footsteps thudding toward the room, moving with obvious urgency.

All eyes turned toward the door, and the warriors tensed, poised for action.

38

Daviyd listened to the heavy footsteps thumping closer, accompanied by deep, raspy breathing. From the sounds, the approaching person was large and heavy. Very large, like...

Like a half-Karkar too old and out of shape to be moving so fast. The toqeph's husband burst through the doorway and, florid and perspiring, bowed before the toqeph.

It was the woman who ordinarily bowed to her husband, so it was tricky for a husband to perform this gesture without compromising his proper authority. But the Karkar somehow managed to bend just deeply enough to convey his respect for the ruler of Gannah without expressing submission to his wife. The feat was all the more remarkable coming from an Outsider.

Pik's apologies in the off-world language also seemed appropriately respectful without being abject. Something about his regrettable tardiness being caused by a problem with the rail system, which wouldn't accept a third pod at the airport terminal. Daviyd couldn't follow it all.

The toqeph kept her thoughts to herself, but he could tell from her verbal and physical response that she was glad her husband was there, however delayed his arrival. She invited him to sit beside her. As he sank into the chair that Daviyd stood behind, the old Karkar exuded an overheated stench of foreignness. Daviyd held his breath, for the giant's head was at nose-level.

The toqeph put her hand on her husband's sweaty arm as if it weren't an insult to the rich Gannahan wood of the table it lay upon. "We shall have Baako look into the problem with the tube. But for now, let me introduce our guests." She directed her attention to the Outsiders and their guards. "Gentlemen, no need to stand there all day. Please, take seats."

THE LAST TOQEPH

Jerry supervised the seating. While the men settled, the toqeph spoke to her husband. "You arrived just in time. Our guests were about to tell me what they're doing here."

They were one chair short, but Jerry strode toward the toqeph and took a position on the other side of her chair, to Daviyd's left.

Daviyd eyed the intruders around the table. The settlers guarding them should be standing. Sitting down, they wouldn't be able to respond quickly enough should the newcomers make a move against them. At least he and Jerry were on their feet.

He watched for suspicious motions but discerned nothing threatening as the toqeph brought her husband up to speed. Pik did, in fact, recognize the other Karkar, and they spoke in their own obnoxious language. Daviyd had never heard such horrible sounds.

Mercifully, the toqeph cut the conversation short after a minute or two. "You'll have plenty of time to get caught up later on. For now, let's hear the others' stories."

Lileela roused from sleep, feeling Faris's heavy arm around her. Against her back, his chest rose and fell in the slow rhythm of sleep, and his breath tickled a spot behind her ear. She wiggled her toes, and no pain assailed her legs. Had she died and gone to be with the Yasha?

She opened her eyes. The round window across the room glowed in the fledgling rays of Gray Dawn, while birds somewhere on the other side conducted an animated discussion. The pillowcase she lay on still carried the fresh scent of the clothesline.

And her bladder swelled uncomfortably beneath that arm draped across her. Yep. She was alive.

Lileela grasped Faris's wrist and shifted the weight. A moment later, his breaths behind her ear turned to kisses, and she rolled over. "What day is it?"

He paused in his kisses to answer, "First Day," but then resumed.

She kissed him back then laid her fingers across his lips. "It sure is."

He took her hand away and held it. "Sure is what?" When he smiled, his eyes glowed as if they produced a light of their own.

"It's like the first day of my life. I feel reborn." She snuggled against his chest. "Is that an effect of the healing sleep, do you think?"

THE LAST TOQEPH

"No." He cleared his throat of leftover sleepiness. "Because I feel the same. I think it's gratitude. I've never been so thankful to the Yasha as I am right now."

She agreed completely. For a fleeting moment, she thought they shared a feeling through their meahs then realized that wasn't the case. The comprehension of the reality, though, brought no disappointment. What she'd felt was the spiritual connection all followers of Yasha share, the indwelling Spirit of the Yasha Himself. He lived in everyone who believed. Even...

She lifted her head. "Did you say Uncle Kughie's recovering?"

"Doing quite well, from what I hear."

"Did you know he and Auntie have worship meetings at their place on First Day afternoons?" Yawning wide, she didn't hear his answer but continued the thought regardless. "I'd like to go."

"To the Kughurrrros? For worship? Now there's a thought."

"Takes some getting used to, doesn't it? But it's true. It'll all be in Karkar, though, so you might want to wear a translator."

"Or earplugs."

In his chamber in the Maddox's apartment, Daviyd pondered the upcoming worship meeting. He'd never heard of such thing before, and he didn't like the sound of it. But his hosts seemed excited, as did the toqeph. He should see what the fuss was all about. At least his comprehension of the Outside language had improved enough that he'd be able to follow the gist of it.

He donned the clothing Jerry and Katarina had given him for the purpose—a formal purple-red skirt that came almost to the ankle, and a lighter red tunic with crisp, even pleats and elaborate embroidery. He smoothed his hair and captured it in the carved elah-wood ponytail holder then surveyed his reflection. The clothing was appropriate. But the occasion?

For the hundredth time since he'd landed in that flying machine, he reached out to Emma in his meah. *Things are very strange here. I shall be glad to return home.*

And when might that be, my son? We all miss thee sharply, none more than I.

I am told it will be tomorrow. The toqeph hath decreed the Nasi named Jax shall fly the machine. The man Adam will not be with us.

Jerry knocked on the door. "It is time to go."

THE LAST TOQEPH

His language was clumsy, but Daviyd understood. He opened the door. "I am ready."

Jerry looked dapper in an outfit similar to Daviyd's, and when they met Katarina in the front room, her tunic and trousers were becoming to her as well. They each picked up a book from a table near the door then Jerry paused. "I believe I have a Bible in the Gannahan language thou may use if thou wishest."

The books must be something called Bibles, and apparently they somehow figured into the meeting they were about to attend. "Would I find it useful?"

Jerry smiled. "Eminently." He strode to the bookshelves across the room, where he quickly found what he was looking for and brought it to Daviyd. Unlike ordinary books, this one was bound along the left side instead of the top.

Despite the odd binding, Daviyd liked the feel of it in his hands. He opened it, and the old, familiar characters he'd learned in his youth marched across the page with solid authority. Strangely moved, he looked up at Jerry. "I thank thee. I should like to explore its words."

"Thou mayest take it with thee, then, when thou goest home on the morrow." Jerry turned and ushered his wife out of the apartment.

Daviyd followed them, more curious than ever about this worship meeting. He knew it to be a weekly event—except, Jerry said, sometimes people would assemble at other times as well. It was something people dressed for, looked forward to, and talked about afterward. Attendance was not compulsory, but most everyone went. They didn't always attend the same meeting, however, as different groups met at different times and places.

This one, however, was a special event because one of the Outsiders, Philip Dengel, would be speaking. Daviyd couldn't imagine what he could possibly say that would be of interest, but everyone seemed to think it the most exciting thing that had happened in years. So many people were expected to attend, in fact, that the location had been moved from the usual meeting room in the palace to an outdoor arena.

As Daviyd followed Jerry and Katarina through the palace halls, several others joined them. By the time they passed through the ornate doors into the courtyard, he was among a group of a few dozen settlers. They each carried a Bible, and their excitement filled the air with a palpable

286

THE LAST TOQEPH

buzz. Though he was aware of some watching him, for the first time since his arrival, he wasn't the center of attention. Their chatter was mostly about the newest visitors, Mr. Dengel especially.

Sunlight filtered through the trellis of flowering vines that roofed the courtyard walkway. It cast a dizzying array of shadows across the people who walked in front of him and the pavement at his feet. Overhead, bees hummed from flower to flower. Daviyd looked up when one of them, laden with pollen, swooped near his head as if too burdened to fly. *Thou art working too hard*, he told it through his meah.

The hive is always hungry, the small creature shot back as it wobbled away with its load.

Daviyd knew what that was like. Not every creature enjoyed such abundance that they could take a day off from their labors.

Someone came up behind him and grabbed his hand. He gave the hand a squeeze as he looked down on Hushai's curly head. "It is good to see a friend."

Hushai grinned up at him. "Ahseethastabible." *I see thou hast a Bible.*

Daviyd grinned back. At last, someone who spoke his language. "Mr. Maddox hast given it to me. He saith I shall find it useful." He guestured toward the book Hushai carried. "Dost thou agree?"

"Verily." Hushai bobbed his head. "More than useful. It is the sun for light, bread for food, clear water for thirst, fresh air for breath, safe shelter in a storm, and a lahab for defense."

Plainly, the boy recited something he'd been taught. He spoke in clear, unslurred Gannahan, and at every analogy, Daviyd felt the meaning of the words. The sensation left him nearly breathless.

He forced his lungs to take in air. "Powerful words, those. Whose are they?"

"The first toqeph's, Atarah Hoseh the Wise."

Daviyd steeled his jaw. Is that what this was all about? Were they on their way to venerate some ancient contamination from Outside?

If so, it was heady stuff. No wonder so many Gannahans had become ensnared.

Hushai waved his book. "What aileth thee? Dost thou think the book to be poison? Emma sayeth the proud will choke on it, but it giveth life to the humble."

THE LAST TOQEPH

Proud? Yes, Daviyd was proud—and he had plenty to be proud of. Pride wasn't a poison, but a thing to grab hold of, to cling to, to cherish. "And who be these proud ones whom thine Emma saith will choke on this book? Those foolish enough to swallow it whole?"

Hushai chortled at first, then sobered. "Perhaps. Mine ab hath said it must be taken in small bits and savored, because it is sweeter than honey. Taking too big a gob can make one feel ill, but mixing a little into each day doth make the whole cup of life more wholesome."

Daviyd frowned. Did all these foolish settlers think themselves sages?

THE LAST TOQEPH

39

Daviyd sat beside Hushai at the worship meeting, trying to make sense of the goings-on.

The toqeph's husband had begun by announcing the arrival of the visitors — as if everyone didn't already know — before giving the floor to the ship captain, Bennett. He spoke a short time then introduced the other visitors. The Karkar merely rose, waved, and sat again, but the bald man and the other pale-skinned one each talked briefly about how they "came to Christ," as they put it.

Everyone seemed excited by what the men had to say, and Daviyd wondered why they would care. What difference did it make what these strangers believed?

Then Jerry got up to pray aloud for everyone. Daviyd didn't understand this prayer business, either. But the Nasi stood there and spoke to the Yasha as if addressing a person. Frowning, Daviyd scratched the back of his neck. If the Yasha were there, why could nobody see him? And if not, why did everyone act like he was? Daviyd's Dathan forefathers had been correct in thinking this was an Earthish form of dementia.

While Jerry prayed, Daviyd communed with his friend Jether in his meah. Unlike the Yasha, Jether was real. Daviyd couldn't see him, but their meahs connected and his communication with him was genuine.

How he longed for tomorrow, when he could return to the sane part of the world. If the villagers agreed to move to Yereq, he'd have to warn them to avoid contact with this alien disease.

After the prayer, the visitor named Dengel rose from where he had been sitting with his wife and two daughters. According to Jerry, Dengel

THE LAST TOQEPH

had earlier sent his family to safety on Gannah while he traveled the galaxy. Yesterday was the first time they'd seen each other for more than six years. It must be terrible to be separated from your loved ones, unable even to communicate through the meah.

Dengel talked about how happy he was to be there, how welcoming everyone was, how wonderful to be reunited with his family. After a few more remarks, the Earther opened the book in his hands.

Adam would have been delighted to hear Philip Dengel speak if he could have kept his mind on the message.

No breezes stirred the sultry air. Despite the shade of the outdoor auditorium's roof, Adam felt overwarm and drowsy. Perhaps he should have slept a couple hours last night, but he wouldn't get anything done sleeping.

Nor sitting here.

He'd come directly from the office after working all night. Earlier in the meeting, the dancing had gotten his blood flowing, reviving him physically and spiritually. But that was an hour ago, and the inactivity since made him sluggish.

He shifted in the too-small seat. At least it was on the aisle so he could stretch out his legs. In the next row, Abba did the same. But he was napping. Adam's ears smiled, thinking how like father and son they must look. But then he quickly straightened himself. Abba was an old man, but Adam was a Nasi trainee and the toqeph's heir. It was important to look the part.

Adam wondered about the ship orbiting the planet. When he was a boy, and Emma's landing craft went down, the visiting starship lent them the technology to search for her. Would this visiting captain—what was his name? Bennett?—be willing to help transport Natsach's people to Yereq? When the meeting was over, he'd take him aside to ask.

Adam had no trouble seeing over the heads of the crowd to search for the man. There he was, seated between the tattooed Cephargian and old Captain Broward—who, like Abba, was dozing. On the other side, Broward's wife, Marianna, nudged him, and he raised his white head and blinked. A few moments later, he rose and shuffled down the aisle toward the exit.

THE LAST TOQEPH

That was an idea. Adam could use a bit of a walk himself. But unlike Broward, he didn't have bladder issues, and his size and rank made it impossible to slip away unnoticed. No, he should stay put.

And he should pay attention. Jax was likely to quiz him about the message.

He drew himself up to his full height, causing the man behind him to make disgruntled noises. Well, he should know better than to sit behind a Karkar. There were other seats, weren't there? He glanced around. No, not really. The place was filled to capacity.

He'd been listening with half his brain, so when he gave Dengel his full attention, he didn't feel lost. If anyone wanted to rehash it, he could pull enough out of his memory to discuss it without sounding foolish.

But he hoped no one would ask his opinion, because the topic made him uncomfortable. Increasingly so, the longer he listened.

The nerve of this guy to come here, knowing nothing about Gannah but telling the settlers what they should do. For half an instant, he empathized with Natsach's abhorrence of "Outside" influences, but crushed the feeling before it could develop.

The problem was, the Bible passages Dengel quoted were true, used in their proper context, and applied in a manner that was wholly scriptural. Adam read the verses before and after and checked cross-references in an attempt to find a flaw with his reasoning. Unfortunately, the argument was sound. Worse, the Yasha's Spirit confirmed it through his meah.

The Yasha had not called His people to isolate themselves in little safe havens where they could lead happy and comfortable lives. Rather, He sent His people into the world—in the present case, into the galaxy—to take the gospel of salvation to those who were dead in their sins. Everyone who followed the Yasha was a believer for one reason: because someone had told them about Him. Then, believing the message, they had received His gift of redemption. If any more souls were to be saved, those who knew the Yasha must continue to spread the word.

There was a huge galaxy out there. The message was to go to the Earthers first, and many were already taking it to them. But the planet Karkar was ripe for harvest, as Kohz had already testified. Even a few on Cepharge had been supernaturally transformed by the power of the God of the universe. The Yasha was opening doors everywhere, and it was necessary that any who felt His call should respond in obedience.

THE LAST TOQEPH

Adam felt queasy. Was Dengel saying Adam should leave Gannah? How could he? He was born here; born to lead these people.

And what if everybody left? Everything his parents had worked for would be for nothing. What Dengel suggested could destroy the settlement as surely as the Karkar ship sought to do six years ago.

The speaker paused. "But the body is not all a hand." He lifted both of his. "Nor is it all a mouth." He pointed to his, one hand still raised. "We all have one Spirit, one Savior, and one God. But we have a variety of gifts, given us by the Spirit for the glory of the Father and the edifying of the Church of our Savior.

"All who believe in Him are individual parts of the Body of Christ Himself. As in your physical body, each part has a different purpose, but each part's purpose is vital to the whole. If the whole body were an eye, wouldn't that be ridiculous? You'd cease to function. If the whole body were a hand, it would be useless without an arm to support it.

"Ask the Spirit what function He's assigned you. He's made it clear to me that I must follow Him across the galaxy to meet the enemy head-on. But I am just one part of the Body.

"My Gannahan brothers and sisters! Do not follow my lead, but the leading of the Savior. Listen to Him with all your being, and obey with all your heart and mind.

"Is He calling you today? Is He drawing you to a life you never before imagined? Then don't just sit there—get up and go. Do you feel Him stirring your heart, but you're not sure what He wants you to do? Don't just sit there—get down and pray. Perhaps He's confirming that you are, in fact, performing the mission He's assigned you, right here on Gannah. If that's the case, don't just sit there—jump up and sing! Praise Him, all you His people. Praise Him with all your being."

Before Dengel reached this point, a few of the settlers had risen, hastening down the aisle to prostrate themselves in the open area surrounding the platform.

Adam's heart thudded so hard it nearly pounded through his sternum. *What part hath Thou assigned me, my Yasha? Am I not to be the toqeph's heir? Am I not to remain on Gannah?*

Though the Yasha didn't speak to him in words, assurance washed over him like a wave. Yes. He was called to stay, not to go. The current of confidence lifted him to his feet and caused his voice to burst out in song:

THE LAST TOQEPH

"O come, let us sing unto the Lord." All around him, others rose and joined in. "Let us sing to the rock of our salvation. Let us come before His presence with thanksgiving."

All over the arena, people rose, singing, swaying, dancing.

The Yasha was not yet finished with Gannah. And Adam was still called to take the throne when the time came.

"The Lord is a great God, a great King above all gods. And Him I will obey."

Daviyd yawned. The man Dengel spoke on and on. Most of his listeners followed along in their books when he read from his. Many took notes in electronic tablets. All of them seemed transfixed by what he had to say.

Daviyd tried to listen, but it took too much concentration. At first, Hushai tried to share his understanding through his meah, but it was wearying for both of them, and Hushai's focus wavered.

All this talk about the Yasha was crazy anyway. He disconnected from Hushai's meah and allowed his mind to wander.

Would his people agree to come here? There would be considerable benefit, but much danger as well. If the Dathan remained alone, they'd survive; they always had. But left to their own resources, it would take many generations for them to reacquire the old Gannahan knowledge, the expertise and resources that allowed these settlers to live in luxury and fruitfulness.

Life in his village was so different from here, so much more difficult. It was a one-step-at-a-time existence in which the future couldn't be envisioned and the past was forgotten.

If they refused the toqeph's invitation—which probably wasn't an invitation, but a command—would she try to move them by force? They wouldn't go easily, so refusal would cause many deaths. Daviyd had seen the character of these people; he knew killing the villagers would cause grief to those who'd be sent to enforce the toqeph's command. Moreover, he knew what pain such an action would cause her. She'd extended the invitation in good faith, out of the proper desire for the good of all Gannah as was her duty as leader. It would not benefit Gannah—neither the Dathan nor the Toqephites—to rebel against that goodness.

He'd thought the promise in the prism's light meant his people's redemption. Now it seemed it would be the undoing of his whole world.

THE LAST TOQEPH

The true Gannahans would be absorbed by the settlers, their pure ways lost forever.

The weight of this knowledge slumped his shoulders, and his head bowed, directing his gaze to the book in his lap. That feeling of lost familiarity, of having seen these things before, prodded his mind like wakefulness nudging aside a dream.

He ran his hands over the book. He had seen one like this, written in the Gannahan language. And he'd seen it long ago. The memory was buried, but it was there.

He raised the book to his nose and sniffed. Ran his fingers along the worn gilt edges.

And saw, in his memory, a book like it open in his father's hands. Abba was reading it. Then he looked up, saw Daviyd watching him, and smiled. "Good morning, little one. Thou art up early today." Daviyd had run to Abba and climbed into his lap. A glance at the open book yielded nothing of interest, for it had no pictures.

He remembered another incident, too, that occurred later, probably a year or more. Abba was upset with Emma. Angrier than Daviyd had ever seen him. He'd tried to hide from the sight and sounds, but he heard enough to know that Abba was furious with Emma for destroying a book that was bound on the left.

A book that looked like the one in Daviyd's hands.

Half fearful of what he might find, he opened it randomly, about three-quarters of the way into the volume. The old Gahannan characters flowed across the page, almost glowing with vibrancy. Daviyd's hands trembled and he laid the open book down on his lap. His eye fell on words that somehow commanded his attention: *Come unto me, all that labour and are heavy laden, and I will give you rest. Take my yoke upon you, and learn of me; for I am meek and lowly in heart: and ye shall find rest unto your souls. For my yoke is gracious, my burden light.*

Dengel's speech worked its way into his consciousness. Daviyd connected with Hushai's meah again for help in understanding. "It matters not where a person is born, where he lives, or what he's been taught to believe."

The Earther waved the volume in his hand. "The God of this book is the Creator of all the worlds and holds the highest authority. He gave the

THE LAST TOQEPH

people of Earth His revelation so that we might all know what our Maker requires of His creation."

Daviyd frowned in concentration. The idea of a creator made sense, for nothing could exist without someone having made it. And if someone made it, that entity did, logically, deserve to be honored, just as a father is honored by his children.

But did this creator actually reach out to people and expect a response? His hands trembled at the thought. The man said this highest authority told the Earthers what he required. What could he want of them?

Dengel answered his question. "As the Spirit said through the prophet Micah, He requires all people to do justly, to love mercy, and to walk humbly with Him.

"The command to do justly is known instinctively by everyone everywhere, though not all obey. I'm told this requirement, in the Old Gannahan society, was called living for the good of Gannah."

Daviyd flushed. The man might be an Earther, but he knew what he was talking about.

Dengel continued. "God also calls all people to love mercy — to realize that none of us is guiltless. As we hope for mercy for ourselves, so must we grant mercy to others.

"In addition, the Creator and King of the universe calls us to spend our life's journey by His side. To walk with Him in humility, recognizing our unworthiness, acknowledging that if He dealt with us as we deserve, He would slay us on the spot."

Struggling to breathe, Daviyd pulled his meah away from Hushai's. He slammed the book shut against the words that glared at him from the pages. Out of the corner of his eye, he saw Hushai turn his head, felt the boy's questioning gaze. In his memory, he saw Adam standing, tall as a tree, in the prism's light. And realized that the redemption offered was far more than the mere return of Natsach to his rightful throne.

Come unto me.

A shiver shook Daviyd's body. The Voice that spoke to Abba was the One who spoke through the pages of this book, and through the voice of the man on the platform.

Take my yoke upon you, and learn of me.

Daviyd reached toward the Voice in his meah. *I come! My Yasha, I come!*

40

Faris wheeled Lileela through the doorway to her aunt and uncle's apartment. Almost before the door closed behind them, Aunt Skiskii swooped down and absorbed Lileela in a loud, blubbering hug.

Kughurrrro, his leg propped on an ottoman and one ear covered with a bandage, made a noise like a squeaky gate then chuckled and spoke in clumsy Standard Speech. "Delcon to dy hone."

Faris made a small bow, understanding the gibberish to mean *Welcome to my home*. "I'm happy to be here, Mr. Kughurrrro. I'm happier yet that you're safely home and on the mend." He turned his attention to Lileela, thinking to rescue her from Skiskii. But Auntie ceased smothering her niece without his intervention.

She shifted her enthusiasm toward Faris. "Oh, Dithta ThairrgHEEES!" He guessed she was trying to say *Oh, Mr. Faris* as she lunged toward him with open arms, then — apparently remembering the Gannahan custom against touching — stopped and dropped her arms, bowing instead. He had to step back to avoid being butted by her spiky-haired head.

Once she stood upright again, still squawking her unintelligible version of Standard, Faris craned his neck to look her in the eye as he tapped his earpiece. "I have a translator, so I'll understand if you speak your own language."

That brought on an excited flurry of voices from all over the room. One of Faris's ears registered the cacophony while the other heard the translation. The combination made his head ache. Would everyone shriek at once during the worship service too?

Lileela joined in with animation, greeting her aunt and her father, inquiring about her uncle's health, and exchanging greetings with the

THE LAST TOQEPH

visitor, Kohz, who was every bizarre centimeter the quintessential Karkar, right down to the brightly dyed hair and extravagant cosmetics.

Faris discerned that on Karkar, introductions must be a long, formal, ear-rending affair. When it came time for him to greet Kohz, his "I'm very pleased to meet you" seemed grossly insufficient, so he added a lame, "I trust your stay on Gannah has been pleasant thus far?"

Kohz expelled a thunderous guffaw that barely registered on his expressionless face. "*Gannah* and *pleasant* so seldom belong in the same sentence, the combination sounds like the lead-in to a joke. But yes, now that you mention it, my stay here has been more tolerable than I anticipated. Nevertheless, I do *so* look forward to returning to my quarters on the *DeLaCruz*. My lungs rebel at breathing raw, unfiltered air. The desolation and loneliness of this wilderness has my every nerve on edge. And, of course, walking about outdoors, with no protection whatsoever between myself and the open sky, is unsettling in the extreme. Yet you people have made me feel welcome to the best of your feeble abilities, and for that, I am deeply grateful. When I think of Dr. Pik's first visit to this wasteland before any attempt had yet been made to rehabilitate it, I marvel that he was able to survive a day, let alone a week. It is a striking testimony to the power and grace of God."

During this protracted speech, Faris alternated between the desire to punch the man and to laugh out loud. The final statement, however, made him settle on a smile. "Indeed it is."

Lileela took his hand, and he looked down at her in the wheelchair. Her brilliant green eyes sparkled with tears. "Thank you for coming here with me."

He bent and whispered in her ear, "I wouldn't miss it for all the Kankakar Jewels."

Adam hadn't been able to snag Captain Bennett after the worship meeting, so when the children were bedded down in the evening, he left Elise and her mother and headed for the palace. The guests would be in the central hall that evening, meeting any of the settlers who wished to speak with them.

To save time, he took the tube. The platform beneath the palace was empty of people, as was the ramp that took him to the main floor. The drone of human conversation reached his ears long before the hall's entrance came

THE LAST TOQEPH

into view. It grew louder as he neared, and light from the open doors promised lively company within.

It wasn't company he sought just now, though; he needed help. If he could convince the captain to assist with the transportation of the villagers, it would make his life a gackload easier.

He'd taken only a few steps inside the room when something rammed into the backs of his legs, buckling his knees. He flailed his arms but fell anyway, pulling down two nearby children and a young woman before landing on his left shoulder and cracking the side of his head. One of the kids, a boy of about eight, lay pinned under his legs.

The child didn't move. It was Jax's son, Kendall. Had he killed him? Half-dazed from the crack on the head, Adam moved his legs from the child. Was he breathing?

Freed from Adam's legs, Kendall groaned. Adam reached for him, feeling him for injuries. "I'm so sorry! Are you okay?"

The child clambered to his knees. "I'm fine. I'm sorry, Dr. Pik." He bowed, face to the floor. "I didn't see you, sir. I wasn't watching, and—"

Adam's head swam and he struggled to make his vision clear. "I nearly squashed you flat. I hope I didn't hurt you."

Jax's wife, Gillian, stood above her son, her image doubled and wavering. "Dr. Pik, I am so sorry." She grabbed Kendall's arm and yanked him to his feet, at the same time addressing Zuri Ayo, who was disentangling herself from the other fallen child—Kendall's twin sister, Kathleen. "Zuri, are you okay? Kathleen, come here. Oh, stop crying, you're not hurt a bit."

Zuri stood, giggling as she brushed herself off. "I'm fine, Mrs. Florida. It was funny, really, the way Dr. Pik—" She cast a quick glance at Adam, then looked away, intent on straightening her clothes. "I'm not hurt. Don't worry about me."

Adam rubbed his eyes. His vision was clearing, to his relief. "Are you sure you're all right, Miss Ayo? I didn't mean to knock you over." Had his flailing hand put that mark on her face?

"I'm okay, really." More giggling. She helped Kathleen climb over his outstretched legs to get to her mother.

He moved his left arm and winced. But with another rotation of the shoulder, he could see the injury wasn't serious. The greatest damage was to

THE LAST TOQEPH

his pride. Fortunately, most people's attention was elsewhere. He rose slowly.

All the while, Jax's wife continued to apologize to Adam, then to Zuri, then scold her children in turn, until Adam raised his hand—as much to balance himself on his way up as to reassure her. "Please, Mrs. Florida. No harm done. Don't give it a thought."

Zuri put her hand on Kathleen's head. "You sure you're okay, hon?"

Eyes wide, the little girl nodded up at her, and Zuri bobbed a small bow to Jax's wife. "I've got to go, Mrs. Florida." She gave Adam a sidewise look, fighting a grin. "Dr. Pik." She turned and hurried away.

Adam's shoulder still throbbed and his head rang, but both would soon pass. What a spectacle.

"Mrs. Florida, I apologize. I stepped in their path. I truly hope I haven't injured anyone. Kendall, especially. I'm surprised I didn't crush him to death."

She looked up at him, her expression uncertain. "Are you sure you're all right? That was quite a fall you took." Squinting closer, she frowned. "Did you bang your face? It looks like you're getting a black eye."

"No, ma'am, I'm getting *over* a black eye. It's several days old." He felt a little giddy. Probably should sit down.

"Well, you don't look so good." She spoke to the children. "You two, no more running. If you want to run, go out in the courtyard with the other kids. In fact, do that." She put one hand on each of their backs. "Go on, get out of here."

They each bobbed a bow then turned and scampered away.

She called after them. "*Walk* to the courtyard! Don't run."

They slowed their steps—but not much. Adam wished he could run away too.

Hushai and Ittai materialized from nowhere. "That was a nice one," said Ittai.

"Yeah." Hushai grinned. "You should have seen yourself. Arms and legs everywhere. I'm surprised you only took down three people." He grabbed Adam's arm. "Come on and take a load off."

Ittai took the other arm, and Adam allowed them to guide him. The people standing about, blend glasses in hand, moved aside at Adam's approach, nodding their greetings. A couple of the men grinned. "You okay? I didn't know you could fly."

THE LAST TOQEPH

"Fine, thanks. Just part of my training." How many had seen that flop? All he needed to do now was faint on his way to that chair up ahead, and he'd be the headline on tomorrow's news report.

His brothers found him an empty upholstered chair at the edge of a group who didn't seem to notice him. He sank into it, but its back was too short to lean his head against, as he discovered when he nearly decapitated himself trying. Straightening, he rubbed the back of his neck.

"We were just going to get some blend. I'll get you one too—hang on." Hushai hurried off, darting among the people like an aphaph bird on its morning hunt.

Ittai climbed beside Adam. "Hey, this is the best day ever. Did you hear?"

Still holding the back of his neck, Adam flexed his sore shoulder. "Did I hear what? That your big brother's a clumsy oaf? I'm sure that'll be the talk of the town in about three minutes."

"No, not that. That was funny, but it's not big news."

Adam scanned the crowd. He knew all the faces but couldn't locate any of those he most wanted to see. "Where's Abba?" That was the first he figured he'd spot, as his head rose above all the others.

"At Auntie's. Him and Mr. Kohz, and Lileela and Faris too. They went to Auntie and Uncle Kughie's for a Karkar worship meeting."

"I thought they did that in the afternoon."

"They're still there, I guess. I haven't seen any of 'em since. But guess what—"

Hushai appeared, carefully maneuvering through the crowd with three glasses of blend.

Ittai took a glass, and Hushai handed another to Adam. "Here you go. That'll make you feel better."

"Thanks." Adam took the glass and sipped. "So if Abba's at the Karkar worship meeting, where's Emma? She didn't go too, did she?"

Hushai answered. "She's up in the tower with Mr. Natsach."

Natsach. As if Adam didn't have a headache already. "What for?"

It wasn't an appropriate question, and he knew it. But the words escaped his mouth without passing through the monitor of his conscious mind.

THE LAST TOQEPH

Both boys' brows furrowed, and Adam blushed. "Never mind. I shouldn't have asked. So what was the exciting news you were starting to tell me, Ittai?"

His brother's expression transformed instantly to joy. "It's Mr. Natsach!"

"He met the Yasha!" Hushai grinned wide. "I was sitting next to him, and I felt it. It was like this jolt went through him or something, and I knew right away in my meah what happened."

Ittai came near to spilling his blend with his gesturing. "You should see him, Adam! He's so excited, he can't stop talking about it."

Hushai's eyes glowed. "And he's got a Bible Mr. Maddox gave him, it's in Old Gannahan, and he can read it, and he keeps opening it up and running his hands over it and saying, 'It is the Voice! The Voice that spake to mine ab!'"

"He says the Voice told his father about you." Ittai studied Adam's face, imploring. "Is it true? What does he mean?"

Adam's head spun, and he was glad he was sitting. But that's all he was glad of. That, and the fact that his Karkar heritage gave him the ability to mask his emotions. He was aware of his brothers' meahs pressing, but he kept himself closed. He didn't dare let them know how the waves of anger and hurt pounded in his head, tightened in his chest, and churned in his gut.

He should be happy for Natsach. But all he could feel was resentment. He hardly heard Hushai's babbling.

"He was all excited about the story in the Bible about the man with two sons. You know the one, where the first son went away and did all sorts of bad things, but the younger one stayed home and helped his father?"

Adam's whirring mind paused and focused on what Hushai was saying. "Hm?"

"Yeah, that's the one." Apparently Hushai sensed he had Adam's attention. "Mr. Natsach said he felt like he was the bad son, the one who went away. And the father in the story was like the Bara. He said you're like the good brother, the one who never left home. He's afraid you'll be jealous of him now that he's returned, like the brother in the story. I'm glad he's wrong about that, though. I just knew you'd be happy for him. It's like he's home now, right? And the Yasha is happy, and we're all happy, and it's like a party to welcome him."

THE LAST TOQEPH

Swaying back and forth in his eagerness, Ittai chimed in. "And all the other Natsach people are coming here too, right? You're not like that other son in the story at all, the one who got mad when his older brother returned. 'Cause you're gonna bring back all the other Natsach people, right, Adam?"

Adam closed his eyes and rubbed his temples. "Right. About that." He lifted his head. "I need to speak with the starship captain. Is he here, do you know?"

"Yeah." Hushai turned to search the area to Adam's right. "I just saw him when I got you the blend. I think he's —" He jumped to see over the adults. "Yeah, over there. Talking to Mr. and Mrs. Dmitry and the Browards."

Ittai bent and peered in the same direction, but at floor level. "I see his feet. He's got funny lookin' shoes." He stood upright. "Want me to go get him for you?"

"No, thanks." Adam rose. "You've pointed me in the right direction, that's all I need." Now that he was standing, he saw Hool, the grinning Cephargian, surrounded by children clamoring to rub his smooth, tattooed head. Beyond that cluster sat a group of elderly folks, including the two old ship captains Broward and Dmitry and their wives. He couldn't see Captain Bennett, but he did see a set of legs and feet clad in clothing that, as Ittai had said, was funny looking.

"Thanks, guys. Hey, where are the girls?"

Hushai shrugged. "They're around here somewhere."

"They're in the courtyard." Ittai drained his blend. "Tamah wanted to play shuffaball, and I don't know what Ra'anan's doing. I'm going out too. You comin', Hoosh?"

Adam gave them a wave. "Go have fun. I'm going talk to our visitors."

He made his way to the cluster of furniture on the far side of the room where the old folks sat with the ship captain. Bennett wasn't elderly, but he probably had plenty to talk about with the two old starsailors.

Sylvia Dmitry was the first to see him. "Ah, there's Dr. Pik's oldest son, Adam. I don't believe you've met him yet, have you, Captain? He's a doctor like his dad."

Bennett turned to look where she pointed, spied Adam, and rose. "I've met too many people to keep track of, but I'd remember this young man." He tipped back his head to greet Adam and extended his hand in the Earthish manner. "How do you do, Adam, is it? The Second Doctor Pik?"

THE LAST TOQEPH

Adam shook his hand then bowed in the Gannahan tradition. "I'm pleased to meet you, Captain Bennett. I am a doctor, but please, call me Adam. It's less confusing." He nodded greetings to the others, calling them each by name and mentally noting how the first generation of New Gannah was showing their age.

Dortius Dmitry, as bald as a Cephargian but without inked embellishments, rose, empty glass in hand. "I need a refill. Anyone else want something from the blend bar?"

They all shook their heads and thanked him. Adam turned to the captain. "I have a question for you, sir. Could I borrow you for a moment?"

"Certainly." Bennett moved with him away from the others. "But if I call you Adam, it's only fair that you call me Dan. I understand you're training to be a Nasi. Fabulous. What's that like, may I ask?"

Adam stepped to an unoccupied space near the wall. The man spoke with an unfamiliar accent, and his scent seemed foreign too. Adam found that strange, since he'd lived around Earthborn people all his life. "I'm sorry, but I'm not permitted to talk about the Nasi training. The only way to learn about that is to become one of us."

Bennett chuckled. "I guess I'll have to live in ignorance. So what can I do for you, Adam?"

The man's foreignness made Adam uncomfortable, and he hated to ask any favors of such an outlandish person. But if Bennett could provide assistance with the transport problem, it would resolve some of the practical issues he'd been wrestling with. "I'm trying to work out a logistics matter, and I wonder if you might be in a position to help. How long will your ship be orbiting our planet?"

The captain shook his head, his mouth a straight line. "Just a few more Standard hours, I'm afraid. We have a rendezvous with another group of believers on Fueraq, and if we leave any later than—"

Adam gasped. "Excuse me—did you say Fueraq?"

The captain smiled. "Surprised?"

"I thought Fueraq uninhabited. And uninhabitable."

"It is." Bennett shrugged. "We're not staying, of course. Just meeting in orbit above it. It's quite exciting, actually. Believers are convening from all over the galaxy to compare notes, to strategize. It'll be a conference unlike anything ever seen before, with Christ-followers from five planets."

THE LAST TOQEPH

"Really!" Adam wished he could hear more, but he had too much to do. "How long did you say you'll be here?"

"In Gannahan time—" The captain's gaze went toward the ceiling as he made mental calculations. "We leave orbit in the middle of the night tomorrow. Not sure what you'd call it, sometime in that dark blue or black band on your timedial thing."

Adam's heart fell, but he nodded, keeping up a pleasant front. "I see. Well, never mind then. That doesn't give us time."

"Sorry, Adam. I'd like to help you out, whatever your question is, but I've got every minute scheduled between now and then." He glanced at something strapped to his wrist that was probably a timepiece, though it had only numbers. "Tell you what. Logistics, you say? I don't know what you're moving or what resources you have, but if you'd like to talk about it, I've got a few minutes. What's the situation?"

Stepping back to make room for a family passing by, Adam swallowed what remained of his pride. "I appreciate that. Let's find a place out of the way of the traffic."

41

Lileela rose from the wheelchair and, with Faris's assistance, moved to their sitting room sofa. Though his help wasn't necessary, she reveled in his doting and didn't wish to discourage it.

He sat beside her. "Too tired this evening to do the exercises Adam gave you?"

He'd missed his second shave today, and between the stubble and his droopy eyes, he looked wearier than she felt. She smiled. "I'm sorry the worship meeting gave you a headache. But it energized me. I can do the exercises by myself if you want to rest."

He chuckled. "No, I'll be fine now that I'm out of the noise. Oh, yeah—" He reached for his ear and removed the translator. "Don't need this anymore."

She answered with the guttural Karkar phrase meaning *one never knows*—but only because it utilized the lower range of the audio spectrum. She'd have spared him if any of the syllables were shrill.

"I don't know what you just said, but you can cut the Karkar, thanks." He went to the kitchen and put the translator in the drawer.

She called after him. "Think you'll ever acquire a taste for it?"

"Sure." He rejoined her. "About the time I develop a liking for being bitten by a nest of weaverrats."

That wasn't what she wanted to hear. How could she bring up what was on her mind if he maintained that attitude?

Her disappointment must have shown, because he quickly turned conciliatory. "Okay, so I'm exaggerating. It's not so bad as that." He took her hands. "Ready to put some weight on those legs?"

"The sooner the better." She let him pull her slowly to her feet. "I feel like I could walk without help, but I suppose I should follow doctor's orders."

THE LAST TOQEPH

"I suppose you should."

For several minutes, they worked on the simple motions Adam had prescribed, but her mind was elsewhere.

She broke the silence. "My legs hardly hurt at all."

"You have no idea how happy I am to hear that."

What was it about his deep voice that made her stomach flutter? She loved him so much, and he'd already shown his devotion to her in so many ways. How could she ask him to sacrifice even more? "Thank you for digging me out of that hole."

"You'd have done the same for me."

She tried to imagine that scenario. "No, I wouldn't. I'd have just sat outside and prayed."

He supported her from behind, hands on her waist. "That's pretty much all I did too. But I did play around with some rocks at the same time."

"That must be the secret to effective prayer. Playing with rocks."

"No. I think the secret is standing on the Rock."

Pain shot through her left leg, and she shifted all the weight to her right. It ached too. "I think I should sit down now."

He helped her to the couch then sat beside her. "That was a longer workout than Adam recommended anyway. You're doing great."

"Lying there in that mine, I never thought I'd be able to stand again. Or see the light of day." Her eyes filled. "Or you."

He took her in his arms and she listened to his heartbeat. How could she tell him what she wanted to say?

"And I'll bet you never thought you'd ever want to go to Karkar again, either."

She pulled back and stared at him wide-eyed. "What?"

His face eased into a half smile. "I might not have a meah, but I can tell what's been on your mind ever since the morning worship." He tapped his temple. "I could see the gears turning."

She bit her lip. "Then why aren't you upset?"

"My darling. What kind of a husband would I be if I didn't want my wife to obey the Yasha's leading?"

"But—how can I leave you?" Her throat tightened around a ball of tears.

"Leave me? What are you talking about?"

THE LAST TOQEPH

She lowered her head, unable to look him in the eye. "I want—I mean, the Yasha wants—" She rested against his chest. "I just know I have to go back to Karkar with Kohz. I've been trying to talk my way out of it, but the Yasha won't budge. He keeps telling me Karkar is where He wants me."

There. She said it. And it sounded as crazy as she'd feared.

"Don't you mean that's where the Yasha wants *us*?"

She sat up and looked at him. "You want to go too?"

"I'm a soldier. I go where I'm sent." He kissed her. "And for now, my orders are to stick with you."

Daviyd jogged through the pre-dawn night toward the airport. Here in Periy, no aphaph birds sang to the sun, but the world around him throbbed with life.

He'd been warned to be wary of animal attack outside the walls, particularly after dark. But he didn't want to take the tube. He wasn't sure how to work it, for one thing. But mostly, the flight home would be long and confining, and he needed the exercise.

Now that he'd started, though, he wondered if it might have been a mistake. Perhaps he'd grown over-confident after living in a land with few large predators. Every pore tightened with the awareness of creatures' eyes and meahs upon him.

So far, he'd only had actual run-ins with insects. They beleaguered him by the swarm. He imagined an observer would see a visible cloud surrounding him and trailing behind like a tail. He covered his mouth and nose with his hand to keep from inhaling them as he ran.

If not for the insects, he'd be unencumbered. Gone were the shoes that pinched, the socks that bunched, the clothing that chafed and made him sweat. Carrying only his newly-acquired Bible and wearing nothing but the breechcloth and skirt he'd arrived in, he felt light and free, ready for anything.

About a ten-minute jog ahead, the airport lights came on. Jax must have arrived. He had preparations to perform before takeoff and wouldn't be looking for him immediately, but Daviyd hastened his pace. The sooner he entered that flying machine, the sooner he'd be on his way home.

He didn't reach for anyone in his meah as he usually did when he thought of the village. What he had to say would be best said in person.

THE LAST TOQEPH

Hearing the front door open again, Ra'anan left her breakfast to greet the visitors.

Mr. Binyamin, Faris's friend, had been the first, before Ra'anan had come upstairs. Abba, in the front room doing his morning devotions, was surprised by such an early visit. Mr. Binyamin had come to petition the toqeph for permission to leave Gannah with the *DeLaCruz*. Abba gave Mr. Binyamin the paperwork and let him sit at the dining room table to fill it out, saying he'd ask the toqeph to review the petition and rule on it immediately.

Shortly afterward, Dale Gazlo showed up with the same request. He was still in the dining room filling out his petition when Ra'anan came upstairs. He'd no sooner left and Ra'anan begun her breakfast than Auntie burst into the foyer.

From the kitchen, Ra'anan heard Abba, still in the sitting room, greet her in the Karkar language. "Skiskii, you're out early this morning. What can I do for you?"

"Oh, Pik, dear, I'm so aflutter. We want to go home!"

"I beg your pardon?"

"Kughurrrro and I, we want to leave on that starship and go back home. We've never really been Gannahans, you know, never really fit in. And now, with what Kohz spoke about yesterday, all the opportunities opening up for the gospel among the Karkar? Well, Kughurrrro said last night, and I agree, that we really should go. We need to tell them, and little Skughokii needs to grow up in civiliza—I mean, around her own kind, and, well, it's not every day a starship comes to Gannah, and if we don't go now, we might never get a chance to, and so that's why I'm here. To find out how we might go about booking passage on Kohz's ship."

If that ear-rending speech hadn't wakened everyone downstairs, Abba's Karkar reply would have finished the job. "The captain has already told us they're willing to take any settlers who want to go. You'll just have to file a petition, and the toqeph will have to approve it. You and Kughurrrro must each fill one out and personally appear at the ruling."

"Oh. But he has a hard time getting around on that knee."

"He can fill out the petition at home and submit it electronically. Since he won't be able to manage the tower stairs, the toqeph will probably be willing to make her official ruling in the dining room. The laws are intended to keep things orderly, not to make life difficult."

THE LAST TOQEPH

After the requisite huffing and squawking, Auntie breezed out, and Abba stood in the kitchen doorway. "Well, this was unexpected."

That was putting it mildly. Ra'anan swallowed her micken. "Imagine!"

Abba's expression was bland as usual. "I keep getting interrupted up here, so I'm going downstairs to finish. Would you mind seeing to any more visitors who happen to show up on our doorstep?"

Ra'anan bobbed her head in a bow of assent. "Of course, Abba."

She poured herself a second cup of tea. All these people leaving Gannah? Mr. Dengel's message yesterday must have really struck home.

Once she thought about it, Mr. Binyamin's response wasn't surprising, as he had never wanted to come here to begin with. Mr. Gazlo, too, had always seemed a little restless, unable to settle into a career that suited him. Ra'anan had never had many dealings with either of them, though, and wouldn't mourn their loss for long. But the Kughurrrros? She'd miss them terribly.

Would any of them ever return? Probably not Mr. Binyamin. Mr. Gazlo might come back eventually, since he was born here. Emma always said a true Gannahan couldn't stay away for long.

The Kughurrrros, though, were Karkar through and through. Ra'anan's micken lay heavy in her stomach. Once they left Gannah, she'd never see them again. Her eyes filled with tears.

That's when the front door opened the fourth time. Who now? Ra'anan rose, but before she left the kitchen, her ears and her meah told her who'd entered the foyer.

"Lileela! Faris! Not you too!" Weeping, she ran to the wheelchair and threw herself into her sister's arms.

Daviyd didn't find the flight home as tedious as the journey to Periy had been.

For one thing, Jax was more talkative than Adam. A lot. And far more likeable.

A student of history, Jax loved to share what he'd learned. But when he asked Daviyd about the Dathan point of view, Daviyd squirmed with embarrassment at his own ignorance. This man had been born on Earth but knew more about Gannah than any Gannahan Daviyd had ever met. He knew a great deal about Earth history, too, and a little of other planets'.

THE LAST TOQEPH

When he expressed his admiration, Jax chuckled — as he did frequently. "To be a Nasi is to be a student. We must never stop learning."

Daviyd waved the Bible he held in his lap. "What know ye of this?"

"No one can ever know all that is within that wonderful book. But I am a student of it." Jax glanced Daviyd's way. "Hast thou a particular question?"

"I have many questions. But one especially. About the matter of this man Noah and the worldwide flood."

"Ah." Jax nodded. "Thou seest similarities with Gannah's flood of six years ago?"

"Yea. The two events are the same in many ways." He told Jax about the Ark display that had been built by the Toqephites many years ago, and how his father had led the Dathan to take refuge in it. "Mine Ab was like Noah. Except it was not he who built the Tebah. And he did not survive the Flood."

Daviyd explained how his father had died when the boat plunged over the cliff. "And the bow in the cloud, as the book doth call it. Doth that mean a rainbow?"

"As I understand it. It was given as a sign of God's promise to never again destroy Earth with a flood."

"Is a rainbow always a sign of a promise?"

Jax didn't answer for several moments. "On Earth, it shall always carry the meaning God gave it. I have often seen rainbows in Gannah as well, and they are beautiful. But I know not if the Yasha hath assigned any significance to them."

Daviyd re-read the pages in the book that described the Flood. He had no difficulty following the basic story, but there were things hidden within the words, mysteries he couldn't make out.

Frustrated, he reached in his meah for the Yasha and realized he was connected already. Was that what the settlers meant by being indwelt with the Spirit? The Yasha was always there and ready to listen? What an amazing thing. But when he asked the Yasha for understanding, the response was much as a father gives a little child who is too young to grasp the explanation. No words were exchanged, but he knew the Yasha would show him the answers in time.

THE LAST TOQEPH

He closed the book and turned to Jax, the Earth-born Nasi warrior-student who seemed to prefer laughter over fighting. He fit behind the vehicle's controls more comfortably than the surly giant, Adam.

"How doth one become a Nasi?"

Jax chuckled. "One like me, not Gannah-born? Or merely how doth anyone?"

"I know the first—thou art Gannahan by choice and thus are Gannahan still. I meant the second."

Jax looked him over. "First, thou must complete the Seventh Level of education and be established in some worthy work for the good of Gannah." Daviyd's expression must have revealed his confusion. "What troubleth thee? The education, or the work?"

"Both. Please explain."

"Surely. We all learn common skills as we grow up, such as how to read, write, and figure. Use of a lahab. How to identify common trees, plants, and animals. Gannahan history, and suchlike."

"Yea. This I understand." He had learned some of that as a boy, but the young villagers had no resources for education.

"In order to determine that a child is learning what he must, he is tested from time to time. If he doeth well on the first test, he is said to have passed the First Level. He doth continue to study and learn until he can pass the Second. And so forth."

"And there are seven of these levels altogether?"

"Yea. Although all seven are not required. Most people pass the Fifth, but the Sixth and Seventh are specialized study."

"I see." Daviyd didn't entirely, but he'd figure it out. "And the worthy work? That is what a man doeth for the good of Gannah, such as the storekeeper or the gardener or the ones who make the tube run properly?"

Jax grinned. "Thou understandeth perfectly."

"I am not certain I do, but I shall learn. To be a Nasi, then, what else must one do?"

"First, he must gain the toqeph's permission. If he be deemed worthy, he must submit himself to the Nasi for further training. And that is all I can say on that subject."

"But a man must be a Nasi before he may take the throne."

Jax raised an eyebrow. "Yea. That hath been true since history began."

311

THE LAST TOQEPH

So much to be learned—and how could he learn if no one would tell him? One step at a time, apparently. "What must one know for the Level One test?"

Jax seemed to have no qualms about divulging those details, in great detail. Daviyd listened with a sinking heart. There wasn't a villager younger than he who could do all those things. Perhaps not even the older ones.

On no level would bringing his people together with the settlers be a simple task. Not in mind or in body. Daviyd had much work to do.

He could hardly wait to begin. "It is a very far distance. How can all my people be brought to Periy? This vehicle is small."

"Thou speakest truly; they cannot be transported on the Hatita. But we have someone working on that question, and I am confident he shall devise a good plan."

Ra'anan stood in the dining room with her arms around the sobbing Tamah. The boys watched from the doorway, eyes wide and faces pale. She took a deep breath. "Mine em…"

Ordinarily, the only time she spoke Old Gannahan was in the course of her lessons. But it seemed a fitting means, somehow, to plead with the utmost sincerity. "Thou wouldst surely not grant Faris and Lileela's petition. We might never see them again."

Emma's green eyes narrowed, and she spoke in the Standard Tongue. "The toqeph does not allow the whims of her children to dictate her decisions."

"It's no whim, Emma." Ra'anan wiped her eyes on a handkerchief. "I love her! I love Auntie too, and Skughokii, and I don't want them to go. But that, I can live with. I understand it. But not Lileela. We just got her back. You can't let her go. You can't!"

Ra'anan had never spoken so boldly to her mother, and the other children held their breaths, meahs cringing. But she couldn't hold her peace.

Emma's voice turned hard. "That's quite enough. Go." She pointed toward the hallway.

Ra'anan released Tamah and prostrated herself as required but said nothing. Just rose from the floor with gritted teeth, brushed past the boys, and hurried down the hall to the Grey Room, where she sat on the hard bench and cried into her handkerchief.

THE LAST TOQEPH

Though she maintained proper silence, she let her mother know through her meah the full power of her frustration. She couldn't be punished for what she felt, only how she behaved.

But touching Emma's meah meant receiving as well as giving. And Emma's grief, which Ra'anan now shared, plunged to depths she'd never known possible.

My Yasha! She groaned within, too stricken for speech. *I'm so sorry! Oh, please, help dear Emma to bear it!*

42

Daviyd stared out the plane's front window. "There ahead." He pointed. "Where the land droppeth away and the river doth fall into the vale."

"I see it." Jax nodded.

Daviyd's throat tightened with emotion, though he wasn't sure why. "That be the place."

The place of many significant events in his life. Few of them good, it seemed. It was, however, the place where he met the young man tall as a tree. The one who did, in fact, lead Daviyd to redemption.

But now it was up to Daviyd to share what he'd learned with the rest of the village. The heirs of those who for countless generations had stood firm against alien contamination.

How can I convince them Thou art the Father of them all? He still didn't understand how best to communicate with the Yasha. He was aware of their connection through the meah—or perhaps the Spirit, as the settlers said—but He didn't speak in the usual way. No one at the palace had been able to explain it to him, either. "When thou callest upon Him, He heareth," they said. "And He speaketh through His Spirit and through His word."

And once in awhile, obviously, through His Voice. Daviyd wished He spoke that way more often.

The machine lowered as it approached the cliff, and the spray from the waterfall misted the window with a liquid prism.

Daviyd blinked back tears. Yea, the Yasha spake in numerous ways.

The ground fell away and the plain emerged from the cloud. It spread flat and green beneath the Hatita, bisected by the river and dotted with

THE LAST TOQEPH

rocks. And trees the height of a certain dour young man. How could anyone who knew the Yasha not be filled with joy?

As Daviyd expected, no one had come to meet him. "There. On the other side of the river, near that large rock. That is where Adam landed."

"Gotcha." Jax sent the plane in a wide arc swinging toward the area indicated. Daviyd remembered Adam had done the same thing. The indirect approach must be a peculiarity of air travel.

So much to learn. "Is the operation of flying machines one of the things a Nasi must know?"

Jax shrugged. "A Nasi must know many things."

Daviyd took that as a yes but said no more. The plain drew closer at a dizzying speed. How many times must he fly before he overcame the terror of this? He gripped the arms of his seat, and every muscle tensed as the plane struck the ground, bouncing wildly.

"Yikes." Jax chuckled. "I might have found a smoother spot, no?"

Daviyd clenched his jaw lest he bite his tongue as the plane chattered a bone-jarring distance before coming to a wheezy halt. "No. I mean, thou couldst scarcely have found a rougher one."

"Sorry." Jax took a deep breath. "Well. The old Earthers had an adage about flying. Any landing from which thou canst walk away is a good one."

The vehicle sighed and hissed, and Daviyd relaxed his grip on the seat arms. "Thou hast done well, then. Though my stomach hath not yet landed." He leaned back in his seat and expelled a long breath. "Ah. Now I am united again with myself."

Touching this control and that, Jax grinned. "Thou art a good man, Natsach." He operated a lever and both doors opened upward. "I shall get out, stretch my legs, and eat a sandwich. Then I must replace the fuel cell."

Daviyd's legs felt a little shaky. Hanging onto the side, he lowered himself down. Once his bare feet touched the grass, strength surged into his limbs. What a relief to be on solid ground. "Ye of Gullach have been most hospitable. I would return the kindness, but—" He hadn't been ashamed to show Adam his home because he had not yet seen how the settlers lived. Now, the knowledge that the true Gannahans lived in squalor while the Outworlders enjoyed every luxury grated on him so deeply his soul bled.

Moreover, there was much to be done. Much to be told. Trying to entertain Jax would not only embarrass him, but it would keep him from the

THE LAST TOQEPH

business that pulled him back to the village with such urgency. Still... "Is there anything I might help thee with before I go?"

Jax didn't answer until he'd finished stretching. "Nay. But I feel—I hate to see thee run off empty-handed." He reached into the plane and grabbed a pack. "Here, let me at least—"

"Nay." Daviyd wasn't familiar with the term *empty-handed*—Jax probably employed a mistranslation from the Standard Tongue—but its meaning was self-explanatory. "The toqeph offered me gifts, as did Jerry and his wife. But I told them then, as I tell thee now, what ye have already given is more than sufficient. I take home a treasure beyond compare."

Jax dropped his pack on the seat then disappeared on the other side of the plane, still talking. "I understand. Did I mention that thou art a good man?"

"Thou didst, yea. I am Gannah, and Gannah is good."

Jax rounded the Hatita and approached. Grinning, as usual. "I like that. Is that an old saying? I have never heard it before."

Daviyd shrugged. "My people have always said it."

Drawing near, Jax extended both arms, palms facing forward. "It hath been my pleasure to know thee, Natsach. I hope to see thee again soon, and to meet the rest of thy people."

Grateful Jax hadn't tried to shake hands like an Earther, Daviyd bumped the heels of his hands against Jax's. Then he bowed deeply. "Thou, too, art a good man, Jacksonville Florida. I wish thee safe travels."

Jax returned the bow. "The Yasha be with thee, Natsach Daviyd Natsach."

Daviyd paused. "Yea, He is." Then he realized Jax's statement must be a farewell, and he returned it with the first response that came to mind. "And with thee."

Jax laughed. "Get thee gone." He made a shooing motion. "I know thou art eager to see thy family."

The man was so much pleasanter than Adam. Daviyd grabbed the Book and trotted toward home.

Hushai sat in the crowded Meetingroom and swallowed hard.

He'd met Daviyd just a few days ago, and the man had only left this morning, but he already missed him. Or perhaps it was Lileela and Faris he

THE LAST TOQEPH

missed, though they weren't yet gone. Or Auntie and Uncle Kughurrrro, though they were still here too, large and loud.

All Hushai knew for sure was that a rock seemed to lie on his chest, and tears gathered, ready to burst out any minute.

No one would have noticed if they let loose, though. The Meetingroom was full of people, and at least half of them were crying.

Emma had approved all the requests, meeting with the petitioners in the dining room rather than the tower for Uncle Kughie's benefit. Which, of course, meant the kids had to leave the apartment. Hushai spent a few hours helping Mr. Mutombo in the fields. Tamah and Ittai each went to play with friends, and Ra'anan, released from the Gray Room, had gone to visit Elise, Everett, and the baby. Everywhere, the mood was gloomy.

The family was quiet at dinner. Emma had invited Lileela and Faris, but they had too much to do before they left. After dinner, Abba and Emma went to help them pack. Ra'anan and Tamah helped Auntie and Uncle Kughie. Hushai and Ittai stayed home and played games, though their hearts weren't in it.

Now, even though they were allowed to stay up late like at Wormfest, there was nothing festive about the occasion.

It seemed like half the planet poured into the Meetingroom. First, Emma spoke briefly. Then, Mr. Dengel and the settlers who were leaving Gannah each made a little speech.

After that, the travelers gathered in the middle of the room while everyone came to say goodbye. Hushai had never heard so much sniffling.

Finally, Emma took the platform again, with Abba, blank-faced, at her side. Everyone gave her their attention. Hushai, Ittai, and their sisters held hands.

"When I was growing up," Emma said, "my father often spoke of his sorrow on behalf of the peoples our forefathers massacred in the wars centuries earlier. Most particularly, the Karkar. They suffered greatly at our hands, and their conqueror, Hoseh the Great, regretted his actions deeply after he met the Yasha. But before he could try to repair the damage, the plague struck, wiping out millions of his people, and he had a world to put back together. He never made it back to Karkar.

"My father and his father before him dreamed of making friendly overtures to that planet, but couldn't discover how to take the first step. Until, that is, my father conceived the idea of bringing up the old, plague-

317

THE LAST TOQEPH

infested warships that Atarah Hoseh had buried in the sea. He planned to retrieve from them the Kankakar Jewels so that he might deliver the Jewels to the Karkar, from whom Hoseh had stolen them. He felt certain the return of that revered treasure would gain him an audience. It was his wish to tell them about the Yasha and impart to them a treasure greater than any jewels.

"But as you all know, his good intentions led to horrible results. The Jewels were returned, but by our own Dr. Pik." She put her hand on his arm and smiled up at him. "And Karkar remained antagonistic toward both Gannah and the gospel."

She took a deep breath. "It gives me great joy, therefore, to learn that some of my husband's people are open to the message and are coming to the faith. My father would rejoice at that. But not as much as he would delight in seeing his granddaughter hearing the Yasha's call to take the gospel to them. I believe it would be his hope that, for every Gannahan who died because of his error in raising the warships and releasing the plague upon this planet, a Karkar would receive eternal life in the Yasha.

"No one can bring Old Gannah back to life, but by the grace of God, I pray that the people of Karkar might be saved, so the deaths of my people would not be for nothing. Mr. Kohz, you are living proof that there is hope. And Kughurrro, and Skiskii. You are in the Yasha's kingdom as a result of the plague. And Lileela?"

Her voice broke and she paused. "Lileela, my firstborn daughter, my heart's delight." She paused again.

Hushai wasn't fluent in Karkar, but he knew the name *Lileela* meant just that: heart's delight. He lost the battle against tears and let them flow.

Emma continued. "It is with great, bittersweet delight that I send you from Gannah to do the work that was on my forefathers' hearts—the work that has always been on the heart of our Heavenly Father. May He make your labor fruitful beyond all imagining."

She turned to the others. "And Faris? Whom I love like a son?" She smiled. "As, genetically speaking, you probably are?" The corporate laugh rippling across the room sounded strained, and Hushai frowned. If the rumor was true that long ago Abba had taken Emma's DNA and sold it to the League of Planets, and that the League had used it to experiment with engineering a race of super-warriors, it would be a matter for shame, not joking.

318

THE LAST TOQEPH

Emma continued speaking to Faris. "I have great respect for you. For your courage in following the Yasha, though it made you an outlaw. For rescuing the Dengel family, though it went against your breeding and training. For your faultless love of my precious daughter. And now, for obeying the Yasha's call. I know this is not what you'd have chosen to do. But you are, above all, a faithful soldier. I salute you."

She made a small bow, then turned to Mr. Binyamin standing beside Faris and spoke encouragement to him as well. Then, on down the line to each of the Gannahans who would soon leave. Mr. Maddox came forward and led everyone in prayer, concluding with a song of hope and praise. Then it was over.

Over. Most of the settlers returned to their homes. Those who would be leaving, along with their families, filed out of the palace and down the ramp to the rail station.

The whole royal family squeezed into one pod. Fortunately they were all small except Abba. Tamah climbed into Emma's lap and fell asleep almost immediately. Everyone was red-eyed and sniffling except Emma and Faris, and they spoke very little all the way to the airport.

Faris had stowed Lileela's wheelchair in another pod, as there wasn't room for it in theirs. When they pulled up to the platform under the airport, he smiled at Hushai. "Hey, buddy, would you mind getting the chair for us?"

"Sure!" Hushai was glad for something useful to do. As soon as the pod came to a stop, he opened the door and hopped out. The other pods were lining up behind theirs, but Hushai didn't know which carried the chair. He was about go back in and ask when Faris called out, "Dale Gazlo has it."

"Okay." As the rest of the family exited, Hushai tried to figure out which car Mr. Gazlo rode in. But then Mr. Gazlo backed out of the pod at the end of the line, pulling the chair.

Hushai ran down the platform, dodging the other passengers. "I'll take that for you, Mr. Gazlo."

The man looked up and smiled. "Here you go." He relinquished the wheelchair.

"Were you the only one in the whole car, Mr. Gazlo? Where's your family?"

THE LAST TOQEPH

He shrugged as he walked beside Hushai toward the first car. "They didn't come."

"Why not?"

"My em is upset with me for going, and she forbade my brother and sister to see me off. They wanted to come anyway, but Cliff's an obedient son and Heather's not of age yet. So we said our goodbyes earlier this evening."

"But what about your abba?"

"He didn't want to upset my em any further, so he stayed home too." Mr. Gazlo spoke as if the situation didn't bother him, but Hushai thought it was terrible. How could a woman not want her son to obey the Yasha, no matter what the Yasha commanded? That was just wrong.

Unaided, Lileela exited the car and lowered herself into the chair, and the whole group left the platform and climbed the ramp to the airport.

The mood was somber. Abba carried the sleepy Tamah, and Ittai clung to Emma's hand. Hushai walked with Ra'anan. In their meahs, the family communed with one another.

That was why they weren't surprised to find Adam waiting for them upstairs. He hadn't been able to get away for the gathering in the Meetingroom, but he didn't want to miss the farewells.

Hushai was always a little jealous of Adam and Lileela's relationship. They were Emma and Abba's first family, the two who were born before Emma was marooned on the other side of the planet. They had kept in meah contact the whole time Lileela was on Karkar. When the other three kids were little, they'd heard about their sister Lileela but had never met her, and so weren't able to know her in their meahs until she returned six years ago.

And now she was leaving again. Hushai could sense Adam's feelings about that. They were somewhat like Emma's—a mixture of sorrow and pride—but less deep and intense. And also tinged with a bit of disapproval. Hushai got the impression Adam didn't think the Karkar deserved the sacrifice Lileela and Faris were making.

But it was an offering to the Yasha, not to the Karkar. Didn't Adam understand that?

Daviyd left the meadow and followed the usual ayal trail through the trees. The ground beneath his feet, the roar of the falls behind, the scent in the air, all welcomed him home. On one hand, it seemed he'd never

THE LAST TOQEPH

left and all that had happened was a dream. But though the land was no different, Daviyd had changed. The last few days had been no dream; they were an awakening.

Some ten minutes from home, Emma rose from a rock where she'd sat waiting for him. "Greetings, my son."

He'd expected to see her, so he wasn't startled at her sudden appearance. He bowed. "Mine em. Before we reach the village, we have something to discuss."

Her brows rose. "So abrupt! One would think thee unglad to be home."

He hugged her. "Nay, I am glad. Very glad. I missed thee, and the others. But I have learned many things and discovered many questions. I would like answers before I return to the village."

Rising to her toes, she kissed his cheek then stepped back to study his face, still holding his shoulders. "I know thy questions, my son. And they do merit answers." She bent down to pick up a chophen fruit from the rock where she'd sat. "Hungry? Thou mayest eat as we speak."

He took the fruit—hard and gnarled, and riddled with worm holes. Typical of the Dathan's fare, but nothing like the plenty he'd grown accustomed to over the past few days. "My thanks to thee. I have not eaten this day." He took a bite. Its taste was bitter, like home.

She sat and patted the rock beside her. "Sit, my son, and we shall talk."

43

Sitting cross-legged on the ground with the other villagers, Daviyd licked the last drops of broth from the rough wooden bowl.

He handed the empty vessel to one of the boys whose task was to collect them then wiped his hands on his skirt. The time had come. *My Yasha, if it pleaseth thee, give me the perfect words.* He rose.

His gaze went from one upturned face to another. "Dear ones." He knew the name of each person gathered around him and loved them like the family they were. "I have already told you many things concerning my visit. The marvelous things I saw, the people I met who are a peculiar mix of Earth and Gannah."

He made a quarter turn to the right in order to face another group of listeners. As was customary, he would make slow revolutions as long as he spoke, so no one would be slighted. "I have told you I met with the toqeph, who did treat me with great kindness. She is not as I envisioned. She is a true Gannahan."

Low murmurs rumbled in his ears as well as his meah. For a Dathan, this was a near-traitorous statement.

"You saw the gifts she sent us when the flying machine first came. She sent them with sincere motive. It doth cause her grief that we struggle here in Yereq, having nothing, while she and the others have so much. I have spoken with her. I have seen her heart. There is no deceit in her."

How could he convince them? He put his hand on his chest. "Search ye my meah and see that I speak truly. Her sorrow is great for the horrors of the past. Knowing it was her father's error that brought the plague, she seeketh to redress the wrong. Her greatest desire is for the good of Gannah. That is what we want as well, is it not? The good of Gannah?"

THE LAST TOQEPH

Despite the shouts of assent, an unspoken *yea, but...* weighed heavy in the air. He didn't let it linger. "The good of Gannah! It is what we were born to uphold!"

They called out with conviction now. "The good of Gannah!"

"Yea, the good of Gannah is our calling. And we shall not let that responsibility fall to the ground. For we are Gannah. Gannah lives." He stood tall with fists raised in the traditional gesture that accompanied the cry. Everyone in the village rose and did the same, shouting, "We are Gannah. Gannah lives!"

Jether's voice rose above the others in a song, and the next moment, all the villagers joined him, dancing. Even as Daviyd danced, he felt the Yasha with him. He hadn't intended the meeting to take this turn, but he couldn't have come up with a better plan. The Yasha had answered his plea.

When the song ended, the people sat again and looked up at him, eager to hear more. He reached for the Yasha and felt as if He held his hand.

Adam yawned. He'd managed to accomplish all his goals for the day. Just one more task, and he could go home and get some sleep.

If you could call it a task. He rubbed his eyes. Physical activity would burn off tension. He'd run instead of taking the tube. He wondered if Elise would still be up.

After closing the lab, he hurried to his apartment. He entered quietly, hoping to not disturb his mother-in-law if she were asleep on the sofa. The room was dark, but her pillow and sheet were folded up neatly, and she was nowhere to be seen. Then he remembered she'd planned to go to the palace that night for the farewell.

He continued toward the hall and his bedroom, where the light was on.

Elise sat in the rocking chair reading while Joseph nursed. When Adam entered, she looked up. "Are they on their way already? I didn't hear the takeoff."

He bent and kissed her. "No. They're not launching until the second hour of Black Slumber." He ran a finger along Joseph's fuzzy head, but the baby was too busy guzzling to be distracted by the touch. "I'll meet the farewell party at the airport." He glanced at the title she was reading. "A galactic romance, huh?"

Her nose puckered. "I suppose you don't approve."

THE LAST TOQEPH

"It's not the sort of reading I go for, but— Wait a minute." He tried to put on a suspicious expression, but his ears smiled, spoiling the effect. "Is there a reason I *shouldn't* approve? What goes on in that kind of book, anyway?"

She laid the tablet on its face, grabbed his beard, and pulled him down to kissing range. "It's just a story. You know, girl meets boy, evil forces pull them apart, they get together in the end. The usual stuff."

"I don't believe I've ever read a book like that." After admiring his new son a few more moments, he stood, rubbing his back. "I need to loosen up." He went to his closet. "Where are my running shoes?"

"Probably outside the front door, right where you always leave them."

His jogging clothes were in the closet, though. "You're probably right." He changed his shirt. "Everything okay? Everett getting along with his brother? You and your mother aren't ready to kill one another yet?"

Elise answered softly as if the baby was falling asleep. "We're all fine. But how about you?"

The question caught him off guard but he continued changing his clothes. "Me? What about me?"

"I know this is killing you. Lileela going away."

"Yeah." The words *Lileela going away* fell on his heart like a hammer. "It is." He steeled his jaw against the emotion welling within him.

"I wish I could at least go with you to see her off. But Emma's not here to stay with the kids."

He squatted beside her chair and kept his voice low. "Not only that, but I need to run. And it's a little soon for you to be running with me."

"This is really huge. For the people going, and for us, staying." She bit her lip. "And we won't even be able to keep in touch with them."

"In most cases, no. But at least Lileela and I can."

"Sure wish I had a meah."

He had little to say except, "So do I. I wish they all did." He kissed her and rose. "I'll go look in on Everett and then be on my way."

As he tiptoed out, she stage-whispered, "Don't wake him up!"

He wiggled his fingers at her through the doorway in acknowledgement then stepped to Everett's door and peeked in. The boy's legs hung down from the bed, his upper half concealed behind the curtain. Had he been trying to get out, or just thrashing around in his sleep?

THE LAST TOQEPH

Adam rearranged the boy in his bed then tiptoed out. He blew Elise a kiss as he passed her doorway, but she didn't respond. Looked like she dozed in the chair.

His shoes were outside the door as she'd said. He put them on, did a few stretches, then thundered down the spiral steps to the courtyard.

The fountain towered in the dark, writhing like a living thing. He turned away from it and headed for the passage that led to the exit. Above, a few stars twinkled behind wispy clouds. The humid air was warm for this hour, and still. The pleasant chirping of *shiyrahs* echoed off the chatsr walls. The insects didn't seem to mind that his footfalls interfered with their song.

He stopped to open the gate then latched it behind him. Once in the open, he put on speed.

Even the mud-and-wattle chatsr walls seemed to listen as Daviyd spoke, telling of his adventures. The clothes he wore, the indoor plumbing, and the bed alcove where he slept behind a curtain.

"I had never seen these things before. Or had I? Surely, I do not see them here." He made a wide gesture with his arm. "But somehow, it seemed I saw them *again*, not for the first time. Did you not feel the same when opening the gifts the toqeph sent? Did it not seem that these were the things of home, but a home you could not quite remember?"

The murmurs of those who were about Daviyd's age confirmed that they felt the same. The oldest ones glanced at one another, their meahs carefully guarded. He shot a glance at Emma, who fixed her whole attention on him, ignoring the furtive looks of the other elders.

"I was confused at first, when I saw water coming out of the wall into bowls for washing. I knew I had seen this before, but could not locate the memory in my mind. Again and again this happened, and I wondered why it should be."

He made another quarter turn, and Emma was no longer in his line of vision. But he recognized her nod in his meah. *It is as thou sayeth. Be truthful with them.*

"After a time, I understood. I *had* seen these things before. Before the Great Flood, when we lived in the east, we had those things. And they were good, and right, and Gannahan. How had I forgotten?"

THE LAST TOQEPH

In the middle of the crowd, the piercing violet stare of Rahabiah, one of the elders, bored into him, coldly emphasizing the meah-spoken command. *Cease this nonsense.*

He glared back. *I cannot. One greater than thou hath command me to speak.* "I had forgotten, because I have ever been an obedient Gannahan. After the Flood, those of our mothers and fathers who survived knew we would mourn, not only for the family we had lost, but also for our homes and our possessions. They could see such things would never again be ours. Therefore they took measures to help us look forward rather than looking back with bitter regret."

The sun sank low in the sky, and, squinting against it, Daviyd made another quarter turn. "Remember ye that day? They took us—each child and young man, every one who was under the authority of his mother—and charged us to forget. They told us sternly that the homes we left were much the same as this." He extended both his arms. "If any of us objected that this was not true, we were punished as liars."

Daviyd saw from the villagers' expressions in the sharp-angled evening light that their minds rebelled at the suggestion. But as he continued speaking, he could tell that the memory of these things returned. "We were commanded to forget, because our mothers believed it was best for us. And we forgot, because we are good Gannahans. A good Gannahan obeys without question."

A few of the people nodded. Some murmured.

"The things I saw on the other side of the world reminded me. My memories would not have returned if not for having seen people living the way we formerly lived. But my memories did return, and I shall not forget again."

As he made another turn, the murmuring spread throughout all the villagers. He spoke above it, and the rumble soon quieted. "I spake of this with mine em upon my return, and she hath confirmed it. We were commanded to forget for the good of Gannah, and for the good of Gannah, we obeyed. As well as they were able, the elders also deliberately lost the memories. But they will now confess to you that what I say is true."

Daviyd hadn't planned to, but he felt this was a good time to let someone else pick up the discussion. He crossed his legs and sat.

Two people stood at once, demanding explanation of the elders. A third, Iri, rounded on Daviyd. "How dare thee make such accusation!"

THE LAST TOQEPH

Others rose to shout Iri down. But Daviyd remained silent. He had spoken the truth as the Yasha had led and would leave the result to Him.

Adam approached the airport where the shuttle from the *DeLaCruz* idled on the tarmac, lights ablaze. As he drew nearer, he could see through the lobby windows that the farewell party hadn't arrived. He jogged to one of the back entrances then walked the halls to cool down before heading for the front lobby.

He stopped in the restroom to splash water on his face. Elise was right. This would be difficult.

He looked for a towel but found none. Drat. He squeezed as much water from his beard as he could then gave his head and hands a few shakes.

In the lobby, Dan Bennett sat in a chair facing the hall through which Adam entered. Elbows on knees and hands clasped, the captain bowed his head as if in prayer, backlit by the starship's glow. Adam slowed and quieted his steps in an effort to not intrude.

Dan looked up. "Oh, hello, Adam." He rose and extended his hand in the Earthish manner.

Though the custom felt strange, Adam shook his hand. "Good to see you, sir. I'd like to thank you again for your help earlier. Are you sure you can spare those housing units?"

Dan nodded. "Absolutely. I've been wanting to get them out of my storage compartment. Space is especially tight now that we're taking on more passengers and cargo, so you're doing me a favor by taking them."

That was the first Adam had heard about goods being transported. "I wasn't aware you were carrying cargo."

"The passengers are bringing more things than will fit in their living quarters, so much of what we've onloaded for them we've put in storage. But there's also the Orvilleware."

Adam blinked. "Orvilleware?" An image of the bumbling Orville Vigneron came to mind.

"Yes, it's fantastic stuff. Not only is it beautifully crafted, but it's made of some of the rarest minerals in the galaxy. Along with each piece, Mr. Kughurrrro has provided a certificate of authenticity as having been handmade on this planet of natural Gannahan flakestone and livingore."

THE LAST TOQEPH

Adam's ears stiffened. "You mean *machalatsah*? Orville uses machalatsah in those plates and things he makes? Where'd he get it? I thought all the mines had been shut down since before the plague."

Dan shrugged. "I don't know about macha... whatever you said. Is that the Gannahan word for livingore? The metal that changes so dramatically in certain temperatures?"

"Yes. It's the rarest element in the galaxy. How did—"

"I'm sorry." Dan put a hand on his arm. "I didn't realize this wasn't widely known."

Adam's head spun and he sank onto a chair. This news was surprising, but the worst part was that it came from an Outsider. Why did the toqeph see fit to tell Captain Bennett these things, but not him? "Yes. Please fill me in."

"Apparently the Vigneron fellow stumbled upon this flakestone mineral, an anomaly even on this planet. As he dug the stuff out of the ground, he uncovered some veins of livingore. He didn't know what it was, but he recognized it had unusual properties. Through several years of experimenting, he came up with a process by which he glazed the stone with a mixture of livingore and crushed, melted glass—genuine Gannahan glass, of course, which is fabled throughout the galaxy. By controlling the thickness of the glaze in certain places to enhance the painted design, he was able to give the artwork the appearance of life and movement."

Adam nodded. He'd seen Orville's work, and it was remarkable, to say the least. "That's the secret? Machalatsah in the glaze?"

"That, and his amazing skill as an artist. Mr. Kughurrrro has analyzed the flakestone, and it contains minute amounts of the same ore. Turns out the work your Mr. Vigneron has been doing out there in that perilous wasteland has greater value than anyone suspected. He's creating a product that's not only beautiful but is of tremendous value anywhere in the galaxy. That's why the toqeph has declared it Gannah's new intergalactic currency."

Adam's mind grappled with the concept. "Intergalactic currency."

"That's correct. She's given us a number of pieces, which we should be able to exchange for goods and services wherever we go. Not to mention—" A sheepish grin softened his expression. "Blinding the eyes of the authorities to our subversive activities. An Orvilleware cup and saucer in the right hands could provide us with a safe foothold on any League planet."

THE LAST TOQEPH

"Even Earth?"

Dan shook his head. "Probably not there, no. That's where the devil has most at stake, so his opposition in that place is insidious and determined. But I'm not concerned about that, because the Lord's people are everywhere there. Just ask your brother-in-law. Earth is where Faris came to the faith despite the devil's attempts to keep him enslaved in darkness from the moment of his Petri dish conception."

Perhaps Adam had such a hard time grasping all this because it was late and his brain was tired. Whatever the reason, he'd have to mull these things over before he'd be able to fully understand.

The captain continued, heedless of Adam's inattention. "I think Mrs. Dengel and the girls will find the worst of their fears are unfounded."

Adam forced his mind to return to the conversation, but he missed what Dan was saying. "Oh?"

"They haven't forgotten the persecution they endured in Africa. Remember, they were kidnapped from their own beds and imprisoned. That's not an experience a person can easily dismiss."

"I wouldn't think so." It took Adam a moment to recall, but yes. It was Faris and his men who had captured them, under orders from their commander. "They were bound for some awful prison space station, were they not?"

"Dengel was. But the ladies' fate would have been worse. Your brother-in-law's orders were to deliver them to the Multicultural Pleasure Center on Station Six."

Adam knew nothing of any of that, but he could guess the ramifications. He thought of godly Mrs. Dengel and the two little girls the settlers had watched mature over the past six years, and his stomach went sour. "The League ordered Faris to do that? How—"

"Unless you've lived on Earth, you can't understand what a spiritual battlefield that planet is. Most of the Earthers don't realize it because they've always been in the midst of it, but Earth is the focal point of the whole cosmic struggle." He shook his head. "I can see why the ladies didn't want to go back to that."

That was news to Adam too. "I thought they'd petitioned for permission to leave along with the others."

"No, they requested permission to stay. But the toqeph turned them down. Apparently they'd never been granted citizenship, only temporary

THE LAST TOQEPH

visitation privileges until the mister came for them. When they petitioned now to stay permanently, the toqeph told them her authority doesn't supersede the husband's in this case. He came to collect his wife and daughters, and she wouldn't stand in the way."

Adam's ears twitched. There was still a lot about Gannahan law he didn't know. "Mrs. Dengel's been terribly worried, not knowing whether her husband was dead or alive. But I believe she thought when he arrived that he'd come here to stay. I don't blame her for not wanting to put the whole family in danger again." His stomach did a flip. "Graver danger than I realized." Was that the sort of thing Lileela would be facing?

"Only the Lord knows for sure, of course. But the peril is considerably less on the other planets, and at this point, Dengel doesn't intend to take his family back to Earth. He sees doors wide open elsewhere and feels called to go through them. He believes, and I agree, that his family will be relatively safe from now on."

"I sincerely hope so."

Dan smiled. "I know you're concerned about the others as well. Your sister and her husband especially. But—" He paused. "Do I hear what I think I hear?"

Adam rose. "If you think you hear a crowd of people coming, I'd say the answer is yes."

THE LAST TOQEPH

44

Adam entered the toqeph's suite and glanced toward the dining room. The light was off and the door was open. His meeting with the toqeph, then, would be in the tower.

His heart sank. That's where she conducted the unpleasant business.

He turned toward the stairway door, straightened his shoulders, and toed his way up the shallow spiral steps. His proposal for moving the Natsachs to Periy had been well researched, clearly explained, and professionally presented. If anyone could come up with a better plan, he'd like to see it.

True, its success depended in part upon forces beyond anyone's control, like the weather. But it was workable. What could she possibly object to?

The throne room doors were open, nestled in their pockets in the wall, and Emma sat at a small round table reading something on a tablet. Two teapots steamed on the table with a plate of sweet-smelling melon cubes between them.

She looked up, her expression kindly. "Come in, Adam."

Somewhat heartened by her pleasant demeanor, he entered and bowed deeply. "Madam Toqeph."

"Sit down, please."

He bowed again and sat, remaining erect and formal. Her meah gave him mixed feelings.

"I've reviewed your proposal." She nodded toward the teapot in front of him. "Have some. It's an herbal tea Mira Macelar concocted. Rather tasty."

THE LAST TOQEPH

He picked up the pot and strained tea into the cup. It did smell good. A mix of fruit and spice. "What does she call it?"

"Periy Pink. I think it'll catch on."

While he stirred in a dribble of honey, she picked up the tablet. "Your proposal is well thought out and contains all the necessary elements. I'll discuss it with the council, but I expect to approve it as submitted."

Flooded with immense relief, he lowered his head in a bow and kept it down for a moment. "Thank you, Madam. I'm honored."

He lifted his gaze into the beam of her maternal smile. "As am I, to have such a son and heir."

He swallowed hard, uncertain how to respond.

"No need to answer. I just wanted you to know." She chuckled. "Try to imagine, if you will, how unlikely I was as a wild Gannahan to marry a half-Karkar. I never would have considered such a thing if the Yasha had not made it clear that He required it." She sipped her tea. "Even so, it took me a while to come around. And, of course, I was the toqeph. What kind of royal heir would a union like that produce? My ancestors would be appalled."

Adam's heart pounded. That's what she was working up to. He was unqualified for the throne because of his mixed breeding. Now that there were real Gannahans available, she no longer had to settle for second best. He set down his cup before he dropped it.

"I couldn't have envisioned how very Gannahan you'd turn out, nor how very proud you'd make me. Obviously, the Yasha knew what He was doing when He commanded the marriage."

He expelled the breath he'd been holding. "It has always been my goal—"

"I know. You've made me the envy of every mother on the planet."

While she ate a piece of melon, he sipped his tea, thankful for something to do, for he could think of nothing to say.

She licked her fingers then leaned back in her chair. "Your proposal is explicit in every detail and needs no clarification. I didn't summon you here to question you about it."

His brows rose.

"There's another matter we must discuss." She crossed her legs. "My meah, as you know, isn't as strong as it was before my injury, so I haven't been able to communicate as well as I'd like. I'm aware that you've felt some, ah, insecurities recently, concerning the Natsachs."

THE LAST TOQEPH

That was for sure. "I'll admit, I have been wondering what it all means."

She nodded. "I am, as you have sensed, drawn to Daviyd in a deep and indescribable way. He is like a cherished memory come to life. I see in his figure and hear in his voice echoes of my first husband, my first love." Her voice grew husky. "The language, the mannerisms, the cultural mores and traditions he embodies are fundamentally my own. They represent an essential part of me I thought I'd lost forever."

Her meah reached toward his, and, weak as it was, he was moved by what it conveyed. He responded in Old Gannahan without intending to. "Thou hast no need to explain, mine Em. It is, I perceive, past explaining."

Her expression eased into a pensive smile. "Verily, thou art a good son." She switched to Standard. "When my shuttle went down and I wandered alone all those months, I made some disturbing discoveries. They upset my equilibrium, and it took me a long time to find my bearings. You'll recall how strange my behavior was when your father found me and brought me home."

Adam nodded. "I was young, but I remember. Abba said it was from the stress of isolation and exhaustion. And then to come home and learn about Lileela's accident and Bushati's rebellion? Abba said it made the floor collapse beneath your feet. But that with proper nutrition, rest, and the support of your family, you'd come around." He took a sip of tea. "And you did."

"But the change this new knowledge worked in me remained." She shifted in her chair. "I must tell you what I learned in the Ruwach Gorge."

Something in her manner unsettled him. He took a piece of melon as casually as he could. "What did you find?"

She explained that the history of Gannah she'd been taught from childhood had been twisted. She discovered this when she came upon the ruins of a place that she recognized from childhood fairy tales. It was Ga'ayown, the fabulous palace of the mythical outlaws, the Rahab. A place she'd been taught didn't exist.

Adam's ears frowned. "But all that was real. They're treated as true in the history the settlers study."

"Now, yes. Because when I returned home, I had the curriculum changed. When I was a child and for many generations before, the history books were in error."

THE LAST TOQEPH

That didn't fit what he'd been taught about the Old Gannahans' obsessive honesty. "How was that possible?"

"I didn't understand either, until recently. Now, however, it makes a little sense. But you haven't heard the worst part."

So far, other than the doubt cast upon the integrity of her fathers, these revelations didn't seem so bad. What did it matter if the Rahab and their fabulous land of Ga'ayown were real? It was all ancient history. It had nothing to do with the settlers today.

She refreshed her tea. "Seeing Ga'ayown with my own eyes, wandering its halls, reading the books in its library, I was forced to realize that the Old Gannah I mourned for had been a lie. The real Gannah was one I hadn't known existed. Once I learned the truth, however, there was nothing I could do about it. All of Gannah was gone. Not just the Gannah I knew, but the truth I'd just learned. They were gone, all gone. Or so I thought."

Her eyes misted. "But the real Gannah wasn't gone. It was merely hiding. Almost within my arm's reach at the time, had I but known it."

She meant the Natsachs, of course. But why were they more real than the Gannah she'd known? "I don't understand any of this."

Emma seemed to study the table a moment then looked up. "In your conversations with Daviyd, did he say anything about the legend of Charach and Natsach?"

"No." He searched his memory, but he didn't recall their discussing it. "I don't believe so."

"You remember the story, of course. The twin brothers, sons of Atarah, who lived early in Gannah's history. When their father died, they fought for the right to succeed him."

Adam frowned. "Yes, and I never liked that tale. Their behavior was so unGannahan."

"Oh, but it's worse than you know. In the story I learned growing up, Natsach was the younger who falsely claimed the throne as his. As a result, he was banished by his brother to the uninhabited north. He and his followers became the Rahab, the proud ones of fable, who were said to have magical powers and devices that performed impossible feats. The rest of the world remained faithful to Atarah Charach and lived simple, peaceful lives."

THE LAST TOQEPH

The name Natsach did seem stained, historically, which gave the legend credence. In fact, Emma had said her father objected to her first marriage, saying no son of a Natsach would ever rule Gannah. "Are you saying the legend's not true?"

Emma sighed. "When I was at Ga'ayown, I found indisputable evidence that the facts as I'd been taught them were wrong. In reality, Natsach was the rightful heir, and his brother Charach deceived the others. Those who joined Natsach at his refuge in the north refused to accept Charach's lie and fled for their lives."

Adam stared at her, searching her meah, trying to sort it out in his mind. "If this brother, Natsach, was the true heir…"

She pursed her lips, her expression grim. "If Natsach was the true heir, then I am not. My father, his father, and many fathers before me were not entitled to rule."

The melon came up in Adam's throat. He gritted his teeth and swallowed it again. "And Natsach Daviyd Natsach —"

"Is in direct line from Atarah Natsach." Face stern, she lifted her hand as if to stop his thoughts. "But he is not *my* heir. You are. And, no matter what travesties were committed in the past, I am the toqeph. I rule in good conscience, and I have told Daviyd that I shall continue to do so until I go to the Hall of the King."

Adam's mouth was so dry he couldn't swallow. He'd have taken a sip of tea, but he didn't trust his hand to not shake. Until she went to the Hall of the King. What then? True, she'd just affirmed that he was her heir. But it wasn't like her to see a wrong and not try to right it. "This makes no sense. How could you come to these terrible conclusions just from visiting old ruins?"

She spent the next several minutes explaining the things she had seen and the overwhelming evidence they presented. He didn't want to believe it, but the facts were persuasive.

He ran his hands through his hair. "That's why you had Jerry change the history texts when you came home."

"That's right. But even after what I'd seen, I wasn't convinced of all of it. I had him incorporate only the parts I couldn't discount. At present, the history books mention the rivalry between the brothers but don't say definitively which was the true heir. I didn't want to believe it myself, for

THE LAST TOQEPH

one thing. But also, I didn't think it mattered anymore, as there was no one left but me."

Adam fought back a wave of self-revulsion. "And then I discovered Natsach. A whole nest of Natsachs."

She smiled. "It was a more significant discovery than even you knew."

Adam studied his em's dear, familiar face. This explained some of the things he hadn't understood before. But it created far bigger questions than it answered. "So where does that leave us?"

Her manner turned businesslike. "For the present, it changes nothing. We will transport the Natsachs to Periy. We will endeavor to integrate them into our settlement. We will meet each challenge as it arises, as we always have, being faithful to the Yasha's commands and to Gannahan law. And you, my son, shall continue your training and become a Nasi, so when I depart this world, I will be confident the settlement is in your good hands."

Despite the surety of her words, he felt adrift in a sea of uncertainty. "You would not—" He couldn't bring himself to say it.

"Once you become a Nasi, you will be my heir, Adam. I don't care how many Natasch nests you dig up, you cannot escape that responsibility. It is the birthright given you by the Yasha, not by me."

Was it? Truly? He wouldn't argue with the toqeph. But something about this didn't seem right.

THE LAST TOQEPH

45

The timedial was only in the first hour of Gray Dawn, and Ra'anan and her family were at the breakfast table, though no one was hungry.

Ra'anan remembered the stories of how, when Adam and Lileela were young, Emma had gone up to the starship to do her Karkar in-laws a favor, and on her return, the landing craft crashed on the far side of the planet. After that, Emma had vowed never to leave again.

But she was leaving.

How could she?

Stirring her micken and trying to convince herself to take a swallow, Ra'anan reproached Emma in her meah with the truth Emma had always impressed upon her children: *The Yasha is faithful to His every promise. As His people, we must keep our promises as well.*

Emma turned her flashing green eyes on Ra'anan. *I never promised to remain in Periy, daughter. I vowed never to leave Gannah.*

Ra'anan averted her gaze. It was true. Traveling to Yereq with Adam didn't qualify as leaving the planet. But she'd be absent from Ra'anan's world, and the thought filled her with fear.

The other children showed their worry differently. The younger two bickered over a cerecfruit, but the argument abruptly ceased as Abba rose from the table. When they saw he intended to go to the bathroom, not to correct them, they radiated relief.

When Hushai complained he wasn't allowed to go with Adam, Emma rose and gathered her breakfast dishes. "We've already had this discussion, and I'll hear no more about it." As soon as her back was turned, Tamah and Attai resumed their wrestling over the fruit. She spun around and laid a hand on each of their shoulders, squeezing hard enough to make them flinch. "Is this the memory you want me to carry to Yereq? My children

THE LAST TOQEPH

fighting over nothing?" Her snapping gaze took in Hushai and Ra'anan as well. "I'm sure children in the Natsach village aren't behaving this way this morning."

Hushai scowled. "That's 'cause they get to go on the trip. Their mothers aren't leaving them behind."

At that moment, Abba returned. "More likely it's because their fathers have not forbidden their mothers to whip them." He stood in the doorway, terrifyingly tall, old, and grim. "Do not give me cause to repent of that command."

The boys bowed, and Ra'anan, struck by shame over her earlier rebellious thoughts, prostrated herself. "I am sorry, Emma. I should not have complained."

As she got up, Hushai glared at Ra'anan. "What are *you* sorry about? You haven't said a word all morning. You're such a goodie-goodie, always—"

He stopped in mid-sentence and scrunched his shoulders, wincing, as Emma grabbed the back of his neck. "I would like to hear nothing further from any of you except goodbye."

Tamah covered her face with her hands, presumably to hide her tears, but her tremulous voice betrayed her. "Goodbye, Emma."

Ra'anan hopped up and hugged her mother. "Goodbye, Emma. The Yasha be with you, and come home soon?"

Emma's stern expression relaxed and she opened her arms to all of them. "Goodbye, children. I'll do my best."

She hugged and kissed them each in turn. "Your father will see me off at the airport, and then he'll be back. I know you'll be good, obedient Gannahans for him while I'm gone."

They each bowed. "Yes, Emma."

"If anyone comes with a question or a problem and Abba is not here to help them, send them to Mr. Maddox. He is head of the Council in my absence, and I have given him permission to use the dining room for meetings."

"Yes, Emma."

Abba cleared his throat as if urging her to come along, but she grabbed each child again in a hug. "Keep up with your lessons. You have your assignments, and I expect you to be up to date with them when I return."

"Yes, Emma."

THE LAST TOQEPH

Clearly, she was as reluctant to leave as they were for her to go. So why was she going?

"They'll be fine." Abba put his hand on her shoulder. "It's time."

She looked up at him. "Yes, my husband. You are right, as usual." She flashed a smile at them then turned and hurried for the door. "I don't want to hold Adam up."

Tamah put her arms around Ra'anan and sniffled into her tunic, but waited until Emma and Abba had left the apartment before saying, "I wish she would stay."

"So do I, sweet. But like Abba said, we'll be fine, and so will she. And just think. When she comes back, she'll have Daviyd and all his people with her."

"Yeah." Hushai picked up the cerecfruit that had been the object of the argument earlier. "That's why I wanted to go. Mr. Natsach likes me a lot better than he likes Adam, and I think I should be allowed to travel with him."

Ittai lunged toward Hushai. "That's mine!" He grabbed at the fruit, but Hushai raised it out of his reach.

"Stop that!" Ra'anan snatched the cerec from Hushai. "None of you can have it if you're going to fight over it." She ran to the counter, opened the compost bin, and shoved in the fruit. It made a dull rumble as it rolled down the chute.

Hushai gasped. "You wasted food!"

"Yes, I did. See, I'm not such a goodie-goodie, am I?" Ra'anan wasn't sure what came over her, but she heard her voice rising. "And what do you mean, Mr. Natsach likes you best? You're just a little kid. He only liked you because he found you amusing. He thinks you're just a funny litt—"

"That's not true!" Hushai lunged at her. "He likes me!"

He tried to slap her, but Ra'anan grabbed his hand. "Don't you dare!"

His other fist slammed into her stomach, and she doubled over. "You—" The blood rushed in her ears and she tried to suck in enough breath to speak.

Hushai spun around and fled the room, almost knocking over Ittai, who tossed a glance at Ra'anan then followed his brother. "'Shai, hold on."

Ra'anan eased herself down to sit on the floor, and Tamah ran to her. "He hit you! I can't believe it, he hit you! Are you okay? Why did he do that?"

THE LAST TOQEPH

Weeping, Ra'anan put her arms around her sister. "I don't know." She gave her a squeeze. "I don't know."

Tamah cried too. "Why is everyone acting so crazy?"

"I don't know." Her mind spun in circles and she could think of nothing else to say. "I just don't know."

Standing outside the Hatita in the wet gray light of dawn, Adam leaned in and slid the passenger seat back as far as it would go. "Are you sure about this?"

Emma settled herself behind the controls. "Absolutely certain." She studied the instruments, touching them lightly as if envisioning their uses. "I haven't flown for decades, though, so you might have to refresh my memory on a few things."

Adam climbed in and tried to adjust the seat more comfortably. "You don't need to, you know. I don't mind flying it." Hm. Apparently this was all the legroom he'd get.

She turned her head and stabbed him with that glittering green gaze. "Obviously you *can*. You've done it. And if I asked you to fly, you'd do it whether you minded or not. That's not the point. I want to fly because—" Her stern expression eased. "I just want to. It's been a long time since I've had an adventure, and I could use a little fun for a change."

Abba stood outside the plane, his ears lifted in amusement. "No point arguing with her, son. She always won even before she was queen of the world, and she's more insufferable now."

"Insufferable, am I?" She reviewed the on-screen pre-flight checklist.

"That's the word precisely." Hanging onto the side of the plane, Abba bent low to speak through the open cockpit door. "I shall suffer immensely while you're gone."

She looked over at him and smiled. "As will I. Now step back before I cut off your too-lofty head with a propeller."

Adam couldn't remember his parents ever acting like this. Was it a new development, or had he just never noticed?

Abba gave the plane a slap and waved farewell. Emma closed the doors and turned her attention to the business at hand as Abba shuffled back to the building with his slow, old-man gait.

Adam thought of Elise still in bed, and the boys. He ached at the thought of another long separation. But Emma, almost childlike in her

THE LAST TOQEPH

anticipation of the trip, didn't seem to mind in the least that she was leaving her family behind.

In Adam's carefully-guarded opinion, she was entirely too wrapped up with those Natsach people.

She was right about one thing: they were her people more than anyone in the settlement. Though she was as old as Abba, her hair was black, her skin smooth, and her boundless energy seemed undiminished. The people he'd met briefly in Daviyd's village were much the same, with their strength and vitality greater than that of the Terrestrial races no matter what their age.

And they were small. Crammed into this Gannah-sized cockpit, Adam felt gargantuan and superfluous.

Emma started the engine on her first attempt. "Good old Hatita. What a machine." Having reviewed the routine, she executed it without hesitation. "Ready, kiddo?"

He resisted the urge to sigh like a teenager. "Ready, Madam Toqeph."

Grinning, she released the brakes and powered the plane a short distance down the runway then sent it leaping into the air. "I love the way this thing takes off. I think your father found it a little too abrupt, though. It seemed to unsettle him."

"I have no doubt." It unsettled Adam a bit too. When he flew it, he took more of a running start.

She chuckled. "Of course when he sat where you are now, he was pretty much at wit's end anyway." She shook her head. "What a time he'd had. I suppose it's hard for you to imagine. But what he did was nothing short of astonishing. A proud Karkar, setting foot on Gannah. Unheard of! I honestly don't know where he found the courage."

Emma was unusually talkative. "I'm sure he questioned his decision every second he was here. But the last day, when we found the Kankakar Jewels? You should have seen him, Adam. His ears twitched every which-way, and his face was just Earthish enough to show his utter astonishment. And then, when we ran across this strange little plane with the note in it from its designer, long dead, saying the Yasha had told him to build it for our use, I thought he'd collapse on the spot. I think he would have, if he hadn't had that seat to squeeze into." She nodded toward Adam. "Which was so tight, what with that big chest of jewels jammed in behind so there was no room to move it back, he couldn't have fallen over if he'd tried." She

341

THE LAST TOQEPH

laughed. "It was when he was finally able to escape the plane that he collapsed, as his legs had fallen asleep." She sighed. "Oh, Adam. You have such a marvelous heritage. I wish I could show you the full scope of it."

He wasn't sure how to respond but settled on, "I think you do a pretty good job." He glanced at the gauges. "I'd like to swing west and fly over Yam to see how the men are progressing with the barges."

"Good plan."

She adjusted the navigation settings. "I'm not sure I did that right. Am I going to wind up where you want?"

He adjusted the angle of the screen so he could see better. "Ah… I don't think you took the continental shift into consideration." He made some adjustments. "That should get us there."

"Good. Thank you. Did you know that when I flew with your father to Yabbashah that day, I almost missed it? If I hadn't realized my error at the last minute, we'd have bypassed the island and flown over the ocean until the plane ran out of power."

"Did Abba put you on the right track?"

"No, he had no idea where we were or where we were headed. Besides, he wasn't speaking to me at the time." A cloud seemed to glide over her bright mood. "That week was pretty hard on both of us. It's tough coming home when everyone's gone and you know they'll never be back. Ever. None of them."

Adam bit his lip. "I've often tried to imagine, but I doubt I fully appreciate what you went through."

"Probably not." She shook her head. "Great sorrow and great joy are the same that way."

Adam's thoughts turned to Lileela, and his meah told him Emma's did too. They communed together, the three of them, though as always, Emma's meah was weak.

When he reached toward Daviyd to let him know they were on their way, he found that he already knew. Emma had been in touch with him earlier, and so had Hushai.

Adam sagged in his seat and closed his eyes. Emma talked on about how the Hatita had made some historic voyages and this trip was just as significant. How Adam had every reason to be proud of what they were doing. It was he who discovered the Old Gannahan survivors and brought Daviyd to Periy. He designed the plan for moving the whole village. And he

THE LAST TOQEPH

would lead the Natsach village on their long trek. Though the toqeph would be there, Adam would be in charge of the travel.

Yes, Adam privately agreed that this was his project from start to finish, and his efforts were changing Gannah forever. Wasn't this what he'd hoped for all his life? To be a strong and wise leader and to help Gannah grow and thrive?

It was what he'd always dreamed of. So why did he feel like this was the end of his life, not the beginning?

THE LAST TOQEPH

46

In the palace courtyard, Ra'anan sat at a table in the shade of the ancient elah, a book open in front of her.

Ordinarily she enjoyed reading, but this morning, she couldn't keep her mind on it. She relived her fight with Hushai. The twitter of the birds above made her edgy, like the whispers of people talking about her behind her back. She wanted to meah-communicate with Emma and Adam to see how their flight was going but didn't want to be a bother.

She had no such qualms about contacting Lileela, though. Her sister told her all was well on the *DeLaCruz*, where she steadily regained strength in her legs. The travelers kept themselves occupied with intensive Bible study as well as routine ship maintenance and housekeeping, as there was almost no crew.

This worried Ra'anan. What if something broke down? Would anyone aboard know how to repair it? Captain Bennett had mentioned something about obtaining the ship because it was obsolete. Not knowing the word, Ra'anan had looked it up. Even reading the definition, she didn't fully understand.

In the settlement, almost everything they used had been designed and manufactured by the Old Gannahans generations before. Items were durable, and if something broke or wore out, it could usually be repaired. She found it inconceivable that anything would be replaced unless it was wholly useless. Especially something as huge and complex as a starship.

Though her eyes followed the words of the epic poem, *Izhar and the Seven Voyages*, her thoughts took voyages of their own. Had Emma and Adam arrived yet at Yereq and the village of the Natsachs?

THE LAST TOQEPH

The Natsachs. She thought of Daviyd, and a thrill shot through her clear to her toes. She thought of him frequently, and sometimes it took concentration to keep her meah from seeking his.

About the time she realized she'd been staring at the same place on the page for several minutes, her friend Fidelity's voice called out. "What're you doing out here, Ray?"

She looked up. "Oh, hi. The kids were bugging me. I just had to get out of the house." She rubbed her eyes. "I'm trying to get this poem read, and then I have to write an essay about it. Have you read *Izhar* yet?"

Fidelity crossed the flagstones then sat on the bench beside Ra'anan, crosslegged. "No, but my brother, Compton? He says it'll put you to sleep in a big hurry. Why do we need to read those silly old poems, anyway? Especially when they're in the old language. Nobody speaks it anymore, so—" She blushed. "Okay, so I guess your family does sometimes, but hardly nobody else does."

Ra'anan replaced the pressed wildflower she'd been using as a marker and closed the book. "We're all going to be speaking the old language soon enough. I hear Mr. Maddox is going to change the Level requirements to include Gannahan language proficiency."

Fidelity's jaw dropped. "No! What on Gannah for? That Mr. Maddox is just the meanest thing ever, stalking around the settlement with that serious look all the time." She made a face that was probably supposed to imitate his stern scowl.

Her gesticulations made Ra'anan giggle. "You'd look just like him, if you had a beard." She grabbed Fidelity's long braid and pressed its wavy plume end to her friend's chin. "There. Now all you need is a purple tongue."

Fidelity hopped up and deepened her voice to speak sternly. "Bow to me, Miss Ra'anan." She stuck out her tongue and wagged her pigtail beard. "Why aren't you working on your lessons, Miss Ra'anan? Must I recommend that your mother discipline you? Answer me! In the Old Language!"

Ra'anan laughed, though she felt guilty for it. She rose and bowed. "But Mr. Maddox, sir, it was the toqeph's idea, not yours, that we should all be fluent in Old Gannahan."

"Really?" Fidelity gave up her act and flopped onto the bench again. "Why would she do that?"

345

THE LAST TOQEPH

"Because we're Gannahans, of course. And Gannahans speak Gannahan."

"Ah." Fidelity wiggled her eyebrows. "Because the Old Gannahans are coming, and we'll have to be able to communicate with them." She crossed her arms. "That's hardly fair. There are more of us than there are of them. They should learn to speak *our* language, not the other way around."

A sudden rush of resentment darkened Ra'anan's mood. "We should have been speaking the language all along. Emma's sorry she didn't require it earlier, but she said all you Earthers had so much to learn as it was. Learning a language no one else spoke might have been asking too much of Outsiders."

"What do you mean? I'm no Earther. I was born here, just like you." Fidelity picked up Ra'anan's book and riffled through the pages.

"Hey, you'll lose my place." Ra'anan snatched the book from her. "What did you want, anyway? Other than to interrupt me."

Fidelity frowned. "Thistles and burrs, girl, but you're touchy. If you want me to go away, just say goodbye and I'm gone."

Remorse formed a lump in Ra'anan's throat. "I'm sorry, Delly. It's not you that's bothering me, it's—I got up really early this morning, and I'm tired. But don't worry about me. Did you want something?"

"Abba got some of that new fabric they made testing out the factory equipment, and I'd like to make a tunic like the one you made last week. Would you mind showing me how to do that fancy neckline? I could maybe figure it out, but—"

"Of course." Ra'anan rose and tucked the book under her arm. Just because the people she loved were abandoning her right and left, that didn't mean she had to do the same to her friends. "I can read this later."

Flying over the island region of Yam, Emma dipped the plane low enough that Adam could see the barges Malcolm Arrantzale and his crew were preparing. She performed a stomach-jolting waggle as the plane passed overhead, and the workmen waved back. Adam wondered how Jax would respond if he'd tried a stunt like that. Once his heart slipped from his mouth and settled back in his chest, he said, "Looks like they're right on schedule."

She pointed the plane's nose back into the clouds. "I knew they would be."

THE LAST TOQEPH

A couple hours later, as they approached the northern Nazal coast, she dropped altitude once more. "See if you can spot the advance party's camp. I'll follow their route so we can see how far they've gotten."

Adam nodded, and before long he spied something. "There, up ahead. Is that the pavilion?"

She peered through the windshield. "Could be." She flew ever lower until the camp came into view more clearly. A round tent pitched on a grassy area near the beach was ringed with numerous smaller structures like a circular rash.

Adam craned his neck. "I see a man down there. Must be whoever they left to guard the camp."

Emma drew closer, and this time, Adam was prepared when the Hatita shimmied a greeting. The man returned the wave.

Adam recognized the long black beard worn in three braids. "Looks like Esposito drew the short straw."

"Good. A hard worker like him deserves some down time."

Adam wondered why she never seemed to have the same concern for him.

She pointed out the window. "I'll bet that's the trail. Let's follow it." She banked and headed for the streak of cleared ground tracing a line from the camp into the wilderness.

It hadn't been so very long since Adam had parachuted into that desolation, which was at that time untrodden and uncharted. Now there was a camp and a trail. How long would it take for the settlement to outgrow Periy and tame other lands? The population had more than doubled in his short lifetime. Soon they'd be bringing in a hundred more. Barring natural disaster or resumption of the ancient wildlife wars, the New Gannahans would increase exponentially, populating the whole planet once again. He watched the wasteland whiz beneath the plane. At what point had he gone from studying history to making it?

With no trees or mountains to hinder, Emma flew lower, as it was difficult to follow the trail from the air. Adam gazed down. "If they're progressing as planned, they should be at least sixty kilometers in by now."

"Keep your eyes peeled for signs of them."

There was little to see, and Emma navigated more by direction than visual cues, heading steadily for the valley with the waterfall where Adam had first seen Daviyd. Where was the advance team? Had the land

THE LAST TOQEPH

swallowed them up? Myles Lyfar was a seasoned adventurer. The brothers Carson and Kitson Armistead were hardly less so, and the youngest Vigneron boy, Johann, had been exploring the wilderness since he was a child, searching out fruits for his father's blend-making. It didn't seem likely they'd have all gotten lost out there.

Finally he spied something that looked man-made. "What is that?"

She saw it too, and flew nearer. "That's a good question."

Adam recalled encountering several places where fallen trees had washed up at the foot of cliffs and drop-offs. He'd managed to get down, but he was concerned about getting the villagers over those logjams. The advance team had apparently solved that problem by sawing through a section of the trunks and branches and building a rough stairway. He told her what he thought it was.

Emma circled around to take a better look. "Yes," she said, "I think you're right. Clever solution they came up with."

She continued following the trail from above. "I wish you could have seen Yereq before the flood. Wave after wave of fertile fields of every crop imaginable. Sometimes when we visited the palace at Saba we'd fly, sometimes we'd take the rail. But one time, Abba wanted to drive so he could see the fields. Our biggest sheber field in Periy is like a window box compared to what we drove past here. The farms of Yereq fed much of the world in those days. The basic grains, anyway, like sheber and *kuccemeth* and *seowr*.

Adam shifted his position. "Seowr?"

"We tried growing it at the settlement early on, but after several successive crop failures, we gave it up as unprofitable. If the seed we have in storage is still viable, perhaps we'll try again."

"Sounds like a project for Hushai when he's older."

"Hm!" Emma flashed him a smile. "That's a good idea. Maybe I'll drop the hint and see if he picks it up." She studied something below her window. "It would be nice to have some good seowr bread again. Nobody made seowr bread like my mother-in-law. She taught me how she did it so I could make it for Rosh."

With her attention on flying and searching the ground, she probably didn't notice his ears tip back in a scowl. He hoped not, anyway. He never liked hearing her speak of her first husband, for it smacked of disloyalty to Abba. He liked it even less now that he'd found Rosh's cousins. Her

THE LAST TOQEPH

eagerness to make this trip, her lighthearted conversation, tended to confirm his fears. She was still in love with her Natsach man, and if she'd had her way, she never would have married Abba. *The Yasha knew what He was doing when He brought us together,* she always said. As if she were trying to talk herself into believing it.

A few moments later, he noticed mist rising not far ahead. Adam sat up straighter. "Is that the waterfall? I didn't see the advance team, did you?"

Emma shook her head. "No. But these are the coordinates where you said we'd find that valley."

"How could we have missed them?" Tension gripped Adam's gut. Could they have gotten off course? He didn't voice his concerns but watched the fall's spray draw nearer.

Emma piloted the plane to the left of the mist, and the valley unrolled below. The river in the middle, the cliffs in the background, the boulder on this side, and on the other, five men lounging in the sparse shade of the saplings. Adam pointed. "Look at that. They beat us here."

"This is good news, then. Why don't you let Daviyd know we'll leave the Hatita here and walk to the village. Do you think you can find it?"

"I'm sure I can." Much as he disliked communicating with Daviyd in his meah, he'd rather do it himself than let Emma do it. Who knew what kind of thoughts they shared?

She brought the plane down on the far side of the river with what, he was coming to realize, was her typical recklessness. In the jarring tumult, Adam's head cracked the doorframe hard enough to make his ears ring.

"Sorry. I guess that was a little abrupt, wasn't it?"

He rubbed his head. "A little."

While she completed the shut-down process, Adam unfastened his restraints and opened his door. The steamy air slapped him like a wet towel. Along with Jarol Dudte, who would be flying the Hatita back to Oatsiyr once the villagers' journey began, Myles, Johann, and the Armistead brothers ambled toward him, arms raised in greeting. He straightened his kinks and waved back.

The next chapter of history was about to begin.

THE LAST TOQEPH

47

There they were. The toqeph and Adam, sunlight and shadow playing across their moving figures as they strode through the brush.

Daviyd sucked in a deep breath then exhaled his tension before stepping forward to meet them.

In the lead, Adam hailed him with an upraised arm that soared higher than any of the surrounding saplings. Behind him, child-sized in comparison, the toqeph made the same gesture, but hers was accompanied by a smile.

As they neared one another, Daviyd stopped and bowed. "Welcome, my toqeph. The people await thee." He straightened and nodded to Adam. "Greetings."

The toqeph spoke. "I have long dreamed of this day, never thinking it might come true. The villagers are willing, are they? They do not resent my interference?"

Daviyd met her glittering gaze. She was a True One indeed, with as fierce a love for Gannah as any among them. "They are eager, Madam. Between your many thoughtful gifts and my explanation of the situation, most of them understand. Those who do not will come with us rather than be left behind. It is my prayer—" He marveled at how naturally he said that, how easily he fell into communing with the Yasha these days— "that they will understand in time and join us in His Kingdom."

The toqeph beamed. "My heart is glad. My feet scarcely touch the ground."

Adam stood as reserved as a lodgepole, his meah shielded.

Daviyd gestured toward the village. "The chatsr is not far."

THE LAST TOQEPH

He turned and led the way, every muscle tensed as if he stalked a qaran stag.

He'd never noticed how the village stank until he returned from Periy. Now, the familiar odor, heavier than usual in the dank heat, wafted to his nostrils before the chatsr's humble outlines came into view. Certainly the toqeph smelled it too, but he sensed no revulsion in her. Just anticipation.

Most of the villagers stood outside the rickety walls watching for the guests. As Daviyd approached with the distinguished visitors, the villagers arranged themselves in two columns to line the path through the gate. Ignoring Daviyd altogether and giving Adam scarcely a glance, their violet eyes drank in the sight of the toqeph.

The only sound was the soft thudding of feet—or, in the case of Adam's, not so soft—on the path. Even the birds and insects ceased their activity. The first of the villagers went to their knees as the trio came abreast of the double column, and the rest followed suit, pressing forearms and forehead to the ground as the toqeph passed by.

Her meah radiated love. Sorrow for the people's long separation. Joy at their reunion. Hope for the future of Gannah.

Daviyd's face ran with tears.

Adam's meah remained closed.

Legs crossed, Adam sat on the damp ground, ignored by the villagers. Only the insects swarming at sunset paid him any attention.

In the center of the chatsr courtyard, Emma sat with the Natsach elders surrounded by every other man, woman, and child in the village. Other than her eye color and the fact that she was fully clothed, she could have been one of them.

Adam was separated from the rest in more than mere proximity. Abba would say he felt like a Nobian sand snail swimming in a crystal punch bowl. Except in this case, the punch smelled like sewage.

The village had served their version of a feast in the second hour of Green Afternoon. It was plain they were proud of the production—except for Daviyd, who knew what a real spread looked like. His manner was more matter-of-fact than pleased when offering the toqeph roasted arych, powlroot with mixed greens in a fish-based broth, followed by honeyed seed cakes.

THE LAST TOQEPH

Despite its simplicity, the fare would have been tasty if not for the background odors. The music and dancing that followed lasted into Blue Night. Long ballads were sung by mixed voices and acted out. Men yodeled back and forth while bounding about with gymnastic moves. Women danced while reciting machowl poems, and group songs were sung in intricate harmonies by everyone, none of whom could seem to sit still.

There were no tables to pound on, but Emma stomped and hooted in appreciation and joined with the villagers to dance the choruses. Because the lowering sun did little to lower the temperature, every face glistened in the moonlight and the new finery made from the toqeph's gifts darkened with perspiration.

Now, having sung themselves hoarse and danced themselves into a happy flush, the people assembled to hear from the toqeph, sipping weak blend from bottles passed from person to person, or slurping cloudy river water from lopsided earthenware pitchers.

Emma was always a good speaker, but she'd never been so eloquent as she was now. Even in her faded, sweat-stained garments and fly-away hair, she was regal. Before she'd finished with her opening remarks, the villagers' meahs reached out to touch hers with awe. They might all be Natsachs, but there was no longer a Dathan in the bunch.

How much of this was due to Daviyd's efforts before her arrival, Adam couldn't say. But he was certain if she'd come wandering in without warning, they never would have given her a hearing.

He glanced toward Daviyd, sitting beside his em, Naom. At the same time, Daviyd lifted his eyes, and they locked gazes. Natsach's meah pressed against Adam's, and the curtain he'd drawn collapsed.

But Adam didn't turn away. Though his soul was bared in that grappling of stares, so was Daviyd's, leaving Adam in doubt no longer: Natsach Daviyd Natsach would not rest until he sat on the throne of Gannah.

Daviyd lay on his mat staring at the stars. This last night in the village, he had no roof over his head, thanks to Emma demanding privacy for her talk with the toqeph. But no matter. Tomorrow night and for many thereafter, they'd all be sleeping under the stars.

There was no practical purpose to his eviction, though, for he could hear them talking as clearly as if he'd been in the house with them. They

THE LAST TOQEPH

chattered like a pair of youngsters. Their hushed, serious conversation sometimes erupted into ripples of laughter, only to settle again into a calm, intimate lapping of words across meah. Among other things, the discussion touched on what they had lost, what they hoped to attain—a daughter-in-law and grandchildren, on his mother's part—and the challenges of raising children. Both women had lost husbands—both Natsach husbands. But if they discussed any particulars of that topic, it was in the privacy of their meahs during the silences that sometimes fell over them.

After one such lull, Emma asked the toqeph, "Your second daughter, Madam. Ra'anan is her name? Has a marriage yet been arranged for her?"

"Nay. My husband will not permit it."

"Why is that? Doth it go against his Outside upbringing?"

"Not at all," the toqeph answered. "It is the Karkar way for parents to choose their children's spouses, and neither son nor daughter hath any say in the match. My husband left Karkar in part to avoid being bound in such a relationship. He will not have his children similarly constrained."

"The girl is what, fourteen? Old enough to show interest in a young man."

The toqeph paused as if considering the question. "She hath mentioned no one."

Daviyd frowned. He had little use for the toqeph's pale, oversized husband, but in this one thing, they agreed: a man should be allowed to choose his own wife, not have one assigned him by his mother.

On his bedroll beside the Hatita, Adam brushed off his face and beard then covered his head with a sheet to keep the insects from swarming over him. The hollow roar of the waterfall crashing against the Tebah and the snores of the men in the advance party sleeping nearby provided background music.

In his mind, he sat in the palace tower in Periy, with the gold circle on the floor lit by a sunbeam from the skylight above, drinking tea with Emma. What she told him about Natsach and Charach made his stomach curdle even now.

Though his eyes were closed, they burned with the memory of locking gazes with Natsach back in the village. According to Emma, the wild man was the rightful heir of Atarah.

Daviyd was heir. Not Adam.

THE LAST TOQEPH

A nightbird sang the refrain. *Naaaht Adam, naaaht Adam, notAdam.*

As another bird echoed the call, Adam recited an article of the Nasi code. "A Nasi lives for the good of Gannah. His highest goal is to serve the throne, to obey with joy, never questioning."

Naaaht Adam, naaaht Adam, notAdam.

Daviyd would have rather the toqeph led them. But she'd put Adam in charge of the operation, and the big man had no qualms about telling everyone what to do.

After going back to the Hatita for the night, Adam had returned early in the morning with four men whom Daviyd had not met before. They were there to help with the transport, Adam said. But they only served to throw the villagers into a tizzy, causing the people to cast reproachful glares Daviyd's way. *This is thy fault,* they accused in their meahs. *We were safe and happy until thou brought these Outsiders to us. Now thou dost expect us to allow strangers to carry our belongings? Nay, no Outworlder hands shall touch our possessions. They would take them away and leave us with nothing.*

Then the Hatita screamed across the sky and landed on the riverbank, the same giant mechanical bird that had brought the treasures the people valued most. In its beneficence it seemed more trustworthy than the flesh-and-blood men with the foreign faces.

As yet another unfamiliar Outsider exited the marvelous machine, Adam showed the Natsachs that the vehicle had brought gifts again: dozens of sturdy but lightweight bags and backpacks such as the people had never seen, with secure closures and comfortable carrying straps.

As he and the pilot distributed them, he explained that the way would be long and arduous, involving great distances and steep climbs. If the heaviest items were loaded onto the plane, the villagers could carry only what they needed for the trip. Otherwise, they'd have to leave many things behind.

The pilot would fly the Hatita to the site on the beach that was the people's first destination. The other three settlers would travel ahead and set up camp on the trail each night. That way, when the people arrived, much of the labor would already be accomplished, and they wouldn't have to hunt or forage.

"This first leg of our journey," Adam proclaimed, "as we travel on foot across Yereq to the Nazal Sea, will be the most difficult. Ye are capable of making the journey yourselves, of course. None can doubt that. But the

THE LAST TOQEPH

toqeph hath commanded these men to help because they are good Gannahans. Ye can trust them with thy belongings as well as thy lives."

So, after a brief discussion of what should be carried by air and what must be hauled on backs, the baggage was sorted and re-packed into the bags the Hatita had brought.

By the second hour of Yellow Morning, they were ready to embark. With a large pack on her back, the toqeph raised her arms for attention, and every violet eye turned toward her, every conversation stilled. "I understand many of you now know the Yasha."

Heads bobbed and smiles brightened swarthy faces.

Emma nodded. "I rejoice with you. Let us commit our journey to His keeping." She raised her arms again and prayed. The villagers who knew the Yasha joined the prayer in their meahs. A few — Daviyd knew each one, and felt their resentment as a personal affront — closed their minds and averted their eyes. They'd agreed to move to Periy because it seemed best for practical reasons. They respected the toqeph and understood that she wanted the best for them. But they weren't ready to accept the foreign concept of God.

As the toqeph prayed for the villagers on their journey, Daviyd prayed for the hold-outs. *Not all will hear my voice*, the Yasha reminded him. The truth of that statement plunged like a spear to the heart. *But let that not prevent thee from speaking to them of Me*, the Yasha added. *For thou knowest not when an ear might be opened.*

After the prayer ended, the people shouted, "Amen! The Yasha be praised!"

A current of anticipation illuminated every face, and Daviyd almost felt he could lift his feet and be carried bodily by its power.

Adam raised his long arms. "Amen. The Yasha be praised. And now, by His grace, I shall lead you, noble Natsachs, to your new home."

The advance men had already gone on ahead, each carrying a heavy load. Adam strode through the rickety chatsr gate. Daviyd followed, with the people flowing behind through the narrow channel in a more or less orderly fashion. When he looked back some moments later, they were still coming with eager steps. Standing by the gate, the toqeph smiled and nodded at each. He lost sight of the procession then, but it appeared she intended to bring up the rear.

355

THE LAST TOQEPH

He faced forward and walked with glad resolve. That which was taken would be restored.

48

Ra'anan lay in her bed alcove, the curtain open.

A heat wave had gripped Periy for the past four days, and the climate control systems were depleting the palace's energy allotment at an alarming rate. The Energy Coordinator restricted the palace's power allowance this evening to an amount that would operate lights and ventilation fans, but little else.

Ra'anan got up and re-positioned the fan sitting on her desk so the air would hit her more directly. Before returning to the alcove, she stood in the breeze, arms and legs wide. After a minute or two, she turned and allowed the fan to cool her back.

The Karkar liked the heat, and the Old Gannahans weren't bothered much by temperature extremes. It must be the Earther in her that was miserable. Either that, or Hushai was right in his accusation that she was too soft. "So what?" he'd said in response to her complaint earlier that it was too hot in the apartment. "Just sweat and keep quiet about it."

Abba's ears frowned. "You might not be bothered by the heat, but that doesn't mean your sister doesn't suffer." Then he got the fan for her. Dear Abba. Emma probably would have agreed with Hushai.

Ra'anan returned to the alcove. The bed felt cool at first, as it was damp from her perspiration, but in sixty seconds she was sweating again.

Looking for comfort, she sought out Emma in her meah, but the connection was weak. She got the impression Emma was sleeping. That was good, because Ra'anan knew from previous contacts that she hadn't been doing much of that on her adventures. Emma was having the time of her life, welcoming the exercise and the travel, seeing for herself the dramatic changes the flood had wrought across the land, and getting to know the

THE LAST TOQEPH

Natsach people. But she was wearying, as were they all. The going was hard at times, and Adam kept them moving at a fast pace.

Because Emma was tired, Ra'anan sought out Adam instead. He slept too, but his mind was active. He expected they'd reach the Nazal Sea the next afternoon, and he looked forward to a short rest on the beach before they boarded the barges. One of the scouts had informed him that all five boats were ready and waiting, and Adam was eager to begin the next leg of the journey.

Communing with him, Ra'anan grew groggy at last. Before sleep took her, though, she wanted to check in with Lileela.

Out there somewhere in space, her sister was wide awake because it was daylights, as they called it aboard ship. There was no night or day in space, so the cycles were artificially imposed through changes in the lighting.

It seemed very strange to Ra'anan, but Lileela had been accustomed to such things before. She had no trouble slipping back into the routine of the artificial daylight, stale filtered air, water recycled through purification systems, and food that came from a factory rather than being grown in the rich Gannahan soil.

Lileela didn't like the food, but she thrived nevertheless. Her healing was complete, and she now walked at least as well as she had before her legs were broken. The *DeLaCruz* had met up with three other small ships and a large one from Eutare in orbit around Fueraq. Everyone met aboard the big starship, the *Entrepreneur*, for Bible study, ministry training, discussion of strategies, and prayer for direction. There were some three hundred believers from all over the galaxy, most of them of Terrestrial breeding. Lileela was excited beyond description to hear their stories, meet and pray with them, and plan for the future.

What ever possessed you to do this? Ra'anan asked for the hundredth time.

The Holy Spirit of God was the expected answer. And Ra'anan detected no sorrow in it. Lileela was content with her decision because, despite the fact that she missed Gannah and her family, this was what the Yasha called her to do. It was, therefore, what *she* wanted.

Ra'anan wondered how she'd respond if the Yasha required her to do something awful like that. Lileela laughed in her meah. *It's not awful, silly. If the Yasha requires it, it's the best thing possible.*

THE LAST TOQEPH

I suppose. But I miss you. She hoped her ache came through clearly enough to make Lileela feel just a little guilty. *And what of Adam and Abba's fertility research? Abba's just about ready to test a procedure on Mr. Esam. If it works — if it corrects whatever the problem is so he can make babies — he and Zuri Ayo are going to get married. If you were here, they could do the same thing for Faris, and then you could have babies too, like Adam and Elise. Aren't you sad that won't happen?*

Lileela responded without hesitation. *I'm going to have lots of children — spiritual children — hundreds more than I could ever give birth to physically.*

Ra'anan's meah kept a thin hold on the conversation for a short time after drifting off. The last thing she remembered was thinking, *I'm happy for you, Leela.*

Sea birds wheeled high on the horizon like slow-moving specks. Their appearance, along with a faint, fishy scent in the air, told Daviyd the Nazal Sea must not be far ahead.

A short time after he spied the birds, a shift in the wind and the dimming of the sunshine warned of an oncoming storm. When he turned to view the sky behind the bedraggled group of travelers, it was black as a bruise, its dark clouds flickering with lightning.

Adam had told them the advance team had set up shelters on the beach, but Daviyd doubted they could reach the camp before the rain fell. Unconcerned by the thunder's ominous rumbles, the barefooted villagers trudged on, their towering manufactured backpacks incongruous with their ragged animal-skin clothes. They'd been rained on before, and, weary as they were, the prospect of being soaked again seemed less exhausting than trying to outrun the storm.

The trail rose ahead then slipped out of sight over a ridge, taking the travelers with it. When Daviyd reached the top, the leaders were once again in view, and beyond them, what may have been a flat expanse of water. The rain was almost certain to catch them first, but the beach — and their first major goal — couldn't be far now. The knowledge was heartening.

Jether, walking beside him, broke the silence. "Look there. Six Outsiders. I thought there were only five."

Daviyd spied them about the same time. Six men hurrying toward them, speaking to Adam, who turned, gesturing toward the people behind. "I believe there was a sixth who remained on the beach to watch over the camp in their absence."

359

THE LAST TOQEPH

"Ah." Jether's words expressed Daviyd's relief as well as his own. "We must be near then."

"So it would seem."

Ahead, Adam stopped and turned to face the people. He raised his arms to get their attention and shouted to all who could hear. "The scouts urge us to make haste lest the storm overtake us. They will ease the burden of any who need assistance." His voice couldn't carry to everyone, but his meah did. "Ye who are able, help those who need it. Make haste. Follow the path to the beach, where shelters await."

A moment of hesitation gave way to an orderly chaos. The five Outsiders ran up the trail to help those with heavy burdens or small children, while the strongest Natsach men offered their assistance to those weaker than themselves. Before long, the whole company was running at nearly full speed, spurred on by the chill wind, darkening sky, and thunderclaps that drew ever closer.

Daviyd ran with a child under each arm, both giggling as they bounced to his gallop.

"Whyyy are we runnning, Uncle?" Four-year-old Chelubai's voice jostled with the impact of Daviyd's pounding feet.

"We race the dark clouds. Who will be fastest?"

Under his other arm, Chelubai's two-year-old sister, Dorbie, cried, "Whee-eee-ee!" when she wasn't laughing too hard to speak.

For several minutes, everything was all slapping feet, bouncing burdens, and breathless anticipation as the people raced down the slope to the beach, which opened up before them as they rounded a bend.

Adam stood to the side, waving them forward. "Ye shall see housing units arranged as they were in the village. Please find the one that corresponds to the home you left behind."

Sure enough, a ring of small shelters formed a circle around a larger tent on the rocky shore ahead. It resembled a chatsr but lacked a wall to surround it. The huts, constructed of some material Daviyd had never seen before, were smaller than their old house but appeared to be completely watertight.

He set first Dorbie then her brother on their feet, but they didn't join the others rushing toward the temporary village until their parents appeared, their ab under a heavy backpack and their em with a baby in her

THE LAST TOQEPH

arms and a pack on her back. The children joined them as they hurried toward the circle of strange little structures.

Making his way to the side of the rushing stream of travelers, Daviyd found himself standing near Adam, who continued to gesture toward the camp, urging the people to make haste. They didn't need more encouragement, though, than the brisk wind whipping up dust and detritus to swirl around them as they ran.

Daviyd searched for anyone needing help but saw no one struggling. These were survivors. They could take care of themselves.

Some of the men herding their families past at a jog shot resentful stares at Adam and Daviyd. Daviyd ignored them and noted that Adam did as well. Over time they would come to see that the move was for the best, that the Yasha was the Creator of all things Gannahan as well as the God of the Outsiders. For now, there was no point arguing over it—but there was no harm in praying for them. *My Yasha, open their eyes that they might see Thee.*

Daviyd's mother came near the tail of this flowing beast of humanity, running with Nechama and her family. And there was the toqeph, last of all. She'd left the Natsachs behind once before and plainly had no intention of losing even one of them this time.

They squinted against the buffeting winds, but the rain still held off. Adam and Daviyd fell in behind the toqeph and followed the last of the villagers. In the camp, people claimed their huts. The few arguments that ensued were broken off by a bolt of lightning striking the water, sending people diving into the most convenient structure. Adam and the toqeph disappeared into the large central tent, and Daviyd and his mother took the building that stood between the huts of the families who'd lived on either side of them in the old chatsr. They had to duck to go through the low opening, but the door fit well in its frame and latched securely, sealing out the wind.

Emma slid off her pack and lowered it to the floor. "This is just like the village. How did they create such a thing?"

Daviyd removed his pack as well then sat and ran his hands along the floor. It was firm and sturdy but not uncomfortable. "Adam asked me how many houses were in the chatsr. He must have then acquired the same number of these shelters." He touched a wall. "What are they?" The structure shuddered a little in a gust but didn't seem apt to collapse.

361

THE LAST TOQEPH

Still on her feet, Emma examined a flap in the wall. It was loose at the bottom, and she lifted it. Behind it was a window made of something clear and flexible, with no visible seam between the window and the wall material. "I know not. But they will do." She fastened the flap in the open position and looked out the window.

Daviyd rose and stood beside her. Everyone was within a shelter now, and all the neighbors seemed to have discovered their windows as well. He couldn't see into the central tent, but the way the wind blew the smoke from its round metal chimney made him feel breathless. Then the rain hammered across the beach and struck the huts in a wind-driven wave.

It was like thunder, multiplied. He peered upward then checked around the door and the edges of the floor.

Speaking above the roar, Emma voiced his thoughts. "It doth not leak. Not anywhere!" She watched out the window a moment. "I smell the cooking of fish. I hope the storm doth not prevent them from getting our meal to us." She bent and pulled a water skin from her pack.

Daviyd dragged a roll of thick fabric from where it lay against the wall. It looked like a sleeping mat, but for now, it would serve as a chair. He sat. "Thou hast little trouble accepting their help, I see. Thou wouldst allow them to feed and house thee forever?"

Watching the rain beat impotently against the flexible window, she drank from the skin. "They owe us. This and more." She stoppered the bottle and set it down. "Those who would refuse their gifts are prideful fools. We have always known, have we not, that Natsach's birthright would be restored?"

Daviyd nodded. But the image of the tall part-Karkar leading them, ordering them, arranging everything for them, filled his vision. It looked more like slavery than restoration.

"**Oh**, sweetie, I'm going to miss you." Lileela gave Essie Trombulak a long hug. "I've only known you a few weeks, but it seems like we've been friends forever. I don't want it to end!"

Essie gave a squeeze before releasing her. "It'll never end, hon. We'll keep in touch, and sooner or later we'll get together again in person."

Beside them, a masculine version of the scene played out between Faris and Essie's husband Tom. Then the Trombulaks joined the rest of their team in the *Entrepreneur's* transport bay.

THE LAST TOQEPH

Faris put his arm around Lileela as they watched through the glass. She sagged against him. "She's the dearest friend I ever had. How could we have grown so close so quickly?"

Faris kissed her head. "Kindred spirits, I guess."

Essie looked her way and waved before entering the *Element,* which would take them to Station 21. Binyamin waited for the others to board before he ascended the stairs after them. A few moments later, the steps folded up and the hatch closed.

Lileela studied her husband's smooth face. He told people he'd left his beard on Gannah. Actually, he'd left it in a trash bin on the *DeLaCruz,* but Lileela didn't correct him.

Even without whiskers to mask his expression, his face showed no emotion as he turned her from the window and walked her down the hall. "And now, on to Zhagskar."

She answered in Karkar. "Yes. To Zhagskar."

"Hey." He pinched her backside, making her squeal and jerk away. "I'm still learning. Don't pick on my pronunciation."

"Nobody expects you to pronounce Karkar like a Karkar. I wasn't criticizing."

He grabbed her and pulled her close again. "You were correcting me. That's what Karkar wives do, isn't it? Nag their husbands and pick on them constantly?"

"Well, yes." She fingered the pink collar she still wore. "But I don't plan on adopting the culture quite that completely."

"Can I hold you to that?"

She snorted. "Like I could stop you."

They walked in silence for a few more paces before she said, "I hope Binya will find someone on Station 21."

He tensed. "What do you mean?"

"He never seems happy. I think he needs a good woman."

When Faris hesitated, she wondered what he wasn't saying. Then he shrugged. "Worked for me. But that's not his problem."

"What is his problem, then?"

He led her to a bench by a broad window where they could watch the *Element* when it took off. "His problem is me."

She sat beside him. "You mean he's still mad that you locked him up and hauled him to Gannah against his will? That was years ago. And he's a

THE LAST TOQEPH

believer now — he knows you did the right thing. He can't still be holding a grudge."

Elbows on knees and hands clasped, Faris stared at the floor. "I've known Binya all my life. We grew up together, trained together, worked together since the beginning. I know him better than I know you. And there's no question about it. He's holding that grudge with both hands."

Lileela couldn't conceive of such a thing. "He wouldn't do that. He's just quiet. Reserved. He—"

"He's been nursing his anger." Faris turned to caress Lileela with a somber azure gaze. "He has no intention of letting it die."

She shook her head. "No. You know what the Bible says. We're to forgive others just as the Yasha has forgiven us. If we love God, we'll love our brothers. And Binya—" A wave of horror struck her. "You're not saying—"

He put his arm around her and pointed out the window. "Look, there's the *Element* exiting the bay doors. Let's give them one last wave goodbye."

THE LAST TOQEPH

49

The storm blasted through the circle of huts and out to sea as if it had important business to the east.

Adam stood inside the tent door watching it retreat. It seemed to take some of his tension with it. "The storm's moving on, Yasha be praised." He turned and spoke to the advance team, glancing from one to the other. "You have done an excellent job. The first leg of the journey went better than I could have hoped. I salute you, gentlemen."

They bowed, each murmuring a version of, "It is a pleasure, sir, to serve you and the toqeph."

Emma's green eyes sparkled in the lamplight as she gazed at each in turn. "You are good Gannahans." She lifted her head toward Adam. "I have much to be thankful for and many reasons to be proud."

Looking past Adam, her expression changed to one of curiosity. "What's that?"

He turned in the direction she stared. Seeing an odd object, he stepped over and picked it up. It looked like a sculpture of some sort.

Johann Vigneron said, "Oh, yes. It got pretty dull around here when I was alone, you know, so I did some exploring. I found that one day, half buried. Looked like it might be something, so I dug it out and washed the mud off, thinking the toqeph might find it interesting."

Adam handed the sculpture to Emma, whose eyes widened. She took it almost reverently, her expression incredulous. "Thank you," she said to Adam without looking up, then turned to Johann and thanked him as well. "You were right. It does interest me." She studied the object with eyes and fingers. "Amazing. There's a little damage, but not much. Amazing."

Adam's ears twitched. "What is it?"

THE LAST TOQEPH

She turned the object upside-down and pointed to etching in the bottom. "This was a gift from the province of Yereq. See that?"

Adam read the Gannahan lettering aloud. "Presented to Atarah Degel Charash, Toqeph of Gannah. From the people of Yereq on his Coronation Day in the 779th Year of the Toqephs." He looked down at Emma. "This was your ab's?" She seldom spoke of her father, and Adam had never heard of a coronation ceremony.

She turned the piece upright and indicated the figure that formed the main part of the sculpture. "This is him, wearing the crown of Atarah. These people with the sheaves of grain represent Yereq. The people behind him represent the rest of the world. He's distributing to them the grain given him by Yereq to show how the province provided much of Gannah's food. It's all carved from one piece of canopy wood. Canopy trees used to grow in central Yereq." She ran her finger along the carving. "My father's standing beneath them here. Do you see these twisted trunks behind him and the branches forming a canopy over his head? At the palace in Saba, the trees were planted in long rows along both sides of the road leading to the front gate. Their branches wove together, as you see here, and formed a continuous canopy. There was nothing like it anywhere in the world."

Adam studied the carving in her hands, wishing to pick it up and get a closer look. "It's a remarkable piece." A longing welled up within him for a time and a heritage he'd never known, and never could.

Curled in a chair in the sitting room, Hushai chewed his lip as he watched Abba on the sofa. Those pale amber eyes behind the reading glasses zipped back and forth along the lines Hushai had written. Abba's face, as usual, gave no indication of his thoughts.

He turned his attention to the ears instead, as they were more expressive. They didn't reveal much either, but he took that as a good sign. If Abba were displeased, his ears would be tilting back or twitching.

Abba looked up at Hushai over his glasses. "Don't you have something better to do? You're making me nervous."

"I'm making *you* nervous?"

"No one likes to be stared at." He smoothed his mustache. "If it would make you feel better, let me tell you that at initial glance, this looks like a good science paper. The format is correct. The experiments we worked on together are reported accurately, and the ones Mikaiah helped you with are

THE LAST TOQEPH

properly documented as well. I haven't gotten to your conclusions yet, but it's organized correctly. I see no reason for you to gnaw your lip over it."

A warm ripple of relief made Hushai smile. "The preparation for Level Four is hard. I'm glad Emma's already made sure we know the Gannahan language, so we don't have to learn all that on top of everything else."

"If you don't pass your exam—" Abba paused, then his ears lifted. "I'll wear Daviyd's arnebeth-skin skirt for a week."

Hushai laughed. "It wouldn't fit."

"Just as the concept of your not passing your Level Four exam doesn't fit in my mind."

"Lileela didn't. I mean, didn't she fail her Level One exam?"

Abba nodded. "Yes. But in the first place—" He lifted one long finger for each point. "You're not Lileela. Two, you're not recently returned from another planet. You've lived on Gannah all your life and you prosper under your mother's tutelage. And three? You have a meah, and I don't. So tell me how they're all doing. Lileela and Faris and Auntie, and Adam and your em. I have no way to communicate with them."

"I know." Hushai gave a vigorous nod. "It doesn't make any sense that Emma's never had the satellites fixed. Why hasn't she?"

Abba laid Hushai's science paper on the end table. "The toqeph always has her reasons, and it's not for us to question."

"Umm—you just did."

"That was an observation, not a question. Since I have no other source for news, please tell me what you know."

"Like Ra'anan said this morning—" Hushai leaned back in the chair, stretching his legs out in front. It was a Karkar-sized chair, and he was surprised when his feet touched the floor. Last time he sat like this, they'd dangled above it. "Did this chair shrink?"

"You're growing. You were saying?"

Hushai pattered his feet on the floor and grinned. "Like Ra'anan said in her daily update to the Ministry of Information Dissemination, they're all okay. Emma and Adam and the Natsachs are still crossing the Nazal Sea. Last time I heard from Adam, they were just coming in sight of the first of the Yam Islands. They had some rough seas, and some kid went overboard, but Adam jumped in and pulled him out. He's kinda busy, I guess, because I'm not getting much from him, and of course Emma's always a little distant. But everybody's okay."

THE LAST TOQEPH

"And the Karkar contingent?"

"They expect to enter League Space in a few days. They've got a long ways to go before they get to that Karkar colony they're headed to—what's it called?"

"Thaiikghackxikar Hzhchmm, the new expansion dome on the moon Zhagskar."

"Yea. That place. They're able to communicate with people there, and Lileela says the people on the colony are looking forward to their arrival because they need Uncle Kughurrrro's expertise, Mr. Kohz's experience in medical administration, and Lileela and Auntie for childcare providers and teachers." He wondered about the niggling worry he'd detected in Lileela's meah. "Lileela says Faris seems concerned about something but won't tell her what."

Abba's ears lowered ever so slightly, indicating he shared the concern. "In the eyes of the League of Planets, he's an outlaw, you know. A traitor. He rescued the Dengel family instead of turning them over to the authorities. As long as he was here, they didn't come after him. Apparently League forces have enough troubles in their own territory that they no longer leave their borders."

Fear sent icy fingers along Hushai's spine. "Nothing's going to happen to him, though, right?"

"It's impossible to predict these things." Abba paused. "I doubt he's in danger, though. The authorities wouldn't expect him to leave Gannah, so they likely aren't looking for him. Besides that, a Karkar colony would be the last place anyone would look for a renegade Earther. No, son, if that's what Faris is concerned about, I think he's worried about nothing."

Daviyd stood watching as the two sailors, standing in rising water below deck, argued over how to make a repair.

Malcolm, the one in charge, spoke through gritted teeth. "If I'd had a spare, I'd have brought it. Do you see anything here we can use?"

"Well, no." The younger man, Abe, cleared his throat then spat into the water they stood in. "But we gotta do something."

"Yeah. But if we ain't got a part, we can't fix it. And we ain't got a part. Nobody's got one, we already checked with the others. It's not like Lucas has a store floating out here."

THE LAST TOQEPH

"I still think we should be able to bypass this and run the pressure through here instead."

Malcolm shook his head. "Sure we could, if we want to blow a hole in the hull."

"I think we should try it. You can't know if you don't try. We gotta do something or we'll just sit here forever."

Malcolm waded to the ladder and climbed up. "I gotta talk to Adam."

Daviyd stepped aside to let him pass, wishing there was something he could do. But, fascinating as all these mechanical things were, he knew nothing about them, and the sailors made it plain it wasn't their business to teach him.

Traveling by sea had seemed like a good idea when Adam first spoke of it. The portable huts were set up on the broad, flat decks, and all the people had to do was let the ships take them to the shores of Periy. No dawn-to-dusk hikes, no steep climbs, no carrying heavy packs or children.

The first day out, the people enjoyed the voyage, resting and playing. But the lack of activity soon made them edgy, and by the third day, children were whining, women were bickering, men were fighting.

And now, with all five barges bobbing in the water going nowhere, tension sparked across the decks like heat lightning. Sooner or later, it would ignite a fire. And Daviyd didn't want to think where that might lead.

It was a long way to Qatsyr. And when they finally arrived, what then? How would the Natsachs deal with being thrust into a city of Outsiders? The way they were behaving now, he had little hope. They'd never come together as a united New Gannah.

Though Hushai brushed his meah frequently, Daviyd didn't reveal much, and he knew Adam didn't either. No need to bother the kid with their troubles.

Ra'anan straightened up and surveyed her work. The new bathroom was the image of clean. Not a sign of construction dust anywhere.

She emptied the bucket of wash water into the toilet, and the clean water washed it away through the channel. As she exited the bathroom, cleaning supplies in hand, the sound of Joseph's gurgles came through on the baby monitor that sat on the front room's barren floor.

Elise's muffled voice came from the kitchen. "Drat. Well, I can't complain. That was a longer nap than he usually takes."

THE LAST TOQEPH

Ra'anan found her sister-in-law on hands and knees, head in a low cabinet. Ra'anan spoke to her hindquarters. "I can finish that, if you want to go."

"Thanks, hon." Elise backed out and rose. "You know how he gets when he's hungry."

Ra'anan chuckled. "He knows how to make his wants known, that's for sure. So this is all that still needs to be done here, right? Just the kitchen?

"Right." Elise wiped her forehead with the back of her arm. "I've finished the upper cabinets, and the lower ones to here. You'll just need to do those last two."

Ra'anan scanned the room. "And the window."

"Right. I'll go get Joseph, give him a snack, then bring him back here." She stepped to the window and looked through the smudged glass. "Everett'll be fine out there playing with the kids. Tamah seems to be keeping them out of trouble." She went into the sitting room, grabbed the baby monitor, and slipped out the door. "See ya."

After cleaning the rest of the kitchen, Ra'anan gathered her things and went out into the hall. The next apartment's door was open and Fidelity's chatter tumbled through it. Ra'anan was about to go in to help until she heard Lisbet O'Dell replying to Delly from another room in the suite. "If they're all as handsome as the Mr. Natsach we saw, I am just going to go *mad*. I don't think I can *take* it! Those violet eyes just *do* something to me, you know?"

Ra'anan sighed and moved on to the next apartment. All the girls seemed to talk about anymore were the Natsachs' wonderful eyes, and she'd heard enough of that subject to last a lifetime.

Next door, someone was vacuuming. She stepped in. "Need any help?"

Pushing the sweeper, Mrs. Broward glanced up and smiled. "Thank you. Yes, there's plenty of work to go around."

Ra'anan walked past her and checked out the kitchen. It obviously hadn't been cleaned yet. She set her things down on the counter. Selecting the ceiling duster, she went to work.

Cleaning wasn't her favorite occupation, but it needed to be done and was a practical outlet for her growing excitement. Emma and Adam and the Natsachs would be here tomorrow, and all New Gannah was in a frenzy of last-minute preparation. Between readying their living quarters, planning

THE LAST TOQEPH

the celebration, and transporting them here, the massive project required the participation of every settler.

Ra'anan's innards did a little jig whenever she thought about the new arrivals, so she concentrated on the job at hand. And on Emma, coming home at last. The past month had seemed like forever. The barges had landed at the old port of Periy a few days ago. The rail tubes hadn't been quite ready for them, but the final repairs were now completed, and several test runs were being conducted today. If all went well, the whole group would load up on the tubes and come into First Town tomorrow. The courtyard was decorated, the central pavilion set up for a party, and dozens of chefs were cooking up a storm. It would be bigger than Wormfest and the Harvest Festival put together.

Mrs. Broward shut off the sweeper and stood in the kitchen doorway. "I've already done the bedrooms, so I'll start in the bathroom next."

Ra'anan, cleaning the ceiling with the extension mop, nodded. "These apartments are really nice. New fabric on the walls and everything. Now that the textile factories are up and running, all the settlers will want wallcovering like these."

"I know I do. I've already asked Edwin to make sure he gets us on the list."

Ra'anan lowered the mop and rubbed the back of her neck. "There's a list?"

"The Lucases had so many people coming in asking for fabric they couldn't keep up with it. So they've asked people to let them know what they want, and they'll be notified when it's ready."

Mrs. Broward ran her hand along the padding in the hallway. "It's so crisp and new. Something like this will really liven up our place." She grabbed one of the towels Ra'anan had brought in. "I think I'll test the commode and make sure it works." She winked and bustled off.

The apartments were nice, but empty. Emma had directed that they not be furnished, saying she wanted the new people to choose everything themselves. Ra'anan supposed it made sense, in a way, but on the other hand, an empty house didn't seem very welcoming.

She filled the bucket at the sink and added a dollop of *shaqued* oil. The residents of this home might not have anything to put in them, but the cabinets would be gleaming. As she rubbed the newly finished wood, she envisioned a bearded face with violet eyes shining out at her.

THE LAST TOQEPH

50

A deep weariness dragged at Adam's bones as the last of the people, chattering with excitement, piled into the cars.

Emma stood watching from farther down the platform. The rail mechanics helped Adam make sure all the pod doors were secure. Once everyone was safely loaded, Adam and Emma entered the last pod with the rail mechanics. John Felix-Mercury, the chief mechanic, programmed the route for the entire string then pressed Start.

The car jolted as the power engaged. A distant rumble indicated the start of the first pod, followed immediately by the next, and the next, until Adam was pressed into the seat as the last pod moved forward. The station soon passed out of sight and the walls outside the windows became a blur.

Adam closed his eyes and tried to relax. They'd be in First Town in just over two hours.

Emma's voice came from across the aisle. "You have done well."

His eyes flew open. "Thank you—" He straightened in the little seat so he could bend forward in a bow. "My toqeph. But I could not have done it without you."

She gave a little shrug. "It was not a job for one man, that's certain. But I'm not sure my presence in particular was required."

"Far be it from me to contradict the toqeph, but I believe you're mistaken." He wouldn't have spoken so formally if the mechanics hadn't been there. "Your presence made all the difference in the world."

"You mean at sea, when everyone started getting grumpy? You'd have come up with something."

Adam noticed his pant leg had worked its way out of his boot and tucked it back in. "Grumpy? Is that what you call a boatload of wild Gannahans with lahabs and hot tempers?"

Emma laughed. Apparently seeing humor was permissible, the mechanics chuckled. John stroked his beard. "Sounds like an interesting situation."

THE LAST TOQEPH

"The people had nothing to do," Emma said, "except worry. We'd hauled them away from everything familiar, and they felt trapped and helpless. It's never healthy to back a Gannahan into a corner."

Another mechanic, Jacob Sisterhen, widened his eyes. "What did you do, Madam Toqeph?"

"I liberated them from the corner. Gave them some control of their destinies."

Seeing the men's questioning looks, Adam explained. "She taught them to read."

John guffawed. "That's it?"

Emma smiled. "I *began* teaching them to read. Most of them already knew the Gannahan alphabet, but I taught them the Standard, as well as a few words in the language. And other things. They're now comfortable with basic manners, which aren't much different from what they already knew, and enough history and science to pass the First Level exam, when that time comes. I made it a game, and they learned quickly." She crossed one leg over the other. "I started all that on my boat. When I saw how testy people were getting on the other barges, I rearranged things to break up the troublemakers and put some of the ones I'd already taught on each of the other vessels. Also, I spent each day on a different barge so I could work with everyone. All that defused the tension fairly quickly, even though it did get rather crowded after we had to abandon one boat and put extra huts on the other four."

She spoke with nonchalance, but Adam saw from the men's appreciative expressions that they knew the feat was not as insignificant as she made it out to be. "They love you," he said.

Her brows rose. "Do you think?"

"I know. They can see you love them."

She leaned back. "I do." Her face took on a far-away expression but then she looked up and smiled. "But you know what I don't love? Fish. Eating fish every day as I have these last couple of weeks reminded me of when I was alone on the other side of the planet. I ate like a qua'athbird. Fish, fish, and more fish, and little else but fish. It kept me alive, but I wouldn't mind if I never ate it again."

Adam said, "Don't tell Malcolm," and the other men laughed.

THE LAST TOQEPH

Emma chuckled. "He's a fine fisherman, a good Gannahan, and he and his crew provide an invaluable service. Our lives are greatly enriched by their efforts. I just prefer to give my share of his bounty to someone else."

She radiated happy contentment, and if anything, looked younger than when they'd left. John must have thought the same. "I'm not sure I heard right, Madam. All those people, kids and everything, walked something like a hundred kilometers day and night through the wilderness to get to the Nazal Sea? And you went with them?"

"You must have misunderstood, Mr. Felix-Mercury. The distance is correct, but we didn't travel through the night."

Jacob whistled. "That's a long walk. And you're—well, pardon my asking, ma'am, but how old are you?"

"I'm not sure." She looked thoughtful. "Time passed at a different rate on Earth, and I lost track of it somewhat."

Adam knew exactly how old she was, because she'd told him. She was seventy-nine. The solar calendar in the palace had continued running while she was gone, so she'd been able to calculate the time of her absence by Gannahan standards. Had she forgotten?

When John and Jacob made noises of surprise, she hastened to add, "Gannahans don't age the same as Earthers do. A few of the Natsach people with us were also alive before the Plague and are nearly as old as I. As my grandfather used to say, a Gannahan keeps going and then he stops. There is no slowing down."

Jacob turned to Adam. "You're a big strapping fella. I'll bet you're gonna do that too. Keep going until you stop."

Adam's ears swiveled. "I am only half Gannahan, so that remains to be seen. Neither my Earthish nor my Karkar ancestors could boast such long, active lives." As weary as he felt after this adventure though not yet thirty years old, he didn't figure he'd make it past a hundred.

In the meantime, he'd have to make sure he left plenty of children to carry the torch. Abba and Emma had five? He and Elise would have seven.

It would be good to see Elise again. His ears smiled. He was never too tired for that.

Daviyd awoke when the pod slowed and a mechanical voice intoned "Qatsyr One." As the car came to a stop, he opened his eyes to the now-familiar sight of the inside of a rail station.

THE LAST TOQEPH

His heart pounded. They were home.

Adam's voice came over the speaker. "Ladies and gentlemen, we have arrived. Please remain seated until your car door opens. Then, ye may disembark at will. And please, be not alarmed at the reception awaiting. The people have come to welcome us."

Daviyd looked past Jether beside him and peered out the window. The entire platform was lined with settlers eyeing the cars expectantly. Their gazes shifted to the car at the end of the line. A moment later the crowd broke into cheers, stomping and hooting. What was that all about?

His question was answered a moment later when Adam came into view. He bowed in acknowledgement of their applause and spoke to one of the men, who appeared to lead the welcome party. Then Adam turned back toward the line of cars, made a gesture, and the door to Daviyd's pod unlatched and slid back.

Still staring out the window, Jether said, "We'll let you out first, Daviyd." The others in the car agreed, so Daviyd grabbed his bag, slipped past his fellow passengers, and stepped onto the platform.

Adam approached. "We shall follow the ramp to ground level and then into the courtyard. To avoid undue alarm, I have asked the people to hold their cheering until all are above ground."

Daviyd nodded. "It is well." Several others had also exited their cars, his mother and the two oldest men in the lead. They cast suspicious glances at the settlers and ogled the surroundings as they moved toward him.

Daviyd extended his hand. "Come with me. I know the way. The people are here to welcome us, not attack."

He needn't have added that last, because the smiling settlers' intentions were plain as they bowed to the new arrivals. Many added verbal welcomes as well, though their speech was clumsy.

Daviyd stretched out his arms and bowed his thanks to the settlers. Then he tucked his bag under his arm and walked up the ramp at the head of the villagers, who continued pouring out of the pods.

Earthish settlers lined the entire route, their expressions eager or curious and sometimes uncertain as they bowed. Daviyd was grateful for Adam's request that they refrain from cheering, for in the confines of the tunnel, the noise would have been jarring.

He smiled when he saw the moving stairway. The settlers stood on either side upon the stationary portions. He mounted the moving steps and

THE LAST TOQEPH

allowed them to carry him. After a moment's hesitation, the elders followed his example. Halfway up, he glanced back to see the whole village rising behind him or queuing up to mount in their turn.

Daylight glowed ahead, and as he neared the top, he heard voices speaking in the Standard language. "They're coming! I see Daviyd! Get ready, they're here!"

Spurred by their cries, he ran up the last few steps and hurried toward the open door. He heard the others close behind, felt their excitement, their trepidation. Their reliance upon him to lead them into this strange new world.

He burst through the doorway into the sunshine, narrowing his eyes against the glare. The courtyard full of people cheered. Their hooting and stomping filled the air. He lifted his free arm in greeting as he walked toward the center of the chatsr.

A banner across the front of the pavilion, written in Gannahan characters, read, "Welcome Home." When he reached the platform, he dropped his bag and turned to watch his people pour into the courtyard, blinking in the light of their redemption.

THE LAST TOQEPH

51

A Year Later...

Ra'anan sat at the sewing machine in the dining room, fabric strewn across the table around her. She finished the seam and snipped off the threads, throwing the trimmings into the waste can on the floor beside her.

As she turned the tunic right side out, Emma walked in holding a narrow strip of white fabric. "I need some emerald green. Do you have any?"

Careful to not see what Emma held in her hands, Ra'anan examined the seams she'd just sewn. "I believe I do." She nodded toward a carved wooden box at the opposite end of the table. "My embroidery thread is in there. Pardon me for not getting it for you, but I'm not supposed to see that until you put it on me on my birthday."

"True." Emma folded the fabric and concealed it in her hand. "There, now you can't see it. But don't get up, I can look for the thread myself." She opened the box and selected a skein of green floss. "Oh, yes, perfect. It matches your eyes."

Satisfied with the seams, Ra'anan stood and held up the tunic. "It still needs a hem, but what do you think?" She turned it around so Emma could see both sides. "I especially like the deep pleat in the back and the flare in the peplum."

Emma's eyes glowed. "It's lovely. You shouldn't do such a good job, though. All the girls will be hounding you to design outfits for their sixteenth birthday parties."

Ra'anan blushed. "I spoke with Mrs. Yuang this morning."

"And?"

THE LAST TOQEPH

"She's offered me a position as apprentice designer."

The way Emma smiled made Ra'anan wonder if she'd asked Mrs. Yuang to make the offer.

"You don't seem surprised."

Emma's brows rose. "Why should I be? You've been making your own clothes since you were twelve and designing them almost as long. It would only surprise me if she *didn't* give you the job."

She extended her arms, and Ra'anan was happy to enter the hug. But lately it surprised her how small Emma was.

Her arms were still strong and comforting, though, and Ra'anan was in no hurry to leave them. "I'm so happy, Emma."

"So am I, sweet."

They broke the embrace, but both continued to smile. "You know, Emma, when I was younger, I didn't think I'd ever want to leave. I dreaded my sixteenth birthday because I didn't think I'd be ready."

Emma chuckled. "Oh, you're ready. And if I'm to have a set of white collars ready to present to you, I'd better finish making them."

She headed for the door, then stopped and turned back, eyes wide.

At the same time, Ra'anan gasped. "Yes!"

Emma became brisk. "Better get this table cleared off. I'm sure the other kids know, but I'll tell Abba. He won't want to miss Adam bringing his *metheq*."

Adam pulled the tray of tarts out of the oven. The fragrance was almost delicious enough to make him lightheaded. Or maybe it was because he hadn't eaten anything for many days. Not since he'd gathered the mossberries.

Though the lay of the land had changed dramatically since the Great Disaster, the rules of the Nasi's Final Quest were essentially unchanged since the earliest known history. The inductee must travel on foot to find the mossberries. He must pick them and bring them home without eating a single one. Then he must prepare the offering, called a metheq, and take it to the toqeph. Once he started homeward, no food could pass his lips until the toqeph had tasted the mossberry offering.

Adam had stumbled home hungry and exhausted but elated at his success. After greeting Elise and the boys, he sent them to her mother's

THE LAST TOQEPH

house so none of them would be tempted to touch a mossberry while he prepared the metheq.

He couldn't keep the unseemly smile from his face as he packed the tarts in a container he'd made for this purpose. The individual compartments would keep the tarts from sliding around when he carried it, and vents allowed the steam to escape so the pastries wouldn't get soggy. He closed the lid, picked up the box by the handle, and hurried out the door, calling Elise on his messenger as he went.

Her eager voice was like an angel in his ear. "Adam? Where are you?"

"I'm on my way. Meet me there."

Hushai scrubbed his hands. He supposed it didn't matter if he showed up with dirt under his nails, but this was worth getting cleaned up for.

Mr. Mutombo came in. "Is it true what I hear? Your brother's back from his quest?"

Grinning, Hushai dried his hands. "Yes, sir. He contacted me when he was taking the metheq out of the oven. If I hurry, I can get to the palace before he does."

Mr. Mutombo clapped him on the back. "Then what are you doing here? Hurry!"

Hushai ran across the newly-harvested sheber field toward the palace and in through the back door by the park pavilion. Inside, he slowed to a walk, straightening his clothes and smoothing his hair as he went. He ran a hand along his chin, enjoying the feel of the whiskers. They were still thin, but it was a beard, and Abba assured him it would fill in soon enough.

He walked tall and briskly, smiling and nodding at Zuri Esam, whose expanding waistline evidenced the success of Adam and Abba's years of research.

He arrived at the toqeph's suite and found the whole family—except for Lileela and Faris, of course, who were still on that Karkar moon colony, and Adam, who had not yet arrived—in the sitting room. They looked up in expectation, and their faces fell as they saw who it was.

"Sorry. Just me." Hushai chuckled. "Looks like I didn't miss anything."

Elise shook her head. She perched on the edge of an oversized chair, her near-bursting belly seeming to pull her forward. "Nope. He's not here yet."

THE LAST TOQEPH

Everett followed Joseph on his toddling exploration of the room, distracting his attention from objects he shouldn't touch. "Any minute now, Joseph. Abba's going to be a Nasi! He's going to get a purple tongue."

"I'm excited about it too, Everett." Hushai joined the family. Ittai, Tamah, and Ra'anan paced the floor. Abba sat on the old, worn sofa with Emma beside him, calmly embroidering. As if it were an everyday thing for her son to present her with a metheq.

Hushai had no sooner sat beside Emma than the door opened and Adam entered, preceded by the most delicious scent Hushai had ever smelled. Hushai hopped to his feet as if the sofa had burned him. Abba pushed himself up with an effort, and Elise rose with even more difficulty than Abba.

Despite Emma's calm appearance, she was the first to reach the dining room doorway. "In here, everybody."

She took a seat at the head of the table. Adam followed but remained standing, and everyone else filed in after him. They found places to stand, with Tamah picking up Joseph and Elise holding Everett's shoulders as he stood in front of her.

Emma had never looked so happy and beautiful as when she gazed up at Adam.

He knelt and handed her an odd-looking container. "Thy metheq, my toqeph."

"Thank you, Adam." She took it from him and lifted the lid. A sweet-sour aroma filled the room, and Hushai swallowed the saliva that rushed into his mouth.

Adam assumed the traditional prostrate position, forehead and forearms pressed against the floor. Emma gazed into the container and nodded. "They're beautiful. I had no idea you were such a talented pastry chef."

The floor muffled his reply. "I have been practicing, my toqeph."

She chuckled as she lifted a tart from the box and sniffed it. "Ah." She took a bite and chewed, and her eyes shone greener than ever. "It is as good as it looks." She finished the tart then looked down at Adam. "Arise, Pik Adam Atarah. Thou art a Nasi of Gannah."

He made a choking sound and rose, tears running into his beard.

THE LAST TOQEPH

Daviyd only went to Adam's celebration dinner to be near Ra'anan. Now that he knew her better, he wondered why he hadn't been drawn to her earlier. True, she was tall for a Gannahan. More lithe and longer of limb. But her green eyes glowed like her mother's, and her dark hair had a proper curl rather than hanging limp and straight like so many of the settlers'. Yes, in appearance and manner, she was the image of the perfect Gannahan woman.

Except she wouldn't be a woman for two more days. Though it was good that she should be free and independent from her mother, her adulthood meant he wouldn't be able to hold her hand, or finger her hair, or kiss her lips ever again, until they were married.

And that wouldn't be until after he'd reached the Fifth Level of his education at the very least. He could, by all rights, marry whenever he wanted. But he didn't want to be husband of a woman who exceeded his status, and so, for this precious jewel, he chose to wait.

The toqeph's family and their adult guests filled the dining room, and the children—all but Ra'anan and Hushai—ate in the kitchen for lack of space. Adam, his tongue stained purple, sat in the place of honor beside the toqeph. His orange-haired wife sat on his other side, bloated with pride and pregnancy.

She kept glancing at Daviyd beside Ra'anan, and from her expression, she didn't approve of his being there. Apparently she didn't realize her opinion meant nothing to him. Ra'anan loved him, his em approved of their courtship, and the toqeph made no objection. That, and the Yasha's blessing, was all that mattered.

After a particularly pointed look from Elise, he held her gaze and put his hand on Ra'anan's right arm.

Because she wasn't of age yet, it was technically permissible for him to touch her, though it wasn't strictly proper. Breaking away from Elise's horrified gaze, he turned to Ra'anan. "This is delicious. Who made it?"

Eyes averted, she pulled away from his touch and picked up her napkin. "It is good, isn't it? Mrs. Maddox made it." After patting her mouth, she put her hand in her lap and ate with her left. In her meah, she scolded him soundly, which made him smile.

Because everyone else was involved in conversations, his untoward touch went unnoticed by all but Elise. He hoped she'd gripe to Adam about

THE LAST TOQEPH

it afterward and that her report would make him angry. The man was a boor and deserved to be irritated.

Daviyd smiled broader. "This noodle dish is delicious, Mrs. Maddox."

She looked up from her conversation with Jax's wife. "Why, thank you, Daviyd."

After the last course, all but the guest of honor and his wife pitched in to clean up. Then they joined Adam and Elise in the sitting room, where the children sat on the floor, leaving the furniture for the adults.

Before taking his seat, Pik walked to the ornate blend cabinet and opened the glass doors. "We've been saving something for this very occasion." He bent to reach in and pulled out two bottles with labels yellowed with age.

Adam eyed the bottles. "Oh?"

The toqeph explained. "It is a blend made by order of my grandfather when Areli, my oldest brother, was born. He gave it to my father to put away for when Areli completed his Third Quest and became a Nasi. But that never happened."

"Why not?" Ittai asked.

The toqeph's face clouded. "He died during the quest. His body was never found, but all of us who were close to him—my family, and his fiancé—" Her eyes darted briefly to Elise. "We knew in our meahs the moment it happened. It was very sad for all of us, but for my parents, it was a crushing blow."

Daviyd felt her sorrow, even now. Yet that was just the first grief in a lifetime of horrors.

Tamah's face puckered in puzzlement. "So why didn't they open it when you became Nasi?"

"That occurred at a very bad time. Everyone was sick. No one felt like celebrating."

While she spoke, Dr. Pik poured a pale pinkish blend into glasses. Even from across the room, its quality was evident in its fragrance and the way it clung to the sides of the goblets. Daviyd rose and went to the cabinet. "May I help? Would you like me to distribute those?"

The old giant nodded. "Thank you. The first go to Adam and Elise."

But of course, Adam being the guest of honor and all. Daviyd picked up two glasses and carried them to the sofa where Adam sat beside his

THE LAST TOQEPH

swollen wife. He bowed as he presented the first glass. "Congratulations, Pik Adam Atarah." Adam thanked him as he took the blend.

With another bow, Daviyd handed the second glass to Elise, making sure to position his hand in such a way that she would have difficulty taking it without touching him. She glared up as she took it carefully with both hands. "Thank you, Mr. Natsach." No meah was necessary to detect her sarcasm.

While Daviyd went back and forth distributing the blend, the others talked about the toqeph's father and grandfather. Tamah jumped up, nearly bumping into Daviyd as he passed by with two full glasses, and ran to a low table. "Tell us about this, Emma." She picked up the wood carving from Yereq and carried it to her mother.

The toqeph explained that it had been a present to her ab. Daviyd had heard the story before, and he figured everyone else had too. But children liked to hear things repeated, and the young ones sat in rapt attention.

Though Tamah was as tall as her mother, she was still very much a child. "What kind of coronation gifts did *you* get, Emma?"

The toqeph looked surprised at the question, and she and her husband exchanged glances. "Well—I was never actually crowned."

Tamah's eyes widened. "You're not the real toqeph?"

"Yes, I'm real enough." Daviyd didn't miss the glance she tossed him for a nanosecond. "I was made Nasi, and then my father put his ring on my finger. That's all that's required. In most cases, there was a big party afterward. People from all over the world would bring the toqeph gifts to show that they loved him. But as I said, when my turn came, everyone was sick. We weren't having any parties in those days."

Hushai fingered the wisps on his chin. "I think the settlers should have had a Coronation Day after you all got here. It doesn't seem right that all the rulers had one except you."

The toqeph gave him an indulgent smile. "It's sweet of you to feel that way, Shai. But it's not necessary. In fact, if I got wind of anyone planning such a thing, I'd put a stop to it immediately. By this time, we've come too far to pretend we're just beginning."

Daviyd detected an emotion slicing through her, though he wasn't sure what.

Then she turned a loving gaze toward Adam. "If the people want to hold a Coronation Day celebration, they can do it for my successor."

THE LAST TOQEPH

Adam blushed, and Daviyd almost sloshed the blend from the goblets he carried. Wasn't the throne to be restored to Natsach? Wasn't that why she'd brought them here, to give back what had been taken?

Later, as Daviyd tipped back his head and allowed the last of that rich, potent blend to make its way from the goblet into his mouth, he made up his mind.

He lowered his glass and locked eyes with Ra'anan in the next chair, communicating his decision to her through his meah. *Thou art mine, now and forever.*

Yea. Thou knowest.

But I shall not marry thee until I am a Nasi.

Her expression mirrored the alarm in her meah. *That will be a long time coming.*

I must devote myself to my training. I will work and study with wholehearted diligence. To have a wife is to be distracted from one's labor, and to work steadfastly toward a goal prevents a man from giving his wife the devotion she deserves.

Still holding his gaze, Ra'anan nodded, sharing with him her recollections of how often Adam had left Elise and the children alone.

I shall not have a celebration such as this when my tongue is made purple; my celebration shall be our wedding day. Willst thou wait for me?

A slow smile made its reluctant way across her face, and her eyes filled. *Yea, my sweet Natsach Daviyd Natsach. I shall wait for thee forever.*

His heart swelled in his chest. *And I for thee. A Natsach can indeed wait forever. But for us, it shall not be that long.*

He made another resolve as well, but he didn't share it with Ra'anan. Not yet.

One day—he knew not when or how—he would sit on the throne of Atarah. But he would not be called toqeph. From his reign onward, the ruler would be called king. That was the way it had been at the beginning, when the Bara first placed Atarah and Em in the garden of Gannah to rule His creation. And that was the way it should be when the throne was restored to the rightful heir.

THE LAST TOQEPH

52

Another Year Later...

"Look, Ziggy." Faris put his hands on his hips and glared up at the blank-faced greenhouse foreman. "I'm telling you, you've got contamination in your water supply. Can't you smell it?"

He'd given up trying to pronounce the language a year ago. But the Karkar understood his Standard, and he could usually get the meaning of their noises, so he seldom needed a translator anymore.

"I smell nothing unusual." Zigkghiizak's ears tilted back. "You would have me run expensive tests for no reason."

"The tests aren't all that expensive, you big cheapskate, and I'm not telling you this for grins." Faris stretched himself to his absolute tallest, though he didn't reach the other man's shoulder, and spoke with the loud passion these people respected. "We supply a significant portion of Karkar's food, and we can't take chances. Too many people depend on us. Besides, I've got to eat the food we produce here too, you know, and — "

The sound of a throat clearing behind Faris made him stop and turn. Having a discussion interrupted was hardly an unusual occurrence, and ordinarily, he talked through it, making the interrupter wait to be heard. But there was such a weight of import in this guttural sound that his skin prickled.

Zigkghiizak's ears snapped back in irritation. "What is it, Jhoch?"

Ziggy's assistant, ears quivering, shifted his glance from his boss down to Faris and back up again. "Sorry to bother you, sir, but there are visitors with President Kukkolok demanding to see Commander Faris."

THE LAST TOQEPH

Faris's stomach did such a violent flip it almost bubbled out of his mouth. "Did you say *Commander* Faris?"

Jhoch cocked his head to the left in a Karkarish nod. "Yes. That is what they called you. *Co-nan-drrr*." His Standard pronunciation was rough, but it got the point across.

All too well.

Faris took a deep breath and let it out slowly, willing his heart to stop racing and his head to stop spinning. "Very well, then. I'd better go." He turned back to Ziggy. "I recommend you run the tests." He tapped his nose. "I know tainted water when I smell it." Then he followed Jhoch out of the greenhouse offices and through the labyrinthine halls to the Thaiikghackxikar Hzhchmm Administration Building.

"How many, um, visitors, are there?"

The answer did nothing to calm his nerves. "Eight."

They'd brought a whole team for him, then. He could consider that a compliment. "Who are they? Do they look like me?"

"They could be your brothers."

He tried to answer, but his voice failed him. He turned his reluctant gaze to toward the landing field and saw a League vessel—Photuris class, much like the one he'd stolen and taken to Gannah—crouched like a beast ready to spring. *My Yasha, give me strength to stand.*

They entered the administration building. "Mr. Jhoch, could I ask you to do something for me?"

The pale giant glanced down at him then looked away, as if the image was painful. "I doubt I can help you."

"No one can. But could you give my wife a message? Tell her I don't want her to intervene. It would be dangerous for her. Tell her it will cause me worry. I'll rest easy knowing she's safe."

Jhoch blinked. "I understand. Yes. I will do that for you."

"Thank you. She won't have to restrain herself for long. These people are very efficient about their business."

"I get that impression."

When they reached the president's office, Jhoch buzzed. "I have brought Faris, Mr. President."

"Very good. Send him in." Jhoch stepped aside and let Faris enter alone. Was it his imagination, or did sympathy flicker across that wan expression?

THE LAST TOQEPH

He had no time to wonder about it. President Kukkolok rose from his chair and spoke his name as best he could. "Ah, Fah-dees." The big man's ears sagged with sorrow. "These gentlemen claim—" He coughed. "I've checked it out, and it is legitimate. I'm sorry, but they have a warrant for your arrest. They are with the League of Planets, and Karkar is a League member, so—"

Faris put up his hand, and somehow, it didn't tremble. "Say no more, sir." The eight men in Special Starforces uniform glared at him with hard, brilliant eyes, their clean-shaven faces chiseled and cold.

"I know the charges." He identified the team leader, Wasim, by his insignia and spoke directly to him. "Treason, am I correct? Kidnapping?"

Wasim's voice was stony. "Commander Faris, you are under arrest for treason against the League of Planets, insubordination, desertion, dereliction of duty, kidnapping, unlawful detainment, and grand larceny in the theft of government property."

While he spoke, the others threw Faris to the floor so fast he never felt himself falling. Before Wasim had finished his recitation, they'd wrenched Faris's shoulders nearly out of their sockets as they clamped his arms together behind his back, bound his legs tightly enough to cut into the flesh, and thrown a hood over his head.

"Take him," Wasim ordered.

A cord tightened around Faris's neck. *And now it begins* was his last thought before he blacked out.

In the toqeph's sitting room, Daviyd heard footsteps coming down from the tower and looked up to see Les Stony emerge from the stairway door.

"Mr. Natsach." He bowed, first to Daviyd, then to Jether. "Mr. Natsach." He greeted Jacob last. "Mr. Sisterhen. The toqeph will see you now. Please, follow me."

The tall young man had been serving the toqeph for several months. Daviyd wasn't sure what she was grooming him for, but it seemed fitting she should have an assistant, and he had the makings of a regal representative. The way Gannah was growing, the leadership needed more support than the three Nasi could provide.

It had been warm in the sitting room, but the higher they climbed, the hotter it grew. A fan at the end of the hall blew air around but did little to alleviate the sweltering heat.

THE LAST TOQEPH

Stony led them to the throne room, announced their arrival, and backed out.

No fans were in this room, though the toqeph had a pitcher nearby and a sweaty glass half-full of ice water. The usual formalities — the obeisance, the proper utterances — were observed with gratifying Gannah-ness. Then the toqeph got down to business.

"I have ruled on your petition, gentlemen, and I am granting it."

All three bowed again. "Thank you, Madam." Daviyd had had little doubt, but it was a relief to know it was official. He informed his em of such through his meah.

"I confess, however, I'm unable to follow all the technical aspects of your plan. You shall work with Roshan Tewodros, who has a good understanding of these things, and I am also asking Dortius Dmitry to assist you as necessary. He has a hard time getting around these days, but his mind is still sharp. Between the five of you, I'm confident you'll be able to accomplish your goal."

"Thank you, Madam."

She gave Daviyd a pointed look. "This has long been my desire as well."

He nodded. "I thought as much, Madam, when thou didst share thy mind with me at our first meeting."

"Yes." She smiled. "If you can discover a way to restore our power production and communication capabilities to what they were before the Great Disaster using no Outside technologies, the whole settlement will be grateful. The Natsachs will be happy because it is wholly Gannahan. Those of Earthish descent will just be glad to have modern conveniences again." She took a sip of water. "And I look forward to being able to communicate with Lileela and Faris on that Karkarish moon."

Faris had been trained in the art of pain. How to give it, and how to take it. None of this was new.

Nor unexpected. It was only right that his crimes catch up with him.

Standing before the tribunal, he pleaded guilty to all charges. How could he not? He was guilty.

The savagery with which his former comrades, Omar and Ya'qub, beat him, was understandable. He'd betrayed them. Sent them on a fool's errand. Ordered them to deliver a false report to their captain. What punishment

THE LAST TOQEPH

had they endured because of his treachery? He deserved every broken bone they gave him.

His sentence was death. But the law didn't specify by what method, nor how long it should take him to die. Faris understood they must drag it out, make him suffer unbearably, because his crimes were so heinous. He'd do the same if he were in their position, if not for the Yasha's grace.

In fact, he had done the same. The mangled bodies of those he had tortured loomed in his vision, their screams of agony rang in his ears. Or perhaps it was his own screams he heard.

"Where is Philip Dengel?" his tormentors demanded. "He is a criminal. He must be brought to justice. Where are he and his family hiding? Where are they?"

At first, he couldn't tell them because he didn't know. He was glad he didn't know. Though he found no bliss in this ignorance, it was a deliverance from temptation. He couldn't give up the Dengels if he'd wanted to.

After a time, he couldn't have told them in any event, because his jaw was too shattered for speech. That's when they started asking him questions whose answers they didn't care to hear. "Where's your God now, Commander? Why doesn't he come down and save you, like you saved the Dengels? If he were so great, wouldn't he stop this? If he loved you, would he let us do this? Or this? Or this?"

Faris knew those answers. Though he couldn't speak, he knew. He wanted to tell them, wanted them desperately to understand. They were him — he was them — creations of man, but with a spark of eternity. How he longed to spare their lost souls the agonies that awaited them if no one told them, agonies that would have no end.

But a body, even a highly engineered one, could only take so much. And, unlike the horrors that await the unrepentant, Faris's suffering was temporary.

"Where's your God now?"

Faris was in His presence. All he knew was joy.

Lileela settled herself in front of the video recorder. Would she be able to hold it together?

Auntie patted her hand. "You don't need to do this, honey. We have no idea when they'll receive the message."

389

THE LAST TOQEPH

Lileela bit her lip and took Auntie's hand. "I know. But I want to tell them. And I want to get it done now. We don't need to send it until their communication systems are working, but I need to say it while it's fresh." She glanced up at Uncle Kughurrrro across the table. Little Skugie sat in his lap with her thumb plugged into her mouth. "I can do it as long as you're here with me."

Auntie's eyes filled with tears and she tipped her head in assent, sniffling loudly. Uncle Kughurrrro's ears smiled encouragement. "We are here for you, my dear."

Lileela nodded. "Thank you."

Skugie laid her head against Kughie's chest and sucked harder.

My dear, sweet Yasha. I love you so much. Help me find the words. Lileela set the machine to Record.

"Hello Emma, Abba, and anyone else who's listening. I love you all.

"I know you've heard what's happened. I shared with those of you with meahs as much as I could, and I know they've told the rest of you. But some things I think are best put into words. So I'm making this recording now and will send it when I can. I know you're getting the communications satellites fixed finally—what took you so long?" She smiled. "So I'll have this message ready to send just as soon as you let me know it's all working."

She took a deep breath. "Soldiers came here a couple months ago and took Faris. He knew they were coming. He'd told me not long before that he expected it, and that when they came, he'd go willingly. He said—" She swallowed hard. "He said it had been eating away at him the whole time he was on Gannah. As much as he loved it there, and loved you all, he felt it was cowardly to hide like a fugitive. So when the *DeLaCruz* came, he wondered if that wasn't his opportunity to go back and make things right. And then when he saw I felt called to take the gospel to Abba's people, he knew right away the Yasha wanted him to do this."

Auntie engulfed her hand in hers and gave it a gentle squeeze.

Lileela tossed her a smile then turned her attention back to the camera. "So they came for him a couple months ago. Binya had told them. After he left us, he contacted the League and told them he'd been kidnapped and had just escaped." She swallowed a sob. "I don't know what all he told them. But Faris—he said Binya would have told them the truth, because he was an honest man. Faris never had anything but good to say about that

THE LAST TOQEPH

Binyamin, and he didn't want me to resent him. I'm trying real hard not to, but—well, I'm trying.

"Faris told me this was coming, but I didn't want to believe it. And then when they took him, I couldn't believe—I mean—how could they do that to him? I heard he was executed, and I tried to think, okay, he's with the Yasha now, that's good, I'll see him again. But then the news reports came, and the videos, and the pictures. *This is what happens to traitors*, they said. They showed pictures, Emma. They said it was my Faris, but it didn't look like him anymore.

"Since then, I've quit looking at news reports. I'm afraid I'll see those pictures again. For a while after I quit looking at them, though, I saw them with my eyes open and my eyes closed. They were always there. And then I remembered how many other people have suffered for the Yasha's name, and how He Himself suffered for me. And as much as I hated what they did to him, I was so proud of my Faris. Proud of him because he loved the Yasha. Because he was willing to face up to what he did and not hide, even though what he called justice doesn't seem like justice to me. Proud of him because he never hated Binyamin. 'My brother Binya,' he always called him. I'm proud of him because—because he was so much like the Yasha. He let the Yasha change him, let the Yasha take him over completely."

She thought of her family listening. This must be as hard to listen to as it was to say. "I just want you to know that I'm all right. Well, not alright-alright, but I'll be okay. And I'm staying here. Auntie and Uncle Kughie, they've been just wonderful to me, so supportive and loving, they're hardly like Karkar at all." She winked at Kughie. "But that's not the best part. What amazes me the most is how the whole colony here is coming to the Yasha. They used to pick on Faris because he was so little, so not like a Karkar, and with those bright Gannahan eyes, they really didn't like him. But he learned to understand their language, and even though he couldn't speak it, he knew how to talk like a Karkar—loud and eloquent and in-your-face." She smiled. "He used to stand on a chair, sometimes, to get close enough to yell at someone nose-to-nose. He wouldn't back down, and he could match anyone with sarcasm or wit or a pun

"And then he was taken. Now people are coming to the worship meetings to see what it's all about, and they're really listening. They're not dismissing it as something from Gannah, but something that applies to

THE LAST TOQEPH

them, as Karkar. And they're coming to the Yasha. First it was a handful at a time, and now it's by the *giktzker* load, as they say around here."

She smiled again. "I hate what happened — it's so terrible, so evil. I feel the wickedness like it's crawling all over me sometimes. But the Yasha needs His people here so we can fight the evil with the truth. And He's chosen me to be one of those messengers. He's been training me for it all my life. I realize that now. It's a privilege to do this, and I won't turn tail and run. I'm staying here until the Yasha sends me elsewhere.

"I miss Faris. I cry all the time. But I'm okay. I just want you all to know that."

She lifted her finger, but before shutting off the recording added, "I love you all.

THE LAST TOQEPH

53

Adam looked up from his desk and rubbed his eyes. He'd had a cloud over his meah the past few days, and he wasn't sure why. Maybe he was just fed up with paperwork.

His messenger buzzed.

"Yes, Abba?"

He heard nothing at first, then a throat-clear. "How are you, son?"

"I'm fine." He frowned. Something was definitely wrong. "How are you?"

"We haven't seen you around lately. Keeping busy, are you?"

Adam leaned back in his chair, reliving the hectic last few days. "You know how it is. Overseeing both clinics and the lab, training more doctors, helping Elise with the boys. I'm sorry I haven't been by." He lifted his teapot to refill the cup, but the pot was empty. "Everything okay? Do you need something?"

Abba paused. "Your mother would like to see you."

He said "your mother." Not *the toqeph*, not *your em*. Something was up.

Adam stood. "I'll be right there."

When he arrived at the toqeph's suite, the whole family was in the sitting room, along with a stranger. Adam took another look. It wasn't a stranger. "Emma?"

Her hair was gray. Her face was lined. The whites of her eyes were bloodshot, and the irises a dull green. He met her in his meah, and his heart plummeted. "Emma!" He squatted beside her chair and took her hand. "Wha—" But he didn't need to ask.

"It is time." She put her hand on his face. "Though I am yet young." Her eyes filled with tears. "This business with Faris, I'm afraid, has done me

THE LAST TOQEPH

in." She looked around at the others, all of whom wore stricken expressions. "Do not grieve. In my brief life, I have been greatly blessed and accomplished much."

Adam's mind reeled. "Emma, this is so sudden!"

She shook her head. "I started turning gray over a week ago, and I knew then the end was near. Your father knew. And Tamah." She smiled at her youngest. "My em used to say the lastborn child is nearest to her mother's heart."

She leaned back in the chair and took in the sight of them, one by one. "I know you'll miss me. And I'm sorry to cause you such pain. But the fact is —" She chuckled. "I've been looking forward to this for a long, long time. A long time." She took Adam's hand. "I've asked Orville to make a new ring. Mine is looking as worn-out as I feel. He's working on it, but it won't be finished before I go." She released his hand and twisted the Ring of Atarah on her finger. "You will get this one, but you can change it out for the new one when it's ready."

Feeling weak, Adam slipped from his crouch and sat crosslegged on the floor. "Emma, what are you saying?"

"Tomorrow morning, we will take a short trip. All of us in this room, but no others. It is for Atarah's family alone to see me off."

Tamah threw herself into Emma's arms. Emma embraced her but looked at Abba. "Tomorrow, at last, I go to the Hall of the King."

They took the bus. How ludicrous.

Adam helped her into the shabby vehicle. "I thought you said when your grandfather made this trip, your father drove the royal limousine?"

"He did, of course." Her voice sounded frail and wobbly. "We had several of them then. One in each province. We also had a royal aircoach and a number of special rail cars. Nowadays, we have a bus. Live with it."

When Tamah claimed the seat beside her mother, Emma gave her a hug. "That's your abba's seat, honey. Adam will drive, and then we sit oldest to youngest, just like at dinner."

Tamah's lip puckered. "I thought I was closest to my mother's heart."

"You are, dear. But you're not a baby anymore, and I know you understand."

THE LAST TOQEPH

Ra'anan ran a comforting hand along Tamah's back as she passed to her seat. "I'd love to sit beside you, Abba, but—may I leave that seat empty for Lileela? She'd be here if she could."

Abba nodded. "By all means."

Adam squeezed in behind the controls. None of this seemed real.

Elise had cried when he told her. "Oh, Adam!" She hugged him long and hard. "I'm so sorry! I am, really. But—" She wiped her eyes. "Does that mean we'll be moving into the toqeph's suite?"

Adam nodded. He understood she wasn't being greedy, just practical, as a Gannahan wife should. "Yes." He swallowed. "Abba and the kids will be moving into Gustafsons' old place in a few days."

He'd been trying to wrap his mind around this all night. He'd known it would happen and had worked hard to be ready. But now that it was finally unfolding, he wished he could stop it.

He started the bus. "So where are we going?"

Emma sighed, considering. "My grandfather took the Har Highway."

Adam stroked his beard. "What's that?"

"The highway that leads to Har, of course. But none of that exists anymore. Well—just start driving. I suppose the Yasha will tell me where to go."

Adam clenched his jaw. All his life, he'd heard about her grandfather's final trip. It sounded so somber and dignified. But this was just silly. "Har was northeast of here, so I'll head northeast."

She leaned back in her seat and closed her eyes. "Sounds good to me."

Adam accelerated, but made no attempt to keep up with the racing of his heart.

They'd taken the tube to the airport and picked up the bus there. All of Gannah had showed up to see them off, tears flowing. Now the people swarmed the road, pounding the sides of the bus, waving and blowing kisses. Adam had to lean on the horn to get them to scatter.

He thought she might smile and wave, acknowledging their love. But the excitement seemed to have wearied her, and she kept her eyes closed.

Adam glanced at her lined face. "I also believe you said your grandfather asked the people to let him make his last journey alone."

"It was a wise thing to do. I'd have issued the same request had I thought of it." She opened her eyes, and, clasping Abba's hand with both of hers, looked out at the crowd. "They're good people."

THE LAST TOQEPH

Abba grunted. "Yes, they are. You chose them well."

"*We* chose them well. With the Yasha's guidance." She closed her eyes again.

The people thinned out as they left the airport, and once they were on the main road, only a few stood by to wave farewell.

Adam drove past Gullach. Without her, it would always seem empty. He swallowed a lump. It would be his domain now. The palace of Atarah.

The boys hadn't said much, but once they were a few minutes past Gullach, Hushai voiced what everyone was thinking. "Doesn't this road stop without going anywhere?"

Everyone looked at Emma — who appeared to be sleeping.

Adam shrugged. "We'll go as far as we can."

They drove in heavy silence for about half an hour, when Adam saw a barricade ahead — the end of the road. He glanced at Emma, whose head lay against Abba's arm. They were both asleep.

Adam drove to the barricade and stopped. Emma remained asleep. While his brothers and sisters watched, he moved from behind the controls and touched the toqeph's shoulder. "Emma? The road ends here."

Both his parents lifted their heads and blinked. She peered ahead through narrowed eyes. "Oh. Yes. I see. Well." She yawned then craned her neck to see out all the windows. "Do you see a hillside anywhere, or a big rock or something?"

"It all looks pretty flat, Emma."

She rose, shakily, and made a complete turn, looking out all the windows. "Ah. I see. We need to go back."

Adam's ears tilted. "Back?"

"Yes, dear, I'm sorry. Did we pass another road back there anywhere?"

"I didn't notice one." A flush washed over him. Was it really supposed to go this way?

"There must be a road somewhere." She sat back down and made an impatient gesture. "Go back. I'll keep a lookout for it."

So much for dignified. Adam sighed. He went to the control platform and spun it around so it faced the other direction, then headed the bus back the way they'd just come.

She stayed awake this time, staring out the window. Beside her, Abba's head nodded. The others glanced at their parents, at Adam, and at each other, puzzlement in their meahs.

THE LAST TOQEPH

He said nothing, just drove, until Emma perked up and pointed. "What's that? There on the right?"

Adam looked. A break in the brush seemed to beckon. "I wouldn't call it a road, exactly. But it's clear enough to drive on." He slowed and turned onto the grass track. Funny, he'd been in this area plenty of times before, but none of this looked familiar.

Emma smiled. "Follow this until it ends. That's where we'll find the cave."

Ittai stared out the window. "What cave? Don't there have to be hills and stuff for there to be caves?"

No one answered, and he didn't ask again.

Five minutes later, the track ended in a cul-de-sac of trees, shrubs, and piles of rock. Adam stopped the bus, his heart pounding. It looked just as he'd imagined it from Emma's description of her grandfather's final trip.

Tamah bit her fist. "Are we here?"

Emma smiled. "Almost, my sweet." She rose, looking as if she were eager to be going.

Adam helped both his parents from the bus then the children exited. Before Tamah's feet hit the ground, Emma was moving toward the largest of the nearby rocks. Adam's skin prickled. This was really happening, wasn't it?

He trotted ahead to help Emma, who balanced herself on the rock as she shuffled around it. Adam took her other arm, and she lifted her hand and patted his hand. "You're a good son."

They stood in front of a broad opening in the rock, with the floor sloping steeply down into a chasm.

"Let me help you," Adam said. He touched Abba's shoulder. "I'll help Emma down, then come back for you."

Hushai spoke up. "No need. Ittai and I can stay with Abba. You just take care of Emma."

Adam glanced at his little brothers. They weren't so little anymore, were they? They'd never be tall as Karkars, but they already towered above their mother. He nodded, then he and Emma plunged into the darkness.

The ground was dry and hard packed, and though the slope was steep, the going wasn't as precarious as it had seemed from the outside. Light came from some location ahead on the path, so when the daylight behind them failed, they were not in the dark.

397

THE LAST TOQEPH

Adam couldn't fathom how all this came to be here so close to Qatsyr with no one knowing about it. But Emma had said it was always like that. Wherever the toqeph was when the call came, the Yasha showed the way — and it was never a route anyone had seen before.

At the bottom was an ancient rail platform with a pod waiting, lights blazing and doors open. The hair stood up on Adam's neck. Though he'd known it would be there, he had a hard time believing it.

Emma's steps had slowed the farther they went, and Adam wasn't sure she could have made it much farther. He helped her into the pod, then the boys assisted Abba, and they all entered and took their seats. Emma grabbed the door handle beside her, and the door slid into place, closing them in.

The interior lights dimmed, a faint rumble tickled Adam's ears, and the vehicle moved forward. Soon it flew along the smooth track with scarcely a sound, carrying them deeper under ground.

Emma turned to Adam. "You know, son, I came by this ring honestly."

He lifted his brows. "I'm sorry?"

"I did not take the throne by deceit. My father, my grandfather, and countless generations before them were guiltless. They believed themselves heirs of Atarah. They should not have been ashamed to sit on the throne. And they were not."

Adam swallowed hard. She'd been reading his thoughts. "I know that."

For a moment, the old familiar glow lit her eyes. "And neither should you. The throne of Atarah is your birthright. I do not ask you to give it up."

So why mention it? "Yes, Emma."

She said no more until the pod stopped some fifteen minutes later.

Emma stood. Adam rose to help, but she waved him away. "Thank you, but this is my journey to take." She hung onto the sides of the doorway for balance and stepped to the platform.

Abba disembarked next. It looked as if his knees were shaking, but Hushai and Ittai hopped out and each took one of his arms, making Adam feel superfluous. Ra'anan and Tamah exited last. Tamah whispered to Ra'anan, "Weren't you supposed to go before the boys?"

Ra'anan put her fingers to her lips.

They stood in a narrow room walled with smooth gray stone, glittering as if embedded with tiny jewels. Though the ceiling was hidden by

398

THE LAST TOQEPH

impenetrable blackness, it gave the impression of being vastly high. Both ends of the chamber were similarly swallowed up in darkness. But the area where the family stood was lit by a portal directly in front of them, opposite the vehicle's open door.

Beyond the portal swirled a sea of bright fog. Adam felt as if he were gazing at the sun through a cloud—just as Emma had described it. Such emotion gripped him he wondered that he could stand.

Emma turned to Ra'anan, speaking in Old Gannahan. "My sweet."

Ra'anan bowed. "Mine em."

"Thou hast been a blessing from the beginning. Thy arrival healed my soul and made me feel alive again. Thou shalt be a blessing to Gannah all thy days."

Ra'anan choked on a sob. "Thank you, Emma. I shall try." She bowed deeply.

Emma spoke to each of them one by one, but Adam hardly heard. His pulse pounded in his head and his heart swelled in his chest.

"Pik." She took her husband's hands. Then she chuckled and, gazing up at him, spoke in the Standard language. "I never could pronounce your full name."

A tear trickled down Abba's cheek.

"And I fear it took me far too long to fully appreciate your goodness. You have been an exemplary husband. An even better father. You are, truly, a good Gannahan. It has been a privilege to work with you in building the New Gannah."

He nodded, ashen and wordless.

She kissed both of Abba's hands then looked into his face. "See you soon?"

He nodded and swallowed. "Soon, my love."

She gazed into his eyes a moment then let go of his hands and turned to Adam. "My son and heir."

Heart pounding, Adam knelt. "My em and toqeph."

When he lifted his head again, her eyes shimmered and her chin quivered as she removed the Ring of Atarah from her finger.

He raised his hand, and she took it, kissed it, then slipped the ring onto his sixth finger. It was too small to go even to the first joint. But being made of machalatsah, it would grow in a short time to fit perfectly.

"Arise, Toqeph of Gannah."

THE LAST TOQEPH

Adam wasn't sure he could, but he somehow managed to stand on weak legs.

"It is my delight to put Gannah in thy hands, and I have every confidence thou shalt hold it well. Be brave, my son. Thou knowest what is right."

Adam bowed again. "Thou hast spoken, madam."

"Yea. And I have spoken my last."

To Adam's surprise, she laughed. "My King! I come!"

She drew herself up straight and approached the portal with slow but even steps. Her foot crossed the threshold, and the cloud swirled away, revealing a scene beyond description. No wonder, in her telling of this tale, that she always stopped here, saying, "You'll just have to see it yourself."

The light was not blinding, but brighter, purer, and more illuminating than anything in Adam's experience. A long table of glowing deep-red wood carved by the most skillful of artisans stood spread for a meal. Chairs like thrones lined the table, each carved of the same unworldly material with the same indescribable craftsmanship. But at the head of the table stood the most amazing throne of all, and at the sight of the One who sat upon it, Adam sank to his knees.

It was the Yasha.

The other chairs were occupied by toqephs who had reigned before. Adam recognized some from their pictures in the history books. Hoseh the Wise sat nearest the Yasha, and the rest were seated after him in chronological order. Adam would have studied their faces, but his eyes couldn't leave the Yasha.

He was aware of Emma approaching the table in the full vigor of youth. The others rose, turned to Emma, and bowed. All but the Yasha. He rose, but He didn't bow.

He smiled.

Emma prostrated herself before the Throne. "My God and my King."

As they reached the bus, Hushai bowed. "It is not seemly that the toqeph should drive. May I do the honors, milord?"

Adam didn't know whether to laugh or cry. "Doest thou know how?"

Hushai grinned. "Mr. Mutombo taught me to drive a farm truck. It is much the same, is it not?"

THE LAST TOQEPH

Adam felt the ring. The band was already expanded enough to push over the first knuckle. "Sure. Let's see what you've got."

Tamah and Ra'anan had been weeping the whole tube ride, but the prospect of Hushai driving seemed to cheer them a little. Ra'anan glanced up at Adam shyly. "I know Emma said to be brave, but this might be pushing it, milord."

Abba stumbled, and Adam helped him enter the bus and settle in a seat. Abba's last words to Emma, "Soon, my love," pierced in Adam's memory, and he gave the old shoulder a squeeze. Abba reached up with a shaking hand and squeezed him back. "She was right, you know. You're a good man."

"She was right about many things. I pray she was not wrong about that." Adam patted Abba's arm then sat down. "Okay, 'Shai. You think you can drive this thing?"

Hushai wiped away tears then sat at the console. "Yep."

He started it up and took off. Plainly, he was familiar with the controls of a vehicle.

Adam shook his head. So much he didn't know. He'd been toqeph for just minutes, and already the world's weight overwhelmed him.

Adam left the driving to Hushai and let his mind wander. It had plenty of paths to explore.

He wanted to fulfill Emma's expectations. To know what was right. *My Yasha, how can I know?*

He connected with Lileela. *Emma is home.*

Amidst her sorrow, he was aware of joy. *Did you see the Yasha, like she said?*

Yes. And now, like Emma, I can hardly wait until He calls me, too.

Thinking of Lileela, of course, reminded him of Faris. Which made him think of Binyamin.

Betrayed by a brother. He glanced at Hushai. He was a good kid. Ittai was too. He couldn't imagine either of them turning on him, nor on each other.

But it was an age-old story. Cain and Abel. Jacob and Esau. Charash and Natsach.

Charash and Natsach. Adam leaned his head back and closed his eyes, Emma's words echoing in his mind. *Thou knowest what is right.*

THE LAST TOQEPH

Ittai's voice interrupted his thoughts. "Hey, Ad—I mean, milord toqeph. Are you going to have a big coronation party?"

Adam looked back and forth between the brothers, then at Abba, whose amber eyes were red from weeping. Abba nodded. As if he knew.

Adam nodded back. "If the people want to hold a Coronation Day celebration, they can do it for my successor."

THE LAST TOQEPH

NOTE FROM THE AUTHOR

In the early 2000s I ran across a little nonfiction book called *The Gospel in the Stars* by Joseph A. Seiss, originally published in 1882. It became the inspiration for my first attempt at writing science fiction.

What started out as a short story became a novel (*The Story in the Stars*), which evolved into a four-book series. I never set out with that intent. I just wanted to illustrate some basic truths that apply to everyone, everywhere, no matter what stars they live under.

Karkar—its language and its people—merely represents me having fun. However, in creating the language of Gannah, I employed *Strong's Exhaustive Concordance of the Bible*, borrowing the Hebrew words used in the Scriptures for the concepts I wanted to convey and adapting (probably more like corrupting) them for the story. *Gannah*, for instance, comes from the Hebrew word for garden. Here are some others:

lahab – blade
meah – sometimes translated bowels or intestines, the word was used in the Scriptures to indicate the place where sympathy and soft feelings originate; the seat of emotions; the heart.
Nasi – prince
toqeph – authority, power, strength
Yasha – Savior

I don't anticipate mankind will ever travel through space as described in this story. I don't believe there is life, let alone human life, on other planets. And I don't believe that the biblical references mentioned in this book apply to extra-terrestrials. That stuff's pure fiction.

But the stars are real, and so is the Creator whose handiwork they show. That's what this whole thing is about.

Yvonne Anderson
www.YsWords.com

Made in the USA
Charleston, SC
18 January 2015